THEY'LL
NEVER
CATCH
US

D0003693

JESSICA GOODMAN

RAZORBILL

RAZORBILL

An imprint of Penguin Random House LLC, New York

First published in the United States of America by Razorbill,
an imprint of Penguin Random House LLC, 2021
First paperback edition published 2022

Visit us online at penguinrandomhouse.com.

THE LIBRARY OF CONGRESS HAS CATALOGED THE HARDCOVER EDITION AS FOLLOWS:
Names: Goodman, Jessica, 1990– author.
Title: They'll never catch us / Jessica Goodman.
Other titles: They will never catch us
Description: New York : Razorbill, 2021. | Audience: Ages 14 and up. |
Summary: Sisters Stella and Ellie Steckler are both determined to win a
scholarship and escape their stifling small town, but their plans are
upset when a new girl joins the cross country team and then disappears.
Identifiers: LCCN 2021017025 | ISBN 9780593114322 (hardcover) |
ISBN 9780593114346 (trade paperback) | ISBN 9780593114339 (ebook)
Subjects: CYAC: Competition (Psychology)—Fiction. | Sisters—Fiction. |
Secrets—Fiction. | Running—Fiction. | Racing—Fiction. | Murder—Fiction.
Classification: LCC PZ7.1.G6542 Tj 2021 | DDC [Fic]—dc23
LC record available at https://lccn.loc.gov/2021017025

Manufactured in Canada

1 3 5 7 9 10 8 6 4 2

FRI

Design by Rebecca Aidlin
Text set in Aldus LT Std.

For Halley—
We'll always be the Goodman girls.

1

STELLA

I HATE THE way my sister Ellie breathes. She doesn't huff or puff or pant or wheeze. No, Ellie's breath is steady and sure and it never changes. Not when she accelerates around a particularly angled turn. Not even when she sprints the final hundred yards. Her breath is as consistent as the time.

I also hate the way Ellie's ponytail never falls out of place. And that she can run in silence without wanting to crush her own brain with her hands. How can my little sister have so many thoughts she actually wants to think?

Me, on the other hand. I just want to shut everything out. That's why I run. To get away. To be free. I just want to pump my legs faster than anyone else's. To feel the burn deep within my lungs and all throughout my thighs. To win. It doesn't matter where I'm going or which course I'm on or anything. What matters is that my brain stops. Completely. And I can only get there if everything's aligned, if I ascend planes, beat records, and speed, speed, speed.

Only when I'm running can I forget about the little things— how my dark hair is so unruly it can only be tamed by a thick medical-grade elastic, or that time in the ninth grade Julia

Heller found out I didn't have my period yet and awarded me the nickname Sterile. I can forget that my parents are constantly worried about money and the too-big house. I can forget that Mom is a recovering alcoholic, who is always a few sips away from overthrowing the delicate balance we've found—and that Dad is constantly forcing us to avoid things that might set her off. I can forget why I'm here, how guilt and horror fizzled in my brain when I first heard the sound of bone unlatching. I can even forget the worst thing of all: that Ellie is just as fast as I am—sometimes even faster.

Shit. I'm doing it again. This happens every time I get hooked on this train of thought. I start listing all the things I hate about my sister, and then somewhere along the way the gears in my brain take a sharp turn and I'm reminding myself of everything that's wrong with *me*.

The spiral continues until I remember something Mom once said: *Everyone hates themselves a little. If you get over that, you survive.* Sure, she said it when she was drunk and I was five. But I think it holds up.

I repeat that mantra over and over as I push toward the final eight hundred yards around the track. The sun beats down on my head and I wonder if my scalp can get sunburnt through my mess of curls. Ellie's fine, silky hair wouldn't protect her against *this*.

"Last one, Steckler! You got this!" Coach Reynolds calls from the sidelines. Her voice is faint, but I can still hear it. I love being called Steckler. It never happens back in Edgewater because there are always two of us.

I lean my body into the inner circle of the track as I glide around the last turn. The finish line beckons. My muscles ache. Makes sense, though. I *have* been running nearly a hundred miles a week. That was what was promised at Breakbridge Elite Track and Field Center. Well, that and anger management courses. But still, I've never slept better. Here, my muscles ache and thrum as I pour myself into bed every night. I don't stay awake reciting my stats or obsessing over the scholarship I lost or listening for gasps in the stands as bodies collide. I just . . . sleep. Is this how I'm supposed to feel? Well rested and happy?

With only a hundred yards to go, I can feel every single lap and every single sprint that have turned my muscles into steel. I've gotten better since June. In the past eight weeks I've seen my times go down like crazy. Sure, I also learned some breathing exercises to help clear my mind and ways to keep me from spiraling with frustration. There's no way Ellie will be able to keep up on the cross country course. A slow smirk crawls across my face as I imagine the fury in my sister's icy blue eyes when I beat her.

This last race isn't really a race at all. I'm just killing time before my parents come to get me. This is my final reminder of everything I've accomplished this summer. My first without Ellie. My first away from Edgewater. I have never felt freer than I do here. Not while running in the woods, or around the lake back home, up by the Ellacoya Mountain Resort. I'm finally, desperately, alone. And I love it.

Here we go. My eyes narrow as the last few yards sneak up on me. I cross them with ease and without ever breaking my pace. I want to keep running. I would, too. If I didn't know Mom and Dad were waiting out front, eager to get home to Ellie, the landscapers, and the home office where they sell real estate to gullible yuppies looking for a second home north of Manhattan, at the foot of the idyllic Catskill mountain range. Or at least where they try to.

They used to have such a hard time closing deals, back when the cold cases were still fresh and the media called our little town Deadwater. In the span of a year, three female cross country stars went missing. Each one was found on the thorny trail up by Oak Tower. All killed in the same way: blunt force trauma, with no signs of sexual assault. They all fought like hell, and our totally incompetent police department never figured out who did it.

But that's in the past now. It's been a decade since anyone went missing. Well, that's if you don't count Shira Tannenbaum, and no one does. Now Edgewater's a place where tristate tourists come to pick our apples, buy our ceramics, and kayak on our lake. Deadwater's just a myth. Something we all lived through but try to forget.

"Steckler, that was your fastest yet." Coach Reynolds skips up to me and wraps her arm around my shoulder. "You're going to crush 'em all back home this year." She flashes a wide, toothy smile, one that I've grown fond of, even though I'm usually not *fond* of much. Her gray-blonde bun flops on top of her head, just above her neon-yellow visor, and her cheeks are flushed and round. She reminds me of Grandma Jane.

"Thanks," I say, barely out of breath.

"Your folks are here."

"I figured."

"Need help gathering your things?"

"Nah," I say. "I'm all packed."

We walk together in silence until the wood cabins come into focus. Behind them are mountains. Dozens of gorgeous, pointy peaks that ascend into the clouds. They're prettier up here, better than the ones back home. Grander. Closer to the heavens. But I'm itching to get going and move on. I want to forget about what happened last year and focus on the cross country season ahead, on winning back my college scholarship. That's my only way out of Edgewater. It's not a *bad* place to live. It's just not the only place.

"There's our Stella!" Mom's cooing voice rings out over the field, echoing into the trees, and my shoulders immediately tense.

"Look at you!" Dad calls. "I swear, you're all muscle these days."

Mom's pretty face turns into a pout and she pushes her dark hair behind her ears. It's long and silky, just like Ellie's. "Sad to leave, sweetie? I know, it's been such a fun summer, such a learning experience." She's right, even though I don't want her to be.

"With the amount we're paying, I should hope so." Dad smiles, but the relaxed feeling in my chest disappears and my face turns a bright shade of crimson as I remember that Coach Reynolds is standing right there.

"I just have to get my bags, then we can head out," I say.

"You don't want to shower before we get in the car? It's a long way home." Mom pinches her perfectly symmetrical nose as if to get the message across loud and clear. *You fucking reek.*

"Nope," I say through clenched teeth. "All good."

"Well, okay," Dad says, nervous. "Shall we, then?"

Everyone nods and we begin walking to the car. "You know, Stella's improved quite a bit this summer," Coach Reynolds says. Mom and Dad look hopeful, like they'd been waiting to hear that I'm still *good*. Good enough to win State again and get back into Georgetown's good graces so I can go to college for free. Coach Gary, back in Edgewater, said if I broke my personal record—we call it PR for short—by a full minute, they'd *have* to pay attention. They *couldn't* ignore me. He said it during one of his million-decibel screaming tantrums, spit forming at the corners of his mouth. But still. I just have to crush that time by State in November. Until then, everything is up in the air.

2

ELLIE

STELLA'S DUE HOME any minute from Crazy Camp. That's what all our teammates call it in the cross country group chat. Assholes. I told them to shut up earlier in the summer, but it's hard to have Stella's back when she goes and does the kind of shit that gets her sent off to a place like Breakbridge.

I try to push my big sister out of my head and enjoy my last day of freedom before preseason starts. I lean back in the plastic lounge chair and feel the slats dig into my skin. Pop music blares from the speaker next to me and sweat trickles down my stomach.

I clench my core, grateful that a summer of swimming and lifeguarding at Sweetwater Lake helped me keep my abs tight, my muscles lean. But as my mind drifts toward work, it *also* drifts toward Noah Brockston. Sweet, kind, strong Noah. Today was our last day working together, which means it was also the last day we could be *us* until he finally breaks up with Tamara Johnson.

We talked about it last night, during one of our midnight walks, after he pressed a copy of his favorite book, *On the Road,* into my hands. I didn't have the heart to tell him I read it last year and hated it. Not after I saw what he scrawled on the first page: *For all we are and what we could be.* He signed it *N.* That's what made me bring it up again: *us.*

"I wish things weren't so complicated," I said, grabbing his hand and squeezing it. We were walking the trail up by Oak Tower, the one that's been closed since the murders happened. And by "closed," I mean "now only used by people who don't want to be found." The only thing stopping anyone from getting to the trail is a flimsy chain-link fence that's easy to fit through. The moon was bright and lit the overgrown path as we made our way to a clearing. There was a big rock in the center, and a deep pit off to one side. Noah sat down on the rock and motioned for me to slide in next to him. He wrapped his arm around my shoulder and pulled me closer. The stars danced in the sky above and it felt like we were the only people on earth. There's no cell reception on that trail, no laughter floating from another group of hikers. Just silence.

"After everything that happened, I just want to be *normal* with you," I said.

I wasn't sure if he was going to flinch at those words. *Everything that happened.* As if what had transpired between us had been a coincidence, a dumb stroke of luck and not a life-altering event. But he didn't. He just cupped my chin in his hand.

"I know, Ell," Noah said softly, his breath warm on my ear. "You've been through so much." He stroked my hair like he was lulling me to sleep and I nuzzled closer to him, pressing my face into his chest. I wanted to do this every day, in broad daylight, on paths we were allowed to traverse without fear of getting caught or ruining each other's lives. "I have a plan, though," he said. "As soon as Tamara's dad makes the call to

Princeton, I'll end it with her. But if I break up with her before, it'll ruin everything."

My skin prickled at his admission. It was no secret—at least to me—that he was using his girlfriend for her connections to his dream school. I almost felt special that he confided in me. It was like he wanted me to know the worst thing about him, that he was capable of using someone. We all are, though. Most of us just don't admit it. But I didn't understand why he doubted his ability to get into Princeton on his own or why some fancy school in New Jersey was the only option.

I let it lie. I didn't want to push Noah. Not after what happened in August, when everything changed, when things became scary and serious. Since then, I tried to keep him close, cling to him and any sense of normalcy. So instead of picking a fight, I let him change the subject to some William S. Burroughs book he just finished. The boy loves long gibberish-y texts about random white dudes losing their minds. After a while, I stopped listening. My eyelids were heavy and I let my mind drift off toward my own future. Maybe it would exist far away, somewhere in Texas or Florida, Oregon or Ohio, where no one knew there were two Steckler sisters. Where I could just be Steckler, not Baby Steckler. Where "Ellie" wasn't always preceded by "Stella."

Last year, my possibilities seemed endless. But after Stella got herself labeled as *violent* and *unrecruitable*, everything changed. Now that I'm a sophomore, the scouts will start looking, and I have to be the one to win a scholarship, to get that full ride Stella had already secured.

But that's a future problem. A tomorrow problem. A next month problem. Now, here in my backyard, I don't have to think about it.

I drape my T-shirt over my face, blocking the bright, hot sun. If Bethany were still here and not off at her new house in Michigan, she would know what to do. She would have understood. I was always able to talk to her about *anything*. But after she told me I was too *needy* when I actually needed her the most, I think it's safe to say I no longer have a best friend.

Something splashes deep within the pool in front of me and in a split second, I jerk forward, drenched from the blowback.

"Miss me?" Stella bobs to the surface, smiling and treading water. She's wearing an EDGEWATER XC cobalt-blue sports bra and white mesh shorts. Her heart-shaped face cocks to one side, and her dark curly hair is piled high into a messy bun, now dripping wet.

"You asshole," I say, shielding my eyes with my hand. "How's your time?" It's the one thing I know to ask her, the one thing that will cut through the bullshit.

"You'll have to find out tomorrow." Stella grins wickedly and ducks below the surface, spinning around before coming up for air.

"Oh, for fuck's sake, Stell," I say. "You're not going to tell me before preseason?"

"Let's just say I improved."

I lie back against the chair, suddenly anxious. "I knew I should have trained with you this summer."

But we both know I couldn't have, that Mom and Dad could only afford to send one of us to a track camp that doubled as a mental health facility. Just like how we know they can only afford to send one of us to college. The other has to bank on an athletic scholarship, which we thought Stella had in the bag. Now it's up to me.

Stella breaststrokes to the other side of the pool and back

again, swimming in time with the pop song on the speaker. "So what'd I miss in Edgewater? Anything of note?"

I could tell her about Noah, how different I feel now, or the little ball of shame buried deep within my heart. But something holds me back. I know she wouldn't tell anyone else, but it's almost like I don't want to show weakness. Plus, Stella doesn't really care about what happens here. Stella hates Edgewater in the summer, when it quadruples in size thanks to all the yuppies who finally come to fill their summer houses and pretend like they're *country* folk for a few weekends a year. She hates Ellacoya Mountain Resort, the five-star luxury hotel up the road where most of our peers work. But who am I kidding? I hate it, too, now that Noah and I are a *thing*. Tamara Johnson's family own the place.

"You didn't miss shit," I say. "Just a bunch of parties you would have hated. No one practiced much except Raven Tannenbaum. Saw her running the trails by Ellacoya basically every day. But she doesn't even register with the scouts. You know that."

Stella chuckles. "Obviously. That poor girl's got no mental game. Too scared of everything." She bobs up and down in the water. "Any word from Bethany? How's she doing in Michigan?"

I bristle at the mention of my former best friend's name and shake my head. "Dunno. Good, I guess."

Stella doesn't say anything. She never liked Bethany that much anyway. Would probably be thrilled to know that she basically ignored me all summer after moving away.

"What time's practice tomorrow?" I ask.

"Seven."

We're both quiet for a second and I tilt my face up to the

sun and wonder what Stella's thinking. If she's running through drills in her head. It may be *her* junior year, her last chance to shine brighter than anyone else and land that spot at Georgetown once and for all, but I have to fight for myself. If I'm lucky, I'll have a spot guaranteed by the end of the season. That's the goal. That's the dream. Especially after this summer, when I saw what life would be like if I let my future slip away.

"Wanna go for a quickie tonight?" I ask, trying not to sound too desperate. "A few miles up by Ellacoya?"

"Nah," Stella says, flipping onto her back to float in the pool. "Gotta rest up."

I lean back, too, wondering what kind of game Stella is playing and just how much she improved while at Breakbridge. But that's the thing about Stella. She keeps her cards so close to her chest, sometimes I wonder if even *she* knows what she'll play.

3

STELLA

"WELL, IF IT isn't the Steckler sisters." Coach Gary crosses his arms over his broad chest and widens his stance. He's wearing a blue Edgewater hat over his bald head and his legs are bronze, as if he's been outside every day for the past three months. When a breeze rustles his shorts, I glimpse his pearly white thighs where his tan line makes a hard stop.

"Miss us, Coach?" Ellie teases. But as soon as she says it, her face turns red, like she forgot she was greeting the dude who earned the nickname Coach Scary after he made a whole bunch of freshmen cry last year. But he gets results. And that's what everyone cares about. That's what I care about.

"You two? Nah," he says, playing along. His dark eyes narrow and he tilts his head toward me. "Breakbridge do you right?"

I nod.

"It better have," he says. "You've got a lot to prove this year."

I straighten my spine and don't look away. "I know."

He snaps a piece of gum. "Looking forward to seeing what you've got." His eyes move over my shoulder and I turn to follow his gaze toward the bleachers. There, sitting in the front row, is a small white woman with gray hair and sunglasses, holding a clipboard. She's wearing a polo shirt and hiking shorts. I don't recognize her from the college recruiter lists.

"What school is she from?" I ask, fear building in my stomach. Scouts aren't supposed to come to practices. Hell, we're lucky when they show up to meets.

"Ours," he says, his voice gruff and frustrated. "School board oversight. They just wanted to keep an eye on things after last year."

Ellie lets out a groan.

"Shut it, Baby Steckler," Coach snaps. "I don't have time for this. You're *my* squad. *My* girls. Just have to show 'em I still have a handle on you lot."

Ellie clamps her mouth shut and looks to the ground. Before we can say anything else, we're interrupted by whooping and hollering. I turn to the parking lot to see Tamara Johnson, Raven Tannenbaum, and Julia Heller tumbling out of a rose-gold SUV branded with a bumper sticker for the Ellacoya Mountain Resort. They pose for a selfie in their practice uniforms and break into a fit of laughter about some inside joke we'll never understand. They start to walk toward us and Tamara smiles, her box braids swinging behind her. Raven's pale, freckled arms hang by her sides like ropes and she glances at Tamara, hungry for approval. Julia's straight, dirty-blonde hair is gathered into a tight high ponytail that looks like it's pulling at her scalp.

This goddamn threesome. Julia and Tamara have been best friends since kindergarten when the Hellers moved to Edgewater to open another location of their fancy sporting goods chain. They became tight with Raven a few years later, which was a good thing, considering that when her sister

Shira pulled that ridiculous stunt, no one wanted to go anywhere near the Tannenbaums. Well, no one except Tamara and Julia. They stuck by her side. It was pretty nice, I guess. Doesn't make up for the fact that Julia still calls me Sterile and continues to just be a straight-up asshole. She and Tamara aren't *that* fast. Raven, though. She could be good but she chokes all the time.

Coach ignores them. "Stella, stretching," he commands. "You are co-captain, after all." He flashes a menacing smile and raises his eyebrows. The school board almost took the title away from me last year, after I got suspended. But Coach got the administration to let me stay on as long as there was a co-captain for the girls' squad. It was no surprise the team voted for Tamara.

I jog onto the patch of grass in the middle of the track and stand tall, waiting for the rest of the team to circle up around me. We're fifteen deep this year, counting the few freshmen who are trying out this week, and the group looks good and lithe. It's obvious I'll make it to State, but if these dummies can get it together, we might have a shot at placing as a team, too.

"Hi, Stella," Tamara says, tossing her braids over one shoulder. "Should we give the girls a pep talk?"

"After stretching, maybe," I say. "You can do that part."

She smiles so wide her molars show, then nods to Raven and Julia off to the side. "Circle up, ladies!" she calls.

I hop up and down and drop to the earth as the others follow. "Left leg out," I call and thrust my leg long. My muscles tense and acquiesce, a familiar feeling of strain and release.

"Switch!" I yell.

But when I lift my head to swap my legs, I see everyone has stopped paying attention. Their gaze has shifted. Their heads are turned to the parking lot, where Coach Gary bounces on the balls of his feet. He taps his clipboard nervously with a pen. A tall girl with high cheekbones stands before him in gray spandex shorts and a black racerback running shirt. An Edgewater-blue bow is tied around her dark, wavy ponytail, which hangs long down her back.

"Who is that?" Tamara asks. She pulls on one of her braids, a nervous tic.

"No clue," Julia says.

"Oh, shit, I know," Raven says softly. Of course she does. Her mom, Mrs. Tannenbaum, is the school secretary, so she knows *everything*.

"Who?" Julia asks.

"That's Mila Keene. I think she moved here over the summer," Raven says.

"*Who?*" Julia asks again.

My heart sinks. I've heard of Mila. Everyone who is competitive in the greater northeast has. She won the Connecticut State championship last year as a sophomore and was rumored to have been talking to the scouts at Harvard. Why the hell is she here? And why the hell is she walking toward us?

"I said switch," I call out, suddenly annoyed and flushed. When I bring my left ankle in to my thigh I realize it's shaking.

"Her parents split up," Raven continues, dropping her voice to a whisper. "I think her mom got a job at the hospital, so they moved here from one of those suburbs close to Manhattan. Her dad's back in Connecticut." She bends down over her knee. "At least that's what my mom said."

"Why didn't she just stay there?" Julia asks.

"Who knows?" Raven says softly. She twists the ends of her

red hair around one finger, exposing a swath of freckles trailing down her neck.

"Shh," Tamara says. "They're coming this way."

I look up to see Coach and Mila jogging toward us. He snaps his gum loudly as he lugs Mila's practice bag over his shoulder. She follows behind him, her gait elegant and graceful. Shit, she's wearing shiny lilac Nikes—*the* lilac Nikes. Even from here, I can see her initials are embroidered on the flat end of each shoelace. My heart drops. I have that pair, too. All the best high school track stars do since Nike gifted them to the top five runners in each state last year. I'm furious I didn't wear mine today. Just these dumb practice ASICS. They don't even come with spikes.

Coach Gary clears his throat. "Girls," he bellows. "This is Mila Keene."

The others raise their heads and offer sweet smiles, saccharine and fake. If Mila senses the charade, she doesn't let on. She just stands there grinning, her arms loose and relaxed by her sides. She doesn't fidget or shift her weight from one foot to the other. She's just happy to be here. How, though?

"Hey!" Mila says. She even gives a little wave.

"Mila just moved here from Hadbury, Connecticut, but you girls are smart; you probably already knew that. She will be joining the junior class and our squad. If you don't watch out, she'll kick your ass." Coach looks directly at me and smirks. "Make her feel at home, will ya?"

Heads bob up and down. Raven stands up first and offers Mila her hand. "Welcome to the team!" she says. I have to suppress an eye roll. Raven has always been *nice*, in the same way vanilla ice cream is nice but you'd rather have cookie dough.

Tamara follows suit, and pretty soon, almost all the girls surround Mila, asking her questions and complimenting her Nikes.

But I stay put on the ground. I stick both my legs out in front of me and lower my head to meet my knees, breathing deeply and leaning into the tugging sensation on the back of my calves.

When I finally lift my head, I squint. The sun is bright, and if we don't get our heart rates up soon, the heat will destroy us.

When the rest of the circle comes into focus, I see only Ellie is left stretching on the ground. She's looking directly at me and our eyes lock in a state of fury.

We're ready for war.

4

ELLIE

EVEN UNDER THE covers, I can hear Stella grunting from her bedroom. Doing squats or push-ups or something that's not required but highly encouraged. I pull a pillow over my face, blocking out the sun, and fumble around for my phone, thumbing through my texts to find the ones Noah sent last night.

Wish I could pick you up and drive you tomorrow, he said. *Like a real couple.*

A dull ache pounds in my chest and I force myself to remember that he *does* want me. He *does* care for me. We'll be together soon.

Without thinking, I run my pointer finger over the thin red bracelet around my wrist. It's made of just a few pieces of thread braided together and tied in a circle. Noah gave it to me on a rainy day in July when we were stuck inside the lifeguarding shack, waiting out a storm. He retrieved it from his backpack and tied it tightly around my wrist.

"I made it," he said, sheepish. I tried to picture him, brow furrowed in concentration, braiding a friendship bracelet in his spare time.

"I love it," I said, turning my wrist around to admire his clumsy work. And I did. It was perfect.

"I want you to look at this when you think I don't care, when you think I've forgotten all about you and that my heart is somewhere else," he said. "Know that I want to be with you."

Before I could say anything he kissed my palm, my fingers, the underside of my arm. Then he pressed his lips to mine, firmly, with intention.

The little bracelet is my only reminder that what I went through this summer was worth it. That we *will* be together in the end, after he gets into Princeton and lets Tamara down easy. I just know that if I try hard enough, I can make this relationship work, even if it means being the other girl for a few months. Otherwise, what was it all for?

I sigh heavily and throw the covers off my bed, knowing that the first day of school is only an hour away. I pull on jean shorts and a white flowy top, and shake out my hair so it falls in waves around my shoulders. I look at myself closely in the mirror and wonder if I've changed as much on the outside as I have on the inside since June. Last year I was so excited to go back to school. I had new notebooks, a fresh haircut, and Bethany. This year, all I have is a secret Noah told me I had to keep and the fear that rises in my throat when I think about sharing it with anyone.

But now I push the thought away and head downstairs to make myself a green juice. Thank god Stella convinced Mom we really did need that four-hundred-dollar monstrosity that pulverizes kale into neon-colored liquid. All she had to do was dangle that scholarship over their heads and they were ready to get her anything she wanted. I have to scream to be heard. Or at least I *had* to, until Stella lost her chance at Georgetown.

Now Mom and Dad are asking more questions about my times, my stats, my chances. It started with a few innocent comments about reaching out to college coaches over the summer, but by the time Mom started grilling me on my PR, I just wanted to curl inside myself and shut them out. Maybe it's easier being out of focus.

The blender shrieks as I throw ginger, celery, half a carrot, and a handful of kale into its bowels. Soon I'm left with a muddy green liquid that tastes like dirt.

"Ready?" Stella appears at the top of the staircase. Her hair is wet and slicked back in a ponytail, and she's wearing an Edgewater tracksuit that makes *swooshing* sounds when she walks. Dork.

"You can't put on something *slightly* cute for the first day of school?" I ask.

There it is. That stare.

"Did you make any for me?" she asks.

I've learned by now. What's mine is Stella's and what's Stella's is also Stella's. I nod and hand her a to-go thermos. She takes it with a grunt and we head out the door into the beat-up navy Subaru Outback Grandma and Grandpa gifted to us when Stella got her license. They shipped it all the way from Arizona, where they moved just before the Dark Years. That's what Dad calls them, when he and Mom were trying to get their lives together, holed up in an Airstream they thought was "cool" over in Bethel.

At first glance, they seemed like everyone else, just trying to get a piece of the mountain-life pie before the yuppies from Brooklyn bought up all the property. But the winter months were long and cold, and the artisanal gin was cheap, since they were friends with all the small-batch providers. They made money by leading brewery tours, taking tourists around, and schmoozing for tips. It was perfect for them, until Mom got pregnant with Stella and they started fighting about money, and Mom's drinking, and their future, and . . . everything.

That's as much as they would tell me now about that time. I had to learn about the totaled car, the one that carried Stella in the back seat, from an old newspaper clipping. That happened sometime in the fourteen months before I was born.

I don't remember much about the way things were before Mom went to rehab. Only that whenever things got bad, Stella would shut the door to our tiny shared room and read to me from picture books. She'd blast the oldies station from our handheld radio. I didn't know we were on the brink of disaster. But Stella did. And for her, those memories turned into a suit of armor.

When I was four, though, Grandma Jane and Grandpa Hal came in from Sedona to stay with us while they forced Mom into treatment. Dad quit partying, too, and hung around as our grandparents basically taught him how to be a parent—how to steam vegetables for dinner and detangle our hair and sing us to sleep. I blocked out a lot of that, too. All I know is that's when the night terrors started. Sleepwalking out into the yard. Screaming in the dark. Most nights, I'd end up in Stella's bed, curled up next to her as she soothed me back to sleep with her steady breath. Everything else, though, I tried to forget.

Mom came back, tan and refreshed, spouting mantras and dancing around the yard. Dad was lighter, too. More hopeful and focused, in love like we'd never seen. They both got back into Judaism, after shunning their faith for years. Soon we were regulars at the local synagogue, where services featured acoustic guitars and all the rabbis wore tie-dyed tallit.

We attended weekly Hebrew school and studied for our bat mitzvahs. Mom and Dad got their real estate licenses and sold their first million-dollar house within a year. It was clear they were natural salespeople, with faces you wanted to trust. That's what everyone said. There was even a small article about them in the *New York Times* travel section a few years back, about how Edgewater had finally ditched its awful nickname, Deadwater, and was becoming an actual tourist destination.

A TOWN ONCE KNOWN FOR ITS GRUESOME COLD CASES BECOMES A SUMMER HOTSPOT! the headline screamed, pasted just above a slick photo of Mom and Dad laughing in front of a refurbished farmhouse over by Ellacoya.

And yeah, Mom relapsed again when I was in fifth grade, but that was minor. She got through it. And no one knew. We Stecklers keep each other's secrets.

At Grandma Jane's funeral a few years ago, Mom cried desperately at the shiva, rocking back and forth, refusing to eat anything from the platters of deli meat. When I hugged her, she held me so tight I thought my chest might explode.

"She saved you," Mom whispered, her voice warbling. "She saved you."

I thought she meant Grandma Jane, how her mother's presence in our lives was what kept us together as a family during the Dark Years. But Mom's eyes were open wide and when I followed her gaze, I could see she was looking straight at Stella.

"She saved you."

I haven't seen Noah since the night he gave me the book on the Oak Tower trail, and by the time I get to chemistry, our one shared class, my fingertips are buzzing. I'm itching to be near him, even if I won't be able to feel the heat vibrating off his skin or run my thumb against the fine hairs on the back of his neck. I get there early, just to make sure I can grab a desk in the back so we'll share a lab station all year. As the bell rings, he jogs through the door.

My heart stops as his eyes find mine in the classroom, bustling with that first-day-of-school energy. A slow smile spreads across his face and he darts through the rows of desks to slide into the seat next to me. His sandy hair flops down over one eye and he raises his hand to push it back.

"Hey," he whispers as he drags his forefinger down my bare arm. I shiver.

"Hi."

My heart races and I can't stop looking at his round green eyes. Or his taut biceps, which are now just out in the open as he unzips his varsity cross country hoodie. He crosses his arms over his chest and presses his knee against mine beneath the desk. I swear I might faint.

"Missed you," he says.

"Me too. At least I have this," I say, nodding toward my wrist.

Noah's brow furrows and his eyes dart around the room. He leans in toward me. "Yeah, Ell. I was thinking. I don't know if it's such a good idea for you to wear that anymore. Maybe you can just keep it in your pocket or something, you know? What if someone sees?"

My face suddenly feels hot. "What do you mean?" I ask, trying to keep my voice steady. "It's not like it says 'Noah Brockston made this.'"

"You never know. I'm just worried, I guess." Noah looks away and part of me feels for him, knows this is hard. But the other part of me is just plain mad.

I open my mouth to protest, but Noah pouts. "Please, Ell. Just for a little."

I soften. He always has this power over me. "Okay," I say, and untie the string from my wrist. Noah looks relieved as I slip it into the pocket of my shorts.

"Ellie Steckler?" Mr. Darien calls. He's standing at the front of the lab wearing a long white coat. He reminds me of that doctor who saw me sixty miles away in Newburgh, where I knew no one would recognize me. The one who pursed his lips when I told him why I was there. He patted my hand and smiled with his eyes. "It's going to be okay," he said as I wiped tears from my cheeks. It was only a few weeks ago, but it feels like years.

"Here," I call, masking the tightness in my throat.

For the next forty minutes I try to listen to whatever Mr. Darien is droning on about, but with Noah's knee suctioned so firmly against mine, it's hard to think about anything. When the bell rings, it's like a spell has been broken.

Noah turns to me as he quickly packs up his bag. "I gotta hit Coach's office, but I'll catch you at lunch, okay?"

"Okay," I say. I don't mention Tamara or how she'll be there, too. I let myself pretend that we're a real couple, a normal couple.

"Bye, babe." Before he stands, he wraps his palm around my thigh and squeezes. I clench my body to remember this feeling.

"Bye," I whisper as he walks out the door.

When I get to the cafeteria, the cross country table has already assembled toward the back of the room. Last year, I hadn't earned a spot at the main table, even though I was the only freshman to make varsity. Now that I've come in the top ten at State and proved myself independent of Stella, *thankyouverymuch*, one of those seats is mine. And now that

Noah's the captain of the boys' team, maybe he'll plop down next to me. Maybe.

"Yo, Baby Steckler. Think fast!" I drop my tray to the table and open my arms to receive something damp and heavy.

"What the hell is this, Bader?" I hold up the ball of fabric and try to shake it out.

"My sweaty boxers," says Todd Bader. He's one of Noah's best friends, but he's still just a dumb jock, dopey and boob-obsessed. Lucky for him, he's blessed with thick golden surfer hair, perfect teeth, and a six-pack that he shows off a little too often at practice. Too bad he's a total dick.

"Ugh, fucking gross," I spit, and toss them to the floor. "Who has hand sanitizer?"

Raven Tannenbaum throws up her fist, which is wrapped around a small plastic bottle. "He did it to all of us," she says. Raven flips Bader off across the table and he responds by turning two fingers into a V and wiggling his tongue between them. "Ugh, gross," Raven says, shuddering. "Wanna sit, Ellie?"

Despite Raven's basicness, I have to applaud her for how nice she is. Stella calls her *vanilla*, the ultimate diss, but she was always sweet to me in Hebrew school. Plus, she trains hard as hell.

Honestly, though, it kind of sucks to be Raven. Her older sister Shira was an Edgewater golden girl until she ran away a few years ago. The police spent all their resources looking for her, canvassing every trail for miles. Everyone thought she was another murder victim, and that whoever turned Edgewater into Deadwater had finally come back. We were in middle school then and the whole town went under lockdown. No bike rides or walks to the diner. No jogs around the lake. We weren't allowed to be alone anymore—well, *the girls* weren't allowed to be alone anymore. The boys could do whatever they wanted.

But a month after she went missing, Shira came back with some older dude who ran the goat-milk yogurt stand at the farmers market. She was wearing a ring and made some apologetic statement about how they had gone to Atlantic City to get married since she had turned eighteen and knew her parents wouldn't approve. She said she needed a break from everything. From SAT prep, cross country meets, and her parents' demands to get into a good college. No one forgave her, though. How could they? The whole town was *pissed* the police department had spent so much time and money looking for her—and that she had turned Edgewater into a news story again, a haunted town that drove away tourists and homeowners and attracted killers.

Shira moved to Philadelphia after that, leaving all the drama behind, and her parents split up, unable to deal with the media attention or the stress. Raven and her mom had to move from their fancy farmhouse to a one-bedroom cottage by the pizza place. No one's heard from her dad since then. Raven stopped going to track camp that summer and started wearing cheap running clothes from the secondhand store in town instead of Julia's parents' shop. Even though Tamara and Julia stuck by her side, everyone talked shit behind her back for a while. It's been five years and Raven never mentions that time. At least not to me.

Now Raven looks at me expectantly. "This seat's open," she says, motioning beside her.

"Thanks," I say. "But I gotta save room for Stella." She turns back to her turkey sandwich. A wilted piece of lettuce hangs over one side.

I make my way around the long rectangular table and find

a seat at the end, where Stella will be able to fit. But when I see who's already sitting there, I groan.

"Mila Keene." Her name comes out of my mouth like a statement, not a greeting.

She looks up at me with wide eyes.

"Uh, hey. I'm Ellie Steckler," I say, like a normal person. "Sophomore on the team. Didn't get to say hi at practice."

Mila's face brightens into a warm grin as she unwraps her lunch. "Nice to meet you. I just moved here."

I bite back the words *I know* right as Stella shows up. "Ell, we have to remember to pick up more heating—" She stops when she sees Mila. "Oh," she says. "Hi."

"Hi!" Mila says. But her smile disappears when she sees Stella scowling. "I can go if this is your seat."

I roll my eyes. "No way. Scoot down, we'll all fit."

I can feel Stella seething, like she wants to drag her nails down my skin, hoping to draw blood. She's done it before. And so have I. But let's be real. This girl's new and has no friends. We can at least be nice to her during lunch.

"So, when did you get to town?" I ask.

"Last week," Mila says. She takes a bite out of what looks like an expertly wrapped burrito and chews slowly.

Stella grunts beside me. "Drama back home?"

I kick her under the table. Seventeen years old, and this idiot will never learn any social skills. But Mila laughs.

"You could say that. Fights with Dad. Mom and I chose each other. They're getting a divorce, blah blah blah, same old sad story. Boring, huh?" She takes another bite.

"I'm basically falling asleep," I say.

Mila swallows and laughs again, a deep hearty one that's actually nice to hear.

Stella is silent next to us, save for the obnoxious crunching sound she makes snapping baby carrots between her teeth.

"What do you think of Edgewater so far?" I ask.

"It's okay," she says, looking around the cafeteria. "Everyone seems pretty nice, but it's a little creepy, I guess."

"Ah, so you've heard about the cold cases." I pop a grape in my mouth.

She nods. "When I told people we were moving here, that was the first thing everyone brought up." Mila pauses and looks at me, curious. "Do you ever worry the killer will come back?"

I shrug. "Honestly, no one really brings it up." I lean in toward her. "We try not to mention the murders around Raven Tannenbaum. Her sister went missing a few years after the last murder and everyone thought she was another victim. It was a whole *thing*."

Mila raises her eyebrows in surprise. "Weird. But things are okay now?"

"Seems that way," I say. "Right, Stell?"

But Stella's looking right past me. She pushes her chair back and stands. "Noah." Her voice is gruff and loud when she says his name, so unlike how it sounds when I roll the letters around in my mouth. She turns it into noise.

Noah walks to us and stands directly behind my chair so I can feel his heat. I want to tackle him right here in the caf.

"Hey, Stella," he says, a little annoyed, like talking to my sister is a chore.

"We need to talk about the Fall Cross Country Formal," she says.

Noah wraps his hand around the back of my chair and I so desperately want to place my fingers on top of his. I sit on them to stop myself.

"Coach already reserved the gym and the caterer," Noah says. "Tamara is on decorations. We just have to figure out the program."

Stella crosses her arms. "Fine. Tomorrow? First period? I have study hall."

"Yes, ma'am," Noah says, doing a military salute. "Whatever the great Stella Steckler wants." Bader and some of the other guys laugh and I force myself not to join in. Noah may be a little bro-y in public, but, ugh, it's kind of endearing.

"Are you talking about the formal?" Tamara asks, appearing next to Noah. "The customized banners just arrived this morning."

"That's right, babe," Noah says. "You're so good at this stuff." He flashes her a wide, toothy smile and my insides curdle as he leans in to plant a wet kiss on her cheek, and then her lips. She rests a hand on his chest and I try not to leap from my chair and yank them apart as they shove their tongues down each other's throats.

I turn back to my lunch and make a mental note to ask Noah to please not make out with his fucking girlfriend in front of me anymore, though I know it's no use. Noah Brockston will do whatever he wants. But most of the time what he wants is me.

The doorbell rings just after dinner, when I'm icing my knee on the couch in front of a brand-new episode of some Real Housewives franchise. Praise be this dumbass show for making me forget how Noah barely looked at me during lunch and that I don't even have anyone to complain about it to now that Bethany's on my do-not-call list, population: one. I'm also zoning out to try to take my mind off the fact that I came down too hard during jump squats at practice and my knee is killing me. Coach Gary even winced while barking out orders. He didn't let me stop, of course, but I could tell he noticed.

"Who is that?" Mom yells from her office. "Ellie, can you get it?"

I heave myself off the couch and drop my dripping ice pack into the sink. By the time I hobble to the door, Stella is already there. "Move, I'll get it," she says.

"Sure, your highness," I mumble.

She reaches for the handle and throws back the door. "Coach Gary," Stella says like she's been expecting him.

"Ah, there she is," he says, arms outstretched. He's wearing the same neon tracksuit he had on at practice and looks like he's spent the past few hours holed up in his office, watching tapes and writing down drills.

Mom basically sprints into the foyer. "Coach! To what do we owe the honor?" She clasps her hands together like he's the rabbi coming over for Yom Kippur break fast. "Can I get you something? Water? Seltzer?"

Coach throws up his hands. "The most hospitable home in all of Edgewater. No, no, I'm fine. I won't be long. I just wanted to talk to Stella about the team. Mind if we post up here?" He motions to the stools at the breakfast bar.

"Not at all!" she practically shrieks. No one asks why this conversation couldn't happen at school or why Coach Gary makes unannounced house calls. But then again, no one questions him. After all, he's brought the team to State all five years since he's been here. His girls—and we're always called *his girls*—have placed every time. People credit him for keeping the program on track, keeping us safe.

But now, after Stella's incident with Allison Tarley, he's on thin ice. Why else would the school board have assigned someone to watch over practice?

Stella and Coach settle into their chairs and I hang around just in case I'm part of the conversation. But then he turns to me. "Give us a sec, Ell, okay?"

I slink back to the living room, but I can still hear them thanks to our home's open-concept plan Mom loves so much. *Assholes.*

Coach waits until he thinks I'm out of earshot to continue. He's one of the only people who knows—or at least *thinks* he knows—how to get through to Stella. But he's a pusher, and a yeller, and what works with my big sister often breaks everyone else. "Listen, Stella. We're both on the chopping block this year," he says. "They're watching us—the school board— making sure we *both* stay in line."

My shoulders tense and I suspect Stella's do, too. That's supposed to be behind us now. Coach promised.

"You've got to behave," he says. "And with Mila being here, I'm not going to pretend that your number one spot is safe. You're not guaranteed anything," he says.

Stella kicks against the stool and I can feel her fury from here. He's riling her up, making her question herself, making her doubt her abilities, her strength. I've seen him do it a million times before. But usually to Raven or the others who don't have Stella's grit.

"You've got to be ready to challenge Mila. Her being here is a good thing, you know."

Stella groans, unconvinced.

"You're going to learn how to push each other, to use your skills to make each other better. You might learn a few things from her, too, like how to control yourself, to channel that fire."

He grows serious. "Stella, you have to remember this is a *team* sport. I can bring this squad to State with or without you, but I'd rather do it with you. You just need to show the scouts you know how to be sportsmanlike and that you won't crack under pressure. Can you handle it?"

"Of course," Stella says in her clipped voice. She sounds pissed, rage curling inside her.

"I know you can," he says. "I see that in you."

I force myself not to turn around and look at their faces, but my heart starts pounding.

"I just don't know why you didn't tell me that she was coming to town. I was caught off guard," Stella says.

Coach laughs and claps Stella on the back. "But wasn't it more fun this way?"

"No," Stella says.

"Come on. You always perform better when you're on your toes."

"I don't like surprises," she says. "You know that. It messes with my brain."

My eyebrows shoot up in surprise. Stella never would have admitted that last year. Maybe Breakbridge really did work some magic.

"Well, you're going to have to learn to deal with it," he says. "Plus, you also have Ellie hot on your tail." My skin burns at the mention of my name. "You can't discount her. She's a fighter and she's got talent. She's hungry, I can feel it."

Stella doesn't say anything. A mixture of pride and fear swells in my stomach. All this will do is fuel Stella. Thicken the lines between us. Coach knows that.

"You know you can win regionals, maybe even State on your own. But don't you want a team title, too? Mila can help with that. Ellie, too. You can show the scouts that you can be on a team. College coaches value that."

Stella pauses and I can barely hear her cautious breathing. "Sure," she says.

"Your head needs to be in the game."

"My head is *always* in the game unless you do something to throw me off."

"Stella," Coach barks, his voice hard and sharp. I flinch like I'm bracing for impact. But then their voices drop and all I can hear is murmuring and the scratching of stools against the floor. Suddenly, Coach is towering over me on the couch, arms crossed over his barrel chest. "G'night, Ell. See you tomorrow."

"Night, Coach," I say. The door shuts and Stella comes back into the living room. "What was that about?" I ask, playing dumb.

But Stella busies herself fluffing pillows like she's Mom or some bullshit. "Nothing," she says. "You wouldn't get it."

"Wouldn't get what?"

Stella throws the pillow down with a violent thud and her fingers dig into the side of the couch. "I said, nothing." Her eyes are dark and for a second I see a flash of something scary. Something I thought was in the past. "Just forget it, okay?"

"Fine."

Stella heads to the stairs and I can hear her footsteps stomping overhead as she moves around her room.

I sink further into the couch and flex my leg. It's all red and tight, like a piece of raw meat. It's only then that I realize Coach didn't even ask about my knee.

5

STELLA

I FUCKING HATE parties. The dark lighting, the over-excited music, the nervous energy pulsing through the air. It's just so sad, like these people have nothing better to do, no goals to achieve, other than to get fucked up and grind on each other. Pathetic. The only one I can stomach—well, have to stomach, since I agreed to plan it—is the annual Fall Cross Country Formal.

"You're wearing that?" Ellie asks, leaning up against my doorframe. Obviously she looks amazing, with her shiny, bouncy hair and off-the-shoulder royal blue dress. She's even put on some sort of lip stuff. It glistens.

I look down at my own getup. A simple black sheath. It hangs off me like a sack. "This is the *team* formal, not the Oscars."

Ellie rolls her eyes. "So?"

I pull my hair up into a high ballerina bun. Whatever.

"Let's go." I brush past her and call to Mom and Dad. "We're gonna be late!"

They scurry behind us, Mom in a sleek navy cocktail dress and Dad in a dark suit. It's basically black tie for Edgewater.

"I heard the Keene girl and her mother are renting over by the farming museum," Mom says once we're on the road.

Ellie groans. "Please do not use tonight to try and upsell someone a house." She doesn't mention that Dad always calls the homes over there "fixer-uppers no one wants to fix."

"I never said I was going to do anything!" Mom whines, getting all defensive.

"No networking," I say harshly. Mom and Dad exchange a look in the front seats and I can't tell if that means they'll abide or just do it behind our backs. They can be *so* annoying. And pushy. And gross.

I try to cut them slack like Ellie does, but it's almost impossible. When they do something—anything—that reminds me of the Dark Years, it's like my brain short-circuits and I'm five years old again, shielding Ellie from the clanking of Mom's empty bottles and Dad's frantic gaze. We were living in the Airstream then, and I can still remember every inch of it. Before we were born they had hung up dumb hippie art, posters of the Grateful Dead and Woodstock memorabilia. Even when Grandma and Grandpa shipped Mom off to rehab, we kept everything, living among the incense holders and the beaded curtains. Ellie walked into them every time she sleepwalked and the noise would wake me. That sound will always remind me of pulling my little sister back to bed, soothing her with head pats and back rubs—of waiting to see if Mom would come back alive, if they could turn into the parents we always wanted.

When Mom did return, Ellie helped Dad make cut-out cards and paper chains. She welcomed Mom with tight hugs and neck nuzzles. She told Mom to never leave her again. But I was cautious. Distrustful.

Ellie was too young to understand why Mom left or what it was like before. She only got the good stuff. The after. The determined, hardworking duo who busted their asses to get their real estate licenses. The parents who worked together as a team to build something, to move us from a home that reminded me of aluminum foil to their favorite house on the market.

She was proud of them and what they accomplished. She wasn't even that upset when Mom relapsed. She trusted Mom would get better, like the last time. I didn't, though. Now it's always in the back of my mind. The fact that Mom's always teetering on the edge of destruction and we're the ones waiting to deal with the fallout.

That's what I kept thinking about when I came out. I sat both of my parents down and read a letter I had written, like I saw on YouTube, unease churning in my stomach. But when I reached the end of the page and lifted my gaze, I was expecting one of the classic reactions I read about on an LGBTQ+ resource website—something resembling disappointment or rage, surprise or excitement. I was worried my admission would send Mom into a tailspin. But instead, she and Dad just smiled pleasantly, unfazed.

"Oh, Stell, is that all?" Mom asked.

"Uh, yeah," I said.

"I think what your mom is trying to say is that to us, it's just not that big of a deal," Dad said, leaning forward to rest his elbows on his knees. "We love you unconditionally."

Mom nodded beside him, but looked a bit distracted, like she wanted to check her phone or prepare for another open house.

"Oh," I said, my heart deflating. "Okay." Suddenly, I wanted the conversation to end. I knew I should have felt things like relief or joy. But the whole encounter was just so underwhelming. I was glad I had done it. It was a good thing. I knew that in my bones. But nothing changed between us. We all just continued on with our lives.

Yeah, they were happy when I told them I joined the LGBTQ+ alliance at school, but it wasn't like I was going to confide in them that it felt like I was being strangled when I was crushing on Lilly Adams and saw her making out with Jade Kensington at practice. I just kept moving about the world, my queer heart another thing that made me whole, and my mind focused on the one thing that could propel me forward: winning.

I press my forehead against the car window and fog the window with my breath. As soon as we pull into the high school parking lot, I pop open the door. "Gotta find Coach and Noah," I call over my shoulder. Even though Noah is completely useless, Coach has always told me that people feel more included when they're . . . uh, included. So I've been trying to make an effort. Doesn't help that I constantly want to punch his face. Or that he looks at Ellie like she's an ice-cream sundae, even though he's basically married to Tamara. Gross.

I walk through the dark hallways toward the gym until I see a light illuminating Coach's office doorway. It's my first time back here since the spring, when I was summoned by Principal Pérez. It smells the same as it did then, like sweat and Lysol. I have to stop to catch my breath for a second.

I thought things had settled down then, that Pérez, Coach, and I were just going to talk about logistics, like assigning booster club roles and fall training schedules. But when I arrived and dropped into the metal chair, Pérez's face was stern, her mouth a straight line.

"Stella, this is serious," she had said. Her dark shoulder-length hair was flecked with gray and she pushed a pair of reading glasses up on her forehead. She had come to Edgewater High after Shira Tannenbaum disappeared. Apparently the school board organized a statewide search to find a principal who could help raise fundraising numbers, increase safety, and send students off to college at an above-average rate. They were determined to make Edgewater a happy place. A safe place. A place that didn't make you think of dead girls.

The superintendent found her in Westchester County, where she had been the principal at some snooty suburban high school for fifteen years. Her district was number one in the state. Mom told me Pérez wanted to move to Edgewater because she liked a challenge. She's the one who recruited Coach Gary to revamp the cross country program *and* persuaded the town council to expand the education budget. She even organized fully funded trips to Mexico City, where her parents were born and her brother works as a curator at the big anthropology museum. In a matter of two years, Principal Pérez was 100 percent beloved.

"Lauren," Coach said. "What are you really worried about here? Stella intentionally breaking someone's neck? She's a *kid*, not a monster. This whole Allison Tarley thing was an accident." His bald head was shiny under the fluorescent light and he gave me a soft smile. *I'm on your side.*

Pérez ignored him, and turned to me. "Stella, there's no easy way to say this. You are a liability. Keeping you here on the team is a risk for all of us."

My tongue became heavy and I swallowed the venom building in my throat.

"But you are also our best chance at winning State next year. And we *have* to win."

Coach let out a puff of air, relieved.

"Cross country is the only team we have that can bring in the PTA money we need to keep this school as the best in the county," Pérez said. "You saw what happened to Tremont a few years back when that new coach ran their football team into the ground. Numbers plummeted. They lost their IB program. College matriculation declined. Families *moved*." She fiddled with the gold wedding band on her ring finger. Her nails were freshly painted, pink and shiny. "All I'm saying is if you fly off the handle again, I'll have no choice but to remove you from the team. And I really don't want to do that."

I nodded. It was the only motion I could make.

"But before that, we need to show the community that you've *changed*, that you've put in the *work*." Pérez reached down into her slick leather briefcase and pulled out a brochure for Breakbridge. She handed it to me. The paper was thick and glossy, heavy to the touch.

"What is this?" I asked, my voice scratchy.

"Where you'll be spending the summer," she said. "It's a track camp that focuses on anger management. Group therapy three times a week. A personalized counselor attuned to your needs. Plus, there's a grueling training program."

I flipped through the pages. It didn't sound so bad. In fact, it was kind of perfect. Until I got to the final page, where a bunch of numbers smacked me right in the face.

"I don't think we can afford this," I said softly, heat creeping into my cheeks.

Pérez and Coach exchanged a look.

"We've spoken to your parents," Coach said. "You're going."

My heart raced, thinking about how much this would cost them, how much I had already cost the whole family. "Okay," I said, and looked at Coach, then Pérez. I had no other options.

"You're good, Stella, but you're not untouchable. No one is,"

Pérez said. She stood then, and left the room, her yellow linen dress swishing around her calves.

Now, right outside Coach's office, I can still feel the warm air from last spring, how it was heavy and hot as I tried to figure out what it all meant. But I made it through. I survived. It's time to get back to work, to get to State, to show them all who I *still* am.

I knock on the door and push it open with my knuckle. "Ready, Coach?"

He looks up expectantly from behind his desk, a stack of papers in his hand. "Stella!" He smooths his tie over his crisp white button-down. "Let's do this."

Together we walk to the gym. My hands shake as I throw open the door, and when I actually see inside, I'm blinded by school spirit.

It barely looks like a gym, with round tables set up at odd angles, plastic folding chairs tucked under them. Each table is covered in a blue or white fabric tablecloth, decorated with big balloon centerpieces. The lights are low and Tamara's customized banners hang from the walls. Members of the team and their families mill about, breaking off hunks of cheese from a mountainous appetizer board and plucking roasted artichokes from an antipasto platter. The soccer formal consisted of take-out pizza and grocery store cupcakes. No surprise, though. Neither the men's nor women's team had won anything in decades. But we're different. We win. We earn this farm-to-table catered dinner for sixty people. I turn away from everyone to the front of the room, where a small podium and microphone are set up.

"Queen Stella, we're at your service," Noah says, approaching with Tamara. He takes a bow.

Tamara rolls her eyes at him and tugs on a few of her braids. "Dork," she says, and runs her hands over her coral-colored dress, which flares out around her hips. She turns to me. "Ready for this?"

"Obviously." I must say it harshly because she takes a step back.

"Hey, hey. Be nice," Noah says. "We're all captains. Let's just not make a scene."

Before I can respond, Coach comes up behind us and slaps my and Noah's shoulders with his palms. It's warm and sweaty on my bare skin. All I want to do is pry him off.

"Ready, guys? My A-team. My captains. Shall we begin?"

"You know it, Coach," Noah says.

"Suck-up," I whisper as we walk to the podium.

He smirks in my direction and strides toward the mic so he gets there before I do, forcing me to stand next to him like a sidekick. As soon as people see Noah in front of the room, with his broad shoulders stretching the seams of his collared shirt, the room goes quiet. People tiptoe to their seats. Respect. That's what Noah has. Must be nice.

I scan the room and find Ellie, Mom, and Dad sitting just off-center. An empty seat waits for me next to Ellie. But then I see who else they're with. Mila. She's wearing a simple sleeveless red dress, laughing with Ellie like they already share inside jokes. I don't know why Ellie doesn't get it. You're not supposed to befriend your competition. Keeping them at arm's length is the only way to win.

I clench my fists and only realize I'm staring when Mila offers her hand up in a little wave. Her mouth is stretched into a smile. I avert my eyes and turn my attention to Noah, who's

probably been fucking up this whole speech while I wasn't paying attention. Great.

"And that's why this year will be the best we've ever had!"
he screams into the mic. The boys erupt in cheers. They pound
their fists into the air and their parents clap, thrilled at their
male displays of aggression. Nobody wants to see that from
the girls.

"Now you get to hear from Edgewater's favorite fighter . . .
Stella Steckler," Noah says. My skin grows hot but I can't let
my fury show. Not toward Noah. Everyone knows what he's
insinuating with the word *fighter*, but that doesn't mean I have
to acknowledge it.

I nudge him out of the way and take my place in front of
the microphone. I know I should try to savor this moment. I'm
finally the captain, even though I'm only a junior. But it feels
hollow, like no one really wants to listen to me, like I shouldn't
be up here. At one point I thought I earned this title. I toiled
away, running drills and lifting weights until I became the best.
But now I just see people who roll their eyes when I call out
stretches during practice. Ellie's the only one I can count on—
and only sometimes.

"Hi everyone," I say into the mic, ignoring the low chatter
in the back of the room. "I just want to welcome Mila Keene to
the team." I grit my teeth as I motion to Mila sitting with her
mom. "Coming from a great squad in Connecticut, she's sure
to be an asset and we're glad to have her." Mila pushes her chair
back and stands, turning and smiling at the room.

Applause breaks out and Coach nods approvingly.

"We have a lot to accomplish this year," I say. "Our first
meet is next week and we have so much to do before then." I

spot Raven and Julia just in time for them to exchange a knowing glance. "So let's have fun tonight and get ready to put in
the work."

Tamara leans in and pulls the mic toward her. "Emphasis on
the *fun*, right, guys?" The tables erupt in cheers and claps and
I slink back, letting her take center stage.

"See you all at the after-party!" she yells. "Cross country
forever!"

The crowd keeps cheering and I want to melt into my too-
tight heels as I rush back to my seat. Ellie barely looks up
when I drop next to her. She's deep in conversation with Mila,
laughing and talking closely over a basket of dinner rolls.

"Give a shit much?" I whisper.

"Sorry," she mumbles, turning to me. "You were great."

I pull my napkin to my lap and turn away.

"Let's go to the party this year," she says. "I want to."

"So go," I say. Famously, I refused to drive her and Bethany
last year and she pouted for a whole week, miserable that she
missed out on a bunch of Jell-O shots and some unsavory time
in a hot tub filled with germs.

Mila, who's sitting on Ellie's other side, leans over. "Are you
talking about the party?"

Ellie nods. "Want to go? I'm dying to."

"Sure," Mila says a bit too enthusiastically.

Ellie glares at me and then smiles at Mila. "Cool."

"I can drive if you want," Mila says.

Ellie's eyes light up and she nods with actual happiness.

"Great," Mila says, and pops a piece of buttered roll into her
mouth.

6

STELLA

WHEN WE PULL up to Tamara's place, all the girls from the team have already changed into jeans and crop tops, or tiny strapless dresses. The boys are wearing their standard uniform of hoodies and drawstring pants. "Easy access," Bader always says. Barf.

Ellie even jumped into Mila's back seat to swap her cocktail dress for high-waisted jeans and a halter top she had stuffed into her backpack.

"Guess we didn't get the memo," Mila says, stepping out of the car. She motions to the dumbass sack I'm wearing.

I pretend like I don't hear her and open the door. Might as well watch the debauchery while I'm here. I never really understood why people like to lose control like this. Why would you want to be anything but peak? Why let yourself fall anywhere below 100? It never made sense to me. Especially after seeing Mom become a different person in the span of minutes.

But maybe I just hate this specific party because of what happened freshman year. That year, Lilly Adams hosted it. She was captain, after all. And I was a rookie, forced to tag along even though I wanted to go home and watch science documentaries.

I stood in the corner, watching my teammates pass around a bottle of something dark and threatening, and tried to make myself as small as possible until I could sneak out, undetected. But something kept me rooted in place.

Lilly was perched on the counter, wearing a denim skirt and a floral top. Her platinum-blonde hair was tied into two space buns and she was sitting cross-legged so you could see a little triangle of her lacy underwear. She was either unaware or unbothered. Both ideas made my skin prickle. Lilly threw her head back and laughed, throwing her arm around Jade Kensington, the senior she diverted her attention to as soon as school started.

Jade tucked a stray piece of Lilly's hair behind her ear and leaned in, kissing her gently on the cheek. My stomach spasmed and something inside me cracked.

It had only been a month since Lilly unceremoniously started ignoring me but it was enough time to make me think the entire summer was a dream. A blip in my imagination. She had been my teammate at the Elite Youth Runner's Club's summer program and we spent most hazy evenings together, driving around in her beat-up Buick sedan, bad country music blaring from her speakers.

There was one sticky night up at Sweetwater Lake when the crickets were out, chirping into the heavy air. We were lying on a flannel blanket on top of the hood of her car, cracking jokes about the people who summer here. The ones who don't bat an eyelash at spending forty dollars on a jar of honey or are willing to wait in line for half an hour to get nitro cold brew at the fancy coffee shop attached to Ellacoya. They crowd the lake in the warm months, then head to the apple orchards to take their autumnal photoshoots come September.

"My parents' clients are always talking about how brave they are for buying property in a town that was once called Deadwater," I had said to Lilly, twirling a leaf in between my fingers. "But they don't live here year-round. They don't realize all the bad shit that comes with it."

Lilly grew quiet and hummed to the music. "At least it's better than it was before. You weren't old enough to realize what it was like when Shira went missing," she said. Lilly was a freshman on the team when that went down. "It was a nightmare. She brought back so many old memories. My parents wouldn't let me leave the house alone until she came back." Lilly sat up and looked around. "I can't wait to get out of this place."

She reached for my hand and squeezed it gently. "I can't talk about this with my friends," she said. "Everyone thinks it's bad luck to talk about the cold cases. Or that I'm being a 'downer,'" she said, using air quotes around the final word. "But they happened—and whoever killed those runners is still out there. How can we forget about that?"

"We can't," I said.

"That's why I'm glad you're here, Stella. You understand." She babbled on for a bit longer, talking about her duties as president of the LGBTQ+ Alliance, what preseason would look like, and how she couldn't wait for me to join the squad. Then she rolled onto one side so she faced me. Her lips were pink and full and curved into a smile. She leaned toward me with such authority, such clarity, that I leaned in, too. I was hungry for her.

"Do you like me, Stella?"

For a second, I wondered if it was a trick question. If she was going to laugh if I said yes, but I couldn't lie. Not to her. So I nodded greedily and held my breath, waiting for her response.

"Good," Lilly said. "I like you, too." She reached for my hand and pressed her lips against my palm, sending a bolt of lightning through my body. Then she intertwined her legs with mine and we stayed like that for a while, whispering into the night.

Later, after she dropped me off, I crept into my room, though I knew Mom and Dad wouldn't be mad. No, they were thrilled that I was hanging out with the varsity cross country captain. But I didn't want to answer questions. I wanted to go upstairs and climb under the covers, so I was alone with just me and my body and the desperate need to relieve myself of the heat between my legs.

We had adventures like that for the rest of the summer, never talking about what we *were* or what it would be like when school started in September. Then, on the first day of preseason, I saw her and Jade together and it was obvious they were dating. When I tried to confront her, she just . . . ignored me.

It was as if the moments we spent together meant nothing now that we were in the Edgewater High ecosystem, where Lilly Adams, the beloved senior captain, couldn't deign to be seen with me, a lowly freshman. She and Jade were Edgewater royalty and I was left with a queasy feeling, unsure of who I could ever trust again.

But Lilly was the first person who made me feel that way, who ruptured something inside of me that I couldn't bandage up. I stayed needy and swollen all season while she flirted with Jade and led us through drills. It helped that they both weren't competition. Lilly and Jade ran for fun, not for need. But at that party, I couldn't help but feel like she was rubbing her relationship in my face.

Now, walking into Tamara's house with Mila and Ellie, I feel like I'm the chaperone. A few sophomores on the team hide their beers when I walk past, as if I would text Coach immediately. But I couldn't care less. Their lack of discipline just makes them weaker.

Ellie leads us through the massive entryway, decorated with funky, handmade pottery and bright, modern paintings, into the sleek white kitchen, where she promptly ditches Mila and me for the make-your-own-margarita station by the farmhouse sink. She never has any problem letting loose. She's convinced the boozy gene won't get her. To be determined, though.

"You want a drink?" Mila asks.

"Aren't you driving?" I say. Top 40 hits blast over the speakers and I spot a shirtless Noah pounding clear shots at a bar set up in the living room.

"I asked if *you* want a drink," Mila says.

I shake my head. "Not my vibe."

"Figured."

For some reason, her words make me furious. "What's that supposed to mean?"

Mila's face grows red. "I just—"

"You just what?"

Mila falls silent, her mouth open just a bit. She looks wounded, which makes me realize that, yeah, I do want a drink just to prove her wrong. "Hey, Ellie, make me one," I say over my shoulder.

She swings her head around and looks at me with raised eyebrows.

"Just do it."

Ellie smiles in a mischievous way and turns around. When she walks back to us, she hands me a red plastic cup filled to the brim with neon-green liquid. "So, it's best to sip—" she starts to say. But who has the time to play by the rules tonight? Not me, not with Mila here, acting like we're friends.

I tip the cup back and chug half of it at once. The booze burns my throat and my eyes start to water. It's sugary and tangy and my stomach is on fire.

Ellie's eyes are bright and wanting as she sips her drink slowly. "Is this the night we finally get drunk together and braid each other's hair and come up with a sisters-only choreographed dance?" Her voice is dripping in sarcasm but there's a lightness to her. Sometimes, I look at her and wonder how the hell we can be related when her default mannerisms are calm and smiley, when her most defining quality is *chill*. But then I see her mouth get small and hear her knuckles crack and it's like I can peer into her brain, where we both think the same thing. *Win.*

I hold my cup out. "Cheers, bitch." Ellie shoves hers into mine, and liquid sloshes onto the floor.

"Man," Mila says. "I always wished I had a sister."

"You can have her," Ellie and I say at the same time. We both break into giggles. It feels good to laugh. To have the sound bubble up my chest and pass through my throat. It feels like practice, like running through cold air, like drinking a milkshake. I forgot the pleasure of cracking inside jokes with Ellie. Whenever Mom would take us to the grocery store or the hardware store, she'd plunk us down in the corner with markers and paper. For the first few minutes we would duck our heads and laugh, elbowing each other softly. "Aren't they sweet," someone would say.

"You can have her," Mom would reply, dead serious, because it wasn't long until our tender movements would shift into a fight. We'd spit and pull and choke until we were restless little puddles on the floor.

You can have her. We never knew which one of us she was referring to.

Mila smiles and cracks open a can of seltzer. Then suddenly Ellie glimpses something or someone over my shoulder and her whole body tenses. "Be right back," she mumbles before pushing past some freshman and disappearing into the crowd. Now I'm stuck with Mila. Great. I throw what's left of my cup back into my mouth and swallow hard.

"Want a refill?" a sophomore manning the bar asks.

I nod even though my throat still burns. He takes my cup and when he hands it back to me, I see the liquid is bright orange. I take a sip and try not to gag.

"Come on," I say to Mila. "Let's find something interesting."

She trails behind me as we walk through the den, where a bunch of sophomores are making out in pairs in the dark.

Mila wrinkles her nose. "Is everyone here always so PDA like this?"

"Yup," I say, wincing. "Shameless. All of them."

She laughs. "Barf." Her response surprises me, but I'm secretly glad that I'm not the only person who can't stand this mess. It's so showy. So obscene. Made for people who aren't exceptional on their own, who need something extra to feel alive.

I take another sip and realize my second cup is empty. I drop it into the garbage and reach for an unopened beer can on the table.

"So what else do people do around here for fun?" Mila asks as we walk out to the deck. "Other than *not* talk about the cold cases?"

"You picked up on that?" I ask.

"I tried to ask the guy at the pizza place about it and he acted like I had just told him to go fuck himself."

I grimace. "Was it Scott Childers? White guy with a gray beard? Orange Crocs?"

She nods.

"Yeah, that tracks," I say. "His daughter Abigail was one of the victims. The second one."

Mila's face pales and she covers her mouth with her hand. "I'm such an idiot."

For a second I feel bad for her. "There's no way you could have known it was him," I say. "They weren't really in the press or anything." She's quiet for a second, looking embarrassed, and I feel the need to fill the space. "Well, there are great running paths up by Ellacoya," I say. "There's one called Foxfire Point that has the best views. The vista's like a painting."

Mila nods and seems to come back to herself just a bit. "Oh, nice. Maybe we can go together sometime. I miss my running buddies back home. Always hated practicing alone."

I'm about to tell her *hell the fuck no*, that I don't run with anyone—ever—and that "running buddies" are not my thing. But all of a sudden, someone bumps me from behind and I stumble, feeling dizzy and disoriented. My beer is knocked to the ground, splashing all over my shoes and I grab the deck railing to steady myself, wondering why the sky is now on its side.

"Whoa, you okay?" Mila asks, holding her hands out as if to spot me.

"Sorry," I say, a flush creeping into my cheeks.

"Do you wanna go home?" she asks. "I can drive you."

I look at the party, at the people I hate chugging shitty drink after shitty drink and—yeah, I really do.

I nod. "Let's find Ellie."

Mila leads the way as we walk from room to room, but my sister is nowhere to be found, lost in the maze of Tamara Johnson's house. "What do you want to do?" Mila asks.

Fucking Ellie. This is so classic. Promising to have the best sisterly night, then ditching.

"Fuck it," I say. "Let's go."

"Do you live far from here? Will she be okay?"

"More than okay." It's only a mile away and Ellie knows these roads by heart. We all do.

"Okay, then," Mila says. I follow her out to the front and into the passenger seat of her used Honda Accord. She revs the engine and turns the stereo to something soft and mellow. A woman's voice sings delicate little notes then explodes, filling the car with longing and devotion as a man joins her for the chorus.

Mila hums as she reverses and pulls out into the street. "I love this song," she says.

"What is this?" I ask.

"'Silver Springs' by Fleetwood Mac," she says. "Reminds me of my old cross country course, my old team."

"You run to this?" I ask. It surprises me. The bridge is slow and melodic, coursing through my blood at half tempo before it crescendos into an explosion. Nothing like the generic garbage that fills everyone else's playlists.

"I run to sad shit. Dark shit. Light-your-insides-on-fire shit. Stuff like Nina Simone and Linda Ronstadt. My best friend, Naomi, used to make fun of me for it," she says. "But it calms me. It makes everything go away. It makes me feel free."

My head is pounding and I want to tell her that's the dumbest thing I ever heard. But I don't. Because I get it. All the Top 40 stuff makes me furious, all the clichés and fake hooks. It's manipulative.

I want to tell Mila I run to weird music too. Classical stuff, like Mozart and Chopin. Science podcasts, sometimes, when I really need a distraction. But Mila speaks first. "Which way?" she asks when we get to the stoplight.

"A left here," I say, nodding toward the dark eerie street. The lights blur in front of me and I wonder if this is what being drunk is like, if I'll feel hungover in the morning.

"You can keep going straight," I say when we pull up to a stop sign.

She maneuvers the car forward and I glance over at her hands. A tiny daisy-chain tattoo encircles her wrist, looping around like a poem.

"When did you get that?" I ask.

"The day we left my dad," she says, her voice a little hoarse and far away. "Naomi and I got matching ones to mark the moment." Mila pauses and grips the steering wheel hard. "He's an addict. Pills. Mom gave him one last chance, but . . ." Mila shakes her head. "It was time for us to leave."

I want to tell her about my parents, about the Dark Years,

about Mom's relapse. How I felt it was my duty to protect Ellie after living with such uncertainty. How we won't really know how it affected us until later, until we dig up that trauma and wallow around in it like mud.

Mila leans back against the headrest. "We were thinking of moving down to New York, where my aunt Deb lives, but Mom hates the city. That's where she grew up after my grandparents moved the family there from Puerto Rico. But Mom always loved the country, and she'd visited Ellacoya once before. So here we are." Mila shrugs as if the move was no big deal, as if her mom decided to make chicken instead of beef. "It feels good to let someone know about my dad. I had a lot of friends in Hadbury, but they were kind of phony, to be honest. I couldn't really trust anyone except Naomi. Learned that the hard way when my ex-boyfriend witnessed one of my dad's episodes. He told everyone and then dumped me, saying I had too much 'baggage.'"

I open my mouth to say that's why I never open up to people, too. You never know who will use private information as ammo. Mila smiles. "I probably shouldn't be saying all of this to you. You must think I'm a freak," she says. "But I don't know. I guess I'm just trying to make friends. Does that make me the biggest loser in the world?"

I know I'm supposed to laugh but I just look out the window, booze buzzing in my brain. "You don't want to be friends with me," I say. "I'm dangerous. That's what everyone says." It's easier to say what someone else is thinking before they do.

Mila's eyes stay focused on the road. "I know," she says. "I read about what happened with Allison Tarley last year."

My heart jumps into my throat. I need to flee, to get the hell out of here. But instead, I press my forehead against the cool window and look up at the sky. "Do you think I'm a monster?" I whisper into the glass.

"No," Mila says, matter-of-fact. "I mean, I might have done the same thing if I was in your position."

My stomach clenches and I motion for her to pull into my driveway.

"Maybe that's why I just told you all of that," she says quietly. "Because I know you also have big shit to deal with. Let's face it. You're a force."

Something about those words makes me tense, makes my fingers curl around the door handle. There's no point in being known like this, not here in Edgewater. "I have to go," I mumble.

"Okay." She starts to say something else, but I can't hear her because I fling myself out of the car and take giant steps up the driveway, listening for her engine to start back up. When it finally does, I pick up my pace and lunge for the door. As soon as I hit the first concrete step, my head lolls and my eyes rest on the ivy Mom planted last year, hoping it would grow a few feet to cover a couple broken bricks on the side of the house. No one expected it to rise from the earth and spread all the way up the trellis so it almost reaches Ellie's bedroom window on the second floor, so it flaunts its strength and resilience. No one knew how much it could withstand. That's what I'm thinking when I barf on our welcome mat.

7

ELLIE

I *WAKE UP* to my phone vibrating next to me on my pillow. I groan but reach for it, wiping sleep from my eyes as I make out the name on the screen. When I see who's FaceTiming me, I smooth my hair down and swipe to answer.

"Noah," I say, angling the phone so it catches my good side. I stick my tongue out at him and he smiles.

"Hey, babe." Noah's propped up in his bed, his chest bare, and I want to touch him through the screen. I shiver, remembering how it felt to have his weight on top of me, shifting back and forth.

"What's up?" I ask.

"I just wanted to say hi before the meet," he says. "Wish you luck, you know, since we can't really be like that when we get there."

My heart sinks. Of course.

"Aw, Ell. Come on," he says, bringing the phone close to his face. I didn't even have to say anything for him to know something was off. "You know this will be over soon. I'll hear about early decision in December, then we'll have a whole semester to be together."

"It just sucks. Sneaking around like this makes me feel like crap, you know?" I don't tell him about the rage I felt watching him make out with Tamara all night at the cross country formal—especially after I spent an hour looking for him at the party. Or how I can't bear to let him go because of the secret we share. Instead I push myself to sit up. "Maybe we can hang out sometime soon? One of our midnight walks?" I try to hide my desperation. The hunger. The need for him to tell me it's me, it'll always be me.

Noah nods but looks away. "Soon, Ellie. For sure, soon."

"When?" I ask, my voice wavering. "This week?"

He ignores the question. "Where's the bracelet, Ell? Remember the bracelet?"

"The one you told me to take off?"

Noah looks away, annoyed. "Come on, that's not fair."

"Yeah, well, this isn't fair to *me*. After what we went through . . ."

Noah purses his lips and runs a hand through his hair. "Can we please not talk about this right now?" he says, his voice an angry whisper. "I've got to get ready for the meet."

"You never want to discuss it," I say, the frustration building in my throat.

"What's the point?" he asks, exasperated. "If people find out, you know this will look bad for *you*." His eyes are shifty, moving away from the camera. "People will talk shit about you more than me. That's just how it is."

Tears form in the corners of my eyes, and I bite my lip to keep from crying. I know he's right. If I told even one person the truth, no one would look at me the same way again.

Noah looks off-camera, bored and irritated. "I gotta go. I just called to wish you luck, okay?" Then he hangs up and my screen goes dark, his face imprinted in my brain. I always forget he can be cruel like this, slick and slippery when he doesn't want to do something.

"Ellie!" Stella calls from outside my room. "Leaving in ten." She bangs her fist a few times on the door for emphasis.

"No shit," I mumble.

I throw my phone down and force myself out of bed. I push Noah out of my brain and try to let the excitement of meet day pulse through my body. I let my mind wander, playing the same *if-then* game I have for years. *If I bring Noah's red bracelet with me, I'll break my PR. If I forget celery in my green juice, I'll come in second. If I don't do forty-five jumping jacks during practice, I won't place. If I . . .*

It's a game I've played with myself ever since the Youth Running Club. Little twisted mantras I repeat over and over. Superstitions that mean nothing, but also everything. I can't stop them and I don't want to. I always follow them, whatever pops into my head.

The wheels are turning and the rules are coming to me as I put on the blue Lycra shorts and the matching racerback tank top with white lettering along the chest. I gather my hair in a high ponytail and stuff my feet into black sneakers. In the mirror, I look like an athlete. A warrior. Ready for battle. *If Noah talks to me at warm-ups, I'll win. If he doesn't . . .* I force myself not to finish the thought.

When I get downstairs, Stella is already stretching in the living room, smoothie blending on high. She's wrapped in a warm-up jacket that crinkles when she bounces into the air, her hair twisted in a tight French braid. She was never into the functional high pony.

I make a beeline for the blender but before I can portion

the green liquid into two cups, Stella comes up behind me.

"Snooze you lose."

"What the hell?"

"Meet day. I need it all."

"Uh, are you kidding? I don't have time to make another one."

She shrugs and grabs the blender from my hand. "Shoulda been down here earlier."

My face heats up and I want to push her and that glass pitcher to the floor and shove her face into the murky mess. But instead, I clench my fists and grit my teeth and reach into the pantry to find our stash of protein bars.

"Okay, no. You definitely can't eat that right before a meet," she says, appalled.

I'm about to shove the wrapper straight down her throat when she rolls her eyes and reluctantly portions her smoothie into two cups. "Fine," she says, handing me half.

Mom appears in the doorway. "Girls, time to go."

I should know better than to fight on meet day. To "rile Stella up," as Mom puts it. But sometimes, when I look at my sister's smug face, I just want to crush her. I hate when she gets like this. Moody and solitary, like she's the only one with problems, with goals. It's how she deals with stress, Mom once told me. She bottles it up and fights off outside forces, even if they're helpful. It's a defense mechanism, Mom said. It must be.

It's what kept her—and me, to be honest—alive during the Dark Years and the short period when Mom relapsed. Mom had been at a wedding of an old high school friend somewhere in the Berkshires. Went alone so they didn't have to hire a weekend babysitter. They were still getting the business off the ground and money was tight. Dad could watch us, no problem.

That Saturday night, he cued up some old rom-com. *When Harry Met Sally . . .*, I think. We were going in on a big bowl of popcorn and each had a glass bottle of root beer when Dad's cell phone buzzed.

At first he ignored it, tearing up as Meg Ryan confessed her love to Billy Crystal. I laughed at him and Dad just patted my head. "Your dad's a big ol' crier," he said, grabbing a handful of popcorn. "Deal with it."

But when his phone kept ringing, he begrudgingly picked up. The mood shifted. Stella noticed it first, staring at him with her big roving eyes. Dad stood up from the couch and went into his office, closing the door.

"Whatever it is, it's going to be okay," Stella whispered. "You and me forever, okay?"

I didn't really understand what she meant, why she was being so dramatic. But then Dad came out of the office in his beat-up jean jacket, flustered. "Everything's fine, but I have to go get your mother. Mrs. Levin from next door is coming over, okay?" he said.

And then he was gone. Stella squeezed my hand in a strange, motherly way. But it helped ease the aches in my stomach. Later, after we went to sleep, the night terrors came back. It was my first episode in years. I woke up in a sweat, sheets tangled around my feet, heart racing. The moon hung high and bright outside my window and I tossed and turned, trying to calm down. But I couldn't. Finally, I heaved myself out of bed and crept into Stella's room. I pulled back her big quilt and cuddled close to her, feeling the warmth from her back. Her breathing was steady and I thought she was asleep. But just as I started to drift off, she spoke. "It's you and me forever, Ell," she said.

It was only later that we found out Mom had allowed herself a glass of champagne, which turned into a few too many, which turned into a drunken rant against her old friends and a fight over the car keys. Dad got there just before she sped away into the dark night. She went back to treatment. Outpatient this time. Started going to meetings every Thursday evening in the basement of the old church in town. But no one wanted to talk about it. Stella and I only spoke about it in hushed whispers, late at night, when I was startled awake from a nightmare and would tiptoe into her room for comfort.

Stella stopped trusting them after that. But I latched on harder. I try not to think about all that now. It's in the past. Forgotten. We Stecklers are indestructible. Mom said that herself.

The first meet of the season is always at Hanover High, where the course is flat and predictable, winding through the woods at the base of Mount Kutz. Stella came in first here last year, dominating the easy terrain. I beat everyone else on our team, but landed in fourth place overall. Nothing to be mad about, but it sure didn't earn me kudos from Coach.

Stella and I climb out of the car and walk in silence toward the team. She's got a dark, menacing look in her eyes—like she wants to watch someone burn. It's that look that scares people. That makes them think she's dangerous. I love it, though. Reminds me we're all carnal on the inside. I get it, too. We have the same DNA, the same hunger. I just know how to hide it better.

Stella pushes past the parents chitchatting on the sidelines to the grassy warm-up area next to the bleachers. She drops her bag and reaches inside, retrieving her enormous set of noise-canceling headphones.

"You're not going to lead us in stretching, *captain?*" I smirk in her direction but she doesn't even hear me.

I scan the group for Noah, and it's only when I turn my head to the bleachers that I see him. Leaning over the metal railing, he's smiling wide, gazing up at Mr. Johnson, Tamara's dad. Noah laughs and throws his head back and Mr. Johnson gives him a hearty pat on the shoulder, like he's proud, like Noah is family.

Mr. Johnson taps his chest. He's wearing his Princeton Alumni windbreaker and Noah nods, staring longingly at that neon-orange *P*. The whole scene makes me gag. Over the summer I learned so much about Noah. That chili is his favorite food, even when it's hot out. That he can juggle, but only for fifteen seconds and not one longer. That after college, he wants to move to DC and work in politics. But one thing I never understood, never could crack, was why Princeton—one school amid many excellent options—was more important than telling the truth, than being with me.

Noah jogs back to the group but avoids making eye contact with me. He winks at Tamara and assumes a quad stretch, bouncing up and down on his left leg.

"You okay?" Raven asks, her voice high and curious. "You look nervous."

"Oh, yeah, I am a little, I guess," I say, playing down my anxiety. Even though she's *vanilla*, her loyalty still lies with Tamara.

"First meet of the season's always a little stressful," she says, kicking her heel in front of her to stretch out her calf.

Raven would know. She landed right in the middle of the

pack during last season's kickoff meet. Would have been fine for most of the girls here. But after, I remember watching as her mom tried to comfort her in the parking lot after the race. "I know you're disappointed," she'd said, running a hand down her back. "Shira used to crush this course."

"Yes, Mom, we all remember how incredible Shira was at everything," Raven hissed, throwing her water bottle to the ground. The parking lot was almost empty but a few heads turned toward the noise. "We get it! I'm a total loser," she spat out. "I'll never be as good as Shira. I'll never get a scholarship. I'll never be number one like she was. The only thing I can do that she didn't is *not* run away." It was a rare break from her submissive demeanor and I froze on the way to our car, watching her body shake as she cried.

Mrs. Tannenbaum looked around warily, trying to contain the scene. She was used to the stares, the ones that came after Shira left town. But Raven was supposed to be the stable one, the one who would put her family back together. It was too much pressure, I guess.

Mrs. Tannenbaum wrapped a hand around her daughter's wrist tightly. "We'll talk about this at home, okay? Let's get in the car." Raven glanced up and saw me standing there, watching.

I tried to think of something nice to say. But I came in fourth. Raven didn't even place.

"What are you looking at?" Raven asked, her cheeks stained with tears.

"Nothing," I said. "Just—you had a bad day, that's all. You'll do better next time."

Raven scoffed. "You'll never get it, Ellie. Not all of us are born Stecklers."

I was left speechless as she threw herself into the passenger seat of her mom's car and slammed the door, wondering what the hell she meant.

Now Raven's all sunshine and rainbows, her usual perky self. She rustles around inside her track jacket and pulls out a bright-blue face-paint stick. "Want some?" she asks, extending her hand. But then Julia stomps over to us.

"I thought we decided face paint was bad for our skin, Rave," she says, rolling her eyes. "It made me break out like crazy last time."

Raven chews the inside of her cheek and shoves the face paint back in her pocket. "Right."

"Of course I'm right." Julia leans down and wraps her arms around Raven's neck in a hug, then winces. "Ugh, you've *got* to stop buying your clothes at Charlie's Vintage," Julia says. "That jacket smells like my grandma."

Raven purses her lips and red splotches form on her pale, freckled neck.

"Not everyone *wants* to spend a million dollars at your dad's stuck-up store, Julia," I say, rolling my eyes as I stretch my arms overhead. "Everyone knows you guys jack everything up a bajillion percent."

"Oh, fuck off, Baby Steckler," Julia says. "It's not my fault we're the only place in the whole county that sells designer athleisure. You wanna go all the way to Westchester to get Lululemon?" She nods over her shoulder at Raven. "Come on, let's get some water."

Raven stands reluctantly and follows her to the cooler. But she looks back at me and gives a small wave, like she doesn't want anyone else to see. In another world, I could actually imagine being friends with Raven. But not in this one, where she spends her whole life repaying Tamara and Julia for taking care of her after Shira left.

Everyone knows that after Raven's sister disappeared, Tamara and Julia spent basically every night at Raven's house, comforting her. They helped her research all the cold cases, memorizing every detail about what *could* have happened to her sister. When Shira came back, they stuck by her side, creating a force field around her, shielding Raven from the shit-stirrers at school. Honestly, now that Bethany's gone, I kind of wish I had friends like that. Some bonds you just can't break.

I turn my face to the sun and feel the warmth seep into my skin. Then a shadow appears, standing in front of me.

"Ready to kick some ass?" Mila says. She extends a hand, helping me to my feet. Her smile is wide and she seems calm, like she's not at all worried about competing for the first time with a team she barely knows, in a place she only just moved to. Something about her whole demeanor makes me lighter.

"I like your attitude," I say.

The rest of the team is huddled up around Coach, near the starting line, so I grab Mila's hand and together we walk toward the rest of the group, where Coach is giving a pep talk. Stella gives me a death stare from across the circle, lowering her headphones. She won't even make eye contact with Mila. Weirdo.

"All right," Coach begins. He leans in and the whistle around his neck swings. "I don't need to tell you how important it is that we take home first today. Everything that happens today determines how we seed for the rest of the season." He takes a breath and closes his eyes. "Run your heart out."

Without missing a beat, we scream back at him in unison. "Run your heart out!"

"Fear no one!" Coach calls.

"Fear no one!"

"Crush everyone!" he yells, throwing his head back, fists by his sides.

"Crush everyone!"

The team erupts in cheers and people throw their arms around each other in the circle, jumping up and down, repeating the mantra over and over again.

"Run your heart out! Fear no one! Crush everyone!"

The first time I heard it, I thought it was so cheesy. But now it's burned into my body. It's the truth. We have no other options.

"You'll pick it up," I whisper into Mila's ear, our arms around each other's shoulders.

"Already did," she says, her mouth curled into a smile.

I sneak a peek at Noah across the circle. He's looking right at me with that annoying sexy grin, all lips. I want to put them in my pocket, despite our fight this morning. He raises an eyebrow at me, daring me to look away, but I don't.

"Remember what you're made of, soldiers," Coach says. "On three. One, two, break!" We walk to the starting line like a unit, our steps in line with each other's.

"Ninety-second countdown!" the announcer bellows through a microphone. I inhale deeply to calm my nerves.

"Come on," Stella says to herself. She stands next to me, blocking the sun as she jumps up and down. Usually on meet day, she's so focused you can barely talk to her. But today she's frazzled. She's fidgeting, playing with her fingers, which she only does when she's scared. Also, her French braid is a little off-center, another sign that something in Stella Steckler's brain isn't working like it should.

"You okay?" I ask.

"Of course," she says, smoothing her bib down over her torso.

Everyone else rolls their necks, picks wedgies, or gets their last stretch in. They make room for Stella and me to stand in the middle of the pack. They're deferential, even after what Stella did last year.

Off on the side, I hear the rest of our team cheering us on. I try to make out Noah's voice above the rest. "You got this, babe!" he yells, and I freeze. Everyone, including me, knows *babe* is Tamara. The thin red bracelet I tucked into my sock for good luck burns against my skin and all at once I realize I'm *nothing*. I close my eyes, pushing everything away. I wait for the signal, the moment to launch.

The ref blows into her whistle, a signal the countdown is imminent. The rest of the runners squeeze in, so we're all squished into the starting box like sardines. Stella's thigh presses into mine. Mila crowds in on her other side and I feel my sister flinch.

"One," the announcer calls out. "Two. Three!" A horn rings out somewhere in the distance and we are off, running from the field into the pathway in the woods that had been whacked wide open to create a cross country trail. There are no cameras in here, no judges. Just us and the trees and whatever we choose to do to each other. Stella knows that best.

This is how it always begins. Stella and me at the front of the pack, followed by scared girls, pumping their legs, wondering how they'll fare against the Steckler sisters. It's a 5K, and everyone knows that the first few hundred meters are pure chaos. To avoid getting swallowed by the group, by everyone clamoring to tear your limbs apart and eat you for fuel, you have to get ahead, and get ahead fast. Then you have to settle into your race pace and glide past the girls who use all their energy up right away. Tamara's usually one of those. She sputters out real quick. But now she's keeping my pace, running so close to me I can hear her breathing.

The pack begins to thin as we trample over roots and fallen leaves, and the canopy of trees narrows overhead. The sky gets darker and the air gets damper as we head deeper into the woods. My heart begins to soar. This is my favorite part, when it's just me and the dirt and the sound of my own feet on the trail. I know Stella loves it too.

Tamara huffs beside me and I can see her arms pumping up and down. Something red flashes in my peripheral vision and I twist to see what it is. A thin string, tied around her wrist. A bracelet. Just like the one Noah gave me, the one I can feel pressed against my ankle.

I'm so dumb.

I turn my head fast, to look away, to forget that I'm disposable. But as I do my foot catches on something and the ground gives way beneath me. My face slams against the earth.

I cover my head for a second as Tamara runs past me. The rest of the girls are starting to catch up and I scramble to stand. But everything is off, and my limbs are shaking at the thought of betrayal. *How could he?*

My eyes sting and the tears are coming. But I need to go, to move. I'm toward the back of the pack and it'll be impossible to catch up. I force myself to put one foot in front of the other, but my gait is all wrong and I can barely see the finish line.

The breakaway is just up ahead and girls spit out into the clearing, sprinting with their heads thrown back. As soon as I hit the slope of grass, I see Coach's face. His mouth is a thin line of disappointment and his eyes are scrunched around his nose like he has a headache. I swat away the shame and try to place everyone else. Tamara didn't get too far, even with Noah's good luck charm—*my* good luck charm. The winners have already been called; I can see that even from here. Woo-fucking-hoo, Stella. Classic.

I speed up. It's the least I can do, not come in last, and race over the finish line, landing somewhere in the back with the losers. It's abysmal, and my heart sinks to my stomach.

But then I spot Stella off by herself, walking in circles, face turned to the sun. Usually when she wins, Coach is with her, giving her an expletive-laced talk about sportsmanship and grace. I swivel my head to find Coach's burly frame. He's off to the side, clutching Mila's hand above her head. Her face is full of elation and her hair is slicked back with sweat. Mila won the race. I turn back to Stella and she's facing me, her eyes wide and her cheeks bright red. She shakes her head, unable to speak, unable to understand what the hell just happened.

She turns around again, to face the woods, as if they will give her answers, and I lift my head to the bleachers. There in the front row. A gaggle of recruiters, making notes on their clipboards and checking their stopwatches. They used to watch the Steckler sisters. They used to come down and congratulate us and chat about our times. Now a handful of the regulars are climbing down from the stands, with their sights set on someone else: Mila.

8

STELLA

"COME ON, EVERYONE. Group photo, whether you like it or not!" Coach is clean-shaven and his bald head is shiny, reflecting the sun. His white dress shirt stretches tight over his chest and he looks like he's about to Hulk out of the whole outfit.

The cross country team, including parents, is on the lawn in front of Ellacoya Mountain Resort, and everyone rushes into place. As the girls crouch, their tiny stiletto heels sink into the mushy grass and stray tulle scratches my calves. The boys straighten their ties and shove each other's shoulders as they hold up grotesque signs with their hands. The mundaneness of it all makes me nauseous.

"Say 'homecoming' on three!" Coach calls out. Behind him, the cross country parents look on adoringly, with hands over hearts.

"One. Two. Three!"

All around me, twenty-four students call out the magic word. *Homecoming.* My mouth stays in a flat, firm line and I try to keep my heart rate down, breathe in and out, just like they taught me this summer. These people, this place. It's not worth the stress.

I turn around and gaze out at the Ellacoya grounds. Even I have to admit it's stunning. No wonder it's a world-renowned vacation destination with a Michelin-starred restaurant and a spa that gets glowing write-ups in national magazines.

"We were the only Black-owned hotel in a fifty-mile radius," Tamara told our class back in second grade. We had been assigned ancestry projects. Most of us explained how our parents had moved to the woods to make time go by slower or because Brooklyn got too expensive in the 2000s. Tamara's family was one of the few who had been here for more than a generation. She came into class with a laminated report and told us all about Ellacoya's history.

Her paternal great-grandparents opened the place as an eleven-room hotel that hosted Saturday-night dances and jazz concerts back in the seventies, just as the glow of the Borscht Belt era was beginning to fade. Ellacoya catered to New York intellectuals and musicians who would leave the dense, steaming city on a Friday afternoon and settle in for a weekend of dinner theater and breakfast buffets.

At first, Ellacoya was just a dot on the map, something new in a landscape filled with apple orchards, Jewish family resorts, and sleepaway camps that taught horny teenagers about Shabbat. But as word got out that some of the best hospitality in the area was coming from the modest Ellacoya Resort, business began to boom.

Famously, Tamara's family perfected the art of East Coast farm-to-table before there was even a name for it. They sourced their own meat from small farms in Ulster and Sullivan

Counties, and only cooked with what was available. Ramps and fiddleheads in the spring. Sweet potatoes and squash in the winter. No one paid attention on a national level, though. Not until Tamara's dad reinvented the place.

Teddy Johnson had grown up here in Edgewater, back when it was something like ninety-nine percent white. He played football and baseball, won Homecoming King, and was even the valedictorian his senior year. He landed a full ride to Princeton, just a few hours away, which is where he met Tamara's mom, Sara. He told her of his dream to turn his parents' bed-and-breakfast into a worldwide travel destination. She was in.

The way I've heard Tamara tell it, they got married right out of college and after a few years in the corporate world, they bought the hotel and the adjacent hundred and thirteen acres.

Within ten years they expanded the place from one cozy building into a pristine compound with dozens of modern A-frame cottages, a full-service spa, four tennis courts, a clubhouse, a swimming pool, a lakeside beach, hiking trails, a blueberry farm, a pumpkin patch, an event space that can hold a three-hundred-person seated banquet, and a main guest building with fifty hotel rooms that cost more than five hundred dollars a night. It's a huge selling point when Mom and Dad try to convince clients to plant roots in Edgewater.

I look out over the manicured lawn as we all shuffle toward the bus and my eyes land on Mila, walking alone, away from the larger group. Her eyes light up when she sees me looking and she waves. But I turn away, fiddling with the buckle on my bag.

Sure, she spilled her guts to me in the car after the cross country formal, but she beat me at last week's meet. It became obvious after that. If she gets too close, everything I've worked for will be ruined even more than it already has been. I've gotten this far on my own in Edgewater, only looking out for myself. I have to stay away from her if I want to win State. If I have any shot at getting back into Georgetown's good graces. I close my eyes for a second and picture their navy uniforms, the white logo emblazoned across my chest.

"Load 'em up!" Coach says. He makes a shooing motion and one by one, the members of the team pile onto the party bus. Ellie climbs up behind Noah and Tamara, a scowl pasted onto her face. Wonder what her deal is tonight. Maybe she misses Bethany. They always stuck together at these things—at *all* things, really. Now she's huddled with a few other girls in her class who take selfies and make pouty duck lips.

I find a seat on the wraparound bench as neon lights flash overhead. Someone turns the music all the way up, and handles of booze and red plastic cups appear from backpacks. All around me, shots are poured and beers are funneled. Who cares if it's only a fifteen-minute ride to the school? We're used to accomplishing a lot in a short amount of time.

I lean back and cross my arms over my chest. But then I spot Ellie nestled into a corner on the bench, a slim bottle of vodka in her grasp. Her long wavy hair pours over her shoulders, so dark it looks like ink. It only makes her silver silk dress even more radiant. She leans back and tips the bottle straight into her mouth. My whole body tenses, as if I can feel the booze course through her body like it's mine. Her mouth is wide and red. But her eyes dart around the bus, landing on Tamara and then Noah and then me. She nods in my direction, but doesn't smile. She's got fire in her tonight. That can only be a bad thing.

The dance is beyond boring. We're all packed into the Edgewater High gymnasium and the air is thick with humidity. The team is wasted, shoving each other and bopping up and down like maniacs. The teachers don't care. The admins don't give a shit. We won last week's meet and that's all that matters. Well, Mila won.

When Principal Pérez walks to the stage under the basketball hoop to announce that Noah and Tamara have been crowned Homecoming King and Queen, the team explodes, bouncing into one another as Pérez places a plastic crown on Noah's enormous head, and a rhinestone-encrusted tiara in Tamara's hair. They pause together on stage, bathed in the sickly bright spotlight, and turn to each other for a slobbery kiss.

"Gross," I say out loud without even meaning to.

Someone laughs behind me and I spin around to find Mila holding her hand over her mouth.

"What?" I bark. I'm so not interested in being made fun of right now.

"You totally just said what everyone else is thinking."

"Oh."

We look at each other awkwardly for a second. "I'm gonna get some air. Wanna come?" Mila asks.

She doesn't wait for an answer and heads to the back of the gym, where a door leads to a playground the elementary school uses.

I weigh my options: stay here alone and watch my teammates make fools of themselves or go outside and get away from all of this mess. I hate that these are my only two choices, but I follow Mila out the door until we're sitting side by side on swings meant for fourth graders.

Mila doesn't say anything for a moment and then she kicks off the ground so she's sailing through the air. I do the same.

"I don't know how you can stand this place," she says, her hair blowing behind her.

Cold air breezes past my cheeks. "Imagine living here your whole life."

"It's just so creepy," Mila says, dragging her foot against the ground to slow down. "The whole *serial killer* thing."

"We try not to say the *s* word," I say.

"They were all cross country runners, right?"

I nod. Marlisse Williams was the first. She was a junior and one of the counselors at the Elite Youth Runner's Club. She babysat us once a month for a whole year, usually when Mom and Dad would do date night at the drive-in. Marlisse showed us how to let chocolate chips melt on the hot kernels of popcorn for an extra-special dessert, and let us fall asleep on her shoulders while watching movies. After she went missing, her family plastered posters all around the town, her smiling face beaming out from the flyers, Senegalese twists framing her face.

But the police were slow to do anything. There were no frantic search parties, no hunting dogs used to follow her scent. They kept calling her a runaway. A misguided kid. But then, six days later, a middle-aged dad found her body hidden behind some brush on the Oak Tower trail while he was jogging.

There were whispers around town about how the police messed up because Marlisse was Black. How they wouldn't have if she was white. But no one in Edgewater did anything. There were no protests. No nasty confrontations at the town council meetings. No op-eds condemning the detectives in the local paper. Just a lot of folks who shook their heads when they passed the police station and dropped casseroles off at the Williamses' doorstep, sheepish as they walked away.

Two months later, senior-class president and captain of the cross country team Beatrice Stiller went missing in the same exact way. She belonged to our synagogue and always played Esther in the Purim spiel. When *her* family put pressure on Detective Parker, who was assigned to both cases, the department obliged, corralling investigators from all around the region. At first they refused to think the two cases were related. But when their dogs found Beatrice by Oak Tower, killed in the exact same way—blunt force trauma, with missing shoelaces, of all things—Parker was forced to acknowledge there was a murderer on the loose.

That's when the press descended.

And things just got even bigger when four months and no leads later, they found Abigail Childers in the same exact location, killed just the same. She had made the varsity cross country team and was a mock-trial prodigy aiming for the Ivy League. The only thing the girls had in common was running.

Everyone in Edgewater had their theories. The most believable one was that Monty Fitzwater, the creepy old white guy who'd led guided hikes up and down the trails for decades, killed them all. He knew the woods better than anyone and his gaze lingered a bit too long on the girls when he passed them in town. He was always screaming about how Edgewater was changing too fast, how there were too many New York City yuppies moving in, driving up real estate prices and fixing things that weren't broken.

Some thought he had an accomplice, his brother Kendall, who ran a fly-fishing program but didn't get much business from locals since everyone knew he had an assault charge on his record. They lived in Edgewater their whole lives, but Monty died of a heart attack after the police found Abigail. Kendall moved away a few weeks later.

The murders stopped after that and police let it go. They didn't have anything they could pin on the Fitzwater brothers directly—no DNA, no faulty alibis, no murder weapon. Basically everyone lost faith in Detective Parker, especially because of the way he'd bungled Marlisse's investigation.

Then, five years later, when Shira Tannenbaum went missing, Parker and his cronies spent all their resources working around the clock to find her and prove that they were capable for once. When the truth came out, everything changed. Girls weren't taken seriously anymore.

Parker brought it up last year when he grilled me about Allison Tarley. "Never again will I have time for the dramatics of teenage girls," he said.

Here on the swing set, I pump my legs to go higher and higher. "You know there's nothing to be afraid of, right?" I say to Mila, though sometimes I'm not even sure I believe those words.

"Yeah, of course," Mila says. "This town's just so small. I feel stifled and I've only been here for a few weeks. At least back in Connecticut, I could say screw it and take the train into Manhattan whenever I wanted. Get out of the bubble. Do you ever feel like that? Like you need to escape?"

I nod and then look at the night sky. "Once you're labeled something, there's no turning back," I say. "Here, you're branded forever." I close my eyes and see all those shocked faces looking at me at the finish line last year, how Allison Tarley tumbled forward as she screamed.

"I'm going to run my way out of here," Mila says. "Be so good, all those college teams have no choice but to pay attention. You know? I can't focus on anything else right now. Just that."

Something inside my chest unlatches. No one's ever spoken to me like this before, like they might possibly understand how my hunger to be number one can trump just about everything else in my life.

"My whole high school experience has been about getting onto the Georgetown cross country team," I say, swinging through the air. "Ever since I met the recruiter freshman year and learned they actually gave out athletic scholarships."

"Why Georgetown?" Mila asks.

"It's just so different from here, you know? It's in the middle of a city where everyone is trying to make something, trying to be better. If you go there, you can do anything when you graduate. My body will break down at some point and there's no way I'm coming back here when it does. I need . . . I want out."

I'm rambling now, which would usually lead Ellie to roll her eyes and zone out, or Julia to make some nasty comment about what a *freak* Sterile Steckler is, but Mila nods slowly, mulling over my words.

"That's what I was like about Harvard," she says, swinging higher and higher. "But when everything happened with my dad, I realized nothing is certain. I thought I'd be finishing up high school with people I'd known my whole life in Hadbury. But now I'm stuck in this small town in the Catskills that's best known for its luxury resort and being the site of a bunch of gruesome murders that were never solved."

I snort out a laugh. I can't help it. "That's the best description of Edgewater I've ever heard."

Mila smirks. "Should we call the tourism board?" She reaches the peak in her swing and jumps forward, sailing through the air, until she lands on her feet in the gravel. Mila turns around and looks at me, hands on her hips. "Things could be worse, I guess."

A silence extends between us and then an English teacher I vaguely recognize comes onto the terrace and clears his throat. "Time to head out, girls."

Mila rolls her eyes but heads toward the door. I follow her into the gym, where we lose each other in the dark mess of limbs and formalwear. I know I could search for her so we could stick together for the rest of the night, whispering about everyone else behind cupped hands. But something stops me. She's my competition and I don't know how much I can actually trust her. I've always thought friends were overrated, stones to weigh you down. Why make one now? So I walk to the door, where the cross country bus is waiting outside.

"After-party at Bader's!" someone yells, and a sea of bodies pushes me onto the bus, toward the back, where all I can do is watch everyone else file on.

As the bus starts to pull out of the parking lot, the music throbs in my ears and almost everyone stands up on the benches to dance. Noah's sitting in the corner, legs splayed, while Tamara curls up next to him, laughing into his chest.

It's all too gross, too much, too showy. I lean back against the window, letting the hum of the drive calm me, but then I hear my sister's voice loud above the noise.

"You fucking scumbag!" she screams. I lean forward on the bench to find Ellie standing in front of Noah and Tamara. Her hair is wild and messy, and her eyes are full of rage. Her fists are clenched by her sides and she's lurching toward them. "You piece of shit. You liar!"

"What's going on?" someone asks next to me.

"Baby Steckler's going Stella on us," a sophomore mutters.

I roll my eyes. "Come up with something more original, loser."

"Ellie, chill out," Noah says, pushing himself to stand.

"Chill out? Chill out?! Have you lost your mind?" Ellie screams. Around me, phones start to come out. The bright screens cast a spotlight on them.

"You're losing it," Noah says. "You don't want to do this."

Ellie steps closer so she's inches from Noah's face. "I could break you, Noah. I could destroy you. Just fucking try me."

Their words make no sense, and Ellie's on fire tonight. I know I should stop her, but I remember what Coach said. *Keep your head down. Stay out of trouble.* I peer out the window and we're almost home. How much damage could she really do in another minute?

"Sounds like Ellie's had a little too much to drink tonight." Noah laughs but the noise comes out like something fake and almost scared.

Ellie crosses her arms. "You're lying," she hisses. "You're a coward and a *liar.*"

Noah's demeanor changes and he takes a step toward her, his back hunched just a bit, like he's ready to pounce. "Lay off, *Baby Steckler.*" He turns his chin up and looks at her in disgust.

Ellie's eyes go wide and she recoils, like she's been slapped. Her mouth drops open and secondhand embarrassment bubbles in my stomach. *Back off,* I tell her in my head. But I know she won't. Because I wouldn't either.

Tamara stands, tugging her dress down. "Ellie, we all know you miss Bethany. But come on," she says, with some tenderness. "This is ridiculous."

That's all it takes for Ellie to lunge straight toward Noah, knocking him to the ground. Tamara yelps and jumps to the side. Her tiara falls to the floor and cracks right in half.

I leap from my seat and try to make it to Ellie, to pry her off him, to stop her from becoming just like me. But she's already there, and there are too many people in my way, shining bright lights on them.

"Fight, fight, fight!" the team calls out.

The bus pulls to a halt in front of the after-party and everyone lurches backward, so we're a pile of hair and heels and ballerina fabric. I fall straight forward into some sophomore's sweat-soaked dress shirt and push him off, scrambling to my feet. When I finally stand, I see the damage.

Ellie sits on the floor of the bus, dazed and red-faced. Tamara is off to the side, shocked as Noah holds her to his chest. The rest of the team files off the bus, making their way to Bader's front door, where they're hoping another party foul takes form. Ellie's breakdown is just another moment to be documented, to laugh at. I try to make my way to her, but the crowd pushes me farther and farther off the bus. My throat is scratchy and I know I should push harder, force myself to get to Ellie, to comfort my sister, but I'm suddenly so tired, so over the drama. I just want to go home.

Noah steps off the bus, shoving my shoulder as he walks Tamara into the party, and I see only Mila left, kneeling down next to Ellie. She wraps her in her arms and rocks back and forth as my sister cries.

9

ELLIE

MONDAY MORNING, TWO days after the party, I still can't bear to look at my phone. It buzzes and hums with chatter from the cross country group thread about after-school practice and next week's meet. But there are digs. There are always digs. And this time they're saying that Ellie Steckler is just as *crazy* as her sister. I hate that word. How the boys deploy it like a bomb, hoping to blow up your confidence, or make you doubt yourself.

CRAZY RUNS IN THE FAM!! some asshole sophomore texted. He followed it up with a blurry photo of me, hair tangled, eyeliner running. My dress riding too high up on my thighs, pointing at Noah as if my finger were a sword. No one could see what happened after, how Mila stayed with me while I cried, even after we got kicked off the bus. How she bent over and touched her fingers to my knee and said, "Hey, you okay?"

"No," I said, spitting out the word in a wet mess of mucus and tears. The story came out quickly after that, in fits and starts, and I told her the *real* reason why I had finally broken in front of everyone, why nothing made sense and my heart was full of rage. Mila didn't say a word at first but her eyes grew wide and her mouth fell open just slightly. When she spoke, she said softly, "I won't tell."

But now she knows the truth. She's the only one besides Noah and I barely know her. My stomach sinks. What have I done?

Stella knocks softly on my door. "Want a ride?" She pushes it open and leans against the doorframe. Wearing head-to-toe track warm-ups and her slicked-back bun, she looks as she always does. Completely unaltered by the worst weekend of my life. I'm jealous.

"Yeah," I say.

She pulls her hand from behind her back and reveals a green smoothie in a to-go cup. "Figured you could use this."

"Aw, Stell." I take the cup from her and my chest fills with gratitude.

"Yeah, yeah. Don't get too used to it," she says, taking a sip from her own smoothie. "School's gonna suck for you today. But school sucks for me every day, so just deal with it."

"Helpful."

I make it through my morning classes without incident; thank god I don't have chemistry with Noah today. But when I get to lunch, I know I have to suck it up and try to make nice at the cross country table if I want to get through this year with some sort of dignity left. I take my time working the caf line, pulling down a veggie sandwich and an apple. After I pay, I survey the room. Off in the corner, I see Noah holding court, his sandy hair falling perfectly over his forehead, and Tamara looking up at him, smiling.

But to their right, I see Julia and Mila huddled together.

Raven sits across the table, leaning so far toward, she's almost in her lunch.

Something fizzles in my stomach and I wonder if Mila's already betrayed me, if she spilled my secret the first chance she got. I walk past them, holding my breath.

"Mila, you *have* to come with us to the drive-in on Saturday," Julia says, clasping her hands. "They're showing the old *A Star Is Born*. The one with Judy Garland. We always sneak in wine and eat fancy licorice, and it's just the best."

Raven nods eagerly across the table. "The last time—"

But Julia cuts her off. "What are you gonna say, Rave? That you fell asleep because you drank too much rosé? That you snored so much we had to cover your face with a pillow? Yeah, we know. This one can't hold her shit."

Raven's cheeks go crimson and she looks down at her sandwich.

"But *you* have to come, Mila," Julia says, wiggling a finger in her direction.

"Maybe," Mila says, and Julia's face falls just slightly.

I make it to the end of the table and slide into a seat, waiting for someone to kick me out and expel me from the team for good. But no one does.

A metal chair leg scrapes against the floor and I turn to see Mila pushing herself to stand.

"Where are you going?" Julia asks, irritated.

"Over there," Mila says, nodding my way.

Please don't cause a scene. Please just stay put.

Julia curls her mouth in disgust. "Your funeral."

Mila plops down across from me and sets her tray down on the table.

"You didn't have to do this," I say.

"Oh, please," Mila says. "Julia's the worst. It's like she was trying to make Raven jealous of me or something. She reminds me of the girls I was friends with in Connecticut. Well, ex-friends. My crew there was pretty superficial and rude, to be honest. But you know how sometimes you're just friends with people for so long you can't see what they're actually like? The only reason I miss that place at all is my best friend, Naomi. She's the coolest. She started the LGBTQ+ alliance at Hadbury High and is this badass Model UN star and . . ." Mila looks up, as if she's surprised to see I'm sitting there. "Wow, I'm just going on and on, huh?"

I want to ask her if she told my secret, if she's playing me now. But I force a smile. "I miss my best friend, Bethany, too," I say. "She moved last year. But we kinda had a falling-out."

Mila winces. "That sucks, I'm sorry. I don't know what I'd do if I didn't have Naomi to FaceTime with every day."

I shrug, not wanting to talk about it anymore.

Mila is quiet for a beat, but then she leans in and locks eyes with me. She lowers her voice. "You know, I wanted to tell you something."

My stomach drops as her expression turns serious. Is this the moment when she admits her judgment? When she starts seeing me differently? A ball of shame forms in my throat.

"Tamara offered me a job at Ellacoya," she says, tucking a piece of long dark hair behind her ear. "Hostess at the restaurant. I just wanted to let you know I'm gonna take it."

My head starts to spin. Does this mean she's now loyal to Tamara? That she's going to tell her my secret? I still can't believe I let it slip—the one thing I swore I would never tell anyone, not even Stella. So, this is how it will all unravel.

But as if she reads my mind, Mila says, "I just wanted to let you know because I'm not going to tell her anything. I'm not going to tell *anyone* anything."

She pauses and waits for me to say something but I don't because my mouth is dry and sandy and no words come.

"I know you said you don't want to talk about it," Mila says, calm and quiet. It's as if she's been in this situation before, as if people just tell her deep, dark secrets and she's totally okay with holding on to them. "But I'm here if you change your mind."

I can't listen to this anymore. I wrap the rest of my sandwich up in parchment paper and push my chair away from the table. It makes a loud screech against the linoleum floor and I wince. "I gotta go," I say. "Let's just pretend it never happened."

Mila looks at me with a small, kind smile. "Okay, Ellie."

I turn away from her and rush out of the cafeteria. All I can think about is making it to the bathroom in time. I push through the heavy double doors and head down the stairs and into the bathrooms in the basement, where the stalls are wide and empty, where you can easily hide. I shove my shoulder against the far door and throw myself inside, falling to my knees. I try to catch my breath, but the chokes come out shallow and rough, and suddenly I'm gasping for air. The metal walls are caving in on me and I wrap my arms around the cool ceramic toilet for support. I try to breathe evenly. It's useless, though, as my chest tightens and my vision grows spotty. My ribs press in on me and I know for certain this is what it feels like to die. This is temporary, I try to remember. This will pass.

It's happened before, the panic attacks. Once after the pee stick came out positive over the summer. And then another a few days later, when I finally got the courage to tell Noah that I missed a period, that I had taken a test and knew what I wanted to do.

We were closing down the lake for the day, tossing soda cans into the recycling and locking our floats inside the small supply shack. I was headed for the door when Noah pulled me to him and pressed his lips to my neck. But before his mouth found mine, I cleared my throat. "I'm pregnant," I said. It came out as a whisper.

Noah froze, speechless, and I untangled myself from him, taking a step back. I searched his face, to read him, but there was nothing there.

"Fuck," he finally said, his voice louder than I'd ever heard. He balled his hands into fists and started pacing the small wooden shack.

I clasped my hands together to try to stop them from shaking. I wanted to tell him I had a plan. I had already found a clinic in Newburgh and it was still early enough that I could get a medication abortion. It was only two pills. Our parents didn't have to know. No one did.

But before I could speak, Noah pulled his arm back and slammed his fist through the wall, leaving a hole where there had once been wood. A cracking sound ripped through the air.

"Noah!" I shrieked. I didn't know whether to run to him and apply pressure to his now-bleeding hand, or to throw my arms up and protect myself.

Noah stared at his fist as blood poured from his knuckles, like he couldn't believe what he had done either. His eyes were wide and menacing, and he looked like someone I didn't recognize, someone I was scared of. "I'm sorry," he said, his voice small. Then he looked at me, fear in his eyes. "This will ruin me, my future, everything I've worked for," he said. "You have to take care of this, you know that, right? I'll pay for it. I'll do anything."

He was right. I knew that much. I just wanted it all to go

away. I wanted to please him. I wanted a future. I made the appointment for the following week.

Noah picked me up early in the morning and we drove the hour to Newburgh in silence. All I could think about was how grateful I was that we lived in New York, where getting an abortion at sixteen years old without telling your parents was something you could actually do. Noah walked me in and sat in the waiting room, a Charles Bukowski book open in his lap, while I met with the doctor.

He had kind eyes that remained free of judgment as I told him why I was there. He told me I could look away during the ultrasound and he made small talk about the weather and how few mosquitos there were for the season. I took the first pill right there with him and he handed me the second to take a few hours later.

"We recommend you not be alone when you take that," the doctor said. "That's when the embryo will pass through you. It can be painful, take a few hours. You will bleed. It's kind of like having a really crappy period. He'll be there?" The doctor nodded to the waiting room.

"Sure," I said, but knew there was no way I would ask Noah to stay with me like that. I knew what he would say.

"Good," the doctor said and took another look at my chart in front of him. "You're from Edgewater, huh?"

I nodded.

"Things seem better there now, don't they?"

"No one's been found dead recently, if that's what you mean."

His mouth formed a small frown. "The Williamses are good friends of mine," he said. "Those cops over there . . . When Marlisse was found . . ." He shook his head as if he didn't have the words. "I shouldn't say anything. Just glad everything's settled down, that's all. Girls shouldn't have to worry about going on runs or exploring their own town on their own. No one should." He looked me in the eye and patted my hand gently. "You go and have a good summer, okay? You're going to be just fine."

I hoped he was right.

When I came back out, Noah stood and wiped his hands on his shorts. "You okay?" he asked. I nodded and waited for him to ask me what happened in the exam room, if I needed anything. But he didn't. Noah just smiled, relieved that we had taken care of everything, that no one would ever know and we could pretend like it had never happened. We stopped for ice cream on the way home, ate our cones on the hood of his car, and said goodbye once we got to my driveway.

The doctor was right, though. Later that night, as I sat on the toilet doubled over in pain and trying not to cry, I wished I weren't alone. I clasped my phone with a shaking hand and called Bethany over and over, willing her to pick up so I could tell her what happened. I wanted her to calm me down and reassure me that everything was going to be okay. But she never answered.

I bit my lip hard as the medication worked its way through me and I wondered what Stella would do if she were home and not hours away at Camp Breakbridge. Stella. My protector. My competition. I pictured her having a neutral, robotic response to it all, bringing me a cold compress, a clean T-shirt, and a green juice. And for some reason, that soothed me. I heard Stella's matter-of-fact voice in my head, the one she used to talk to me during the Dark Years. *You and me forever, Ellie. You and me forever.*

I bled for a few more days and called in sick to Sweetwater

Lake. But other than the physical discomfort, the absence of what had been, all I could feel was relief. I just wanted to forget that the whole thing had ever happened. It helped that Noah and I never spoke about it again. That he always wore a condom and I got a prescription for the pill. We just moved on. Everything was okay.

But all these weeks later, sitting in the bathroom stall, it's as if a dam has broken inside me. I finally realize that everything is *not* okay, that *I'm* not okay, and that Noah was wrong about everything. I remember what he said in the lifeguard shack: "This will ruin *me*, *my* future, everything *I've* worked for." Noah didn't care about me. He was only worried about what a pregnancy would mean for *him*. I was just an afterthought. My future and my health were secondary to his. And because of that, I can finally admit I don't want him anymore.

Within a few seconds, minutes maybe, the panic attack passes. My chest loosens and my fingers relax. My vision clears and my head ceases to throb. I rest my elbows on my knees, my head between my legs, and tell myself, *It's going to be okay*.

Noah leads the boys in stretching and I try to ignore him as he leans over to one side, his shirt lifting up to expose a small patch of muscle, flexing against the sun.

Coach jogs over to me and I realize I'm the last one to arrive at practice. "You're late, Ellie. Whatever the hell is up with you, I'm not interested," he says, tapping his clipboard against one palm. "Knock this shit off. I can only deal with one Steckler on the edge. Take a lap, Ell," he says. "Then another. Don't stop until I blow the whistle three times."

Horror Laps. That's what we call these drills. Usually he lets you go after four or five rounds, but I once heard that he made Lilly Adams keep going way after dark, hours after everyone left, just for rolling her eyes at him during drills. Coach only blew his whistle after she stumbled and puked.

He lowers his gaze to the clipboard in front of him and I roll my head around my neck. I put one foot in front of the other and start. That's the only way to do it. Just start. That's what Stella always says.

I pound the gravel as I make my way through the first quarter of the oval. I can hear the boys behind me, charging at me, ready to drown me in their dust. When they come up close, they part and run around me, leaving me vulnerable and up for grabs. I keep my eyes forward, but I can feel Noah lagging behind the group, falling into step with me.

"Hey," he says.

"Fuck you," I say.

"I'm sorry."

"Again," I say. "Fuck you."

"Come on, Ell. You know that wasn't cool, what you did on Saturday."

I laugh. "You know what else isn't cool? Pretending like I *didn't* get pregnant and have an abortion this summer." After a beat I don't hear his footsteps anymore. But I don't turn around. I keep going, picking up speed, as I feel the anger that's been simmering below the surface course through my veins.

Then he's there again, catching up to me, in step with me, our feet pounding in time.

"So that's what you blew up about," he says softly. "I thought you were past this."

"Yeah, well, I'm not."

"I figured this might happen," Noah says. "Delayed trauma. I've heard about it. Look, it sucked for me too."

Bull-fucking-shit. As if his body went through what mine did, as if we were both affected in the same way. I don't answer him as I lean into the inner ring of the track, going faster and faster.

"No one knows, though, right?" Noah asks. His heart is so close to mine. I can feel his breath hot on my neck and he turns to look at me. I hate this about him, how he can see straight into me and press all of my soft parts, hold them in his hands and mold them like putty. "This would look so bad for you."

I grunt and keep pushing around the track.

"Who, Ellie? Who did you tell? Was it Stella?"

The final stretch of track comes into view.

"Mila," I say softly, her name drifting into the wind.

"You told Mila Keene?" he hisses. "You don't even know her. How did this happen?"

I try to pick up speed and outrun Noah and his questions, but his hand grabs mine and for a second I think we're back on the lifeguarding chair, when his fingers would graze my thighs under the thick white floats we kept over our laps, how they would sometimes find their way inside me right in front of everyone, our little secret.

I yank my hand from his grasp and don't say anything. I keep going, leaning into another lap around the course, leaving Noah behind. I focus on my own breath and the gravel and the birds chirping overhead. If I listen carefully, they all become one bleating siren. They call to me and only me. *Run. Run. Run.*

10

STELLA

MOM USED TO say that I wasn't really a "people person," whatever the hell that means. I first heard her say it on the phone years ago. She was talking to whoever. A cousin, a teacher, a friend from high school. Whoever it was, she said it with the flippancy of someone who just discovered their child didn't really like mushrooms, or preferred to read than swing on the monkey bars. Like it wasn't a big deal. And part of me believed her. Still does. The whole people thing is great for Ellie. She gets energy from them, uses them like batteries. But me? I prefer to remain unattached, unencumbered.

So I don't really know how to deal with this predawn text from Mila.

> *Wanna run before the bell? I've been meaning to try*
> *the trail up by Ellacoya. Coach said it's good practice for*
> *regionals.*

I groan and wipe the sleep from my eye. I hate running with people. Especially people who beat me. Who cause me to start my season in second place. I stare at the words and wonder what it would be like to get inside Mila's brain and figure out what makes her tick. Maybe then I could beat her. I type out the word *Yes.*

Twenty minutes later, I'm walking up the dirt road to the service entrance to Ellacoya, which leads to one of the best paths in all of the Catskills. Mila's there, wearing black leggings and a well-loved, mint-green, long-sleeve shirt, clearly one of the free ones they give out at races. I expect her to turn around, but she's hunched over, her phone pressed tightly to her ear. The red plastic case is bright against her hair.

"No, Dad," she says sharply. "You have to stop doing this."

I hang back for a second, not wanting to butt in.

"Seriously," Mila says, pleading now. "I don't want to see you anymore. You can't come here again. Not yet. It's not okay." She registers my presence but she doesn't look surprised or even embarrassed. She just shakes her head in frustration and motions for me to come closer. "Fine. Okay, bye," she says curtly before hanging up. She stares at her phone for a beat and I see a crack slicing through the screen. She shakes her head and slips the phone into her pocket.

"Asshole."

"Wanna talk about it?" I ask, awkward.

"Nope," Mila says. "He's just . . . intense. Let's go."

Relieved, I start up the path. It only takes a few strides before I feel her next to me, keeping in line with my stride. I wonder if I'm supposed to say anything, if we're supposed to talk, or if the silence is okay. A few birds caw overhead and there are droplets of dew on the moss, squishing underfoot. It's calm and lush out here, behind the modern A-frames and freshly cut lawns. It's only when we hit the first mile mark that I realize neither of us have said anything, and that there's no tension, no fear. My mind relaxes and heads into that place I love, the place where nothing exists outside of my steps, my breathing, my heartbeat.

Mila must feel it too. Our feet pounding against the ground as we head up an incline, the one that cuts deeper into the woods, where the trees narrow overhead and the temperature drops about five degrees. It's the perfect time of year for this trail. Late September. Apple season. Crunchy-red-leaf season. Cross country season. *My* season.

As we reach the trail marker, she speeds up, moves faster, pumps harder. It only makes me pick up my pace, push forward, and surge ahead. My mind floats, as if suspended in air, like nothing can break the spell. It drifts to where it always does: the future. What could be. If I let my vision go just a little bit blurry I can picture it. Me at Georgetown. Walking through campus. Gazing up at the colossal gray neo-medieval buildings. Entering a charming brick townhouse full of teammates who are excited to see me. Reminding myself, *This is where you belong.* That's how I felt after the scout took me on a tour last year, pointing out where I would eat lunch with the squad, where I'd take classes. It was all so certain. Until it wasn't.

When we get to a massive maple tree in the middle of the clearing, I shake my head, discarding the memory. I motion to Mila to follow me to the right. We start up a narrower path where we have to run in single file, I try hard not to stumble over knotty roots. Mila's breath is heavy behind me, steady as we climb higher and higher.

Sweat trickles down my back as I make a hard left, turning into the clearing. It's a route I know by heart, could run in my sleep. And this is the best part. Just beyond the cliff's edge a vista appears, the horizon stretching wide until the fluorescent leaves meet it on the other edge. Mila must see it because when I turn to her, she's looking past me, her eyes wide and her mouth forming an O shape as she gazes out at Foxfire Point.

I slow and clasp my hands behind my neck as the scenery comes into focus. "It's the best view in Edgewater," I say, catching my breath.

Mila turns in a circle and stares out over the trees, their leaves on fire with stunning reds and bright oranges. We can see fields and reservoirs, and the sun peeking out behind the clouds. "Wow," she says. "It's like a painting."

"That's why people love it here."

"No," Mila says, shaking her head. "Like an actual one. The Hudson River School. The Romantics. Late 1800s. They would paint mountains and valleys here in the Catskills, over in the Hudson Valley, and up in the Adirondacks. But all anyone ever remembers are the dudes. Thomas Cole and Frederic Church and those guys. They were rich pricks who loved nature and palled around with Emerson. But Susie Barstow painted this one." Mila takes a few steps closer to the ledge of the lookout point and shields her eyes with her hand. "I saw the sketches when my mom took me to Philly a few years back. They're in a museum there. They look just like this. Massive. Extraordinary. They're meant to make you feel small. Human. In real life . . . It's breathtaking."

I'm quiet, not knowing what to say.

"Everyone always erases the women from the Hudson River School. Not surprising, obviously. But I love them. It's why I wasn't *totally* bummed out when I learned we were moving here. I thought I'd get to see some of the landscapes for real, all the time. And look . . ." Mila motions around us. "It's . . ." She trails off and I glance over at her. Her eyes are misty and she crosses her arms over her chest, taking it in. "My dad got me into them, you know. He had a massive coffee-table book about the Hudson River School. And a dozen puzzles of views like this. We put them together all the time when I was a kid. That all stopped when things got bad."

I say what I'm thinking before I can stop myself. "My mom, too. Alcohol. Sober for twelve years. Well, she was. Had an episode a few years back."

Mila doesn't say anything but she sucks in a breath between her teeth.

"It's weird. Wondering if she'll slip again. Like standing on shaky ground. It changes everything, you know. Being the kid of *that*. Living through it. Makes it hard to trust people." My stomach flips, kind of not believing I just said all that. I've never talked about Mom with anyone but Ellie and Dad.

Mila laughs. "That explains it, then."

"What?" I ask.

"Why you and Ellie are easier to be around than everyone else here. We always find each other."

"Do we?"

Mila turns back to the horizon and watches the wind ripple through the trees. "We're the messy ones. All tough on the outside, but mushy in the center."

"You don't seem so tough," I say, scoffing.

Mila laughs, her face turned to the view. "And you don't seem so mushy." We're both quiet for a second, and then Mila nods at where we came from. "Race you to the trailhead?"

11

STELLA

I MAKE IT home and out of the shower just in time for Ellie to bound down the stairs a few minutes late and shoot me a look like *Let's go.* When we pull out of the driveway, both our phones buzz with an email from Coach. Ellie whips out her phone to read it.

"Oh, shit. Longshot's this week," she says.

"Already?" I groan.

Longshot is supposed to be a twelve-mile race up and down the hills beside the lake. It's a brutal course, so Coach only schedules it once a year. But no one actually runs Longshot. Well, no one but me.

I learned about the tradition freshman year. As the only rookie on the varsity roster, I thought it was just a regular practice, but on a different course. I showed up to find Lilly Adams's girlfriend, Jade, handing out hair glitter and face paint and all the senior girls dressed in matching neon sports bras. The boys had traded their usual uniforms for muscle shirts with long, droopy arm holes and sweatbands that matched the girls'. This wasn't a race. It was a party.

When we got to the course, everyone lined up and Coach brought his whistle to his lips. Without warning he blew into it long and hard and we were off. As we raced up the first hill, I could already tell who would lose steam before the halfway mark. I chugged ahead, putting one foot in front of the other, steadying my breath and focusing only on the trees in the distance. The leaves were starting to change, from forest greens to brilliant reds and oranges.

At first I didn't notice the reveling behind me, the incessant cheering that carried over from the bus. But as we flew down the first hill, it was impossible to ignore.

I pushed forward, keeping my gait steady as I braced myself for the next hill. But when I reached the top, I realized I was alone. The singing had all but stopped and my skin began to tingle. I had outraced them. I had won, I thought, and the race wasn't even half over.

The next two miles were a delight, as I sped up and down the rolling grass on my own, with only soft earth and the setting sun to keep me company. Edgewater at its best.

But soon, I noticed that I hadn't passed anyone, not for a long time. I couldn't even remember the last time I saw a flash of neon. Suddenly, I heard the singing pick up again. I pressed on until I reached the top of the next hill, the one that would signal I was almost finished with this hellish terrain. I stood on at the top and looked down into the valley.

There at the base of the first hill in a small grassy valley was the rest of the team, dancing and laughing, the glitter on their cheeks sparkling in the sun. CamelBaks that I had assumed were filled with water were littered on the ground. The scene reeked of alcohol.

No one had run past that point. Possibilities swirled in my

head but none of them made sense. Why waste all this time? Coach's time? I couldn't piece it together.

When I finally reached the group, I decided to keep going, to bypass them all and claim the number one spot. But as I ran past Lilly, she tugged on my sleeve.

"Slow down, Steckler," she said. She smelled like Mom in the Dark Years, and her face paint was a messy smear. She looked so different from the girl I spent time with over the summer, the girl who cracked open my heart. "Have fun for once," she said.

Jade came up next to Lilly and slung an arm around her shoulder. "We were wondering when you'd come back," she said with a laugh.

I panted and tried to catch my breath. "What . . ." I started

"Oh, no one really *runs* Longshot," Lilly said. "Thought you'd picked up on that."

I swiveled my head around to find it was true. No one else was sweating or red, exhausted from pumping air in and out of their lungs at a rapid pace. Instead they were sucking down liquor and passing around joints. A few juniors had paired off and were making out, pressed against trees.

"I don't get it," I said softly, still trying to catch my breath.

"It's fun," Lilly said. "That's it. That's the whole point." She flashed me a smile and reached for my hand, but I kept my fingers limp by my side. Something boiled up inside me. Hatred for them all, for the disregard and lack of respect they had for the race, for Coach, for putting in the work, for winning.

I turned my back to them and started to make my way back to the finish line. I wasn't planning on *telling* on them. I wasn't planning to say anything. I just wanted to go home, to lie on my bed and tune the world out as I listened to Bach or Yo-Yo

Ma or one of my science podcasts Ellie always calls a "snooze-cast."

"She can't do that!" some dude barked. I turned and saw it was Calvin Parker, a senior with broad shoulders and a few first-place trophies. He was heading to Michigan for sprints. "She has to wait for us or else Coach will know. We'll be fucked."

"Dude, you have to stop her," someone else said.

I heard the footsteps coming, but they seemed farther away, farther down the hill. It wasn't until I felt a hand wrap around my arm that I even began to worry. But then everything happened so fast. Calvin grabbed me and tried to lift me off my feet. I resisted, lurching forward. It wasn't enough, though. Calvin pulled, and I went tumbling back down the hill, head over feet, hitting rocks and roots all the way down.

I can't remember much from the actual collision, just that when my body finally stopped spinning it was because something hard and cold struck my stomach like lightning. When I came to, I was lying curled up next to the rock, a sour stench climbing up my nose. I opened my eyes, or at least I tried to. Everything was blurry and out of focus. I flared my nostrils and caught a whiff of something putrid and off. A puddle of vomit lay next to me, green and runny.

"Is she . . . okay?" someone asked.

I opened my mouth to respond, to shout, *No*, but no words came out.

"She's awake. She's breathing." Lilly stooped beside me and pushed my hair out of my eyes. She looked at me with a tender mix of horror and concern. "You're gonna be okay," she whispered. She turned away and motioned for Jade to come over and squat beside me. They each wrapped their hands around my arms and pulled me up so I was sitting on the rock.

Lilly asked me a series of questions that sounded garbled, like we were underwater. But I remember trusting her. Whatever she said, I trusted her.

"She ruined it," someone muttered, off to the side.

"Dude, you could have killed her," Lilly said to Calvin.

I shook my head, but that hurt more than anything. I must have winced because Lilly took my hand in hers and started speaking. "I think you have a concussion." She looked me up and down. "Some bruises, too. Bad ones. But you're gonna be okay."

"What are we gonna tell Coach?" someone asked.

Calvin widened his stance. "That she fell and we took care of her, that's all."

"You can't be serious," Lilly said. "Look at her!"

"The terrain is wild and super steep," Calvin said. "He knows that. It's not a big deal."

"You're just trying to save your own ass," Lilly said.

"Lilly, come on. You're captain. You think Coach is going to be okay with this happening on *your* watch?"

Lilly turned to me, crumpled on the ground. "Shit." She bent over and took my hand in hers. "I'm so sorry, Stella."

Everyone was quiet and started packing up, stuffing portable speakers and glow sticks into their empty running backpacks, and before I had a chance to do or say anything, everyone was racing again as they sprinted the final mile back to the finish line.

I followed behind them, forcing my body to move. I kept my gaze on Lilly as she looked over her shoulder, making sure I was still moving. I was too broken to feel the shame of finishing in last place and didn't even mind when Coach slapped me on the back so hard I thought my knees would give out.

"Next time, kid," he said, totally unaware of what had transpired.

That day showed me the whole team thing was bullshit. It was impossible to rely on anyone but yourself. I thought I could keep it a secret. I really did. But a few days later, Coach called me into his office and asked me why I was stumbling at practice, why I seemed out of it. I broke down, wet, sloppy tears spilling down my face.

"Stella, spit it out," he said, arms crossed. "Did something happen at Longshot?"

I nodded but the words were caught in my throat.

"Look, I know the seniors can be a little rough on you," he said, his tone sweetening just a bit. "You can tell me, Stella." I looked up at him and his eyes were kind for once, like he cared about me as a person, not just as a number, a pair of fast legs.

"Calvin," I started. "He pushed me on the course." I tried to find a way to tell him about the drinking, the party, the way no one else seemed to care that they were all wasting their precious time sucking down alcohol and twisting their bodies to the beat of the music. But something stopped me. Coach didn't need to know all of that.

"Calvin Parker?" he asked, like he couldn't believe it.

I pulled up the back of my shirt, so he could see the purple bruise that had spread across my skin.

Coach cleared his throat. "Well," he said. "I'll have a word. Take tomorrow off, and I'll see you Monday ready to rip, got it?"

But everything changed after that. No one spoke to me at practice for the rest of the year. Not even Lilly. I was a leper. *Coach's girl.*

Mom and Dad freaked when Coach told them what happened and there was a heated meeting between them, the Parkers, and Principal Pérez. But we all knew Calvin would only get a slap on the wrist. After all, his dad is Detective Parker—the same guy who still runs the police department even though he bungled the cold cases.

Calvin was forced to skip a meet and a few weeks of practice. By the time he got back on the course, his PR had dipped, his focus rattled. He still got to go to Michigan but he only lasted half a season before they cut him from the team. Heard that one through whispers on the course.

It was only last year, when Detective Parker was questioning me about Allison Tarley, that I realized he still held the whole thing against me.

12

ELLIE

A *SOFT GLOW* emanates from Johnson Tavern, the restaurant at Ellacoya, on Wednesday night when I arrive to meet Mila. We had been assigned to work on a history project together, which kind of broke the ice on the whole *I told you I had an abortion even though I barely know you* thing.

"Why don't you meet me there after my shift and we can figure out what we're gonna do?" she said, leaning over my desk earlier today.

I really didn't want to run into Tamara, but Mila was looking at me with those big, hopeful eyes, and I realized none of this was her fault. I said yes. Maybe I wanted to punish myself for being the other girl or torture myself by being in Tamara's presence on her turf. Or maybe I was just tired of fighting. I don't know. For whatever reason, that's how I end up walking toward Johnson Tavern just after dark.

The night is crisp and chilly, and I bury my fingers deep inside the fuzzy pockets of my fleece. The resort is quiet since it's midweek. Even though fall is peak season for city people to come up and leaf peep, pick pumpkins, and drink cider, no one ever seems to do so before Friday. Suckers. They miss out on all the stillness.

The way the trees rustle gently in the night. And how the moon hangs low, rolling out its blanket of stars like a canvas.

As I approach the restaurant, I tilt my head up and listen for the faint sounds of cutlery bumping up against itself, plates hitting reclaimed farm tables, and benches scratching against the wood floor. The big gray building is warm and inviting with high ceilings and thick rafters. Raised beds full of gourds and pumpkins line the porch next to rocking chairs filled with guests waiting for their tables.

I've been here a few times with my family over the years, for Mom's birthday or Father's Day. But Bethany's parents had a standing reservation. Every Friday at seven p.m. until they moved. I joined them a few times, always marveling at the mounds of smoked fish her mom, Sally, ordered to start. She would slather a piece of dark toast with a creamy trout dip, dotting the mountain with a spoonful of bright red roe.

"Heavenly," she'd say with a full mouth, before reaching for a glass of white wine. What was a luxe breakfast in our house was her starter.

Bethany didn't get along with her mom for the usual reasons. She didn't let Bethany have a cell phone until high school and grounded her when we dyed Bethany's bangs pink in eighth grade. But I always liked Sally and her husband, Doug, both of whom worked at some fancy law firm over in New Paltz. They were normal. Simple. They always came to our cross country meets, and patted Bethany on the back even when she didn't place, which was often. "As long as you had fun, kid," Doug would say. And she did. That's why Bethany ran. She never expected to beat me, and I never expected her to move a million miles away.

She broke the news to me on the last day of school in the

spring, appearing at my locker with her green eyes ringed in red, like she'd been crying.

"My dad's being transferred to Ann Arbor," she said in her high-pitched voice. "We have to leave next week." It was all she could say before she broke into tears.

I don't remember much about the conversation, just that it felt like all the air had been let out of my lungs. Later, we sucked on Popsicles in my backyard, dipping our toes into the pool. "I wonder what your new friends will be like," I said as a sticky red trail dripped down my thumb.

"What new friends?" she said, pushing her aviator-style sunglasses up her nose. "I'll be too busy missing you." She knocked her shoulder with mine.

"Ugh," I said. "Please don't go." I sniffled to try and stop the tears from coming.

"You'll be fine," she said. "By this time next year you'll be best friends with Tamara Johnson, dating some hot senior, and lapping your sister on the cross country course."

"I just want you to stay."

But when we said goodbye in her driveway a week later, Bethany seemed excited, not sad. Someone from her new school had DM'd her, she said. The girl was her "welcome buddy." I tried to be happy for her. I really did. Especially as the summer progressed, when she would only respond to my texts late at night, after a day full of tubing or hiking with her new friends. She was never available to talk on the phone. I only let her go when she finally called me back, days after I had taken my second pill from the doctor in Newburgh.

"About time," I said, scoffing into the phone.

"Oh, come on, Ell," Bethany said, her voice annoyed and far away.

"I really need you," I said. "You're supposed to be my best friend, but you're never around. I just . . . I need you, okay?"

"What could possibly have happened?" Bethany asked. But before I could answer, she said, "One sec, Ell." I could hear her cover the phone and laugh to someone else beside her. "This'll only take a minute," she said to someone else. That's what broke me.

"This will *not* take a minute, B. It's like ever since you moved away I'm a ghost to you."

"Jeez, when did you get so needy, Ellie?" Bethany's voice sharpened and I knew then that our friendship would never go back to the way it had been, that there was no way I was going to tell her about the abortion.

"Forget it." We hung up and haven't spoken since. After a few weeks of school without an anchor or a best friend, I can finally admit it sucks.

Especially now.

I plop down on a bench outside of Johnson Tavern and wait for Mila, trying hard not to think about Bethany and her mom shoving smoked fish into her face.

"What are you doing here?" I turn my head and see Tamara standing at the kitchen's side entrance, wiping her hands on a dishtowel. Her braids are tied in a thick, tall coil on top of her head and she's wearing her server's uniform, a chambray button-down and high-waisted jeans.

"I'm waiting for Mila," I say. "She said to come by. We're partners for AP US History. Sorry, I . . ." I stand and start to gather my things, my cheeks hot with shame.

Tamara's mouth puckers but she doesn't ask me to leave. She takes a step toward me. "Look," she says. "I just want to say that I get that things must be tough for you since Bethany left, but that doesn't mean you can go around getting drunk and making a scene. You were such a mess at homecoming."

My face burns and I try to find the words. But I don't even know what they are. *Your boyfriend's an asshole who was cheating on you all summer* seems to be the most appropriate. So does *I was his willing sidepiece and now I feel like shit about it.* But it's easier to lie. "You're right," I say. "I'm really sorry. I guess I'm just kinda lonely without a best friend anymore."

Tamara crosses her arms over her chest. "That must be really tough."

I know she means it, too, because she's never been without one. She and Julia have always been a unit, and once they took Raven into the fold, that was that.

"I seriously hope that was a one-time thing," Tamara says. "No one has time for that garbage."

"It was," I say, quiet.

"Well, good thing you're hanging out with Mila now. She's the best. We take all our breaks together. Maybe we should all go for a run together sometime?"

Having to lie to Tamara over and over again turns my stomach. I don't know how Noah does it. But, well, yes, I do. I've seen him do it every damn day. I learned what a great liar he is over the summer, one Wednesday in July. He and I were supposed to close down Sweetwater Lake for the day, which led to some messing around in the lifeguarding shed. Noah had pushed me up against the wall of floats and his hands were everywhere—in my hair, on my thighs, creeping into the bottom of my bathing suit. That's when we heard her.

"Noah?" Tamara called. She was just outside the shed.

"Shit," Noah whispered into my neck. He stepped back and

I could see the fear in his eyes. "Get yourself together," he said. "Quick."

Shame crept into my stomach but I did as he said, pulling on my jean shorts and smoothing down my hair. Noah emerged from the shed first and I could hear him greeting her in a bouncy voice. I followed him out of the door.

"Hi, Tamara!" I said, smiling wide. "Haven't seen you much around here this summer."

Tamara's eyes narrowed and she looked at me quizzically, then to Noah, then back to me. "Yeah, Ellacoya's been super busy this season. We've got weddings every other weekend."

Noah nodded and we all shifted awkwardly in the silence.

"What were you guys up to?" she asked, crossing her arms over her chest.

Noah shrugged. "Closing up for the day. We had to retie a bunch of the buoys, so it took a while. Right, Ellie?"

My insides melted and I wanted to dissolve into air, to tell Tamara the truth. But I lied, just like Noah. "Yep."

Tamara winced. "Ugh, that's so annoying," she said. "If you're done, we were gonna go to Sweet Tooth for cones. Wanna join?"

"I should be getting home," I said, avoiding Noah's gaze, his relief. She didn't push it and they left me alone to lock the shed with shaking hands, trying to figure out why it was so easy for Noah to lie. He'd been able to pull an excuse out of thin air, like it was nothing. But I did too, I realized. Wasn't I just as bad?

Now, outside Johnson Tavern, Tamara looks at me with those same inviting eyes. I just want to tell her the truth. The main entrance opens with a creak and Mila appears in her hostess uniform, a linen blazer and the same high-waisted jeans as Tamara. "Chef gave me a doggie bag," she says. Her face is flushed from the warm dining room and she's carrying a small paper bag with the Johnson Tavern logo stamped on the front.

"Ooh, I hope it's the chicken livers with apples," Tamara says. "Or the burrata and beets. Both are in season right now. So good."

Mila laughs. "Smoked trout, actually. With the pumpernickel bread."

Tamara brings her fingers to her mouth and makes a kissing noise. "A classic. Bethany's mom used to get that every week, right, Ellie?"

"Mm-hm," I say. "She loved it."

"Well, we'll just have to share," Mila says. I force a smile, but my stomach sinks. I can't believe this is my new life. One where I blurted out my biggest secret to my competition, who is *also* becoming friends with my secret ex-boyfriend's actual girlfriend. How did this happen?

13

STELLA

ELLIE'S ALREADY IN the kitchen, sitting at the table with her phone in hand, when I rush down the stairs on Friday morning. She's wearing one of her *I look cute* outfits, a cropped sweater over a short denim skirt, even though it's too cold for bare legs now.

"You're awake," I say with genuine surprise.

Ellie sips from a mug in front of her and doesn't look up from her phone. "Coffee's still hot," she says.

"You know I don't drink coffee on race day."

"It's Longshot," she says, as if that changes anything. "It's not *really* a race."

We went through this last year, Ellie's inability to understand why I *still* don't partake in the ridiculous ritual of running a mile, partying, then running a mile back to Coach with boozy breath. At least no one tackled me last year. That's what happens when you become the best, when people get scared of you.

I look at Ellie closely as she scrolls through her phone. Worry lines form between her eyes and she's wearing more makeup than usual. Something's off but there's no point in asking. She won't tell me.

"You look like a clown," I say. Ellie lifts her gaze and her mouth, painted pink, puckers, like she's bitten into a lemon.

"You're mean."

"What else is new?"

"God, you know, sometimes I wish I had a sister who was actually nice to me," she says, anger rising in her voice.

"Well," I say. "You have me."

Ellie snorts. "Fucking hell."

"Come on. I'll drive you."

When we get to school, I weave into the only parking spot left, and unfortunately it's right next to Julia's rose-gold SUV.

"So tacky," Ellie says.

"Seriously."

Ellie pretends like she's going to puke and then laughs. I relax, relieved that being sisters means it's always so easy to get over a fight, to toggle between annoyance and intimacy.

Julia opens her door and makes a grossed-out face when she sees us. "Well, if it isn't the loony tunes," she says. "Cute, right? I made that up."

"So cute," I say. "Just the cutest."

Julia smiles in a satisfied way that makes me uneasy. "Excited for Longshot?" she asks.

"Sure, Julia," I say, trying to move past her.

"I mean, we know you're the only one who runs it," she says, shaking her blown-out hair over her shoulders. "But I guess you need the practice these days, especially if you're going to try to get Georgetown to pay attention to you instead of Mila."

"What did you say?" I ask, turning around so I'm facing Julia.

"Oh, you didn't know?" Julia asks, feigning surprise. "Oops." But she doesn't look sorry. She smiles wide and swipes a coat of lip gloss across her mouth. "Tamara told me that Mila's having lunch with the Georgetown recruiter today. Thought you knew, since you guys are, like, friends or whatever." Julia starts walking toward the school entrance. "Guess not."

I shake my head. This doesn't make sense. Mila knows what Georgetown means to me. I fight back the rage building inside me.

"Are you okay?" Ellie whispers beside me. She reaches for my arm, but I pull it away.

"Whatever," I say. Like it doesn't hurt. Like I'm *fine*. Like I'm made of stone and metal, not flesh and bone. "Go ahead without me."

Ellie nods and walks quickly toward the door, glancing over her shoulder at me before she disappears into the building. I bury my hands in my jacket pockets to stop them from shaking. Then I grab my phone and begin texting, the words flying from my fingertips, fury appearing on the screen. I don't even think before I hit send.

Georgetown? Are you serious, Mila?

I can't believe you would backstab me like this.

I trusted you and you betrayed me.

I thought you were different. But you're just like the others.

You're going to wish you hadn't done this.

The bus ride to Longshot is fizzy with anticipation. Per tradition, which I do not subscribe to, the captains are supposed to procure the alcohol and rally the troops, but no one even asked me about it. I assume Tamara and Noah took care of everything, which is just fine.

"Here we are," Coach says as we pull up to the first hill of the course. He turns. "What are you waiting for? Go!" The rest of the team cheers and he opens the door so we can head over to the makeshift starting line between two oak stumps.

I shield my eyes from the autumn sun and look out over the terrain. It's as wild as it ever was, steep and browning, with twisted roots crisscrossing along the ground, up the incline. That first hill is the hardest, the tallest. It's what keeps the sound of the parties at bay. Coach gives his usual marching orders and I try to ignore the younger girls, the ones who wear pink face paint that looks like gashes along their cheeks. Mila never responded to my texts about Georgetown but I can hear her laugh floating above the group.

"Huddle up!" Tamara calls. Everyone moves into place and Coach blows his whistle. We're off.

The first mile is a mess, everyone exploding with cheers. The boys gallop ahead, discarding their usual focus for fun, and the girls follow, cheering as we climb the first hill.

"Run your heart out!" Noah calls.

"Run your heart out!" the team responds.

"Fear no one!" he screams.

"Fear no one!"

"Crush everyone!" Noah throws his fist into the air and charges ahead like we're at war.

"Crush everyone!"

I tune them out and keep my own pace off to the side. They'll all disappear if I just try hard enough. When we reach the top of the first hill, everyone descends like cars on a roller coaster, momentum and adrenaline pushing us down, down, down into the valley. It's a rush like no other, the wind shoving me forward, my feet flying beneath me. A smile spreads across my face. I remember why I love this, why I run, why it's worth it. I feel the others stop behind me, as they start to open secret containers of liquor and press play on a speaker. But I don't turn around. I keep going.

Another mile later, I listen for the silence, for the absence of people, of footsteps, of sneakers hitting the tough earth not meant for runners. But that's when I realize there's still one set of feet slapping the ground a little ways behind me. I turn my head just a bit and see Mila, her dark hair piled high into a ponytail and her brow just starting to sweat, flecks of glitter stuck to her eyelids.

I train my eyes back to the course ahead of me, but she stays by my side. We run like that for another mile, and I keep waiting for her to turn and head back to the group. I'm not interested in making amends or hearing her excuse. But she runs next to me, keeping my pace. I feel her there, her arms pumping, the air pushing and pulling through her body.

I wait for the anger to build inside me, for something to snap so I can make her leave. But all I feel is the desire to go faster, to speed away, to challenge her to beat me one more time. *I dare you. Just try it.*

When we reach the top of the second hill, she slows just a bit and stops. She interlaces her hands behind her head, catching her breath. "Hang on a sec," she says.

I don't want to pause. I want us to keep pushing each other, to race until we're faster than anyone else has ever been. But if I keep going, there will be no one left to beat. So I stop.

"What?" I ask.

"Uh, don't you want to talk about those texts you sent me? About Georgetown?"

"There's nothing to talk about," I say. "You're just as fake as everyone else. Pretending to be my friend and then going after *my* dream. I never should have trusted you."

"This isn't about you, Stella," she says. "I have to get out of here too, you know. I don't even *want* to go there. But I *had* to meet with them."

I shake my head, my braid flapping between my shoulder blades. "That was supposed to be *my* spot, *my* future."

"You're being selfish," she says, shaking her head.

"Fine. I'm selfish. That's who I am. So why are you even here, then? Why don't you accept it and go chug a beer like everyone else?"

Mila pauses and looks straight at me, like the answer's obvious.

"Because you're the only person in this town who's not full of shit."

Something bubbles inside my chest and I wonder what it might be like if we weren't fighting for the same thing. If we could just be *friends* instead of competitors.

But none of that matters because we *are* fighting for the same thing. Only one of us can come in first, and if she's able to crack me right open, I'm afraid of what might leak out and who I might become. A loser.

"This is all a game to you, isn't it?" I say.

"What are you talking about?"

"I see what you're doing. You're trying to get in my head. See how far you can bend Stella Steckler before she breaks. Is that right?"

Mila laughs. "That's ridiculous." She crosses her arms. "Look, I'm just doing what I have to do to survive here. Just like you are. But I don't hold grudges. I forgive you for those texts, okay? Come on, let's just head back and join everyone else."

I turn away from her and look up into the trees.

"Aren't you sick of being alone all the time?" Mila says.

I wish it were so easy to say yes, to shrug it all off and let her in. But . . . it's not.

"Being alone is better than wondering if you're being used."

The words slice through the air and Mila takes a step back like I've just tried to hit her.

Her eyes grow glossy and for a split second I think she actually might be for real. But before I can find out, she backs up even farther, turns around, and starts down the hill, toward the rest of the team, to the party she abandoned. I watch her disappear under a brush with crisp orange leaves, see her sidestep gnarled roots, and hop over logs. Instead of going after her, I spin around and run the other way.

14

STELLA

WHEN I WAKE up on Monday, I feel guilty as hell about Mila. Coach told me not to make any waves this year. To play nice. But I did the opposite. I roll over in bed and replay that final stretch of Longshot, how she *did* actually make me go faster. It was just like what happened at Foxfire Point. She runs like I do. Like she's on fire. Maybe we *could* work together. Maybe today's the day I learn to apologize.

I've never really played the groveling bit with anyone except Ellie when I stepped on her phone by accident, smashing the screen into a million pieces, or when I told her Bethany was more interested in finding the right padded bra than being a good friend to her in the eighth grade. I never worried about Ellie *not* forgiving me. She had to. Blood is just like that.

But when I slide into AP Calc just as the bell rings, Mila's seat is empty. I look out the window, toward the parking lot, to search for stragglers. All I see are thick sheets of rain pummeling the asphalt.

Mrs. Crayton shuts the door closed. "Shall we begin?" she says, a smile spreading across her wrinkled face.

I pull my phone out of my pocket and check for any messages. Nothing.

"She's probably sick," someone whispers behind me. I swivel in my seat and see Raven leaning forward in the desk behind me. Her strawberry-colored hair is tied sloppily in a topknot.

"Who?" I say, letting the nonchalance drip from my voice. No need to give *Vanilla* Tannenbaum any reason to go running to Tamara and Julia, telling them I was being weird.

"Mila," she says. Raven turns her head back down to her spiral notebook. "My mom said mono's going around. She got like three doctors' notes today."

I turn back around and try my best to ignore Mila's empty seat for the remainder of class—and the sinking feeling in my stomach. The rain is loud against the window and I can't shake the feeling that something isn't quite right.

At practice, Coach scans the lineup in the weight room. "Where's Keene?" he barks.

"She didn't call in sick?" Tamara asks, concerned.

"Nope," Coach grumbles and looks to the window. Big drops of rain continue to fall, plunking down on the earth. "Eight-hundreds," he yells. "All of you. Now."

Everyone groans but follows orders, heading outside. We're all drenched within a minute and mud splatters everywhere as we pound the wet earth. Pretty soon I'm breathing heavy and my muscles are working like they should. But I keep turning toward the parking lot, expecting to see Mila appear with an explanation for her absence. She must have one. But Coach seemed just as surprised as I was that she didn't show up.

What if . . .

I don't let myself finish the thought. No one's been missing in Edgewater for years. No one's been found dead. Monty Fitzwater was responsible for the cold cases. Everyone knows that. And he's dead. Monty is dead. His brother Kendall, though . . . He's alive.

But no. It's just not possible. Edgewater will never become Deadwater again. We all know that. People get sick and forget to call the school all the time.

After practice, I check my phone for the millionth time, but the screen is blank. I type out a text as I walk to the car, shielding the screen under my windbreaker.

I know things are kind of weird right now, but are you okay? Can we talk?

I hit send and wait for the message to be delivered, for my text bubble to turn blue. It doesn't, though. It stays green, indicating Mila's phone is turned off. Weird. Probably nothing. But . . . weird.

When I get home, I head straight for my room, but Mom catches me by the door.

"Salmon, broccoli, and brown rice?" she asks. "That's what you want for dinner, right? Training food?"

"Yep," I say.

"Nothing extra? No pizza just for fun?"

"Nope," I say, trying to shut down the conversation.

"Sometimes I think I'll never understand you, Stell," Mom says, pulling a bag of orange fish filets out of the freezer. "But I will always love you."

In another world, I'd be able to talk to her about everything, how I was a total asshole to Mila when she didn't deserve it and how shame is buried in my chest for how I acted. I'd be able to tell her that I'm worried about where Mila is now.

But in this world, we're not like that. She doesn't understand me and I don't want her to. How could I ever explain that my desire to win, to be the best, comes from her? All she wants is for Steckler Homes to be synonymous with "Yuppies, come buy your second house and raise all of our taxes with your expensive renovations!" That's winning in its own way, too.

She and Dad were both so fragile for a while after the Dark Years, like any mistake or misstep might push her back to the bottle. And then when Mom relapsed, I spent weeks wondering if it was because of something I did. If only I had won the Spring Invitational that year. If only I made life easier for them. If only I didn't tell them about the little moments of middle school drama, like how I pushed Bader into the stone wall behind the playground for calling me a dumb bitch, or how everyone on the middle school track team rolled their eyes at me when I tried to lead stretches. But they always worried when I told them these things. And worrying made her drink. At least that's what I thought since Mom went to the wedding only a few days after I made the mistake of telling her about the Bader thing. Since then, I found it best to just detach, disassociate, fend for myself.

"Any word from the guidance counselor? The scouts?" Mom asks, her voice steady.

I shake my head. "Not yet. It's only mid-October."

"I know, I just thought maybe they'd wanna lock you in, you know?"

No one wants me, I want to yell. There's no way the Georgetown scout will pay attention to me. Not when he's obsessed with Mila. There's only one alternative. Break my PR by a full minute. Then he'll have to. That's what Coach said. And I only have ten more seconds to shave off. I just have to do it at regionals, which is only a few weeks away.

"Why don't you go wash up?" Mom says when I don't respond. "I'll call you girls when it's ready."

When I get to my room, I close the door behind me and flop down on the faded yellow gingham duvet, even though I usually have a strict no-outdoor-clothes-on-the-bed rule. I kick my sneakers off and grab my phone, tapping over to Instagram. I pull up Mila's feed. She hasn't posted a Story in the past twenty-four hours, nothing about being sick and marathoning *The Great British Baking Show,* or a post about visiting her dad in Connecticut. The nothingness is somewhat jarring. The lack of Mila. It's everywhere, and for some reason I feel like it will only keep expanding.

The last photo she posted on her feed was from the meet where she won. Where she beat me. I bring the screen closer to my face and zoom in on Mila's smile. In the picture, her wavy hair is sweaty, slicked back over her skull, and her eyes are bright and wide. The first-place medal hangs around her neck from a bright blue ribbon, and she's holding the gold circle in her right hand, up close by her face.

First meet down. A million go to. #EdgewaterXC #newteam-sameme, she wrote.

I scroll down and tap to expand the comments. Ellie's is first. Hate that you beat me but ILU! I roll my eyes. As if Ellie had stood a chance at that meet. For reasons she still won't get into, she practically ended up in last place.

Tamara had pasted a string of runner-girl emojis, and Julia had written a hashtag: #fastbitch. Even Raven had posted too: Queen!!

The rest of the comments come from names I don't recognize, with no connection to Edgewater. Then I see one that sounds familiar. @NaomiRuns, just like Mila's best friend she mentioned in the car after the cross country formal. That's my girl! Naomi had written.

I tap over to her feed, more out of curiosity than anything. I click on the first photo, which was posted last week, to find an Asian girl with a short angled bob and deep brown eyes rimmed with bright blue eyeliner. She's standing with three guys around our age in front of a stark-white brick wall, and wearing a chic pink boilersuit and gold platform sandals. Gold hoops dangle from her ears and she's caught mid-laugh, like whoever was behind the camera just made a joke. She looks happy and calm, like a hug from her could wash away just about anything. Nothing like a visit from your cousins to make your month, she wrote.

I keep scrolling, half looking for hints of Mila, half looking for more glimpses into what Naomi's really like. There's a smattering of race pics, a throwback photo to a Lunar New Year celebration where she's a kid wearing a yellow-and-white hanbok, and a post at the Stamford Pride Parade, where Naomi poses in rainbow-colored overalls and sticks her tongue out at the camera. Further down, there are group team shots and purple-and-white spandex uniforms. Hadbury colors, Mila's old team.

I stop when I get to a photo of Mila and Naomi sitting on the bleachers, leaning toward each other in matching uniforms. Their foreheads touch and their legs are crossed toward each other. But they're not looking at the camera. They're smiling, stifling laughs, like no one else would ever get their jokes. I check the date, and it was only posted a few months ago, in May. Right at the end of the school year.

Gonna miss this girl more than words, the caption reads. I sit up, hinging at my waist.

Don't go, Mila! someone had written below the post.

BFF goals.

This suuuccckksss.

I scroll further down to the last comment. It's only a few hours old, according to the time stamp, and it's from a user with garbled mush for a username. Just a string of random letters and numbers. Come home, Mila. Come home to me.

My heart beats fast as I tap that handle. There's something so strange about the comment. Something off. But the profile is bare, with zero posts and zero follows; no tagged photos either. There's not even a name attached. I pull down to refresh, but nothing's there, so I tap back to Naomi's profile.

It has to be from her dad. Mila did say he was *intense*, that he had tried to come visit her. I refresh again to see if anyone else has replied.

But when the photo loads again, the comment is gone, a bare slice of screen in its place.

Mila's not at school on Tuesday, and at lunch, the team is talking.

"It's mono, I'm telling you," says Raven. She leans back in her chair and crosses her arms over her chest. "Three juniors have it." Raven might be meek but she also loves to be right.

Tamara bites her bottom lip, her brow knit with worry. "I'm not so sure. I heard from one of the Ellacoya guards that someone called 911 yesterday and reported an incident some-where in the woods. A missing runner, maybe." She leans in closer. "I heard him say Oak Tower."

Julia gasps. "Tam, no. Are you sure?"

Tamara nods, a grimace on her face.

Noah slumps down next to her and slings an arm over her shoulder.

"What are you taking about, babe?"

"Mila," Tamara says. "I think she's missing."

"What?" Noah asks. "She's probably just sick."

"No way," Julia says. "If Tamara says she heard there was a 911 call, it has to be true."

I swear I see Raven roll her eyes as Tamara flashes Julia a grateful smile. Julia's always been Tamara's gofer, even in elementary school. But Julia isn't magnetic like Tamara, or a people pleaser like Raven. She's cruel and insecure, always grasping to keep her place at the top by kicking others in the shins. Sometimes that means making up names like Sterile. Other times it means copying off Raven's pre-calc test, getting caught, and crying her way out of it with a load of BS about not being able to study enough after working a shift at her family's overpriced sporting goods store. True story. But most of the time it just means shitting all over everyone and everything.

"Has anyone seen her?" Noah asks. He shifts in his seat and his eyes scan the table.

Julia shakes her head no. "Hopefully she's not pulling a Shir—" Her mouth falls open midsentence when she realizes what she's saying.

"Seriously, Julia?" Raven says, her voice small.

Julia's face reddens and for once she's embarrassed. The whole town had been turned upside down looking for Shira

Tannenbaum. She was Homecoming Queen and captain of the cross country team. She even still holds the county record for the 5K, the one Ellie and I are always trying to beat. When she came back unscathed, everyone talked about how Shira had ruined it for the next girl in trouble. Detective Parker was even quoted in the paper: "We all know teenage girls are capable of lying," he said. "But now we know just how far they'll go to protect themselves. Since the Edgewater killer is gone, we'll think long and hard about how we look for the next girl who goes missing." Asshole.

"I'm sorry, Rave," Julia says. "But, I mean, she freaked everyone out. Had us all thinking Kendall Fitzwater was back, looking for new victims." She shivers dramatically. "It was scary."

Raven picks at the roast beef sandwich in front of her. "They don't know for sure it was the Fitzwater brothers," she says. "There were holes in Marlisse's, Beatrice's, and Abigail's cases."

"Weren't they each missing one set of shoelaces?" Tamara asks.

Raven nods. "Died from head wounds. But the police didn't have a slam-dunk case. No DNA evidence, either. Monty and Kendall didn't even have alibis, and the cops still couldn't pin it on them."

"No one ever talks about the fact that those girls looked nothing alike," Julia says carefully. "And they were killed at different times of day."

Raven nods, a small sad smile crawling across her face. "Aren't you guys glad we spent weeks memorizing all the details?"

Tamara throws an arm around her. "You were just looking for answers, Rave," she says. "We all thought Shira was dead."

Julia nods. "You're right, though. Mila's probably fine. Like you said, I bet she just has mono."

"Totally," Tamara says, like she's trying to convince herself.

"I'm gonna go to the bathroom," Raven says softly. She hustles off, wiping her nose on her T-shirt.

"Ugh. I should not have brought up Shira," Julia says, shaking her head.

"I know, but . . ." Tamara looks around and leans in toward Julia. "Mila *might* be missing. She was supposed to cover a dinner shift but she ghosted. I texted her but the message wasn't delivered."

I freeze. That's what happened when I tried to text Mila, too.

"Someone at Ellacoya called her mom but they couldn't reach her at the hospital," Tamara says. "That's when the security guard brought up the 911 call. He thought maybe *she* was the missing runner from the call. But it was pouring rain all night, so who knows what the police found."

"What'd I miss?" Ellie says, appearing by my side. Her hair is tangled around her shoulders and she looks pale, her skin nearly translucent under the cafeteria's fluorescent lights. She sets her tray down across from me.

"They're wondering where Mila is," I say, leaning back in my chair.

"Oh," she says.

"Tamara says she heard there might be a runner missing in the woods." I roll my eyes, trying to convince myself that Mila going missing *is* ludicrous. After all, Deadwater is long gone. What are the chances that some psycho killer would come back just for Mila? It doesn't make sense. "Isn't that absurd?"

Ellie nods emphatically. "Ridiculous."

"Have you heard from her?"

"Nuh-uh," Ellie says, and rips open a bag of pretzels, spilling some on her tray. Her face gets red and splotchy, like it does when she's anxious or uncomfortable. She glances at her phone and her eyebrows shoot up in surprise. "Crap, I gotta go. Spanish prep." She gathers her shit and bolts for the swinging cafeteria doors, leaving a bunch of pretzel crumbs behind for me to clean up. Classic.

I bite my tongue the rest of lunch and try to listen in on the chatter. But hearing Mila's name over and over again makes me nervous and irritable. I slide my phone out of my pocket and type out another text to her.

If you get this, can you please respond?? There are some rumors going around school. Can we talk??

I wait for the message to be delivered, but it just stays green, stuck somewhere in space.

With five minutes left in the period, I push the caf doors open and make a left, toward the athletic hallway, looking for Coach. Maybe he'll know where Mila is. He usually spends free periods working on lineups, or watching tapes from previous meets. Last year, after the Allison thing, shit got really bad and he let me hang out there during lunch. He wouldn't speak to me, but he just let me sit. It was his way of saying, *It's going to be okay.* At least that's what I hoped. More likely, he just wanted to make sure his star runner would be back and ready the next year.

I pass the field hockey office, the lacrosse room, and the volleyball closet, before seeing Coach's room ahead. The door's closed with no light on inside. *Shit.* I'm about to knock anyway, when I hear the squeaky sound of sneakers walking along the tile floor behind me.

"Stella Steckler?" someone calls. "Is that you?"

I turn to find a tall woman with medium-length dark hair, tied back into a low ponytail. She's wearing blue hospital scrubs, a peacoat draped over her shoulders. Her cheeks are high and round like Mila's, and her nose has the same notch that Mila's does, right on the bridge.

"Are you Mrs. Keene?" I ask.

The woman nods but doesn't smile. She clasps her hands tight in front of her. "Call me Shawna," she says. "I was coming to look for Coach Gary. He's not here?"

I shake my head.

"You're Stella, aren't you?" she asks, looking at me with curious eyes. "Mila's mentioned you. She said you were weird. In a good way, I promise. Mila likes weird."

I snort. "I guess I am."

Mila's mom nods and looks to the ceiling, her eyes round and tired. "Have you seen Mila? Talked to her in the past couple days?" she asks.

"No," I say. A pit forms in my stomach.

"She hasn't been home since yesterday," Shawna says. I can tell she's trying to be strong, but her shaking hands betray her. "She texted me that she was leaving on her run in the morning, but I worked an overnight shift so I didn't see her before school. Then I got a call from Ellacoya that she didn't show up for work last night. I assumed she would be home this morning, but . . ." Shawna trails off.

"You haven't heard from her?" I ask.

"No," she says. "And this morning, Mrs. Tannenbaum called

saying Mila hasn't been in school. I called the police right away."
Her voice grows louder and more urgent with each word. "And
Detective Parker told me to just sit tight and wait, that she
would come home, that that's just what teenage girls do."

Of course Parker is working this case. Fuck, Mila is now a
case. Parker covers everything about minors, no matter the
situation, even though he's obviously so biased against us. But
that's what happens when you live in a small town with an
even smaller police department. Everyone knows everyone—
and everyone's connected, most often through their indiscre-
tions.

"But that's not what my Mila does," Shawna says. "She
doesn't just *go missing*. I found her wallet at home. She
wouldn't leave without it."

My heart races. *Where is she?* "What about her dad? Or
Naomi?"

"Naomi hasn't seen her. I asked. Her dad? Fat chance.
Thomas is probably holed up in some country club passed out
in an overstuffed leather chair right now." She looks at me.
"Sorry. Probably shouldn't say that."

I shrug. "I've heard worse. Seen worse."

Shawna gives me a knowing look and I wonder what Mila
told her, if she knows I can relate. "Plus, I called him and he's
not answering, which isn't unusual for him."

My mind flashes back to the random Instagram comment
on Naomi's post. Come home, Mila. Come home to me.

"It's just, everyone keeps saying Edgewater is safe now,"
Shawna says. "But what if it's not? What if someone took my
little girl?"

Could Mila become just another headline in Edgewater? It's
impossible.

Shawna lets out a puff of air. "All those girls wound up dead," she says quietly. "Well, except for that Tannenbaum girl. But I know how they treated Marlisse Williams's case." Shawna scoffs. "It's no coincidence they didn't take her disappearance seriously until one of the white girls in this town went missing. My daughter is half Puerto Rican. You think they're going to pull out all the stops?" Shawna clucks her tongue. It's almost like she's talking like I'm not even here, like she's unleashing her worst fears into the world, like saying them out loud will make them sound too outlandish to be real. But what she's saying doesn't sound outlandish. It sounds like it could be true.

"She'll turn up," I say. "She has to."

Shawna crosses her arms over her chest. "Detective Parker said I should be wary of you."

I wince. Of course he did.

Shawna doesn't say anything else, but she looks off, past me and down the hall, and I wonder what she's thinking. If she's sizing me up as a suspect, or if she's doing all the mental math we've been trained to do when we hear about a *missing* girl. We all know the stats. They're drilled into us during every *Dateline* episode, every true-crime podcast. The first twenty-four hours are crucial in missing persons cases. You have the best shot of finding someone within seventy-two hours. After that . . . it's a crapshoot. And it's already been a day. Soaked in rain.

Shawna looks down at her phone. "I have to go. My sister is coming up from the city. If you or anyone else on the team hear anything, you call me right away, okay?"

But she doesn't wait to hear my response. Shawna turns on her heel and walks quickly down the hallway, out the door and into the parking lot.

I back up against the cold cinder-block wall and slide down

until I'm sitting on the ground. My mind spins and I wonder where Mila is, what *happened*, and how Parker will find a way to fuck me over yet again. Memories of last year flash through my brain. The popping sound of bone unlatching. The ambulance wailing through the mountains, on its way to rescue Allison Tarley. How Parker smelled of mint and tobacco when he sat down across from me inside the police station, looking at me with disdain.

But that's in the past. It's all behind me. We've all moved on. Just in time for another disaster. What if Mila is in trouble? What if she's hurt? I rest my head back against the wall and try to steady my breathing. That's when I realize that I've been crying.

15

ELLIE

THINGS START TO get out of control on Wednesday. That's when Coach calls a **pre-bell** meeting. Show up at six fifty, he wrote in his late-night email to the entire team. Attendance is mandatory.

Stella and I are the first ones there, and Coach looks drained when we enter the room. His usually flushed skin is a grayish color and beads of sweat gather above his lip.

"Are you okay?" I ask.

He wipes his arm across his face, gathering perspiration in a neon terry wristband. "Yes," he snaps. "Why wouldn't I be?"

I try to make eye contact with Stella, but her gaze is trained on the door. She sits, spine straight in her chair, watching as the rest of the team files in.

I used to be able to tell her everything with just one look. We used to have a secret language, back when we were tiny, when our bodies collided with love and also with pain on a more regular basis. We didn't use words or sounds, or anything that could draw attention. Our language was based on looks and gestures, and fingers that curled into fists. With the raise of an eyebrow, I could tell how Stella was feeling, if she was angry or hungry, or if she wanted me to tell Mom a small white lie to get us out of something boring like an open house or piano lessons. And she read my mind, too, when I bit the inside of my cheek, turning my mouth into a lopsided pucker. How it meant *Let's escape, let's run.*

"It's been two days," Tamara says, sliding into a seat nearby. "Mila would have texted if everything was fine." She's wearing an Ellacoya Mountain Resort hotel sweatshirt that has STAFF embroidered on the front and JOHNSON printed on the back. Everyone knows the Johnsons give them out at the resort's annual holiday party. I wonder if Mila will get one this year. But as soon as the thought flickers in my brain, my heart rate quickens.

"My mom said the school staff and faculty had to stay late last night, that they had some meeting with Detective Parker," Raven says, her eyes wide and her skin paler than usual. She always turns nearly see-through this time of year.

I suck in a mouthful of air and kick Stella's seat in front of me.

"What?" she hisses. When she turns around, her lips are curled into a snarl.

Julia, Tamara, and Raven turn to stare and I know there's no way to warn her about Parker now. If he's involved, Stella's in trouble. He was the first detective on the scene last year, who *dealt* with Stella.

"Never mind," I mumble.

"Freak," she mutters under her breath.

"Asshole."

"You guys okay?" Raven asks, leaning over, her red ponytail swinging behind her.

"Mm-hm," I say quietly. If only Stella and I could still read each other's minds. If only we still cared to.

Julia scoffs. "Let 'em tear each other apart, Rave," Julia says, waving her hand dismissively. "Who cares?"

Just then, Coach clears his throat at the front of the room.

The door swings open and in walks Principal Pérez with a tall, burly white man. He has a splotchy complexion and a thick neck that strains against his collared shirt. I would recognize him anywhere. He walks with a purpose, like he doesn't have time for your bullshit, which he definitely does not, as he told me last year when he questioned me about Stella.

My sister's breath catches and I lean forward, toward her. Even when she's being a dick, she doesn't deserve to get blindsided by this guy, who basically ruined her life last year. Parker scans the room and looks at us a little longer than he should.

Principal Pérez speaks first. "You must be wondering why we've gathered you all so early in the morning," she says. Her long hair is pinned back and she's wearing a muted beige dress, even though she usually favors bright colors. "As some of you may have noticed, Mila Keene has not been in school this week."

The room buzzes as people begin murmuring to each other.

"What we're about to tell you is *not* public knowledge yet," Pérez continues, a little louder than before. "So we are trusting you to keep this information to yourselves until we can alert the entire school."

Fat chance.

Pérez clears her throat. "Mila Keene is officially a missing person."

I grip on to the sides of my desk and hold tight, hoping to ground myself. In my periphery, I see Noah shake his head in disbelief.

"We are only telling you this because you are Mila's teammates," Parker says in a low voice. "Her *cross country* team-mates, and we have reason to believe that Mila may have gone missing while she was out for a run."

Coach's mouth thins to a straight line and his knuckles turn white, grasping his clipboard. I know he's watching the season flash before his eyes—regionals, State, his fundraising numbers. A missing runner throws a wrench in all his plans. A missing Mila ruins his chance at excellence.

"Her mother noted that the last time she heard from her was . . ." Parker pulls out a slim black notepad. "On Monday morning around five a.m., when Mila set out for her usual morning run. She didn't come back after that." He clears his throat. "Right now, we have no reason to believe that Mila's disappearance is connected to the cold cases. We've dealt with missing girls and runaways before. More times than we'd care to," Parker says with a strange nonchalance. His eyes flit to Raven just for a second and I feel a stab of sorrow for her. But no one says what we're all thinking. *You never found the killer.*

"We're asking you to be safe out there on the paths in the woods," Parker continues. "We don't know what we're dealing with just yet."

Heads nod around me. The Fitzwater cases are all burned into our brains. I may not know as many details as Raven or Julia, but I've watched the sensationalized documentary that barely featured the families, and listened to the true-crime podcast episodes that were mostly about the reporters—not the victims. I know the killers chose the Oak Tower route because it has no cell phone service, and that Marlisse, Beatrice, and Abigail were found with their shoelaces missing. I know that for years, no one let girls out on their own.

It was hammered home season after season that even though going out for a jog can make you feel alive and whole and powerful, it also leaves you vulnerable and alone. But we keep running anyway. Because we have no other choice.

We run in spite of this. We run knowing the dangers, knowing who we are and why we could be targeted. But that won't stop us.

"We need your cooperation," Parker says, "If you saw anything, if you heard anything. If you know anyone who might want to harm Mila, we need to know. I understand she was new here in town, but she's been on this team for six weeks now. That's enough time to make some real connections, some real friendships."

Coach huffs and shifts his weight from foot to foot.

"It's also enough time to rise to the top, to make enemies," Parker says, his eyes lingering a bit too long on Stella. "I'll be on campus all day today, in Mrs. Tannenbaum's office. Find me if you have any information you think might be useful. Anything at all." He cracks his knuckles and the sound reverberates through the room, bouncing off the walls.

"I know this must be very scary to hear," Pérez says. "And that you might have a lot of questions. My door is open, as is Coach Gary's. Right, Coach?"

He nods and lets out a grunt of agreement.

"We are all here for you, and we will do everything in our power to find Mila," Pérez says. "Anything else, Detective?"

Parker widens his stance and tilts his chin up. "That's it for now," he says.

He and Pérez turn and leave the room, closing the door gently behind them, and as soon as they do, everyone erupts in high-pitched gasps and whispers that veer into conspiracy-theory territory.

"Dude, you know she's already dead," Bader says. He runs a hand through his bright blond hair and his mouth forms a creepy smile so the gap between his two front teeth shows. "I read that you're basically fucked if you're left out in the woods overnight. Plus, it was raining."

I want to punch him in the face.

"Nah, man. She's so hot. Whoever took her would let her live just a little," Noah's friend Matt says.

"You fucking pervs!" Julia calls out.

"Have some respect, you dick." Tamara elbows Noah in the arm, as if he can do anything to stop his friends.

Noah looks at Tamara, then at me, and then back to his crew. "This is serious," he says softly, his eyes narrowed and somber.

It's the way he says it that makes me lose my shit. The gentleness with which the words come out makes my head spin and I press my hand to my stomach. It's the same way he spoke to me when everything felt out of control, when a bundle of cells was growing inside me.

Stella turns around in her chair, her face slick with terror. She wraps her hand around my wrist and squeezes so hard, it hurts. I know she'll leave a mark but I don't care. Not this time. In an instant, I understand her. What the longing and the fear in her eyes might mean. We're back to how we were when we were kids, communicating on the same plane, in a different dimension, where no one else can get in. I see her and she sees me.

Stella drops my wrist but not my gaze, and I swear her lip quivers just a bit, just for a second. I know what she's asking, but I don't know how to answer. Because suddenly, the room is spinning and I'm falling out of space and everything . . . everything goes black.

By lunchtime, my fainting is a punchline. The kicker to the end of a horror story that has *obviously* gone around school by now.

"And then Ellie Steckler *fainted*!" I hear some sophomore squeal in the hallway outside the math wing. "Like, sure, make it about you. Go right ahead!" She and her friend burst into giggles without even realizing I'm right there. A few months ago this wouldn't have happened. A few months ago, they would have pouted and cocked their heads and asked in earnest tones, *Are you okay?* And if this were last year, Bethany would have been by my side, screaming at anyone who dared say something cruel.

If Bethany were here, none of this would have happened. If I just had someone to talk to . . .

I slam my locker shut and rest my head against the cool metal. *Get it together. Breathe.* I lift my forehead and turn around, watching a sea of students go by, some turning their heads to gawk at me then quickly looking away.

I spot Noah in the crowd, ignoring me as he ambles down the hall.

"Noah!" I call. "Wait."

The bell rings and everyone else starts rushing to class. For a second I think he's going to keep going, but then he turns and walks toward me, a frustrated look on his face. "What?" he says through gritted teeth.

His tone startles me even though it shouldn't. I know where we stand. But still I open my mouth to speak. "I think we should talk—"

"Talk, Ellie? Are you serious? All you've done is talk—about us and *your* secret. Don't you think you've done enough, huh?"

I want to scream and lunge for him. I want to tear at his skin and gouge out his eyes. Because it didn't have to be like this. It only is because of *him*. But before I can say anything, Noah turns and walks away.

I force myself to be strong. *He doesn't control you.* That's what I tell myself as I make my way to the caf for lunch. The cross country team is all huddled together around our usual table. Everyone seems to be listening to something Tamara's saying.

I nudge in beside Raven, whose eyes are narrowed in concentration.

"What's going on?" I ask.

"Tam's going to organize a search party with Mila's mom tomorrow," she whispers. "Shawna's worried Parker and his department are useless, since they never solved the cold cases."

My throat feels scratchy and I crane my neck toward Tamara to hear the plan.

"I figure we can case the perimeter of the lake tomorrow," she's saying. Her wrist flies over a legal pad in front of her, where she's drawn a map. She taps the back of her pen against an outline of a massive structure on the north side of the water. The Ellacoya Mountain Resort. "We can meet at the lodge at nine a.m. tomorrow," she says. "The hotel will provide coffee and bagels for everyone, so come hungry, okay?

We already have permission from Mrs. Keene, but she said she would love some privacy at this point, so no one even think of ambushing her right now."

Heads nod around me and Raven wraps her arms around her middle, murmuring her agreement.

"Any other thoughts?" Tamara looks up with wide expectant eyes and scans the circle. Her face falls when she gets to Stella. I didn't notice her on the other side of the table. But Stella's rolling her eyes and shaking her head.

"What, *Sterile*?" Julia says.

My sister doesn't even flinch. "I just don't get why we're doing this. It's not like we're going to *find* anything. You think there are random *clues*?" She scoffs. "It's pointless."

I suck in a puff of air through my teeth and wish I could disappear through the floor. I try to catch Stella's eye and tell her to *shut the fuck up*, to stop drawing attention to herself, to *us*, but she holds her ground.

Tamara sits up straighter. I can almost feel her spine stiffen. "What about trying to find Mila is pointless?"

Stella shrugs. "I just—"

"She's *missing*," Tamara says in a firm voice. "Aren't you two friends? Don't you care?"

I feel like I'm going to faint again. I knew this would happen. *Come on, Stella. Back down.* Her face turns into a scowl. As she readies a retort, I blurt out, "Of course she cares. We'll both be there. Obviously."

Everyone turns to face me and Tamara swivels her head, her box braids swinging around her shoulder.

"Fine," she says in a muted tone.

I don't look at Noah but I can feel his eyes on me. I avoid

Stella for the rest of the period, and the rest of the day. It's only when I meet her in the student parking lot, looking for a ride home, that I'm ready for her wrath.

But she's silent as I climb into the car. "What?" I say, a spike in my voice. "Let me have it. Just yell at me, already."

"I don't know what you're talking about," Stella says without looking at me.

"Come on, Stell. I know you're mad about lunch."

Stella turns the key in the ignition, reversing out of the lot. "There's nothing to say."

I know what she's doing. This is her favorite trick. Gaslighting me, as if I don't know when she's about to erupt, as if sixteen years of being her sister hasn't prepared me for her ire, hasn't made me anticipate her every move.

"Look, I know you think Mila's not actually missing, but we have to be part of the team. We can't give them a reason to come after you like last year," I say, a million possibilities swimming in my head.

Stella bangs a hand on the dashboard. "You think you know everything, Ellie, but you don't," she says quietly, leaning toward me. "You're so deep in your own drama wishing Bethany were here that you can't pay attention to anything else, like the fact that I *do* think Mila is missing, and that Parker's working the case, and that I'm fucking terrified." She blows out a stream of air through her nose. "You don't give a shit about anyone but yourself right now."

Her words are like a knife in my side. We've always been aligned, even when we were little and horrible, in that foggy period after the Dark Years, when Mom came back and Dad was trying desperately to hold everything together with frozen meals and seltzers with lime.

Mom would take us everywhere with her, trying to piece together some semblance of normal. To the bank, the post office, the Jewish bakery. Often, she would tell us to stay outside, on a bench, or by the front door where she could see us, and within a few minutes, Stella would pull my braid. Or I would elbow her in the side. That's all it took for us to tumble into each other violently and with abandon, pushing and pinching and rolling around on the sidewalk, our little bones colliding with concrete or dirt, our carnal rage seeping out of us and onto the sidewalk. New moms would pass us and watch, curious if the precious babies in their strollers would turn into tiny monsters at some point too.

The world hadn't yet told us that little girls don't fight with fists, but with words. Laughable now, though, after everything that's happened. The idea that girls don't fight.

After a while, when Mom had finished with an errand, or when someone alerted her to the two wrestling beasts out front, she would burst through the door and pull us apart, forcing her body between ours. It was useless to scold, she found. We didn't listen. We never did. It was her penance for leaving us, Stella told me once. One of us would walk away with a lock of hair or a torn sleeve curled in our fist. A scratch on one arm. A bruise blooming on a shin. We'd growl and snarl until a calm settled in, and after that, we could continue throughout the day, holding hands and skipping around the house, as if nothing had happened at all. As if that's just how sisters act.

But it is, though. How sisters act. Brutal and tender and out for blood.

16

STELLA

On Saturday morning, Ellie and I drive to Ellacoya in silence. There's a pit in my stomach, and the weather is crisp but warm, almost like spring instead of fall. It reminds me of the only time Ellie beat me. The Johnsons had invited the whole town for a barbecue out on the main lawn of Ellacoya to celebrate the Johnson Tavern's first Michelin star. There were thick, juicy hamburgers made from grass-fed beef, enormous bowls of pasta salad, and vats of limeade sweetened with agave. Prize-winning biscuits sat in towers on the edge of the table, where you could slather them with jam and butter or strawberries and cream.

It was a gorgeous weekend in May, with just a light, swaying breeze. It was also only six months after Mom had relapsed and I was furious at the world.

Bethany was gone for whatever reason, and Ellie wasn't interested in dealing with my gloominess. She ignored me for most of the day until finally Mom bent down, exasperated. "Play with your sister, Ellie," she said, her voice unsteady.

Ellie crossed her arms and stared down at her paper plate full of food. "But I don't want to play with Stella! She's no fun!" she yelled so loud, I was sure the other kids could hear it too. Who would want to be with me when my own sister didn't even want to?

Mom leaned in close over the wooden picnic table and narrowed her eyes.

"Ellie, you do *not* speak that way about your sister," she said. "You must take care of each other. That is what sisters do." Mom rubbed her temples and swung her head around, looking for Dad. I spotted him, off by a canoe they had turned into a cooler, schmoozing the out-of-town guests, trying to sell them on a house not far from Ellacoya. *Deadwater is in the past*, he was probably saying. *Look how great everything is now.*

"I can be fun," I said softly to Ellie.

"Oh, yeah?" she asked, disbelieving.

"We can race," I said. I scanned the field, looking for a flat expanse of grass. "How about over there?" I pointed to a volleyball net, set up next to one of the A-frames. "From that line to the lake."

A mischievous smile spread across her face. "You're on." My heart lifted and I felt hopeful for the first time in a long time. Ellie leapt from the picnic bench, her shiny ponytail swinging side to side, and we hustled to the court, ready to start.

"On your marks!" Ellie yelled. "Get set! Go!"

Together we sprinted, our little legs pumping up and down across the grass toward the clear, sparkling water. Other kids turned to watch us go, and my chest felt like it was about to explode. I loved the wind rushing through my hair, the way my feet hit the ground in an easy rhythm. This was what I was meant to do, this was . . . everything.

But as we neared the water, I turned back quickly to see how far behind Ellie was. Only just a bit, but she looked crushed, like she couldn't believe I was going to beat her, like she was devastated to be stuck with me, of all people, as her only sister.

So I slowed down. Not all the way, but enough that she could have a chance, enough that she could hope. Her eyes widened and she picked up her pace, realizing she could catch me, she could win. In a flash, she was at my side, and then as we reached the finished line, she raced across it first, beating me by a hair.

"Ha!" she yelled, jumping up and down, panting just a bit. "I beat *you*! And you're *older*!"

I tried to play along, to stomp out the part of me that wanted to rip her hair from her scalp and pin her to the ground. "You did it," I said softly.

Ellie skipped away, parading all around the field, relaying what happened to whoever would listen. A rage stewed inside me and by that time, I knew if I made a scene, if I pushed Ellie to the ground and started pummeling my fists into her side, that Mom would be mad. And I didn't want Mom to be mad. I didn't want Mom to drink, or to disappear again. I wanted Mom to be on *my* side in all of this, to love me. So instead, I walked to the lake and picked up a shiny flat rock, and tossed it into the water. I grabbed another and threw it, harder this time. I did it over and over, repeating the same words as the little pebbles soared into the horizon.

I will never let her win again.

Now Ellie and I walk along the same field at Ellacoya, wearing leggings and oversized fleeces monogrammed with the Edgewater XC logo, ready to join the search party.

The grass is damp and a blanket of fog hangs over the lake. But the sky is still and quiet, a murky mix of blue and gold. It's so peaceful, like one of those Hudson River School paintings Mila loves. If I were Tamara, I would never leave the grounds.

I can see why people shell out half a grand a night for rooms.

"Look," Ellie says softly. "The whole town is here." I follow her gaze to the left of the restaurant and see the entire cross country team, plus dozens of other students, people who never even knew Mila's name or that she had a tiny tattoo circling her wrist. There are reporters, too. You can always spot them thanks to their roving eyes, hungry for a scoop. We got to know their kind well over the years. They basically took over the Starlight Motel back when everyone thought the police would be able to pin down Monty and Kendall Fitzwater and get justice for Marlisse, Beatrice, and Abigail. They came back when Shira disappeared, too. Now they look eager and hungry for the next chapter in the Deadwater chronicles. They shoulder laptop bags and clutch recorders, phones pressed to their ears.

As we get closer to the crowd I look for Mila's mom, with her dark hair and worried eyes. I see her toward the back, huddled with Coach Gary and Detective Parker. My stomach lurches.

Shawna comes forward and steps onto a small wooden crate near the front of the circle. She clears her throat and closes her eyes. Her skin is sallow and her hands are shaking. My stomach is tied into a knot. *Where are you, Mila?*

"Hi, everyone," Shawna says. Her voice is small and wavering. "I don't know many of you, but I'm so grateful that you are here." She pushes her hair behind her ears and lifts her chin, catching a glimpse of sun. "My daughter, Mila, is grateful you're here. I say *is* because I know she is still out there. I know she's waiting for us." Her voice catches and another woman, who looks like she could be her twin, emerges from the crowd. She's dressed in faded jeans, a worn sweater, and hiking boots. She takes Shawna's hand in hers and steps up beside her, their shoulders touching. It's so obvious they're sisters.

Shawna nods and continues. "I want to thank the whole Johnson family for hosting us here this morning and for allowing us to search the grounds." She turns to Mr. and Mrs. Johnson, who stand off to the side, wearing matching Ellacoya vests and holding hands.

"Anything for one of our own," Mr. Johnson says in his steady voice.

Shawna smiles weakly and steps back, her shoulders shaking.

Mr. Johnson clears his throat. "Detective Parker will split you into groups and give you routes to canvass," he says. "You will each get a whistle and if you find anything, anything at all, any sign of her, use it to call Parker over. He'll be circling the area."

Parker gives a quick nod and starts distributing little plastic whistles, each one hanging from a thin string. One makes its way into my hands and it feels like a toy, something a child would play with. Not a way to save someone's life.

"Please, let's find my baby girl and bring her home," Shawna says, her voice floating above the group. She leans up against her sister for strength and I glance at Ellie. I picture us years from now in the same situation, me comforting her, making everything better, cleaning up whatever mess we had gotten into. That's the only way it would be.

Parker takes his place on the crate and starts barking instructions, splitting the group into packs of four and handing out trail maps. He sounds just like his son Calvin when he led us in stretches. Ellie and I get stuck with Raven and Julia, who cross their arms in unison like miffed little soldiers.

The detective walks through the crowd handing out maps on laminated sheets of paper, as if we don't all know this land by heart. As if we haven't spent years running over roots and whacking brush back to make our own trails. When he gets to our little foursome, he hands our map to Julia and avoids making eye contact with me. Ellie too.

"You four will take the banks on the far side of the A-frames, by the boat launch," he says in his clipped monotone. "Form a line and walk your assigned area three times, then come back for another assignment." When Parker moves to the next group, Julia and Raven turn to us.

"Come on," Julia says briskly. She and Raven walk in front of us, but not so far that I can't hear their mumblings. "God, I can't believe we got Stecklered."

Ellie winces and falls into step with me as we trail behind them. I nudge her shoulder, hoping she understands. *Fuck them.*

She elbows me back and tilts her chin up to the sky. *Fuck them.*

"Here," Julia says, stopping in her tracks at the base of the last A-frame. A chill picks up and she wraps her arms around her middle, pulling her fleece tight. If Mila really *was* out here alone, there's no way she'd survive the cold. Not at night. "You heard Parker. Spread out and walk to the banks."

"What are we looking for?" Raven asks.

I want to laugh because it really is a good question. No one told us.

Julia opens her mouth once and then closes it. "Uh, clues?"

I snort. "Clues? What is this, *Nancy Drew?*"

Julia's mouth grows small and her eyes narrow. "Got a better idea?" She's always looking for a fight, even when no one's there to see it. She just wants to be able to say that she put the Steckler sisters in their place. "Go find something that proves she's *actually* missing. That she didn't just go for a joyride and forget to call home or something."

Raven winces, but Julia doesn't even notice. They start walking, their gaze glued to the grass.

"I'd rather have no friends than have a friend like Julia," I say.

Ellie giggles that little-girl giggle of hers, the one that used to melt my heart when we were kids. Now when she does it, it's a reminder that I don't make her laugh so much anymore.

Julia looks over her shoulder and scoffs. They're getting closer to the water now, sidestepping kayaks that guests left haphazardly on the damp sand.

"I cannot believe you two are *enjoying* this," she says, loud enough for the group next to us to hear. Heads turn. Eyebrows raise. "And in front of Raven, too. You are so heartless."

The smile falls from Ellie's face and her lip quivers. "Sorry," she says quietly.

"Come on," I say. "Let's check the canoes." Ellie follows behind me, eyes tracing the shoreline. The boats are piled on top of each other and I look behind the stand. Nothing. Obviously. I move to the rack of paddles and part them with my hands. Again. Nothing. I wonder how long I can pretend this has a point.

I motion to Ellie to move on and we head closer to the water. The ground is muddy and my sneakers begin to sink into the soil. I hear Julia and Raven behind us, whispering in worried voices, but I ignore them and join Ellie, who's crouching down near a bush, looking toward a thicket of branches.

"Find the key to unlock this mystery?" I ask, half kidding. Ellie opens her mouth, but then I hear a gasp from over by the canoe paddles where we just were.

"What?" Ellie calls, a frantic pitch in her voice.

Raven's face has gone white. Her mouth is open and she

turns around frantically, hair flying in the wind. She's clasping a phone with a bright red case. From here, I can tell there's a thin, long crack along the screen. It's Mila's.

Julia rushes to Raven's side. "Don't move!" she calls. Then she raises the whistle to her mouth and blows as hard as she can, sending a piercing wail over the lake and across the grounds. Birds ruffle their feathers and take flight overheard.

"We found something," Julia yells.

Shouts ring across the lake and the wet sound of sneakers squelching in mud gets louder as half the search party descends on our foursome.

"What is it?" someone asks.

"Mila's phone," Raven says, her voice quavering.

Parker pushes through the crowd until he's standing right next to Julia and Raven. He frowns. I try to read his face, but there's no emotion. He just lifts a bulky camera from his bag and snaps a photo of the phone. "Where did you find this?"

Raven nods to the paddle stand. "Right there. On the ground. Under the paddle, so it was still mostly dry. It's dead, though."

Julia whips her head around. "Stella, how did you not find this? Weren't you *just* looking here?"

Parker looks at me quizzically, almost with delight.

No no no no no. My throat is dry and scratchy and I have no answer.

Parker leans down and snaps some more photos. Then he pulls a plastic bag from his pocket and motions for Raven to drop it inside. She looks reluctant, but follows instructions. She was always one to play by the rules.

Parker zips it closed and stashes it in his satchel. "I'll need you to answer a few questions about this," he says to Raven. "In the lodge, maybe?"

She nods, eager to help. "Whatever you think is best," she says.

Parker turns to the rest of the crowd and waves his hands for a few other officers to come forward. "Everyone else, step back. This is now a potential crime scene."

Raven nods and starts walking toward the lodge, clearing a path through the group. Parker follows her lead but before they get to the grass lawn, he turns around and and looks at me. "Stella," he says. "We should chat. Soon. I'll find you."

I try to keep my face neutral but I can feel dozens of eyes staring at me. I can feel their questions. Their suspicions. Their wonder.

Did Stella Steckler do something to Mila Keene?

17

ELLIE

THE ANNOUNCEMENT COMES just after Raven and Julia find Mila's phone. The whole cross country team is summoned into the lobby bar at Ellacoya, where we sink into plush armchairs in front of hulking wooden coffee tables, covered with mugs of hot cocoa. Tamara walks around with a tray full of marshmallows in silver bowls and tiny silver spoons used for stirring.

I always did love coming to Ellacoya, loved the decorations, how it painted a scene of what Edgewater *should* be like. Pairs of snowshoes march up the far wall by the staircase, and sets of skis cross behind the bar. Baskets of soft blankets sit on both sides of the couches, and recently fluffed pillows rest on the windowsill. Dozens of board games are stacked in a bookshelf against the wall. The room is as comfortable and cozy as someone's actual living room, not just made up for guests and out-of-towners willing to shell out a few grand for a make-believe mountain experience. Ellacoya is a promise and it delivers.

Parker walks to the front of the room and barks at us. "Settle down. We have a visitor." It only takes a few seconds before

Creed Dickerson, the town mayor, walks through the grand French doors. He's wearing what he always wears, ratty hiking boots, cargo pants, and a well-loved navy fleece zip-up. His white beard covers his neck and his hair is wild, sticking out from all sides of his head.

"I'm sure you all know Mayor Dickerson," Parker says in his booming voice. "But he has an announcement that we'll be sharing with the rest of the town immediately after this. Mayor?"

"Yes, hello. Edgewater's fastest. What a delight," he says, clasping his hands behind his thin, wiry frame. "I so wish this was under different circumstances, but it seems I have no choice. Until we find Miss Keene, we are bringing back an old rule. Effective immediately, young women are not allowed to run by themselves on the trails, and you cannot run before sunrise or after dark, even with a partner."

A quiet murmur spreads throughout the room and anger builds in my stomach. The town instituted this rule after the murders, when people were too scared to even go to the farmers market alone. But it's bullshit that the girls are the ones who have to suffer, who have to change our behavior. I glance over at Noah and his crew. They're all looking down or away, unfazed. This doesn't affect them. It never affects them.

Mayor Dickerson shuffles from foot to foot and his waterproof pants rub together in a swishing sound. "Any questions?" He smiles in a way that means he does not have time for questions, nor does he want to give us the answers. He wants us to shut up and listen.

"Isn't that sexist?" Julia says. "Just the girls have to run together?"

"It's not like boys are the ones disappearing while out for a jog, Miss Heller," says Dickerson. "We'd rather err on the side of caution."

Julia narrows her eyes. But she knows it's no use to argue. Not in this town—and not about missing girls.

Back when we hit puberty, I learned nothing about running was free, not the wind in our hair or the fire in our lungs. That's when people started looking at me differently. Started staring as I ran through town. I wondered if it was because of my chest. If my sports bra wasn't as supportive as it should have been. If my shirt was sweaty and stuck to my skin in a way that suggested *something* I wasn't even aware of. That's when I started noticing how us girls were the ones who had to watch ourselves. Girls out for a jog. Girls trying to get their times up. Girls trying to chase the electric high that comes with pumping your legs up and down for miles on end. Girls trying to get away, to feel something, anything, that we can't while sitting still. Girls in motion.

The mayor glances down at his watch and looks back up again. "Well, I'll be off. Pit stop at the Elks Lodge. Stay safe, runners." He walks out of the lodge quickly, leaving all of us in a stunned silence.

I sort of expect Coach to stand up for us. Or to secretly whisper *Don't listen to him* after Dickerson leaves. But he doesn't. He doesn't do anything. Instead, he gathers his things and looks at us with furious eyes, sitting above big purple circles.

"I've been told we have to cancel practice Monday" he says. "But I expect you to keep moving. Weights. Core work. Stretching. Do it inside. In your living rooms, on your floors.

I don't give a shit. Just show up on Tuesday ready to get your asses kicked. This changes nothing."

I can feel Stella tense beside me. She knows as well as I do that he's wrong. This changes everything.

I wake up shaking, my sweaty sheets balled in my fists and my jaw clenched. It takes a second before I can breathe normally again, before I realize the night terrors are back. My vision is shaky and I squeeze my eyes shut. *Breathe,* I tell myself. *Just breathe.* But it hurts to inhale. I just want to calm my nerves, to push away whatever demon was chasing me.

I roll over onto my side and stare out the window into the inky darkness, stars dotting the sky. This was the same view I had all summer, waiting for Noah's signal, a tiny pebble chucked this way. A classic move, but it worked. With every little knock, whether it came on a Wednesday when I had to be up early the next day for a shift at the lake or a Saturday when I could sleep in, my stomach fluttered and contracted. It had become a Pavlovian trick. He came calling. I answered.

The first time he did it in June, I thought it was a branch. I didn't hear it right away. But then another stone made contact and the sound was bigger, louder. I shuffled out of bed and moved to the window, peeking down to the yard. Noah stood there in a dark hoodie, his bike on the grass next to him. He waved.

It was easy to climb up to my window along the trellis on the side of the house, but I motioned that I would come to meet him. I pulled on a sweatshirt and tiptoed downstairs and out the sliding side door. When I emerged, Noah tackled me to the ground in a playful bear hug, kissing my neck and running his cool hands along my stomach.

"Shh!" I said, suppressing a laugh. "My parents could wake up."

"Wanna go for a ride?" Noah asked, his eyes twinkling with possibilities.

I nodded and stood on his bike pegs, arms wrapped around his neck as he pedaled to the entrance of Sweetwater Lake. I breathed deeply, trying to absorb him, never forget him.

When we got there, Noah stopped and unlocked the gate with his head lifeguard key. He pulled out a blanket and we sat there together on the sand, watching the sky for the first hint of sun. Noah pulled out a beat-up paperback filled with lines of poetry and started reading aloud. *Howl* by Allen Ginsberg. I wasn't sure if I liked the poem itself, but I liked the way Noah read it, that he read poetry at all. I liked that he surprised me. I closed my eyes and drew my knees to my chest as he recited the words as if he were performing a play. When I opened my eyes, the sky was purple and blue and seemed to emerge straight up from the still lake, serene and warm. I wanted to record every second, remember this is what it felt like to be loved, to be treasured, to be wanted.

"It's perfect," Noah said quietly, his arm looped around my shoulder. "You're perfect." He shut the book and set it down next to us. He leaned in, kissing me with his whole hungry mouth. It was then that I knew what was about to happen. We had been messing around for a few weeks. This was the obvious, natural conclusion. I wanted it. I wanted him.

We moved quickly from there. His callused finger pads pressed against my bare stomach and made me shiver. "I've never done this before," I whispered into his neck as our skin suctioned together like rubber.

"I know," he said. "I've got you." He nudged my legs apart and slipped himself inside me, without anything between us.

"What about a—" I started. I wanted a condom. I knew we needed one.

But Noah just smiled and kissed my neck. "It's so much better this way," he said. "I'll pull out."

I knew I should have pushed, should have demanded protection, but I didn't. I said nothing. Soon, his gaze moved from my face to my chest, to where he disappeared inside me. Then he closed his eyes finding his way to the finish line.

His biceps rippled and crested, and his torso moved in a wave. It hurt just a little, but after the initial shock subsided, I felt nothing. No ecstatic pleasure or burning need. There was no blood, no broken body part. No great change or awakening. Just two sacks of bones intertwined with one another, stuck together by sweat.

"Wow," he said, when he finally rolled over. "Wow." Noah panted just a bit, catching his breath as the sun rose from the horizon.

"Uh-huh," I said, pulling the picnic blanket up, over me.

I always hated the idea of "losing" my virginity, as if it were something that I had misplaced between the couch cushions. It seemed deranged that it was something someone could "take" from you, as if it were up for grabs and not wholly yours. Back in middle school, I often pictured how it would be, fantasizing about who it would be with and how it would happen—in a bed made with silk sheets or a camping tent decorated in twinkly lights. But that was before I learned the reality is so much more normal. Basic. Carnal. There was skin and sweat and smacking sounds because, of course, we were both simply human.

There was only Noah, his hulking, damp body, and the sticky goo between my legs. I wiped it off with a bandana and balled the fabric in my fist. Noah reached for me and kissed my forehead, my cheeks, my nose, and my chin. He caressed my hair as I struggled to fight sleep, to remember every moment of what had happened between us. It was only later, when he dropped me off at home, that I felt the wetness still between my legs. That was when I realized he had forgotten to pull out.

I spent so much of the summer waiting and hoping to hear the sound of pebbles against my window, inviting me on an adventure. I never thought to be the one to knock on *his* window. I didn't think I was allowed. I didn't think I had the power to do that.

But Noah stopped coming around like that after we went to the clinic in Newburgh. That's when I started running in the earliest hours of the morning, the ones that could still be considered night.

I get it now, why Stella only ever wanted to run before the sun came up. It's when everything is new and damp, and just a little creepy. The air is harsh and biting and untouched. And when the sun starts to peek out over the horizon at the lake's edge, I always catch a hitch in my throat and feel tears prick my eyes. It's so beautiful it stings.

The clock says 4:05 a.m. and I give up on finding sleep again. This morning is different. This morning is defiant. This morning is in direct opposition to Mayor Dickerson and Detective

Parker. I'm not going to stop running. It's the only thing left that's mine.

I roll over and feel around in the darkness for joggers and a sweatshirt. I pull them on without turning on the light, and tiptoe down the stairs, through the back door, farthest from Mom and Dad's room.

When I step outside, it's freezing, as if it's become winter overnight. By noon it'll warm a little, but now in the witching hours, the air is ice.

My muscles are tight, unworked and unloved after a few days without practice, so I take off slowly, through our backyard and down the street toward town, hearing Mayor Dickerson's words beat in my brain. *It's not like boys are the ones disappearing.*

Everything in town is closed. Nothing stays open twenty-four hours here. Not the unbranded pharmacy, run by Old Ned who was born in Edgewater, nor the gas station, which hasn't changed its neon script signage since the seventies. The folks who come up from Brooklyn are always posting photos of it on Instagram.

I run by it all. Past the diner, where the lights turn on at five a.m. for the farming crowd, and the natural wine shop that opened when a bunch of mustachioed hipsters moved up here a few years back. Past the soap store and the cheese purveyor and the bakery that specializes in sourdough and rye. Everything is still dark. There aren't any streetlights here. Everything is lit only by the moon. When it wanes, you can barely see your hand move in front of your face. No wonder Edgewater inspires killers.

I get to the end of the main drag, speed up, and turn left, heading up the hill toward the service entrance at Ellacoya, where the gravel becomes dirt and then a slick path, looping around the lake.

I run toward the sun, which is finally starting to appear. At first the sky is a haze of milky purples and dusty blues. Everything is magic and I feel nostalgic for a few moments ago, when it was only me and the stars. I can see the water by its reflection, sparkling and shiny in front of me. It's calm, lapping at the shore and the sound brings me back to every other night like this, when I know I'm all alone with just my skin, my muscles, and my heartbeat. When I can forget what I've done, when I can just be.

I've never felt afraid on these runs even though I'm told I should be. It's people that scare me. The ones who look at me from stern to stem. Out here in the dark, at night, I'm part of the brush.

But then my mind drifts to Mila. She didn't get to know these places. Not like I do. What would she say if she were running next to me? I don't even want to imagine. I pick up my pace and try to push her away as I round the bend toward the dock.

All of a sudden a branch snaps and I stumble, landing in a pile of crunchy leaves, bracing myself with my hands. I gasp and whip my head around, expecting to see Mila running toward me. But when I turn, there's no one. Just the breeze and the water, rippling outward. I push myself to stand and try to steady my heart. There's a rustling in the woods and for a split second I can't breathe. What if the killer is back?

But I know that's impossible.

I blink hard and shake my head. I keep moving up the path and away from the resort, away from the woods. My breathing is shallow and tender, and I circle back through town, where one of the line cooks at the diner flips on the overhead lights and turns on the griddle. I take a right and push myself toward school to take the long way home.

The sky is now flecked with oranges and yellows, bursting as day begins to break.

That's when I start to hear voices. They're small at first but clipped and flecked with sharp tones and hard inflections.

I can hear my breath in my ears and start to slow my pace as I reach the Edgewater High parking lot. I clasp my hands behind my neck and feel the sweat roll down my back, my sweatshirt sticking to my skin. I try to catch my breath, but panic rises in my throat.

There in the middle of the parking lot are trucks. Half a dozen. With satellites poking out the top. Women in smart pencil skirts and silk pants, made up with lipstick and blownout hair. They're standing around holding microphones and clipboards. Dudes in suits and earpieces dot the scene. There are cameras. So many cameras. And they're all gearing up to film us when we arrive for school in a few hours.

I take a few steps closer, craning to hear what they're saying, how they are going to describe us as we become the perfect backdrop for their news segment.

One woman with honey-blonde hair is running lines, practicing her little monologue into the space in front of her. She wraps a scarf around her neck and closes her eyes.

"I'm Gertie Adler from Channel Twelve News, and I'm here at Edgewater High School, where yet another young woman has gone missing while on a run," she says, her brow furrowed. "You might remember Edgewater as the town where female cross country stars were brutally murdered while running nearly a decade ago. Police believe all three girls were killed by the same perpetrator, but the cases remain unsolved. We have to ask, is the Edgewater killer back? Is there a serial killer on the loose in this idyllic mountain town once nicknamed Deadwater?" she asks, her voice rising with the question. "And what is it about Edgewater that makes people want to harm little girls?"

A rage builds inside my chest and my fingers curl into fists. I want to hurl myself at her middle and throw her to the ground. I want to whisper the truth into her ear.

We're not that fucking little.

18

STELLA

BY THE TIME I get to school on Monday, all I want to do is practice. It's been almost a week since Coach held an all-squad session and I can feel my muscles rebelling, softening. But when I see the reporters, relegated to the patch of browning grass across the street, which is technically *not* Edgewater High property, I know this week will be shot.

Principal Pérez looks like she's giving them a stern talking-to, but that doesn't stop a perky woman with a mousy-brown updo. "Raven Tannenbaum!" she yells. "Do you think Mila ran away like your sister?" Raven blinks but doesn't say anything as she picks up her pace, hiding her face behind a shield of red hair.

"Stella Steckler!" calls a white man with pimples and curly blond hair. "How did you feel about losing to Mila in the first meet of the year?"

I grit my teeth as Ellie wraps her hand around my elbow, a signal to not engage, to keep moving forward.

"So what if I lost to her?" I mutter under my breath. "That doesn't mean anything."

Ellie nods solemnly, but twitches with discomfort. Dark bags hang under her eyes and her shoulders sag like she's exhausted by all of this. "They want to turn you into a monster," she whispers.

She said the same thing last year, after I came home from the police station, where Parker kept me in that cold, stark conference room for hours, questioning me about Allison Tarley, making me relive the worst five seconds of my life, telling me things about myself as if I were a specimen, an object.

"You're competitive, Stella," he said, his voice calm and deep. "We've known that for years. You'll stop at nothing to win, to be the best, to take others down. Isn't that right?" He looked so much like his son Calvin in that moment, tough and broad, handsome and cocky.

That's what made me shut down and stop talking. I wasn't going to convince him of the truth. It was obvious then. My silence didn't help, I learned later. But it was *my* coping mechanism. How could it have been the wrong one?

"They want to turn you into a monster," Ellie said at the time. Both of us had hair that was wet from the shower and she curled up against the foot of my bed. "You should pretend you're not."

Now, in the halls, lockers slam with urgency. Everything seems to be moving slower, like we're all wading through molasses. There's a heightened sense of worry simmering below the surface. Students look at each other with wide-open eyes, as if to ask, *Again?*

We were all in elementary school when the murders happened, and middle school when Shira went missing. But I remember what it was like, how even the wind blowing a door open would make teachers jump, how the girls were given curfews, how our parents installed deadbolts on the doors.

When we get to the junior lockers, Ellie shoves an elbow in

my side and gives me a look. It's that *Don't do anything you'll regret* look. The one reserved for when she knows I'm on the verge of a full-on freak-out meltdown. I'm not, though. Not today.

After last year, a few reporters won't scare me.

As I make my way down the halls, I see a flash of neon blue once, twice, and then a million more times. The flyers are plastered all over, on corkboards, on lockers, and littered on the floor. I stop in my tracks and pick one up, the cardstock heavy between my fingers.

JOIN US FOR THE
MILA KEENE CHARITY RUN

5K AROUND THE TRACK

TUESDAY

3 p.m.

$15 ENTRY FEE

**ALL PROCEEDS GO TO
THE MILA KEENE SEARCH FUND**

**SPONSORED BY
THE EDGEWATER VARSITY XC TEAM**

My jaw drops and my face feels hot. I know this is *nice*, but what about practice? With regionals so close, we've already lost so much training time. Doesn't anyone else want to win as much as I do? That's what Mila would want. I turn around and hustle through the halls until I make it to Coach's office. The door is open and he's shuffling a stack of papers, flustered and unshaven.

"Stella," he says with little affect. "What?"

I hold up the flyer and open my mouth. But Coach raises his hand as if to stop me.

"Don't say a word."

"But—" I start.

"But what?" he asks. His voice is tired and impatient, like he's been up all night or subsisting on only coffee and protein bars, both of which could be true. "Sit, Stella."

I do as I'm told, but cross my arms over my chest as I drop into the plastic chair across from him.

"We've lost almost a week of practice," I say. "Everyone's going to be rusty as hell by the time we get to regionals." But we both know I don't care about *everyone*. I care about me.

"Look, Stella. Things are a bit dicey after last year. Parker still has it out for you, and I don't want you making a stink anywhere near this." Coach leans forward. "I don't have to remind you that your chances of landing a scholarship are almost gone. You're a junior. This is when the scouts make their final decisions. You'll be lucky if they take another look at you. You know that, right?"

I fight the stinging in my eyes, the burning in my throat, and nod. I do know that.

"The last thing we need is you looking like a suspect or raising any eyebrows," he says. "You gotta show them all you can be on a team. I need you to support the efforts to find Mila but not get too close to the case. Do you understand me?"

Of course I understand. I just want to find Mila, to laugh

about all this and push each other to the finish line. But if I say any of that out loud, I know I'll cry. "So if tomorrow's taken over by a *charity* run, how are we supposed to get better? How am I supposed to win at regionals? Show them I'm too good to ignore?"

Coach raises his arms over his head and stretches. "Get in the weight room or something. Go on the treadmill. This is bigger than practice, Stella." He lets the empty space sit between us. Then he leans in and lowers his voice like he knows he shouldn't share whatever it is he's about to tell me. "Apparently Mila's dad has been totally MIA," he says. "And so even though he's got a whole trust-fund situation, Mila's mom now has to raise money for a private detective to get some extra resources. They don't trust Parker's team to get it right. So I expect you to be there and *not* make a scene. Okay?"

"Fine," I say.

"Good. Just think of it like practice, okay? Work on your time. Stay in your own lane. Don't fuck it up."

"Okay, Coach." I pick my bag up and turn to leave.

"Oh, and Stella?"

"Yeah?"

"I know this isn't really your *thing*, but it wouldn't kill you to show some emotion."

"Emotion?"

"You know. *Feelings.*" He smiles, like he's just made a sly joke, but in a second, it slips from his face. "A girl is missing, after all."

I grit my teeth. How I wish I could throw him to the floor and rip that smirk off his face. Coach has no idea what the fuck he's talking about and I don't know how to explain it to him. So I don't.

The flyers seem to follow me for the rest of the day, scattered on desks in World History and French. As the bell rings for third period, I trudge back to my locker to dump my books from my morning classes, but I keep seeing those neon papers out of the corner of my eye. It takes everything in me not to rip down every single one.

"Hi, Stella."

I turn to find Tamara leaning up against the locker next to mine, cradling a stack of paper in her arms.

I grunt hello and spin the dial on my lock.

"Just wanted to see if we can count you in to come to the charity run," she says.

I turn to Tamara, wanting to say something sarcastic or flippant, but when I look at her, there's fear in her eyes. She fidgets, twisting one of her braids around her finger.

"I'll be there," I say, softening my tone.

"I know we're slacking in the practice department, but . . ."

I shrug and mimic Coach's words. "This is bigger than practice." The pained look on Tamara's face confirms it's true and something inside me softens. "Thanks for organizing this whole thing," I say. "Coach told me Mila's dad hasn't helped at all."

"It's so messed up. I just hope we can do something to help Shawna."

"Me too," I say as I pull my locker open and reach for my physics textbook. But before my fingers can grasp the thick spine, something hard and plastic drops to the ground.

I bend down to pick it up. My heart nearly stops. It's Mila's Edgewater High School ID. Flecks of dirt stain the edges and a smear of mud nearly covers her face. *How did this get here?*

Quickly, I scoop it up, praying that Tamara didn't see, that she won't ask any questions. I shove the ID back into my locker and slam it shut. But when I look up, Tamara's eyes are wide with shock. Down the hall, I see Noah, Julia, and Raven coming toward us.

"I gotta go," I mumble. I head for the gym, the only place where I can wait out the lunch period and just think. How did Mila's mud-stained ID get in my locker? Who put it there? For the first time since Mila's gone missing it occurs to me that *someone* must be behind this. And whoever it is wants me to take the blame.

In physics, I count the seconds on the clock above the door as the period ticks by. As soon as the bell rings, I head back to my locker. But when I approach, Principal Pérez is there, arms crossed over her chest. Detective Parker stands at her side. They're both staring at my locker, as if their steely gazes will cause it to spring right open.

I wonder what will happen if I run. But the hallway is crowded and there's no way out unless I want to bulldoze a bunch of freshmen.

"Stella Steckler," Pérez calls when she sees me approaching. The halls go quiet. "A word."

I hold my breath and walk to the locker, horrified by what's inside.

"We have reason to believe there may be some evidence in your locker, Stella," Parker says with a cool, steady voice. "Do us a favor and open it. Otherwise we'll have to get the master key."

I don't know what to do. Heat pulses through me and I

clench my fists. There's a crowd now. Freshmen whispering behind cupped hands. Sophomores rubbernecking on their way to class.

"Move along, everyone. Don't you have places to be?" Principal Pérez says, but nobody listens.

I spot Noah with Tamara, Raven, and Julia, staring at me with curious looks at the other end of the hall. I wonder which one of them threw me to the wolves.

I have no choice. I enter my combination with shaking fingers. The locker pops open and I hold my breath as I step back, letting them search for Mila's ID, for anything else that someone may have planted.

A few moments pass but nothing happens. No one gasps or shrieks or holds up that plastic card with any sort of relief. Parker slams the locker shut. "Nothing interesting, Steckler," he says. "Guess we got a bad tip."

What? Parker and Pérez turn back toward her office, shooing students to class on their way.

Once the hallway is empty, I rush to my locker and fling it open again, digging around to see where the ID may have gone. I take a step back.

Suddenly, I see Ellie's dark hair in my periphery. She walks toward me. Huddling close, she leans in and whispers into my ear. "I took care of it."

"What?" I hiss.

But the late bell rings and Ellie's gone, rushing to her next class.

"Ellie!" I yell, trying to get her to come back, to explain what the hell is going on. But she keeps walking. She doesn't look back.

19

STELLA

THE CHARITY RUN takes over the entire school for twenty-four
full hours. Every wall is plastered with Mila's class picture. The
same photo that was on her ID. Her *missing, mud-stained* ID.
The one that was in my locker—and then wasn't. I try to shake
the strange feeling as I reach into my gym bag and pull out my
sneakers. The rest of the team jostles around me, peeling off
their jeans and fleeces and changing into our uniforms.

"Here," Tamara says. I open my eyes and turn to face her.
She hands me a purple ribbon.

"What am I supposed to do with this?" I ask.

Julia rolls her eyes from behind Tamara. "Whatever you
want," Julia says. "Tie it in your hair, or around your wrist.
Wrap it around your neck for all I care."

"We're all wearing them," Raven says, tying hers into a bow
around her flat ponytail. "Purple is Mila's favorite color."

"How do you know that?" Anger pools in my stomach. I
still don't know which of them told Pérez about the ID in my
locker, but based on the crimson color of Raven's cheeks, she's
my best bet.

Raven shrugs and scurries away. The ribbon is soft and

shiny, thick and frayed at the edges where Tamara must have cut them with scissors. I don't want to attach this fake bullshit to my body, but I remember Coach's words. *Don't make a scene.* I gather my hair into a low pony and knot the ribbon at the base. The ends tickle the back of my neck and I know it will annoy me while running.

"Let's get out there," Tamara calls. "Let's do it for Mila!" The rest of the team follows her out to the track. I'm left alone with the smell of stale sweat and the tinny echo of slammed lockers. That is, until Ellie barrels into the locker room, nearly knocking over a wooden bench as she drops down onto it.

"Nice of you to show up," I say.

Ellie lifts her leg and presses it into the lockers as she leans forward to tie her sneaker. "Fuck off," she says, not making eye contact.

"What's with you?" I ask. But Ellie says nothing. I lower my voice and try again. "Hey, about the ID—"

"Don't mention it," Ellie says, keeping her head down as she straightens her sock.

"How did you know?" I ask. "What did you do?"

Ellie stands and reaches one arm across her chest in a stretch. "Raven saw and was practically telling the whole school about it," she says. "After last year, I thought Parker would jump at any chance to place blame on you for *something.* I knew your combination and I took care of it. That's it."

"But—" I want to tell her I had nothing to do with Mila's disappearance, that I'm just as confused as everyone else.

Ellie holds her hands out in front of her. "We don't need to talk about this anymore, Stell. I got your back always," she says. "And you got mine." She pauses for a second, chewing on her lip. "You and me forever, right?"

"Right," I say, softening.

"Come on," she says. "Let's go."

I don't know what I thought I would expect, but the scene on the track makes me stop. The bleachers are filled with Edgewater students and faculty, holding signs that say things like BRING MILA HOME and FIND MILA KEENE. The marching band has formed in their usual roped-off area in front of the bleachers and they're all wearing purple T-shirts that say WE MISS YOU, MILA. The pit, where the away team usually readies themselves, is packed with reporters and cameras, microphones and recorders. All around us, Mila's face, that same class photo, is staring out at me, smiling as if nothing's wrong. But none of these people knew her. None of them knew about her dad, or that she loved art history. I bet they didn't even notice the daisy chain on her wrist, or that she has the same fierce ambition inside her as I do.

"Whoa," Ellie says under her breath.

"I know."

But when I follow her gaze, I see she's not looking at the reporters or the instruments in the marching band. Her eyes are locked on the front row of the stands, where six scouts holding clipboards sit side by side, wearing baseball hats.

"What are they doing here?" Ellie turns to me. "Did you know?"

My throat is scratchy. "No," I say.

One of the scouts, the dude from Yale who was at the first meet of the season, sees me and elbows the other. Soon they're all looking at us, at the Steckler sisters, to see what we can do.

"Un-fucking-believable," Ellie mutters. "I thought this was for *charity*."

I spot the scout from Georgetown and kick my pre-race

routine into high gear. My breathing becomes rhythmic. My brain begins to clear.

I follow Ellie to the rest of the team, where Coach gathers everyone in a huddle. He's surrounded by the varsity team, but also a few JV runners and a bunch of other participants, who willingly signed up to complete the race on Mila's behalf.

Detective Parker is off to the side, near the scouts, sitting with his arms crossed over his chest. I vow to block him out. I can't think about him today, not when the scouts are here.

Shawna Keene is next to him, watching as her sister moves in front of a microphone to make a speech. She speaks slowly, with confidence, about how much Mila loves running, about how her old teammates are holding their own charity run in Connecticut at this very moment. After a minute, she takes a deep breath and closes her eyes. When she opens them, she scans the crowd of strangers and grasps the microphone.

"Bring our baby home," she says. "Bring her home."

My chest tightens and I jump in place, trying to keep warm, trying to keep my cool. I picture Mila and I wonder where she is. What she's doing, because she must be doing *something*. She must be alive. *What would she do if she were here?* I ask myself. And the answer comes instantly: she would try to win.

Principal Pérez joins her in front of the microphone. "I'm pleased to announce we've already raised four thousand dollars for the Mila Keene Search Fund!" Cheers erupt from the stands and Mila's mom offers a weak smile. "But we'll continue collecting donations throughout the evening, if you feel so inclined." Pérez then brings a whistle to her lips. "Without further ado, runners! Take your marks." The massive group pushes to the starting line and I shuffle to take my place, closest to the inner ring of the track. My heart rate steadies, and I close my eyes for just a second. "Get set!" Pérez yells. "Go!"

The word sends me speeding. I've run around this track a million times before. I know its cracks and slopes like I know my legs, my muscles, my heart. As I take off, the world fades around me. The cheers disappear. I'm in a black space of darkness, fighting for air, for breath, for space in the crowd. I can't see anyone else or anything. It's just . . . me.

The first lap around the track goes by, and then the second, and by the third, I can't tell who I've already lapped, who is at my level. People are walking. Parents and cousins, freshman theater kids who are here just trying to do something *good*, some volunteer work. They're just here to get out of doing homework on a Tuesday. But I keep sprinting. I fight and I push, and these randoms, these people who mean nothing, move to the side as I go by. They hear me before they see me flying past them. They feel the air move between us. I am wind and I am speed and I am one with the road.

Until I'm on the sixth and final lap, the one that I know I can crush. I can stomp it out and beat my time and show all of those scouts that *I am Stella Steckler* and I am a star.

The finish line looms overhead, and my lungs are on fire. I am skin and bones and pain will not stop me. I blow through the finish line and slow as I know I should, to conserve my muscles, to relish the victory. I tilt my head back and look up to the sky, a clear swath of blue just beginning to darken. I think of Mila and how if she were here, she would have kept up with me. She would have been right beside me, throwing herself over the finish line.

Then I look to my watch to check my time. Shit. I obliterated my PR. Blew past it. I want to cry, I feel so free, so good, so alive. I can't help but let my face erupt into a smile, a broad wide grin reserved only for breaking records and winning medals. But when I look up to find Coach, his mouth is a hard line of fury. He motions for me to come over.

"That was my best," I say. I'm still trying to catch my breath, but I look up to the scouts to see their reactions. They betray nothing, their eyes on their clipboards.

"I told you not to make a scene, Stella," he says.

"What are you talking about?"

"You were the only one running," he says. "Look." He points to the track, where everyone, including Tamara and Noah and the rest of the Edgewater varsity track team, are just . . . walking. Well, walking and looking at me, whispering to each other.

"But . . ." I say. "The scouts."

"They're paying respects, Stell," he whispers. "They're not here to judge you."

"But you said if I beat my PR, they'd have to pay attention." The delight I felt a few seconds before is now replaced with shame, all muddled with adrenaline and fear and the unfairness of everything. How unfair it is that Mila isn't here. How unfair it is that I can't control my body or my brain.

"Leave," he says, his voice a harsh whisper. "Just go. It'll be better if you do."

The sweat on my back grows cold and I want to protest. I take one last look at the crowd, where Parker and Mila's mom sit next to each other in stunned silence. Both of them stare at me, but with different expressions. Shawna's mouth is open, and her eyes are sad, bewildered puddles. But Parker's brows have narrowed, and he looks like he's trying to take me apart and put me back together like a puzzle. I remember Ellie's words.

They want to turn you into a monster.

I think I just let them.

I turn to walk to the locker room and try to avoid the eyes. But just as I pass the group in the middle of the track, I hear Julia's voice, loud and clear from behind me. "Stella definitely had something to do with it," she says. "But that's obvious. We all know what she's capable of after the whole Allison Tarley thing."

A few weak laughs follow, and the rage rises into my throat. I can't let what happened last year happen again. But I have to defend myself. No one else will. I start back toward the group, but before I get to Julia, Ellie emerges from the crowd and blocks my path. "What the fuck did you just say?" she asks, turning to Julia.

"Relax, Ellie. It was a joke," Julia says. "Your *sister's* just being a competitive freak again, but what else is new."

Ellie leans in so she towers over Julia. "I cannot stress this enough, Julia. Fuck. Off."

Julia takes a step back, crashing into Tamara who's looking at Ellie with confused, almost admiring eyes. Raven stands slack-jawed by their side.

"Jesus, Ellie. What's wrong with *you* these days? You're turning into a mini Stella," Julia says.

A smile spreads across Ellie's face. "Maybe that's not such a bad thing."

Julia's mouth falls open and she turns back to her friends. "Did you just hear that? What . . ." But I stop listening. Ellie holds her chin high and her face is hard like stone. She retreats from the group, ignores the stares from the stands, and walks over to me. She throws one arm around my shoulder and whispers into my ear, "Come on."

I follow my little sister's lead for once and focus on the metal doors to the locker room up ahead. But I can feel Ellie's heart racing through her chest, her fingers shaking as they graze my arm. When we get inside, away from everyone else, we both pause. I search her face and she searches mine. It's back to like when we were little. I see her and she sees me. I hear her and she hears me. And I know what we're both thinking.

We'll protect each other.

We'll hide each other's secrets.

20

ELLIE

IT'S HARD TO remember when Stella and I stopped being the same, when our interests diverged, then swerved and criss-crossed on the track. I don't have many memories of the *before*, when Mom was "sick" as Grandma liked to say. When Dad was too depressed and frazzled to even make us eggs. Stella bore the brunt of that period, convincing me to play with her in our shared bedroom in the Airstream. She was only fourteen months older and couldn't do *that* much more than I could, but she would pretend. Read me books upside down, while really just making up stories. Draw on the back of old bills we found in the kitchen.

I only remember the *after*, how Mom came back shiny and new, with clean clothes and a fresh haircut, glowing skin and a real smile. How she smelled good, like vanilla and sawdust. How Dad came up with a plan for them to sell houses, to re-build our lives. When they earned their real estate licenses, I remember clapping at our Formica dinner table, eating a wedge of cake made from a box. I was proud of them for being like the other parents, for being *normal*. But that's when Stella got angry. Angry that I was happy and she couldn't be. Angry at them. Angry at the world.

That was also when Mom started dressing us in matching outfits. Fitted floral dresses with buttons down the front. Neon baseball hats and soft denim overalls to wear around town. We always had the same everything. The same hiking boots. The same swimsuits. The same backpacks. But something shifted when Stella got good. When she got *fast*.

Maybe it happened the summer after first grade. Stella made the summer travel soccer team. I did not. Mom comforted me by saying Stella was older and that only one first grader made it. But I was still devastated. Mostly because it meant Mom and Dad dragged me to every single one of Stella's games, even if they were all the way down in Westchester. I was forced to sit on the sidelines with a granola bar and a chapter book and watch Stella have all the fun.

She wasn't *great* at soccer. She always kicked the ball too hard, out of bounds. And she had a tough time working with her teammates, other little girls from neighboring schools. Girls who wore ribbons in their smooth, shiny hair. Girls who sang Disney songs on the bus and searched for earthworms in the mud. Girls who made each other flower crowns out of dandelions and braided strands of grass. Stella didn't care about all that. She just wanted to win. She wanted to be strong. She wanted to be *fast*.

Her coach at the time noticed it first. After one of her final home games, he pulled Mom and Dad aside. I didn't hear the conversation, but by the looks on their faces, it was good. And within a few weeks Stella had stopped playing soccer and was enrolled in the Hudson Valley Elite Youth Runner's Club.

She started coming home with fancy, shiny sneakers with bold labels on the sides. Soft synthetic T-shirts made with aerodynamics in mind.

Once, when I whined that my sneakers were too old, Mom bent down to meet my gaze. "Are you jealous of your big sister, sweetie?"

Her words stung. Was I jealous? Stella's willingness to play house or cards with me had disappeared. Instead, she had taken to knocking over my block mountains and snipping locks of hair off my dolls before racing around the yard. I tried to stay away from her. I read a dozen books in a month. I met Bethany. I found my own way. So of course I wasn't jealous of Stella.

But maybe I was. Of the attention she received for being *good*, for *winning*. Of the blue ribbons she brought home every Saturday. Of the mud stains that streaked her white mesh shorts and the electricity that seemed to shoot through her body during the final seconds of a race. Of the way her eyes narrowed when she saw the finish line up ahead.

So I told Mom yes. "I want to run, too," I said. She sighed the sigh of someone who was too busy to think about the minutiae of a child's inner thoughts, but a few days later I was enrolled in the juniors' program at the Elite Youth Runner's Club.

Soon, I got good too. I brought home fancy new sneakers and soft T-shirts that were supposed to make you soar. I won medals in my division. I was *fast*. Not as fast as Stella. But close.

I only beat her once in elementary school, during some just-for-fun race at the Ellacoya Mountain Resort. But catching up to Stella had become more than a game by then. It was a necessity. It was survival.

Now, though, none of that matters. I've learned how to move forward on my own.

The day after the charity race, we finally have practice. The locker room is still and somber when I arrive. Everyone pulls on their spandex, and some of the girls break out their fleece headbands and gloves, even though it's not yet Halloween. I usually try to wait until November to get cold. Otherwise you're fucked come December. I lean up against the locker and close my eyes, counting to ten, then twenty, willing myself to stay present, to stay grounded, to keep control.

Only Julia speaks, but her voice grates against the sounds of lockers slamming and sneakers sliding against the tile.

"I guess it's a good thing, getting back out there like normal," she says. "We've been still long enough, you know? Mila would want us to run. She definitely would. Don't you think?"

Raven nods silently next to her, her face pale and her freckles prominent. She ties a purple ribbon in her hair.

"It's a good distraction," Tamara says definitively, but she looks concerned.

"The reporters out there are vultures. I wonder if they'll be watching us," Julia says. She stands in front of the mirror and pouts, dabbing her mouth with a lip gloss wand.

"I bet you'd love that," I say. The words come out of my mouth in one breath, a surprise even to me.

Julia whips her head around, her blonde ponytail swinging to one side. "What did you just say?"

"Oh, come on. You're literally putting on makeup right now."

Julia's eyes flare and she crosses her arms. "You better watch yourself, Baby Steckler," she says. "People are onto you, you know. If the Fitzwater brothers aren't back, all eyes are on you and your freaky sister." Julia takes a step toward me so my back is up against the locker, cold and hard even through my long-sleeve shirt. "Parker's been calling all of us into Pérez's office one by one asking us questions, wondering what happens when the Steckler sisters get too close to someone. Did you know that?"

My throat grows dry and my fingers begin to tingle. I could push her away. Hard, so she falls. So her skull collides and crashes with metal. But I curl my hands into fists to keep them steady. I sidestep away from her and try to hide my trembling fingers, tears pricking my eyes.

"Only a matter of time before they get you two in there for some real talk." Julia snorts, then pauses, thinking for a beat. "Where were you anyway, Ellie? Where were you the morning Mila disappeared?"

By now the rest of the team has gathered to watch and I feel their eyes drilling holes into my skin, fear rising in my throat. That's when Stella appears, fully dressed and ready to run. She drops her bag down onto the floor with a thud.

"She was with me," she says. "We were doing circuits at home. So fuck off."

Julia rolls her eyes. "Like I'd believe *you* anyway," she says, a smirk crawling across her face. "Whatever. I'm heading out there."

The group disbands and everyone follows Julia out the exit over to Coach and the boys, who stand huddled around a clipboard in the center of the track.

Stella turns to the door, but I grab her arm and pull her to me. I want to say something but there's nothing, no sounds. Just her dark eyes, searching mine.

Stella wiggles out of my grasp and smooths out her low, frizzy ponytail. "You'd do the same for me," she says.

What do you know? I want to ask. But Stella turns and jogs to the rest of the team. I follow her slowly but my legs are made of stone and my ears are ringing like I've just been hit.

"Sprints, Ellie," Coach barks when I get close. The exhaustion in his voice is gone and replaced with a gruff disconnect. He's trying to make everything normal. Make us forget.

But we can't. Not when there are dozens of reporters standing as far away as the school can make them, recorders and cameras in their hands.

I jog toward the rest of the group and line up to run hundreds across the clay-red track. I duck low and shoot out into space, pummeling the ground beneath me.

Coach paces up and down the sidelines, yelling at us to *hustle* and *fight for it*. He holds his clipboard over his barrel chest and tilts his head toward the sky, looking for answers or salvation. It doesn't take long before my heart is pounding and my muscles ache.

I'm out of practice. Off. I can tell. I push myself, squatting down to touch the clay with the tips of my fingers before exploding again back in the opposite direction. It feels good to burn, to have my body rebel against everything I'm trying to do. It makes me think of Mila. The way her muscles arched along her back as she fought for every single stride.

"I don't have to remind you that regionals are next week," Coach yells. "If we have any chance of winning, of bringing home something good, something to be proud of, you're going to have to work harder than this."

I explode again, sprinting back to the starting line. Regionals. A way out, one that will take me far, far away from here. A future that doesn't involve Noah or Mila or being in Stella's shadow. All of a sudden it seems essential.

But we all know what regionals mean. That's the meet that

won Stella her spot at Georgetown. After the race, the scout dressed in blue followed her to the parking lot. Coach asked me to hang back, to let them have some time, and I could only see it from afar, how he shook her hand and nodded enthusiastically, slapping her on the back. Stella's face lit up. Her whole body relaxed for the first time in what seemed like ever.

When we got in the car to head home, Mom looked at her, eyebrows raised. "So?"

Stella nodded in the passenger seat. "I'm in."

Mom's hands flew to her face, covering her eyes, and her shoulders heaved up and down. "Stella," she whispered. When her hands dropped, we could see she was crying, so proud, so relieved. "You did it."

None of us knew then that Stella would only hold on to the spot for another month or so. It was out of her grasp before she could even order a T-shirt from the campus bookstore.

This year, regionals was supposed to be my turn. My chance to impress the coaches enough to get a handshake deal as a sophomore.

Mila should be finalizing her scholarship too.

That's the thought that slows my legs and nearly makes me collapse onto the ground.

"Pick it up, Ell!" Coach yells.

I trudge along, but my mind begins to spiral, playing the *if-then* game against my will. *If I do two hundred squats today, I'll shave ten seconds off my PR. If I don't get eight hours and three minutes of sleep the night before regionals, I'll lose. If Mila comes home tomorrow, I'll come clean about Noah. If I . . .*

The rules are coming to me, but that's when I spot a man walking toward us from the school's main building. Dressed in a dark suit and an overcoat, he can't be a teacher or a member of the staff. Everyone wears fleeces and hiking boots. As he gets closer, his face comes into focus and the glint of his silver badge catches the falling sun. Detective Parker.

I keep running but my eyes stay trained on him as he motions for Coach to join him by the water station. They talk for a few seconds and Coach smacks his clipboard against his thigh. He grimaces but then nods and turns to us, to where Stella leads the pack, finishing her hundred-yard sprint. When she crosses the finish line, she slows to a walk, hands on her hips, until she looks up and sees Coach and Parker.

Coach holds up his hand and cocks his head. Stella peels off the track, annoyed to be taken out of practice. I can tell by her gait, the way her feet flop in front of her. She wants to keep running. She's not done.

But when she gets closer to Parker, her posture changes. She straightens her spine, rigid and still, and stays silent as Parker's mouth moves in small motions. The reporters notice, all at once, and a flock of heads turns to watch the interaction. After a few seconds, Coach pats Stella's shoulder and she starts walking with Parker back toward the school—no, the parking lot. Parker opens the back door of a black sedan, an unmarked police car, and motions for Stella to slide in. He walks around the front, and soon they speed away.

21

ELLIE

"WHAT HAPPENED?" *I* yell as I barge into the house, not stopping to kick off my muddy sneakers or drop my training bag in the hall. I bowl through the first floor, looking for Stella, or Mom, or Dad, or anyone who can tell me something about where Parker took Stella. But the living room is empty. The kitchen is too. It's dark by now and usually Mom is here, opening up delivery from Tofu Garden or throwing a chicken breast in the oven. If all were right, Dad would be typing on his keyboard in the office, a comforting *click-clack* floating through the house. Stella would be lifting weights downstairs and I'd be catching up on trashy reality TV. But everything is not right.

The air is still and there's an unwashed head of lettuce on the counter. A kitchen knife set beside it, like someone would return at any second to finish the task. I grasp my phone so hard it starts to make indents in the side of my palm. No one has returned my texts or my calls.

I pull out a stool at our breakfast bar and a chill creeps up my neck. I hate being alone. Always have. That's why I sought out Bethany when Stella disappeared into running. Why I gravitated toward Noah when Bethany left.

But that's when I remember the reporters. They were all there, capturing Stella and Parker's interaction. I flick on the TV and fumble for the local news. Some blonde lady is talking about apple pie up at the old cider mill, tasting various kinds of Honeycrisps and Galas, as if this is the hard-hitting content I crave.

I tap open Twitter on my phone and search Mila Keene with shaking fingers, afraid of what might pop up. At first, I'm greeted by her face. Her beautiful smiling face. Everyone used the same photo, the one from the meet where she won. Red cheeks. Huge grin. My heart beats hard but I push away the memory, the grief, the shame, and keep looking.

Finally a few thumbs down, there are a few tweets from one reporter. Trish Rollins. She looks young from her avatar. She sent the first one at 5:45 p.m., a few hours ago.

BREAKING: Edgewater PD has brought a 17-year-old member of EDG XC team in for questioning in #MilaKeene case.

Another one followed.

Per sources, the runner, who we aren't naming bc she's a minor, sent #MilaKeene threatening text messages before she disappeared. No word on what they said, but this story is still developing.

She posted a photo with the message. It's grainy and shot from far away, as if she were running to get a better look. You can't see Stella's face, but I can make out her dark, frizzy hair as she bends to duck into the car. Her knuckles are clamped around the metal door, white with rage.

The house is quiet and dark when I finally hear the front door open. No one says anything but I can make out footsteps diverging. Mom and Dad heading to their room. Stella climbing the stairs. I look at the clock on my phone. It's near midnight. Stella pads into the bathroom and turns on the shower. I wait for her to finish, and then a few minutes more, before I tiptoe out of my room and over to hers, knocking softly against her door.

She doesn't answer but I see a sliver of light peeking through the crevice between her door and the floor. Gingerly, I push it open and there she is, sitting cross-legged on her bed with wet hair and an oversized T-shirt bearing the words RUN LIKE HELL.

"Oh, hey," she says. Her face is blank and her eyes are distant.

"'Oh, hey'?" I ask. "Are you kidding?" I rush to her and throw my arms around her, hugging her tightly. She feels foreign under my touch, all bone and muscle, tense and unyielding. But I hold her closer because we don't do this often.

Stella recoils. "Off, Ell."

I inhale the clean scent of her hair before releasing her, and sit back on her yellow bedspread. "What the fuck happened?" I ask.

"I'm sure you saw the news." She shrugs as if none of this is surprising, as if none of it's a big deal.

"What did they ask you? What did you say?"

Stella's face falls and she looks tired and a little broken in a way I've never seen her.

"They think I had something to do with this," she says. "But that's not a surprise after last year. After those fucking texts."

"What texts?"

She purses her lips and hesitates for a moment. Then she digs her phone out from beneath the covers and tosses it to me with her messages to Mila open on the screen.

Georgetown? Are you serious, Mila?

I can't believe you would backstab me like this.

I trusted you and you betrayed me.

I thought you were different. But you're just like the others.

You're going to wish you hadn't done this.

My face must say *something* because Stella looks directly at me and her mouth falls open. "I didn't do anything to Mila, you know. I just want to say that out loud. I didn't."

My throat tightens. Of course Stella wasn't involved. I know that. She sniffles beside me, a raw, strangled sound. It's not one born out of self-preservation. It's one of loss. Of fear.

"It's going to be okay, Stell." We both know it's a lie, but what else is there to say?

Stella tilts her head up to the ceiling. Her bare walls are stark white except for the row of race bibs taped up above the bed. The moonlight drifts through her window, casting a golden glow on her face. Stella looks so small, so fragile, so unlike the girl who won State last year, unlike the girl whose rage is a sweeping, rolling sea, who wears armor made of barbed wire. This is what my sister looks like when she's stripped of all her superpowers.

Stella closes her eyes and tries to suppress a shudder. Her shoulders still shake. When she opens her eyes, she tilts her head toward me. "So, are you going to tell me the truth, Ell? Where were you the morning Mila disappeared?"

It's not an accusation, but I can't help but stiffen. My mouth is dry and my hands are clammy. It's the one question I didn't want to answer. The one that could cause everything we've worked for to unravel.

"I covered for you," she says. "In the locker room before practice, I said you were with me, working out. I told Parker the same thing tonight." She looks at me quizzically. "Where were you, really?"

I rack my brain for the truth—any truth—until I know what I have to tell her. "I was with Noah," I say softly.

Stella's face twists in confusion. "What? Why?"

"We were together all summer," I say. "Sneaking around behind Tamara's back. We were lifeguarding together and it just . . . happened."

"Ew, Ellie."

I laugh because that's the most Stella response ever. *Ew.*

"So you guys were, like, hooking up or something that morning?"

I shake my head. "I was breaking things off with him. Something happened over the summer." Stella's quiet, waiting for me to explain. The words are slippery on my tongue and my stomach flips as I gather the courage to say them out loud. "I got pregnant and had an abortion," I say in one breath.

Stella's eyes go wide. She reaches for my hand and holds it tight in hers. My heart snaps and I wonder why I waited all this time to tell her, why I didn't realize back in August that she would be there for me, that she was the one person who wouldn't care or judge or say a goddamn word. If I had, then maybe none of this would have happened.

"I'm okay now," I say, lying with a shaking voice. "But that changed everything. It just took me a little while to break it off, you know? So that's where I was."

Stella leans forward and wraps me in a hug. Her wet hair is cold against my bare skin but I don't let her go.

"It's fine," Stella says, her body so close to mine. "Everything is going to be fine."

But we both know it's not. A girl is missing and Stella has a target on her back. But for tonight, just one night, we'll pretend like everything is just that. Fine.

22

STELLA

NEWS LEAKS QUICKLY in the mountains, where the coroner also sells wildflowers at the farmers market and the CSI tech moonlights as a fly-fishing guide. That's how rumors spread around here. Slowly in the beginning, whispered in the Hellers' sporting goods store and in the rows of plants at the nursery. Almost unnoticeable. A soft breeze drifting through town. But then it becomes a rolling tide, sweeping through living rooms and locker rooms, rushing through the open air so all at once everyone knows: Stella Steckler is a suspect.

That's what the front page of the *Edgewater Eagle* says. It's lying facedown on the kitchen counter and when I flip it over, a headline jumps out at me. RUNNER QUESTIONED IN KEENE DISAPPEARANCE. Just my story alongside Mila's. The article goes on to mention what happened last year, that the unnamed runner had a *history of violence*, and that she—I—had sent "threatening" text messages to Mila. Those fucking text messages, sent in a fit of rage. Even I can see how bad this looks. Sure, the press can't name minors, but everyone knows it's about me.

The story ends with a rehashing of the cold cases—how three runners were found dead on the Oak Tower trail only days after going missing. How the killer left nothing at the crime scene, but took shoelaces from each of their sneakers. How a madman may still be on the loose.

The final paragraph mentions Shira: *But police haven't ruled out the possibility that Keene simply ran away.* "*We spent weeks looking for Shira Tannenbaum five years ago,*" *Detective Parker said.* "*Maybe Miss Keene will return to us on her own.*" I can practically hear the smirk in his voice, like he's already decided who Mila is.

Everyone hated Shira for what she did, but still I wish Mila's fate will mirror hers. That she ran away to have a weeklong vacation with her best friend, Naomi, or that she just wanted to clear her head before regionals. But with each passing day, the chances of finding Mila, of having her back, are getting smaller and smaller.

"Give me that," Mom says. She rushes out from her office and snatches the paper from my grasp.

"It's not like it's a secret," I say.

She throws it in the recycling and presses the start button on the blender so a sawing sound rips through the entire kitchen. "Whatever," I mumble.

"Here," Mom says as the noise cuts off. She pours the green liquid into a glass and slides it across the counter. "We can at least pretend to be normal."

"Thanks," I say. I perch on a stool and look at her for the first time in a while. Her hair is unbrushed and a little greasy at the scalp, and she's traded her usual trousers and blouse for a loose cotton tee and jeans. Her skin is thinning around her eyes and sags at the corners of her mouth. I wonder how close she is to the edge. How much I've already caused her to break, to spiral.

She was like this for a while after Allison Tarley and her

coach pressed charges. I worried it would cause her to relapse, to find some way to forget the fact that her daughter Stella was trouble. But she held strong. I just need her to do that now, too.

"You know I didn't do anything to her," I say. "To Mila. You believe me, right?"

Mom exhales deeply and looks to the ceiling. She waits a second too long and my heart sinks. "Of course, Stella. This is all just a misunderstanding. It has to be. Mila will turn up soon."

Before she can say more, her phone rings in her pocket. She pulls it out and I can see Principal Pérez's name bold and blaring. Mom slides her finger across the screen to answer and brings the phone to her ear. She turns away from me. "Lauren, hi!" Her voice is lighter, an act of self-preservation. It's the same one she uses when clients are on the fence, unsure if they really should spend their hard-earned money on a second home in a town once called Deadwater.

"Yes, yes, I thought you might call." I crane my neck to hear Pérez's side of things, but Mom walks farther away, through the door, and into her office. "Well, yes, I can understand . . ." Then she shuts the door.

"Who's that?" Ellie drops her bag on the floor and climbs up on the stool next to me.

"School." I take a sip of the smoothie and let the cold freeze my throat.

"Are you coming today?" she asks.

I can't tell what's worse, walking through the halls with icy stares piercing into my back, knowing everyone thinks I'm a monster, or staying home and letting everyone assume I have something to hide.

Ellie picks at her already-chapped lips, flicking a white piece of dead skin onto the floor. She's all nerves and live wires. I want to tell her things are going to be okay. To protect her like I know big sisters should. I can't let go of the feeling that I failed her this summer, that she was so alone when she needed someone the most.

The door to Mom's office opens and she comes out, clutching her phone to her chest. "You're going to school today, Stella," she says. "Lauren wanted to keep you home, but I convinced her it's best for you to be there. It's not like they've *arrested* you. Plus, you've got regionals coming up. You can't miss another practice. Neither of you can." She throws on a fake smile.

By the time we get to school, my numb sense of calm has been replaced by a pit of dread. The stares are worse than they were last year and no one even hides their whispers as I walk through the halls. I try my best to ignore them, but I catch snippets of conversation.

"I heard she threatened to kill her in those text messages."

"She would do anything to win."

"Mila just wanted to be her friend."

"They should have locked her up last year."

My ears ring and I clench my fists at my sides. I want to yell at everyone and explain that I didn't do it. I want to scream that I *was* working out at home that morning—and that I *miss* Mila. Shit, I'd do just about anything to know what happened to her. That's the worst part—not knowing. But unleashing my anger will only make things worse. I know how everyone will react. I know because I've seen it all before.

It was the last meet of the year, the postseason, just-for-fun race that took place every December. Coaches from all over the county would trot out their best players and invite scouts to come to get one last look at us, the potential prospects, the slabs of meat up for slaughter.

Coach used to say it was a way to send the teams off for hibernation so we could emerge eager and hungry in the spring for track and field. But I always hated it, how we were paraded around. The coaches would always hang in one corner, talking shop about whose form was best, whose endurance would last in the NCAA, who recently puked on a practice run in the woods. We were prizes to them. Cattle to be raised and shipped off to colleges, to better boost their high school fundraising numbers, the districts' college admissions stats. It wasn't for us. It was for them.

That day was cold, even for December, and I hopped up and down to keep my body temp up, noise-canceling headphones suctioned to my ears. Our race wouldn't start for another ten minutes, but I knew I had to stay warm if I wanted to stay loose. That's when I saw the coach from Langston out of the corner of my eye. He was known for being an asshole with a penchant for screaming at his runners. His mouth was curled in a snarl and he pointed a stubby, angry finger at one of his girls, a junior, Allison Tarley. She came in fourth at State, but she could have nabbed second if she had run her best time. Big Ten schools were eyeing her but there was a rumor going around that her coach was pushing her to go further, to try to make Nike's elite training program, to go pro. Her bottom lip quivered and she kept her head down as he yelled close to her face. Allison looked smaller than when I saw her at State. Frail. Almost gaunt. A funny feeling crept up my spine and I shivered to keep it away.

Ellie said something beside me and I pulled down my headphones.

"That guy's such a dick," Ellie muttered.

I nodded in agreement but snuck a look at Coach Gary. He'd pulled similar shit before. With Raven and Lilly Adams, runners who had potential but never quite met it.

Soon, they called the varsity girls to the starting line and we all hopped on the balls of our feet, finding warmth where we could. I took my stance and when the whistle sounded, I let my muscles do the rest, taking me into the lead. I don't remember much from the beginning of the race or how I wound up in the final moments of the thicket, neck and neck with Allison. But what happened next is burned into my brain. As the finish line appeared in the distance, she said something under her breath, just loud enough so I could hear.

"I hate this. I hate it all."

I blinked a few times but knew if I turned to her, it would ruin my time, it would throw me off. So I kept running, kept moving, kept winning.

But she spoke again through choked, panting breaths. "Before we get to the clearing, I want you to take me out," she said. "Hurt me. Make it so I can't run. I need to get out."

"What?" I gasped.

Her words startled me, a ghastly shock of pain and fury and understanding all wrapped up in one choked-out plea. I thought of her coach and how desperately some of us need to run like we need to breathe, while others dread every single race.

"Do it," she said. "Come on." But Allison didn't slow, and neither did I.

I kept my gaze forward, focusing on me, my time.

"Stella," she panted. "I need this. I'll say it was an accident."

There was hunger in her voice. A pain that shot through my veins and pierced my ears. I recognized it because I knew the feeling myself. I wrestled with the options, of what to do, what to say.

But it didn't matter. Allison's mind was already made up. Just as we approached the clearing, only a hundred yards from the finish line, Allison closed the space between us. She gritted her teeth and steeled for impact as she crowded my path and forced her body into mine. I tried to stave her off, to stop the damage, but as she veered into me, her foot caught on something and she tumbled off the trail. The crunching sound was loud enough to cause the hair on the back of my neck to stand up straight and to crack open my heart wide enough to swallow me whole.

A high-pitched wail rang out and I was alone, stumbling across the finish line.

I didn't know that Allison's bones were so brittle, she would break her collarbone. Or that she would be rushed to the hospital. I never could have predicted that she wouldn't follow through on her promise and that she would end up pointing her finger at me. How could I have known that her coach would pressure her to press assault charges?

Parker brought me in for a marathon questioning session a few days later, after Allison filed her suit. But once it was just him and me across from each other in that small, cold conference room, I realized Parker wanted to talk about more than just Allison Tarley.

"You have a history of violence, Stella," he said, his hands folded neatly on the table between us.

I didn't say anything, just tried to focus on a water stain on the ceiling and wait for Mom and Dad to arrive with a lawyer.

"You always find yourself tangled in these things, don't you?" he said. "A few years ago, you almost ruined my son

Calvin's life, his future. Thank goodness he was able to stay at Michigan. Sure, his life as an athlete is over, but at least he's on track to graduate." He sneered at me, baiting me into admitting something, anything.

"What do you have to say for yourself, Stella Steckler? Why can't you just leave your competition alone?"

I opened my mouth to defend myself, to tell the truth, but then I remembered what happened the last time I did that, with Calvin. Everyone would blame me anyway. So I stayed silent until Mom and Dad finally burst through the door.

"We're leaving," Dad said, a public defender by his side.

Allison eventually dropped the charges, but I had to write a formal apology to her and her coach. Pérez suspended me for a week, and it was only a month or so before I lost my spot at Georgetown. The order to spend the summer at Breakbridge came in the spring.

Allison became a sad news story while I was branded violent, aggressive, a monster. She knew it was easier to blame me than endure the wrath of her abusive coach. I became a warning of what can happen when girls get too competitive, when we want too much.

In a way it was okay. Allison healed quickly and finally got the courage to ditch track in the spring. And I learned how much I could take, how I could survive even if I lost everything. I learned I was a warrior. I was indestructible.

But in all the other ways, it was a disaster. After Parker realized he wasn't going to nail me for this act of aggression, he hung around Edgewater High. He stationed himself at our practices, popping by every few days just to *check in*. He never spoke to me, only watched from the sidelines, hands clasped behind his back as he paced up and down the sidelines.

"A petty, petty man," Mom said after he drove past our house on a random Wednesday night. "You'd think he'd get over what happened with his son and leave you alone. Why does he feel like he can torment you like this?"

I shrugged and mumbled a response. "I don't know."

But I did know. Because before my parents got to the station, before Allison walked away from the charges, Parker stared at me with those dark, menacing eyes and said only one thing. "You girls are all the same."

I kept my mouth shut but I knew what he meant. *You girls.* The obsessive ones. The focused ones. The ones who have enough grit and determination to break things and crush people and rip worlds apart. The ones who call bullshit when things aren't fair. The ones who speak up and demand better. The ones who don't fit into neat little boxes.

There were girls like me at Breakbridge. Girls who kicked and screamed and worked their muscles until they became hard as steel. Girls with steady eyes and stoic faces who took pride in the pain, the ice baths, and the wall sits. Girls like Shira Tannenbaum and Allison Tarley who would do anything to run away from the lives that caged them in.

Parker had dealt with so much agony in his line of work— so much death and uncertainty. And he had also dealt with girls like us. He had seen us repeat our mistakes, lunge at other victims, break skin and draw blood. He had seen us all march toward the same goal: self-preservation.

But I was the first one who touched his family, who threatened to destroy his son's life—even though Calvin was the one who should have paid. And for that, for his son's mistakes, I was to blame.

23

ELLIE

I WATCH FOR Stella out of the corner of my eye, but as the minutes in our lunch period tick by, I know she's not coming. I send her yet another text, my fifth of the hour.

Where are you??? I'll come eat with you, just tell me.

She doesn't respond and I'm left alone at the cross country table with both seats next to me empty. The rest of the team has shifted down, toward Noah and Bader. Their voices are hushed, but I can hear fragments of conversation. They're talking about Mila, about Stella, about what they think she may have been capable of.

"I heard Parker questioned her for six hours," Julia says. She looks down at her palms and picks at a few spots of red paint probably left over from art class.

"I don't know, dude," Bader says. "She's fucking feisty. Bet she murdered her somewhere in the woods for even talking to Georgetown."

I glance at Noah, wondering if he'll defend Stella, if he'll say anything at all. But he just shrugs and stares down at a bag of chips. "Who knows, man."

I blink back tears and fight the scratching, raw feeling in my throat.

"I heard Parker found another lead," says Tamara. "Something about Mila's dad, maybe."

"Damn, this is about to get extremely *Unsolved Mysteries*," Bader says, grumbling into his hamburger. "Next thing you know, they'll be saying Kendall Fitzwater is back in town."

I can't listen to this much longer. I'm zipping up my bag and gathering my things when someone comes up behind me.

"Hey." I turn to find Raven standing behind my chair, her bare freckled arms hanging limp by her sides. "You okay?" she asks.

Julia's staring daggers our way, but Raven doesn't seem to care. "I'm fine," I say.

Raven tucks a stray piece of red hair behind her ears. "You know," she says, "just because your sister's a mess doesn't mean you are, too. I should know."

My mouth drops open in shock. Was that supposed to be nice? To make me feel better? I push my chair out and a screeching sound echoes through the cafeteria. Heads turn and there's a hush that fires up my insides.

I know what everyone's thinking. They want to see if Baby Steckler is really just like Stella, if that dark and stormy DNA is as strong as it seems. But I won't give in. I won't let them win.

I stand and take a step closer to Raven. Her cheeks flush and she backs up, timid as always.

I lean in so our foreheads almost touch and grit my teeth. "Fuck you, Raven."

Then I rush to the door and exit into the science wing, gasping for air, for freedom. I check my phone again, looking for Stella, but no word. I decide to try her locker and make a right when I reach the end of the hall, heading toward the junior row. There's a group of students circled up, right where Stella's locker is, and my stomach sinks. *What now?*

"Move," I say, pushing a bunch of freshmen out of the way so I can see the damage. When I can finally get a good look at Stella's locker, I gasp. Scrawled across the metal, in dripping red paint, is just one word. MONSTER. Around it, someone has taped up printouts of the news articles from last year. The ones about Allison Tarley.

I shake my head, tears stinging my eyes, and lunge toward the lockers, ripping down every piece of paper I can. I ball them up and throw them on the floor. Muffled, nervous laughter rings out behind me, but I don't care. I know I have to save Stella, to shield her from this. I wipe my palm against the paint, but all that does is smudge it, make it look messy, like blood. I think I might throw up.

I turn around at the gawkers. "What are you looking at?" I yell. "Get out of here." Everyone rolls their eyes and the group breaks apart, heading to their next classes. Then I see Stella, leaning against a doorframe across the hall. As she steps closer to me, her face is still like stone.

"Stell—" I start.

"I've been called worse," she says. "Don't worry about it."

That's when I remember the red paint I saw on Julia's hands at lunch. "It was Julia," I say. "We have to tell someone."

Stella purses her lips. "The last thing I need is to tattle on someone right now. Why don't you go wash up."

The next time I see Stella is on the track during all-girls practice at the end of the day. The wind has picked up and whips my ponytail around my face when I turn to see her jogging out from the locker room. Her eyes are narrowed and she looks determined.

"Are you okay?" I whisper.

"Of course." Then she clears her throat. "Let's huddle up for stretches."

A few of the girls' mouths drop open, as if they can't believe Stella Steckler is actually going to put on her captain hat and pretend to lead everyone.

Julia makes a grossed-out noise under her breath and Raven winces. But still, they walk toward us. Tamara doesn't say a word.

I half expect Stella to make a speech about how she's innocent and how everyone is full of shit, to unleash her temper onto the team. But that's not her style, at least not right now. Today she's showing, not telling, and she keeps her cool, calling out hamstring and quad stretches as if this were a regular sort of practice.

Coach Gary watches from the sidelines, rubbing his temples every so often and shifting his weight from foot to foot. Dude has no idea how to deal with anything besides doling out orders to win. I wonder if Parker and Pérez told him to stay back, to let Stella hang herself.

"All right, it's mile repeats day," Stella says, a joyful lilt in her voice. "We've got regionals on Saturday and I don't know what you all have been up to. Let's get this shit into gear."

The team looks at one another, confused at the prospect of taking instructions from a *monster*, but I hop to my feet and follow Stella toward the course to take off on our first fast mile. She smiles back at me with her eyes and I know she's waiting to see what everyone does, if they have enough spunk to say no, or if they, like her, want a distraction. If they want to win.

"Fuck this," Julia says. She throws up her hands. "Coach!" she calls out. "Coach Gary!"

He looks up from his clipboard on the sidelines and walks over to us with reluctance.

"Why is she still here? I'm not taking orders from *her*," Julia says.

Coach throws his clipboard down on the ground. "Yes, you are." he says, his voice nearing a bellow. "Because I said so. Because you're a goddamn team. Because one of you is *missing*. And because we have a huge meet this weekend, which many of you seem to have forgotten. Do I really have to remind you that if you win this one as a team, you qualify for the State championship? Not just as individuals, but as a goddamn team. Don't you want that? You know who would? Mila."

Julia pales and looks down at her sneakers. Next to her, Raven's eyes widen and she chews on her bottom lip.

"So if I were you, I would listen to Stella for one day and hustle." A stunned silence spreads over the group and Coach speaks again. "What do you want me to say? That you should do it for Mila because she's not here to do it for herself? Sure, let's go with that. But come on. You're all young and selfish and you know what? That's fine. Do it for yourselves. Get yourselves out of this place. Find a pathway out of here. No one else will do that for you."

The team is quiet and I know Julia is desperate to retort with something nasty. But Tamara clears her throat. "He's right," she says. "Let's work our asses off this week. Win everything on Saturday."

"Okay?" Coach asks.

"Okay," the team says in unison.

"Mile repeats," Stella calls. "Let's go."

We take our positions on the track and when Coach blows the whistle, we fucking run.

24

STELLA

THE DOORBELL RINGS and sends a spasm through my stomach.

"Stell, could you get that?" Mom calls from the office.

I suppress a groan and trudge to the door, making mental notes of what I have to do this morning before we leave for regionals. *Make smoothie. Find lucky sweatshirt. Charge head-phones.*

I pull back the door, expecting to see one of Mom's clients or the mail carrier. But when I see who's there, I take a step backward.

"Coach."

"Can I come in?" he asks.

I move aside and Coach Gary doesn't wait for an answer.

"Who is it, Stell?"

"Hi, Carla," Coach says, peeking his head into Mom's office.

"Gary!" she says, getting up from her chair quickly. "What's up? Is something wrong? The bus for regionals doesn't leave for another hour." She frowns and looks at her watch.

"No, no," he says, pumping his hands. "I'm only here to chat with Stella for a little bit. That okay?"

"Oh," Mom says. "Of course." She looks at me warily and

I know we're both thinking the same thing, that Pérez might have finally asked Coach to make me sit this one out. "Go right ahead." Mom retreats into her office but keeps the door open so she can hear.

Coach leads me into the kitchen and leans up against the counter.

"Please let me run." The words tumble out of my mouth so fast I can't catch them. "I just want to compete."

Coach frowns. "Of course you're running. Don't be ridiculous."

Relief floods through me. But then I remember winning is what's most important to him, too.

"I just wanted to talk about the scouts," he says. "They're all going to be there again and they are *not* happy with you, as you can imagine. Not after what happened at the charity run, and certainly not with what's been in the news."

I open my mouth to defend myself, but Coach holds up a hand.

"Of course I know you didn't do it. Those text messages prove nothing. You're intense, but you are not . . . whatever they say you are. Unfortunately, what I know doesn't change what *other* people think. You need to keep that in mind. Be sportsmanlike. Stay calm. Keep to yourself. Run your own game, and don't worry about anyone else, okay?"

"Okay."

"Stella, you're the best runner we have. Best since I started this job. Don't let anyone else mess this up for you. You're on your own out there, no matter how much bullshit I spew about teamwork, got it?"

I nod. I've known that since the beginning, since Calvin Parker gave me a concussion during Longshot, since Lilly

Adams lied to Coach about what really happened to me that day, since Allison Tarley tried to blame me for breaking her collarbone. "Got it."

"Good," he says, standing up straight. His track suit crinkles as he walks toward the front door. "Let's bring home gold today."

Ellie and I sit sandwiched together on the bus as we pull into Tremont High's parking lot. It's one of those neighboring towns where everyone is super woodsy, even more so than Edgewater. These kids were practically born on the trails, scrambling over rocks and crossing waterways with just a few wooden planks. Their cross country loop is known for being root-heavy and uphill, with no patience for amateurs. The JV teams don't even run here—the high school sports association won't let them.

When we file off the bus and onto our bench, I scan the bleachers. The usual crowd of scouts are seated in the front row, huddled together in fleeces and windbreakers, holding thermoses of coffee and munching on apple cider donuts. They look practically jolly, jostling the clipboards on their knees, comparing stats of students they already picked up.

In an alternate reality, I would be chumming it up with the Georgetown guy, the one who called my house last year to say I wouldn't be joining them and that he was *so sorry but my hands are tied. Maybe you could walk on somewhere else when things settle down?*

Now he looks straight through me, on to the next class of prospects. His gaze stops on Ellie, who's stretching beside me, and he clicks his pen to make a note on the piece of paper in front of him.

I nudge my sister. "Did you see that?" I ask. "Georgetown dude looking your way."

Ellie's eyebrows shoot up. "Really?"

"Mm-hm. Made a note."

Her cheeks flush as she tries not to look toward the bleachers. "Fuck." She picks at her lip, revealing a scab.

Coach signals to us that it's almost go-time and we whip off our sweatshirts, toss our track pants to the side. My bib is pinned securely to my tank and I hop in place as the wind bites at the bare skin around my ankles. I try my hardest to tune out everything else. The scouts, the other girls elbowing beside me, the nagging pulsing in my brain, reminding me that Mila should be here, too, that we *still* don't know where she is—or who's to blame.

And everyone thinks I had something to do with her disappearance.

But there's no time to dwell on that now.

We line up, huddled together as a group, and when the whistle blows, we all explode onto the course. Girls who are usually slower than I am take off, accelerating for the first quarter-mile uphill. They're dumbasses, though, and they're miscalculating. They won't make it to the back half with that same kind of vigor, that throbbing, rushing pace. I place myself in the middle of the pack, hoping to throw everyone off, to conserve my energy.

When we reach the peak of the first hill, there are already girls losing steam, gassed out by the treacherous Tremont course. They didn't practice. They should have run Longshot. I wince a little thinking back to that day when it was just me and Mila on that hill. She should be here now.

I shake the thought away as we descend and swivel my head

slightly, trying to find the other cobalt jerseys to see where everyone else is in the pack. Tamara is behind me, while Raven is off to the side, taking shallow sips of air. But I don't need to look for Ellie to know where she is. I can feel her pulling up next to me, our feet slapping the ground in unison.

I used to hate these moments where Ellie tried to copy my gait, put forth her best Stella imitation. But after running like this with Mila, I want her to propel me, to push me. We don't look at each other, but slowly, as we ascend the second hill, we pull away from the rest of the pack, breaking free until we're on our own, with just the open air and sky and trees in front of us. My heart races and I know we're going to win. One of us will win.

The finish line is up ahead and I can hear the crowd cheer as we break into the clearing. The scouts are on their feet, their hands shielding their eyes as we emerge. Everyone else is so far behind now, I can't hear them, can't feel them, don't know them.

All I hear is Ellie's steady breathing, our spikes slicing through ground beneath us, the air whooshing by as we cut through it with our bodies.

It's now or never and I dig in, pushing, pushing, pushing as a little voice whispers in my ear. *You're a force.* Mila.

I give it one last bit of effort and heave myself over the finish line before Ellie pulls in behind me.

25

ELLIE

IN THE FINAL moments, Stella's braid flies in front of me, so close I want to yank it and pull her to the ground. I lose my breath as I push over the finish line and register what has happened.

Stella won.

Stella knew the scouts were there to watch *me*. And Stella won.

Stella wins every time.

26

STELLA

I COLLAPSE ONTO the ground and bury my head in my hands, willing Mila's voice to come back to me, to speak to me one more time, to tell me what happened to her. But she doesn't. She's gone.

Ellie stands over me, hands on her hips. I can feel her shadow casting darkness over me and I look up to find fury in her eyes.

She extends a hand and grits her teeth.

"Be humble. Don't make a scene," she hisses.

I grab her fingers and rise to my feet.

27

ELLIE

I PULL STELLA in for the fakest hug of my life.

She feels stiff at first in my arms and then wraps herself around me.

It only lasts a second but when I steal a glance at the scouts, they're all writing on their clipboards, silent as the coffee in their thermoses grow cold.

Coach runs up to us and slaps one hand on each of our backs.

"Stecklers!" he yells, excitement ringing in his voice. "You broke your PRs! Both of you!"

Stella's eyes grow wide. "Really?"

I want to slap her. Of course we did. She's never run like that. I've never run like that. It's infuriating that we only make each other better.

Coach calls out our times, and for a second, I think I've misheard him. But he repeats the numbers and rubs his hands together.

Fuck. I didn't realize it was *that* good. "Good enough to qualify for State," I say.

"State?" Coach says, incredulous. "That's good enough to impress every single scout here. Your worlds just opened wide up."

28

STELLA

COACH IS TALKING, but I can't hear him through my own pounding brain. *Mila. Mila. Mila.* Then I hear the number. The sweet number that could change everything.

Mila, I think. *That number should have been yours.*

29

ELLIE

COACH WAS RIGHT. As soon as we get home, the emails come rushing in. But they're all for me. No one seemed to care that Stella technically won. They only saw the young and fresh-faced sophomore with two more seasons to improve. Someone they could mold. Someone untouched. They know I have time to get my PR even tighter, and, unlike Stella, I don't come with any of the baggage from last year.

Let's talk! the coach from Michigan wrote.

You've got a bright future, said the woman from Villanova.

Mom makes me wait until after I shower to read them all, and then together we settle down into the couch in the living room. My brain buzzes as I begin to picture my future, finally, somewhere far, far away, where no one knows me or what came before.

"Well, this is *exciting*," Mom says, snapping a piece of dark chocolate between her teeth. "Stella, want to check these out?"

My skin burns and I want to elbow Mom hard in the side for being so careless. Of course Stella doesn't want to *check these out*. We both know this was her final shot at a scholarship. If they wanted to take a risk on Stella, we'd know. But no one does. That's obvious now.

Stella grunts in the kitchen and starts banging around, opening cupboards and slamming utensils down on the counter for dinner.

"Don't mind her," Mom whispers. "She'll come around."

But I know she won't. When I look back at Stella, her eyes are narrowed and her fists are clenched so hard I know she's making marks on her skin. I turn back to my computer. A few more emails had come in over the past few minutes and I click through messages from a small private school in Minnesota, a college in Washington, and some place in Boston I've never heard of.

But then Mom sucks in her breath and points to the screen at a new email that sits at the top of my inbox. It's from Georgetown.

Fuck.

I lean my head back against the couch and try to remember all the pep talks we were given over the years. They were always aimed at Stella, but I got to hear them because I was there too, always in the periphery. The backup sister.

Every single coach always told us that high school was our only shot. It was the tiny sliver of life that could determine every single thing about our futures.

But they never told us how to deal with the pressure of trying to set up our entire lives in just a few years. High school should come with a warning, told in hushed whispers to those who deserve to know.

This is the best you'll ever be.

It doesn't matter if it's true. But believing that and flying a flag of unbridled confidence is the only way to get what we want, to fulfill our prophecies.

The world breaks little girls. It stomps out our will, our joy, our curiosity—and replaces them with disdain, cynicism, and the need to fit into neat and tiny boxes. I learned that young, in kindergarten, when the other kids called Stella a *show-off* for raising her hand during class, or when the boys in first grade said I was *bossy* for leading a reading circle. When Stella and I would overhear the other moms at the Elite Youth Runner's Club: *The Steckler sisters are just a little much.*

That's how we were described while the boys were sprinting around the playground kicking and screaming, breaking and biting. The world doesn't celebrate girls who take up space, who demand to be heard, who are *just a little much.*

But sometimes, in tiny fleeting moments, like when I'm sprinting a fast mile alone up near Sweetwater Lake, I feel that power. That urgency. The sparkling, glittery feeling that cloaks us all when we least expect it. Those are the moments when I know for sure. *This is not the best I'll ever be. I'm only getting better.*

Later that night, after Mom and Dad go to bed, and Stella disappears upstairs without saying goodnight, I sneak into the hallway to see if the light is still on in her room.

"Stell?" I ask quietly, my forehead pushed up against the door.

"What?"

"Can I come in?"

"No," she says, but I do anyway.

She's propped up under the covers with her back up against the headboard, a thick textbook open in her lap.

"What are you reading?" I ask.

"Nothing," she mutters, but holds it up so I can see the cover.

The Hidden Women of the Hudson River School. "Are you taking art history?" I ask.

"Mila's into this stuff," she says, her voice small and far away. "Thought I'd see what all the fuss was about."

"Oh," I say. We're both quiet for a beat and I realize we haven't really talked about Mila. Not about their burgeoning friendship, the only real one Stella's had, or the tragedy of being labeled a suspect. But I know if I say anything now, then the truth will tumble out and I'll unravel.

Just thinking about it, I feel the tears coming hot and fast, and suddenly all I want is to be close to Stella, to feel her hard body curl around mine and hold me like she did when she caught me sleepwalking, or when the night terrors came. I pull back the corner of Stella's bedspread, shoving my limbs under the covers. I rest my head up against her middle and I expect her to flinch, to shove me off the bed. But she doesn't. Instead she rests her hand on my hair and smooths it back, over and over.

I close my eyes and let myself feel free for just a moment, to forget about everything. But I know I can't.

"Georgetown reached out," I say.

Stella doesn't say anything but her hand freezes in place.

"I don't want to go there, though." It's the truth. It's too close, too full of Stella. I want something that's mine, all mine.

Stella stays silent and my stomach flutters.

"You know, the schools want you, too," I say, trying to find the right words. "You're gonna walk on *somewhere*, especially after today."

That's what makes Stella rustle. She brings her hand back to her book and shifts her weight so I fall back against the pillow.

"We can talk about this, you know," I say. "Schools and scholarships and stuff. We're sisters." But even as I say it, I know the words are hollow. There's still so much we can't say.

Stella knows it too. "If that's true, then why do we keep so many secrets?"

30

STELLA

I WAKE IN the middle of the night with a jolt. Something isn't right. I can feel it in my muscles, the way they cramp as if to summon me from sleep. I clutch my calf in pain. A charley horse. The worst. I kick my leg back and roll over to look out the window. The moon is just a sliver of a crescent tonight.

But something moves in my periphery. A white T-shirt, stark against the dark sky, a ponytail swishing in the wind. My stomach sinks. Not again. Not now.

I throw the covers back and swing my door open, rushing down the stairs. There's no time to grab a sweatshirt or shove my feet into slippers. I learned that when we were little, back when Ellie's night terrors peaked. Mom had just gone to rehab and Ellie had moved from wetting the bed to screaming in her sleep to sleepwalking. Once, she wound up in the herb garden near the Airstream next door. We only knew because she fell over, crashing into some flowerpots, at two a.m.

I was always the one to find her, to coax her back to bed, usually by swaddling her in my big quilt and letting her spend the night huddled next to me with her fists balled into my back.

I swing the side door open and frigid wind whips me in the face, stinging my cheeks and my neck. I scan the yard to see Ellie facing away from me, walking awkwardly in circles on the lawn with her head lolled back. I rush toward her, my bare feet slipping in the dewy grass, and try to remember the best ways to guide a sleepwalker back to bed. Those old WebMD articles said never to wake them, to just sort of nudge them along. And that usually worked when we were little. I press gently on Ellie's back, maneuvering us both back toward the house. But that's when she starts talking.

"I'm sorry," Ellie says, her voice authoritative and loud. "Don't worry, I'm coming. I'm coming for you."

I inhale sharply and my heart weighs heavy in my chest. I've been so wrapped up in my own feelings about Mila disappearing, I didn't realize Ellie was freaking out too. That she feels as alone as I do.

A lump forms in my throat, and just as I reach forward to grasp the door handle, Ellie's eyes flicker open. "Stella?" she mumbles, swiveling her head side to side. "What?"

"Shh," I say. "It's okay, Ell. We're going back to bed."

Ellie looks around, nervous and uncertain, but lets me lead her up to my room. "Can I stay with you tonight?" she asks.

I nod and guide her upstairs to my bedroom. She slips under the blanket and I crawl in next to her, waiting for her breathing to become rhythmic, her body to relax. "You and me forever, Ell," I whisper into her hair. "You and me forever."

As soon as we get to school, the loudspeaker crackles overhead. "Attention all Edgewater students," Raven's mom, the school secretary, calls in her high-pitched voice. "Homeroom is canceled this morning. Please make your way to the gymnasium for an all-school assembly."

A wave of students move in unison, and I start walking, letting the crowd push me down the hall. I turn to ask Ellie what she thinks this is all about, but then I realize she's not beside me anymore. I scan the sea of bodies for her long dark hair, but she's nowhere. I go on alone.

By the time I enter the gym, the air is cloudy from dust particles swept up by students clamoring for a spot on the bleachers. There are hardly any seats left, but I find an empty perch in a row full of kids in the marching band and ignore their stares.

I crane my neck to see if Ellie wandered in with the rest of the stragglers, but I don't see her. Suddenly the room quiets. Principal Pérez and Detective Parker emerge from the door in the corner and make their way to the microphone at the half-court line. Pérez steps up first and clears her throat. The audio system shrieks and she offers us an apologetic smile.

"I wish we were here under different circumstances," she says in a soft, steady voice. "But I am devastated to inform you that Mila Keene's body was found early this morning."

Gasps ring out beside me and my vision blurs. I must have misheard. Pérez's voice sounds odd in my ears—distorted and garbled—as she continues speaking.

"Detective Parker and his team are continuing their investigation as we try to find out what happened to this special, bright young woman. But in the meantime, all of us here at Edgewater High want you to know that our guidance counselor's office is open for you. Classes will be canceled for the rest of the day, and all of the teachers and faculty will be here for your support. Seek each other out in these moments. Band together. Do not be afraid to ask for help."

A few small sobs echo in the rafters and the quiet sounds of crying fill the empty space. But I can't even cry. I *won't* cry. Because this must be a mistake. Mila is alive. She has to be. Her laugh was too big, too full for me to never hear it again. I never got to tell her I was sorry. I never let her play me more of that sad music she liked, never got to tell her that I read all about Susie Barstow. I never let her in.

Detective Parker moves in front of the microphone. "Like your principal said, we will continue our investigation, and your support is more crucial now than ever before," he says. "If you know *anything* about where Mila was before her disappearance, or if you have any idea of who might want to harm her, we need to hear from you. I will be stationed in Principal Pérez's office and we will protect your privacy."

Parker pauses and clasps his hands in front of his chest. "I must also tell you to be safe, safer than you have been in recent years." Suddenly, the air is still and no one seems to even breathe. "We haven't ruled out the possibility that Mila Keene's death is related to the other cold cases."

Someone gasps and Principal Pérez looks away, her brow knit, as Parker continues. "So, again, if you have any information about Mila Keene, please come forward."

For a second, no one speaks. My heart pounds in my throat and I don't know how to even process this information. Then a few hands shoot up. Someone in the back speaks first. "So you're saying she was found on the Oak Tower trail?" they ask in a too-loud voice. My ears ring.

Pérez looks warily at Parker and he responds. "We will not be sharing any more details at this time."

"Did she die like the others?" someone else calls out. "Were her shoelaces missing?"

"Like I said, we will not be sharing any additional details."

Pérez nods at him and they retreat through the doors, to her office, where undoubtedly they will be waiting for tidbits of information from my peers, these rubberneckers, people who didn't know anything about Mila. They're the onlookers, the ones who can't wait to post about how much they *loved* and *missed* Mila. Who are already itching to mourn her publicly and celebrate all of her achievements. Who are desperate for attention, for bits of conversation to share with their cousins at Thanksgiving, crap to talk about in their college application essays. They are the people who love living in Deadwater, who will use it as a fun fact for the rest of their lives. They're the people who don't even remember Marlisse, Beatrice, or Abigail, but will continue to say things like, *Those dead runners? Yeah, that was my town. Can you believe it? It could have been me.*

But it couldn't have been *you*. It couldn't have been *just anyone*.

Because something about this isn't right. It doesn't make any sense. Why would Mila's disappearance be related to the cold cases? Why would the killer lie dormant for years, only to come back and take Mila as his next victim? It's impossible. Someone wanted Mila gone. Someone couldn't take her messing with the Edgewater ecosystem, turning everything upside down. Someone wanted to hurt her, to kill her. But who?

After the announcement, the halls are on fire. Little clusters of students huddle together, leaning against their lockers, weeping into each other's jackets, performing the role of grieving friend.

Others whisper with looks of hunger plastered on their faces as they scroll through their phones, looking for tips or tweets about Mila. And all I can do is keep walking, moving one foot in front of the other because if I stop . . . if I pause . . . I don't know if I'll ever be able to start again.

I walk past the lockers and the entrance to the cafeteria, until I reach the athletic hallway. I take a right, past the science wing. I want to run. I want to run so fast and so far that my legs collapse and my heart breaks free from my chest, red and raw and pumping. But I know if I leave, if I take one step out of this building, it will be news. *Stella just up and left. Can you believe it? She must have been running from something. Heartless. Bitch. Monster.*

That last word was already smeared across my locker like blood. But I'm used to it now. My shell is hard like a turtle's. My skin is made of stone.

I lean against a trophy case, catch my breath, and close my eyes. But all I see is Mila. Her mischievous, friendly smile. Her eyes looking at me, seeing me for who I am, who I wanted to be. I didn't let her look at me that way.

"Stella." Tamara strides up to me, her arms wrapped around a stack of books. Her eyes are red and soft.

"Hi," I say warily.

"We're going to have a little get-together at the resort to, I don't know, just be together and talk. Like a support-group thing. You should come." Her voice cracks and she tucks a stray braid behind her ear. "We're gonna head over there soon," she says. She looks around at our crying peers. "Being here is freaking me out. Mila would have laughed her ass off at these vultures."

She's right. Mila would have.

"Okay," I say. "I will." We're both quiet for a sec. "Why are you being so nice to me?" I ask. "I've been an asshole about the search party, the charity run . . ."

Tamara looks right at me. "You were an asshole. But I get it. I miss her too," she says. Then she lowers her voice to a whisper. "Plus, I wouldn't trust anyone either, if I knew someone was trying to frame me by slipping Mila's ID into my locker."

My heads snaps up. "You think someone was trying to frame me?"

Tamara shrugs. "I've always been right about my gut, and my gut is telling me that *you* had nothing to do with Mila's disappearance. I've sent mean texts too, you know. Everyone who thinks you did this is just trying to find a simple excuse so we don't become Deadwater again."

"So you didn't tell Pérez about the ID?"

She shakes her head.

"Tamara!" Julia calls to her from over by her locker, where she's huddled with Raven.

"I gotta go," Tamara says. "See you at Ellacoya."

My heart pounds desperately and I know I need to run or else I'm going to lose my mind. I rush out of the building as sneakily as I can and dump my backpack into our car. It's only four miles from here to Ellacoya, but if I take the long way, around the lake and up through the boat launch, I can turn it into six. I'll arrive sweaty and beet-red, breaking all of Mayor Dickerson's rules about running alone, but who cares at this point? My brain is about to explode and I need this. I need to clear my head. I need to find a way to make sense of this.

I take off behind the gym and quickly find the dirt path. It darkens as I creep farther into the woods. The trees canopy above me and within a few strides I feel calm, relieved. The leaves are shocks of reds and oranges and yellows and the fallen ones crunch underfoot. Soon my breath is steady and I tread over roots and logs and little moss kingdoms. I feel at home. I don't think of Mila anymore. I don't think of anything.

My watch vibrates against my wrist, clocking the beginning of my third mile, and all of a sudden I hear something rustle in the woods. It's too heavy to be a deer, too soft to be a bear. They're feet, human feet. And then a voice rings through the silence.

"You have got to keep your shit together."

My body slows and my limbs are heavy. The voice is coming from my right, male and deep. Harsh and focused. Instantly recognizable. It's Noah. I peer through the trees but it's hard to see clearly. His voice peters out and then I hear rustling again.

I run another quarter of a mile up the elevation to get a better view.

"You don't understand. You never could. This isn't about *you*."

I freeze in place, my feet glued to the ground. I'd know that voice anywhere. Ellie.

I crouch down and separate the branches with my fingers. She's leaning up against a tree, facing away from me. Her pale neck is bright against the foliage and her long dark hair blends into the bark. Noah's to her left, kicking the brush at his feet. His hair is messy, tousled, and he throws his backpack to the ground in rage. I cover my mouth to keep from calling out.

"Look," he says. "You're being dramatic. Everything is *fine*. No one knows about us."

"It's not fine," she says. She's terrified but speaks with the same defeated tone she uses when I play my podcast on the car speaker or decide what's for dinner. She's not ready for a fight. She doesn't have it in her. She knows this is one she won't win. "I'm sick of lying," she says.

I rise to my feet and inch to my left, trying to get a closer look. But as I step, a branch snaps and turns in my direction. "What was that?" Ellie asks, fear in her voice.

I stand so desperately still, willing myself to blend into the branches.

"Nothing, babe," Noah says. "You're being paranoid."

Ellie turns back to him and points a finger in his face. "Don't call me *babe*," she spits. "You don't have the right. Not anymore."

I feel breakfast coming up in my throat. I want to run into the clearing and shove him away from her, tell him to leave her the hell alone after all he put her through. But something stops me. What if Ellie lied to me about breaking it off with him? Is this really a conversation you'd have with an ex? What if they're still together? I can't stomach that, on top of everything else.

I know I need to get away, to leave this scene, and burn the memory of it. There's no use in tiptoeing back to the path, so I make a break for it and run. I run like I always run and race myself to the road, flying through the trees, the brush, the woods, until I make it to the boat launch where Mila's phone was found.

There's still yellow police tape around the canoe stand, crisscrossing over the paddles.

I sidestep it all and try my hardest not to stare, not to imagine how Mila's phone got there. I bolt for the side door to the lodge, where I know there's a single-use bathroom. And as soon as I make it inside, I fall to my knees and vomit into the toilet.

I'm taking a few minutes to clean myself up when someone knocks on the door.

"Stella? Is that you?" Tamara calls out.

"Just a sec," I say. "Ran here. Just washing my face."

"For sure," she says, and I force myself to unlock the door. "Everyone's over in the den," she says.

I steady my breathing and follow Tamara through the lodge and into the same room where Mayor Dickerson warned us not to run alone. About a dozen other members of the cross country team have assembled on the plush couches and cozy armchairs. The fireplace glows with sturdy flames and an unfinished puzzle sits on the wooden coffee table.

"We were just talking about how Mila had begun to really settle in here at Edgewater," Julia says, a hint of snootiness in her voice. "How she was so adaptable."

I bite my tongue and just nod.

But to my surprise it's Tamara who snorts. "Sure, Jules."

Julia's face grows red and she shuts up quick. The others go around and say generic things about Mila, how she was smart and funny, fast and nice. One girl, a sophomore, tells a story about how Mila saw her struggling to screw in her spikes during practice one day and helped her, as if that was the greatest, most meaningful moment in the world.

As they talk, my stomach cramps in revolt. My chest tightens and I twist my fingers around themselves, trying to sit still. To not *do* anything. To not make a scene.

After a while Raven turns to me, her freckles pronounced on her pale skin and her head tilted in concern. "What about you,

Stella?" she asks with little affect. "Do you have anything you want to share?"

I squeeze my eyes shut as I try to block everyone out, to remember Mila's smile, the way it felt to talk about our parents, about the need to win. What it was like to find someone who might understand.

"I never met anyone like her," I say. It's all I can manage.

"Nice," Julia says, rolling her eyes. "Original."

But I ignore her and continue. "I've never run with anyone like her. She was so determined. So free. Even practicing with her was like racing at regionals."

The room is tense and I wonder if I'm making a mistake, if I'm giving everyone even more ammo against me, if I'm playing into the narrative they want to believe. But I keep going, determined to give Mila's talent its due. "She was better than I was," I say. "She made me better. She made us all better."

"So is that why you threatened to kill her in those text messages?" Julia mutters under her breath.

I push the chair back and stand. "You have no idea what you're talking about."

Julia quiets for a second, almost scared, and the room is silent, everyone waiting for one of us to make a move. Julia's eyes flash fire until Bader clears his throat in the back of the room.

"Anyone else ready to *not* talk about their feelings for a while?" he says.

The tension breaks and the others laugh. Someone slaps him on the back.

"My parents are running the bowling alley all night. Throwdown at my place!" Bader yells.

Julia jumps up. "I'll go for a beer run." Pretty soon the room is empty and it's just me and Tamara left in the cozy den.

She starts folding blankets and placing them back in their baskets, then kneels in front of the massive coffee table and sweeps an armful of puzzle pieces back into their box.

I don't know if it's her red-rimmed eyes, or the way she's breathing like she might burst into tears, but a lump forms in my throat. "Here," I say, grabbing some pillows our teammates left on the floor. "Let me help you."

"Thanks," Tamara mumbles without looking at me.

"It sucks, right?" I ask, trying to find the right words. "Everyone treating Mila like a news story."

Tamara cocks her head and looks at me. "You know, you're the first person who's acknowledged that," she says. "The others . . . they're just pretending they were best friends with her now that she's gone."

"People want a story," I say. "They all want to whisper about how we're going to become Deadwater again. Everyone's forgetting she was a person and that someone *did* something to her." I shake my head and swallow the lump in my throat. *Please don't cry*, I tell myself. *Not in front of Tamara.*

But she notices. "You don't have to be so tough all the time, Stella."

I straighten my spine and don't answer.

"Neither do I." Then Tamara laughs. "Well, yes, I do, actually."

"What?" I say. "Everyone loves you." The words spill out like water. "Your parents are obsessed with you. So is everyone at school. You might not be the fastest, but you have . . . everything."

But then I look at the amused expression on her face and realize how dumb that all sounds. I don't know what her life has been like as one of the only Black people in town, or how I, as one of the white girls on our team, might have made it even harder.

"Sorry," I say quietly. "That was a ridiculous thing to say."

"You couldn't understand," Tamara says. "But you know who did? Mila." She sits down on the couch and rests her head back against the cushions. "It was nice to have someone who just got it. We didn't even have to talk about it, you know? Obviously we had to deal with different kinds of garbage, but she understood things like why it was so messed up when Coach told me not to get so *angry* at practice. I didn't even bring it up. She came up to *me* and said she was sorry that happened. Raven and Julia would never do that."

I sit down too and let my jaw drop open. I've never heard her talk shit about them before.

Tamara laughs. "What? You think they're my favorite people in the world?" She shrugs. "We all do what we have to in order to survive. You know that. Mila was so refreshing. We talked about running and art," she says. "She was just . . . easy to be around." Maybe Tamara knew Mila better than I did. Maybe I wasn't the only one who saw Mila for who she really was.

"It sounded like her life back in Connecticut was similar to mine," Tamara continues. "She hated the people who had become her best friends, but didn't know how to ditch them. And she never really felt like she fit in. But at least she had Naomi. One true friend. More than me, I guess."

I pause at the name *Naomi*, Mila's best friend from Hadbury, and Tamara glances at me sideways. "Look at me, spilling my guts to Stella Steckler of all people," she says.

A smile creeps up my face. It's unlikely, this moment.

"I'm sorry for . . . everything," I say. "I wasn't . . ." I start. "I don't . . . It's hard for me to trust people, I guess."

Tamara nods and we're both quiet until a vibrating sound slices through the silence. Tamara pulls out her phone to look at the screen. Her whole body tenses as a block of text appears on the screen. "Fucker," she says under her breath.

"Everything okay?" I ask.

"Noah," she says. "I haven't seen him all day. Probably pumping in the gym or something. Idiot. He knows he should be here. I've texted him like fifty times."

I could tell her exactly where he's been and with who and what they were saying. I almost do. The words are on my tongue and I can taste them, salty and potent. But I think of Ellie, propped up against the tree, the hurt in her voice, how she shook in the cold. Tiny goose pimples forming on her flesh. My baby sister alone with that cheating asshole. No. I need to talk to her first. I can't betray Ellie. She's my blood.

Tamara shoves her phone back into her pocket. "You don't think the killer is back, do you?"

I mull over what Pérez and Parker said at the assembly today. They definitely insinuated Mila was found on the Oak Tower path, just like all the others. But the idea of Mila being a victim of a serial killer feels absurd.

"It doesn't add up," I say. "Why would Kendall Fitzwater or whoever come back after all this time, right when Mila moved here? Blaming it on something like that is the easy way out. It absolves anyone who actually lives here, who actually knew her."

Tamara ducks her head to me. "Naomi has a theory."

"You spoke to Naomi?" I ask.

Tamara nods. "We've been talking a little bit since every-thing happened. Shawna gave me her info. It's been nice to hear from someone who knew Mila—like, really *knew* her, you know? They were best friends since kindergarten."

"Yeah," I say softly.

"She thinks Mila's dad might have been involved. Wild, huh?"

Then I remember the comment I saw on Naomi's Instagram a few weeks ago. Come home, Mila. Come home to me. It's cer-tainly something a father would write, a father desperate to see his daughter. Plus, there was that weird call I overheard, how Mila told him to never come here.

"You should talk to her," Tamara says. "Naomi, I mean. Might bring you some comfort or closure or something." She pulls her phone out again. "I'm sending you her number."

My phone pings softly and a humming starts in my heart.

"You might be right," I say, and push myself to stand.

Tamara nods and gets up too. She looks me straight in the eyes, her gaze unflinching. "Do you think we're going to make it through this? The shittiness of being cross country runners in Edgewater?"

I mull over her words, but I know there's only one answer. "We'll have to."

When I make it outside, the air is cold and whips against my cheeks. I want to run home, but instead I take slow steps and stare at my phone, trying to think of what I could possibly say to Naomi.

Will she even respond? Is it worth it? Will she take it to the police? Tell me to go fuck myself? But at this point, I need an-swers about Mila. I want to find out what happened to her and

I want to clear my name. Maybe Naomi can help. What choice do I really have?

I take a deep breath and tap out a message, something that feels real and true.

> *You don't know me, but my name is Stella Steckler. You might have read about me in the paper or heard my name from the cops, but despite what they say, I was Mila's friend. I'd really like to talk to someone who knew Mila better than I did. Maybe we can meet?*

I close my eyes and hit send.

31

STELLA

MOM TRIES TO convince me not to go to the funeral. She says it would inspire *talk*, as if everyone isn't already gossiping about what I did or didn't do anyway. But Ellie said it would be weirder if I *didn't* go, which is how I end up wearing the same itchy black dress I wore to the track formal, the one I wore when Mila and I sat in her car listening to Fleetwood Mac.

We arrive at the old church near the hardware store just as one of the ushers starts shutting the doors, and plaster ourselves up against the back wall. It's standing room only. The other Edgewater students, people who didn't know Mila until she was a dead girl on posters, pack the pews. They're the ones who gawk, filing this away as another detail about their strange hometown.

I spot Tamara, Raven, and Julia sitting up toward the front with Noah and his bros, Coach, and some JV runners. And in the first row, I see Mila's mother, Shawna, her shoulders tense and high, up around her ears. Her sister sits next to her, one arm wrapped around her, as if she's the only thing holding Mila's mother up. I try to find Naomi. I'd recognize her from her Instagram, but it's impossible to see her in the dimly lit church.

The priest walks to the center of the stage and begins talking, reciting traditional prayers and examining the difference between heaven and hell, right and wrong. He doesn't say much about Mila at first. He doesn't mention how much she loved art history or how she had a tiny tattoo circling her wrist. He doesn't sound comforting or sad. He sounds like a man doing his job, who has presided over many funerals. A girl gone too soon? Just another Sunday. But then he pauses and looks to the front row where Shawna's face tilts toward her lap.

"Mila's mother has asked one of Mila's best friends, Naomi, to say a few words," the priest says.

There she is, in the second row, just behind Mila's mother. She's wearing a silk black headband over her short dark hair and a long-sleeved black lace dress that hits just above her knees. It swishes when she walks toward the front of the room. She climbs the stairs of the dais and turns around once she reaches the podium. Her lip trembles a bit but she smiles at the crowd.

"Mila would have loved to see you," Naomi says into the microphone. "She would have loved to know that so many of you want to remember her. She was a connector, someone who was always bringing people together, on the cross country team or in the classroom. She wanted people to be happy."

A hitch catches in her voice. "I don't need to say how deeply upsetting it is that we are here today and she is not. Mila and I became best friends in kindergarten. Even then, she loved with her whole heart. She would spend hours at my house, helping my mom slice cabbage for kimchi or working out long-division problems with my little brother. He always liked her more than me. Even after she moved here, we spoke every day. On our last call, the night before she disappeared, Mila said something I'll never forget." Naomi lifts her chin and one hand floats over her mouth. She blinks back tears. "She told me, 'I'm finally starting to feel like Edgewater is home. I think everything really is going to be okay.'" Her gaze drifts to where Mila's mother sits and even from the back of the room I can see her shaking in her seat.

Naomi straightens her back and looks at the piece of paper in front of her. "I will leave you with this quote, which Mila slipped into my locker one day after practice last year." Naomi closes her eyes and recites the words from memory.

"'Life is so short, I am finally learning. But if I can love and be loved all at the same time, I'm not sure I mind.'"

People murmur their agreement and I feel like I'm naked, disemboweled, and served up for feasting. Like my whole world has been wiped out at once. When Naomi opens her eyes, I swear she looks right at me, all the way in the back of the room, behind a few hundred other mourners. And as she descends, her gaze stays put, holding mine until finally she turns away.

After the service, everyone crowds under a tent on the back lawn of the church, nibbling on crackers and drinking hot cider in the cool fall air. The crowd is thick with students from Edgewater and Hadbury, dozens and dozens of people I don't know. Naomi is off to the side, picking at a platter of cucumber sticks, bundled in a puffer coat for warmth. She looks exhausted.

I dart through the crowd and stop right behind her. "Hi," I say. "I'm—"

Naomi turns around, an unfazed expression on her face. "I know who you are," she says. "Stella Steckler. I've seen photos." She looks over her shoulder like she doesn't want to be seen with me, like she's scared of getting caught speaking with the enemy.

"Then why didn't you respond to my text?" I ask, desperation creeping into my voice.

"We can't talk here. Let's meet in an hour. Is there somewhere we can go?"

"The diner on Main," I blurt out. "No one goes there except the old farmers. There's a booth in the back that's private."

She nods and turns on her heel, sucked back into the crowd.

I duck out of the funeral and get to the diner early enough to grab the booth and order an iced tea. I sip it gingerly, my teeth clanking against the ice. My heart thrums loud and fast in my chest. The diner is empty save for a few farmhands who come here for bowls of chili every day after their shifts. I love this place. Used to come by when I was suspended last year. Here, no one asked why I hurt Allison. Or how it felt to break another person. No one whispered things like *crazy* or *monster* as I ate my chicken Caesar wrap with waffle fries in peace. They just ignored me, which is how I liked it.

The bell on the door chimes and I peek out of the booth to see Naomi looking around. I wave my hand once and she rushes toward me.

"That was a nightmare," she says when she sits down, unzipping her coat. She pulls off her headband and shakes out her short hair, running her fingers through her bangs.

"You spoke beautifully," I say, but the words come out formal and odd, as if I'm an old lady or a stranger, which I guess I am.

Naomi snorts. "Mila was right about you."

"What do you mean?"

"She said that you were kind of weird and I would like you

immediately. Mila always liked weird. That's why we were best friends for so long."

My face gets hot as Naomi flags down the waitress. She wiggles her fingers as she orders a plate of mozzarella sticks and a Diet Coke, and I notice her nails are painted all different shades of purple. Mila's favorite color. "I love diners," she says as the waitress disappears behind the griddle.

I know the proper response is *Same* but different words form in my mouth. "So, why didn't you respond to my text?"

Naomi leans back against the leather booth and looks to the ceiling, like she's trying to decide which version of the truth to tell. "I wasn't ready to talk."

"Are you now?"

Naomi shrugs and looks over at the glass case of pies by the cash register. "We all want answers, right? Doesn't seem like Parker and the detectives here are doing much good. Shawna is still looking for a PI to help, and let's be real, this *is* the town of cold cases." Naomi smirks. "Bullshit, really. Seems more like they just bungled the Fitzwater thing and then pretended those murders were unsolvable." Then she cocks her head and holds my gaze, her dark eyes piercing my skull. "Did you do anything to hurt Mila?"

"No." I shake my head emphatically. "No."

"I have no reason to believe you."

She's right.

"But I do. I can tell you're just as freaked out as I am—about Mila. Not yourself."

I relax my shoulders and feel relief. I don't know why, but I need Naomi's approval. For some reason I want her to like me, to be on my side.

"Got any other leads?" She leans in close and I can smell

her vanilla shampoo. "This can't be a serial-killer thing, right?"

I shake my head. "I just can't wrap my head around that. I mean, I guess there's always a possibility, but it doesn't make sense."

Naomi nods slowly.

"Do you think her dad had something to do with this?" I ask. "I overheard him calling Mila once and it didn't sound good."

"Ah," she says softly, crossing her arms over her chest. For a second, Naomi's wrist is exposed and I can see a tiny daisy-chain tattoo circling her wrist. It's identical to Mila's. "How much did she tell you about him?"

"That he's sick, that he's an addict. That they moved here to start over without him." I remember the strained, sad look on Mila's face. Her determination to move past it all. Something about Naomi makes me want to tell her my truth, too. Maybe it's the way she doesn't break eye contact or that she looks at me like we're a team, an alliance. "My mom is in recovery," I say. "It was something we talked about."

Naomi nods slowly. "Good," she says. "Mila always wanted to find people who understood. I only could a little, you know? My parents have no vices. Their only real flaw is that it took them a little while to get on board with the whole *I'm a lesbian* thing." She smiles and I notice a dimple on her left cheek and the way she's twisting her straw wrapper in her delicate fingers. Suddenly I want to know everything about her. Naomi shrugs. "But even that was just a few weeks. Now my mom plans the Fairfield County Pride Parade." She laughs like there's more to say on that topic. But I don't push. "Honestly, I think Mila was the one to help her get it. She just had a way like that, you know?"

I nod. I barely got to see it, but I do know.

"Anyway," Naomi says, wiping her eyes with her palms. "You asked about Mila's dad, right? Well, when Shawna told him she was filing for divorce, he lost his mind. Like, tear-the-house-apart lost his mind." Naomi tucks her hair behind her ears. "He was high. He wasn't himself. There were holes in the wall. Broken chairs. Glass everywhere. Mila called me sobbing that night. He didn't touch Mila or her mom, but they fled to her aunt's apartment in the city that same night. Never went back. I think that was the last time she saw him."

"Whoa," I say. Mila gave me the watered-down version. My chest tightens at the idea of her scared and worried, afraid for her father.

"Her mom's the best. She kept everything stable. Within a few weeks they were off, over here in Edgewater, which they thought was far enough away from her dad but close enough that Mila's aunt could visit. Nearly broke Mila, though, to leave her dad when she knew he needed help."

"Had you seen her recently?" I ask.

The waitress comes back with Naomi's order, sliding everything onto the table before walking away without saying anything.

Naomi smiles and dips a mozzarella stick into a steaming bowl of marinara sauce. "We FaceTimed a lot. Talked about everything. I kept her in the loop of all the drama at Hadbury. She was like my sister." She pauses, then points her mozzarella stick at me. "You have a sister, don't you?"

I nod. "Ellie."

"Yeah, she knew you two were complicated. But she liked you both. *Scary Stella wasn't so scary*, she said." Naomi breaks the fried cheese in half and steam floats above, circling in front of her face.

I bite the inside of my cheek. Mila saw me. She did. And I pushed away her friendship.

"She felt awful about meeting with Georgetown, you know."

I shake my head and try to find the words. "I shouldn't have . . ."

But Naomi cuts me off. "I get it," she asks. "You're competitive."

That doesn't even skim the surface of the raging desire inside me to win, win, win. But it's easier to agree that's all it is. A competitive streak. "It hurt." My voice shakes as the words come out. "I had to stay focused this year. It was my last shot. Everything . . . I had to leave everything on the trail, and Mila knew that. Or I thought she did."

Naomi leans back and crosses her arms. "I never understood you runners, the ones who wanted to do this forever, who never want the speed to stop. I just run to keep my anxiety away. To get some endorphins. But you and Mila. Both so serious, so obsessed."

"It's my entire life."

"I guess I'm like that with Model UN," Naomi says. "I'm Poland this year, and if someone tried to steal it from me, well, let's just say they'd never see it coming," she says, ripping a bite out of one of her mozzarella sticks as if to demonstrate tearing her competition apart. But she can't keep a straight face and all of a sudden we're both laughing.

I'm surprised to hear the sound coming out of my mouth. To feel my lips turn into a smile. Maybe it's because Naomi has totally disarmed me. Maybe it's because I can't stop staring at her smile, painted with a pink lip gloss, or the way she runs a thumb along her wrist tattoo as if it's a real bracelet. For the first time since I found out Mila died, I feel a little bit lighter.

But then I remember she never answered my original question. "So do you, though? Think her dad could have hurt Mila?"

Naomi looks to the ceiling. "Maybe."

"That kind of sounds like a yes."

Naomi fumbles for her phone. She taps a few times then turns the screen toward me on the table so I can see a headline from the *Hadbury Local*: NOISE COMPLAINTS RAMPANT ON ROLLINGTON LANE.

"This is where the Keenes lived," she says. "It doesn't mention Thomas by name, but everyone knew this was about him."

I scan the page and see the date is from earlier this year. A few key phrases jump out at me. "Repeated domestic disturbances." "Fearful neighbors." "Constant calls from concerned citizens." It even cites a few police reports that were filed the same year.

"Mila was devastated when this came out," Naomi says. "Awful to see it in print."

"Wait, was he not at the funeral?" I ask.

"Well, get this," Naomi says, leaning in and resting her elbows on the table. "I heard that when the police went to his house to notify him, they found it abandoned. Totally empty. He had left town and no one noticed."

"What?" I ask. "How did I not know this?"

Naomi shrugs. "His parents, Mila's grandparents, are like Connecticut royalty. Tessie and Daniel Keene. Have lived in Greenwich forever. They cut Mila and her mom off when they left her dad, but I bet they found a way to bury it," she says. "They weren't even here today. Felt too guilty, Shawna said. I think it's bullshit. And no one knows where Thomas is. Super suspect."

"Extremely," I say.

Naomi picks up another mozzarella stick and breaks it in half, letting the glossy cheese droop between both sides. She looks up at me with sweet, calming eyes. "I know you didn't do it," she says, twirling the cheese on her finger. "I hope everyone else does too."

32

STELLA

I THOUGHT FINDING Mila's dad would be easy. A quick Google search. A phone number lookup. I had no problem with the research portion of library class. But Thomas Keene seems impossible to find. Naomi was right. He has gone off the grid completely. There's an old LinkedIn account that described him as a "businessman," that faceless now-deleted Instagram, and a bunch of photos from some prep school reunion a few years back. But other than that, he's a mystery.

I close my laptop and tap my feet against the footboard of my bed, running through different scenarios, each one more gruesome than the last. The morning sun peeks through my window and I know I only have a few moments left before I have to leave for school.

I'm about to give up and start packing up my backpack when something pops into my head. Naomi said no one was at his house, but if his family's rich as hell, maybe he's living at someone *else's* property. A cottage in the Keene name or something. I flip open the computer and head to one of Mom and Dad's real estate databases. My brain spins as I enter the Keene name and Mila's grandparents' estimated ages before narrowing the search to Connecticut. Within a few seconds, multiple listings pop up. There's an apartment building in Stamford that looks like an investment property, a mansion in Greenwich that must be the family estate, and a handful of other places that have been owned since the nineties. But when I sort by most recent, my heart begins to pound.

The first listing is brand-new, purchased only a month ago in cash by Tessie and Daniel Keene, Mila's grandparents. I copy and paste the address into the search bar and hold my breath as the page loads. From the satellite view, the house looks like a sleek mid-century ranch nestled in the woods, up in the northwest corner of the state where the border meets New York and Massachusetts in the Berkshires. It's less than ninety minutes from here.

My fingers tingle as I try to decide what to do. I could call Detective Parker and plead with him to make a house visit. But would that hurt me even more? Parker already wants to blame this on me. Maybe sharing the information would make me look even more suspicious, like I was trying to divert the investigation away from me or something.

There's only one option. I whip out my phone and send Naomi a text, my fingers flying over the screen. I don't wait for a response as I run down the stairs, jacket in hand.

"Bye, Stella!" Mom calls as I head out the front door. "Have a good day at school!" I wave and head to the car. But I'm not going to school. I'm going to Connecticut.

"Wasn't sure if you were kidding or not." Naomi sits on the hood of her beat-up Toyota Corolla, wearing a puffer coat, a plaid skirt, and black Doc Martens boots, paired with knee-high hunter-green socks. She rubs her gloved hands together to keep away the cold, but her smile is wide and warm like she's glad to see me. "This better be good. I'm missing a Model UN meeting for this."

"It is," I say, trying to ignore the butterflies swarming my stomach. We're in the parking lot of a health food store, where one sign promises organic avocados even though it's November in the Northeast. But it's smack-dab in between Hadbury, Edgewater, and Thomas Keene's probable new address. "I found him," I say. "Thomas Keene is home."

Naomi rolls her eyes. "Uh, no he's not. The cops checked last week. Remember?"

I shake my head. "I think he moved." I reach into my pocket and pull out a crumpled piece of paper, where I had written his address in my chicken-scratch handwriting. Naomi's eyes widen as she scans the page. "Looks like Tessie and Daniel Keene bought this house a month ago," I say. "In cash. Don't think Thomas Keene could have done that on his own, right?"

"Well, shit." Naomi pulls out her phone and searches the address. "It's in the Berkshires."

"Does that mean anything to you? Did they ever go there?" I ask.

"When Mila was little, they had a country house in Litchfield County," she says. "I went there once. They had a pool and a big grill built right into the deck. Her dad had been trying to replicate some bulgogi recipe he'd had in Manhattan. I think he was trying to impress me or something. It was so bad, way too sweet, but he was trying." Naomi's eyes get misty for a second and she bites her lip. "Mila thought it was hilarious. She scrounged around in the freezer until she found some old hot dogs we could toss on the grill instead. He showed us how to catch fireflies that weekend, and how to toast marshmallows so they turn golden, but don't burn. It was the only time I saw her dad relax. It was like being there, he could just be free."

"So you think he could be living up there?"

"Yes," she says without hesitation.

"Road trip?" I ask. Naomi hops down off her car and rushes around to open her door. She pauses and flashes a smile, her dimple coming into view.

"I'll drive."

The house is big and wide, an elegant one-story building nestled far back into a wooded lot, full of tall oak trees, ferns, and weeping willows. The front is all glass and clean lines, and a stone pathway leads to the front door.

Naomi pulls the car into the driveway slowly, gravel crunching under the tires, and shuts off the engine. We both sit silently for a second, the reality of where we are setting in.

"Should we ring the bell?" she asks.

It seems like the logical thing to do. The *only* thing to do. Then the kitchen floods with light. Naomi inhales sharply beside me.

"He's home," she says.

I reach for the passenger door to step outside.

"Wait," Naomi says. She grasps my arm tightly. "I'm just a little nervous. I haven't seen him since before . . ." She trails off and looks toward the house. We can't see anyone inside, no shadowy figure or hulking man, but I can sense her fear, her pain. Naomi's voice is small and far away. "He was mean and sloppy when he was high." Naomi shudders and she closes her eyes. "I'm just scared, that's all."

My stomach flips with rage and despair for both Mila and Naomi, for what happened to Mila, for . . . everything. I take Naomi's hand in mine. "I'm with you," I say. "We're doing this together."

She looks at me, surprised, but then squeezes my hand right back. "I'm so glad you're here," she says, a small smile spreading across her face.

I want to say something back, but the enormity of what we're about to do washes over me. If Mila's dad really hurt her—if he was able to kill her in cold blood—then what would he do to us? Two girls who are trying to learn the truth?

I look to the house one more time and see a small man wearing gray sweatpants and a white T-shirt padding through the kitchen. Through the window, I can see his salt-and-pepper hair is thin, and his shoulders hunch as he walks. I take a deep breath in. "Let's go," I say.

I push the door open into the cold air. I walk steadily, knowing if I show any fear, it's all over. Naomi must know it too because I hear her feet behind me, rushing to keep up.

"Ready?" I ask as we reach the front door.

"Yes," Naomi says. She whips out her phone and taps over to the voice memo app. She hits record.

I curl my hand into a fist to knock, but before I can make contact, the door swings open to reveal Thomas Keene looking surprised and a bit scared, his gray eyebrows high on his forehead.

"Naomi Lee." His voice is raspy, like he's a smoker, and his skin is sagging around the edges of his mouth. "I was wondering when you would find me." Then his gaze lands on me and he stares straight into my eyes. "You must be Stella Steckler."

I open my mouth to respond but he holds up his hand. "Let's

do this inside." Naomi looks at me and mouths *What the fuck?* I shake my head, bewildered, but we do as he says and step inside. The door swings shut behind us.

Thomas walks along the hardwood floors in his white drugstore socks until he reaches the sunken living room. It's open and bright but bare, with nothing on the walls. One potted plant sits in the corner. He flops down onto a tan suede couch facing the floor-to-ceiling window and extends his arms along the back of the sofa. "Please," he says, nodding toward the matching armchairs across from him. "Let's chat."

Naomi and I sit at the same time, and when she leans back in the chair, staring at Thomas in shock, I know I have to take the lead. I perch on the seat's edge and rest my elbows on my knees. "How did you know we would show up?"

Thomas smiles thinly. "I've known you your whole life, Naomi," he says, nodding at her. "It was only a matter of time before you came looking for answers."

Naomi stares at him, her mouth open.

"And I've heard about you, Stella, that you and Mila were each other's greatest competitors. I just figured you and Naomi would find each other. Looks like I was right."

Something about the smugness in his voice makes me want to scream, to break every piece of glass in this house. "Then why have you been in hiding? The police are looking for you, you know." The words are coming up like vomit and I don't know how to reel them back, to play this strategically. I want answers.

Thomas sighs, his face weary. "I know."

"Why didn't you contact anyone when your only daughter went missing?" My voice rises, but I can't help it. My anger bubbles to the surface. "Where have you *been*?"

Thomas cracks his knuckles. His fingers are slender, with

clean, trimmed nails and palms that look like he's never done manual labor in his life. Why would he have to? With a house like this and a trust fund he kept from Mila, he's all set.

"Look, Stella," he says, putting on what must be his dad voice. "You may have only heard terrible things about me as a father. How I was neglectful and angry, how I only cared about numbing everything." He rubs his eyes with his thumb and forefinger as if he has a headache. "But she was my daughter. My only daughter. As soon as Shawna left, that was the wake-up call I needed."

Naomi shoots up out of the chair and I can see her hands curl into shaking fists by her sides. "But you *made* them leave," she says through tears. "You said you would get help but you didn't. Shawna couldn't take it, and Mila was terrified that you would hurt yourself or them. And now you sit here playing the grieving father?" Naomi crosses her arms over her chest. "Bullshit. I know you had something to do with Mila's murder." She spits the last word like it tastes like poison.

Thomas stands and starts wringing his hands, a concerned look on his face. "Wait a minute," he says, his voice rising. "You think *I* killed Mila?"

Naomi steps closer to him, her combat boots thwacking against the shag rug. "Prove that you didn't," she hisses. Her spine is straight and she no longer looks scared. In fact, she looks strong, like she has nothing left to lose. I can see why Mila liked her. Naomi has the same kind of fury as I do, but she's better at using it for good.

Thomas drops back onto the couch and rests his head in his hands. "I was in rehab," he says softly. "Out in Malibu."

"Malibu?" I ask.

He nods. "After Mila and Shawna left, my whole life fell

apart. I couldn't eat or sleep. I was using more than I ever had. I knew I had been so wrong in all of this. It was just a shame spiral. But you have to understand. Addiction is a disease. I couldn't stop." Thomas shakes his head and his eyes become glassy, like they're about to spill over. I try to remember the last time I saw a man who wasn't my father cry, and I can't. Dad has always been a crier, tearing up at sappy movies about grandparents and dabbing his eyes during rom-coms. He lets it flow, not caring who sees.

But seeing someone else's father break down may qualify as torture. I push down the awkwardness and remember we still need answers.

"I tried to visit Mila once, surprise her and Shawna at their house," he says. That must have been why Mila was talking to him on the phone before our run. *I don't want to see you anymore. You can't come here again*, she said. Remembering sends a shiver down my spine.

"But it was a disaster. They kicked me out as soon as they saw I was still strung out. Mila wouldn't speak to me after that. It was the last straw." Thomas looks at me, his eyes pleading. "I called my squash buddy Jim and had him arrange it. He had me sent to Malibu for a month. It was hardcore rehab. One of those over-the-top places where you're totally cut off from the world, with counseling, detox care, and yoga. No Wi-Fi, no cell service. You can't even write letters."

"Bet it cost a hundred grand," Naomi says under her breath.

Thomas snorts. "Almost. But I would do it again in a heartbeat. I came back ready to mend my relationship with Mila and Shawna. I reached out that day, you know? The day they found her." Thomas breaks down then, a sob rippling through his body. He hunches forward and clasps his hands in his lap.

Then he breathes deeply and continues. "I was on my way back east and called Shawna from the center. She didn't pick up but I left a message. I found out as soon as I landed. Couldn't bear to go to the funeral. Every day's a struggle to stay sober, and I knew if I went . . ." He shrugs and his shoulders slump forward.

No one says anything for a second, and then Thomas leans over to the side table and reaches for a marble keepsake box. He flips up the latch and riffles through some papers. "Here," he says, pulling one from the stack. "Proof. I stuffed all my travel documents in here when I got back." Thomas slides a piece of paper over to us and immediately I can see it's a receipt for the place in Malibu, confirming Thomas was there for weeks, including the time Mila disappeared.

"So you couldn't have hurt her?" I ask. After hearing so much about him, this guy had turned into the bogeyman. But seeing him here, up close, he looks frail and timid, a grieving father who never had a chance to make things right with his daughter. A man with regrets.

Thomas doesn't answer, but he doesn't have to. Naomi moves from her chair to the couch and sits next to him, leaving a little room between them.

"I'm so sorry," she says softly. "This must be unbearable."

Thomas lets out a whimper and it's almost too soft, too raw, too vulnerable. I want to run. He turns to Naomi through tears. "I'm the one who should be sorry," he says. "If I hadn't been . . ." Thomas's voice trembles as he trails off. "None of this should have happened. Mila should still be here."

Naomi blinks back her own tears. "You can't rewrite history," she says. "All we can do is figure out the truth. Find out who hurt Mila and bring them to justice."

I know she's right, and the sentiment is sweet and tender, but there's one thing still bothering me, one thing that just doesn't make sense, especially since he says he didn't have Wi-Fi out in Malibu. But he could be lying. He could have snuck away. The bill could be fake.

I clear my throat, forcing an awkward pause. They both look up like they're surprised I'm still there. "I just have to ask," I say. "Did you leave this comment on Naomi's Instagram?"

I slide my phone over the coffee table to a screenshot of the comment where that random user had written Come home, Mila. Come home to me.

Thomas turns red and he rubs a hand on the back of his neck. "Uh . . ."

Naomi raises her eyebrows.

"You wrote this?" she asks, incredulous. "I totally forgot about this, but it freaked me out."

Thomas looks down. "I'm so embarrassed," he says. "I did write that. Right after Mila said she didn't want me to come to Edgewater." He looks down at his lap. "I just . . . I wanted to reach her."

"With a creepy comment from a gibberish account?" I ask, perhaps a little too bluntly.

Naomi stifles a small laugh but Thomas doesn't flinch. "That was the day before I went to Malibu. I was in a rough place. I just thought . . . I don't know," he says, small. "I deleted it a few hours later when I realized how dumb it was."

Naomi looks at me with pity in her eyes and I know we're both thinking the same thing. *This man isn't a killer.*

"We should go," Naomi says, turning to Thomas. "Mila would have wanted to get to know the new you," she says. "So would Shawna. You should call her."

Thomas starts to cry again, mopping his face with his white T-shirt.

I stand and extend a hand for an awkward shake, not knowing what else to do. But Thomas pulls me in for a tight, urgent hug. When he releases me, my limbs feel like jelly.

"Thank you for coming by," he says. "It's good to remember Mila. To talk about her."

Naomi nods. "I think so too."

"Now," he says. "Let's find the fucker who did this."

33

ELLIE

I USED TO love Halloween. You could be anyone. A superhero. A politician. A pop star. Anyone but a Steckler. Stella was never into it, but me? I planned for months. By the first week of the school year, Bethany and I had our matching costumes planned perfectly. One year we were Arya and Sansa from *Game of Thrones*. Last year we were Romy and Michele from Bethany's favorite movie, *Romy and Michele's High School Reunion*. No one got it, but that made it even funnier to us.

But this year, everything's different. Mayor Dickerson canceled the town parade, trick-or-treating is banned after dark, and all anyone can talk about is how there's a *murderer* on the loose. I walk into school on October 31, and with every step, I hear Mila's name whispered behind cupped hands. Even though I have no costume, my desire to be someone else is at an all-time high.

It's been a week since they found Mila, and the police have nothing. It all makes my stomach flip, my head spin. I pick at my chapped lips and wince as I draw a bit of blood. *Shit.*

When I get to my locker, I peek over my shoulder and spot Detective Parker, hanging around the doorway to Pérez's office, leaning up against the wall. He's been like that since the funeral, just standing around, watching.

"Hey."

The word startles me and I nearly yelp. Noah stands behind me, his backpack slung over one shoulder. Here, by the lockers, we're so out in public I feel naked. Anyone can see.

"What?" I ask, stuffing my history textbook back into my bag.

"I just want to know if we're cool," he says. "After everything."

"Cool?" I ask. "That's not really the word I would use." I slam my locker shut.

"Look," he says, exasperated. "Can we just bury the tension, okay? Tam is freaking out about basically everything, so on edge about Mila and the investigation. And we can't afford to have any more drama between us. Right?"

His words hang between us. The secrets we've kept. The truth we know. All my nerves are on fire, and I can feel Parker staring in our direction.

"I'm having a Halloween party this weekend," Noah says. He shifts from one foot to the other.

"How is *that* going down?"

"It's a fundraiser," Noah says. "Everyone's gonna pay ten dollars to get in, and we're going to donate all the money to Mila's mom to help fund the private investigator. Dickerson okayed it."

My cheeks flush. "You sure you want to do that?"

Noah doesn't say anything and I slam my locker shut.

"Bury yourself," I say. "But leave me out of it."

"Come on Saturday, okay? It'll look weird if you don't." He rests his palm on my arm and I jerk away at once, a reflex that draws a few stares from the people around us. Parker stands up straight and takes a step toward us. But I can't have any more attention on me. I can't have him questioning me.

"I'll think about it." I turn and walk away, quickly, trying to stop the bile from coming up through my throat.

"Are you sure you don't want to come too?" I ask Stella, who flops on my bed, belly-down, on Saturday night.

"Absolutely not," she says, crinkling her nose and shaking her head violently.

"Come on," I say. "Don't make me go alone." I know there's no use in trying to convince her otherwise, but Noah's words stuck with me. *It'll look weird if you don't.*

"Nope," Stella says. "But I'll watch you put on whatever ridiculous costume you decide to wear."

I roll my eyes and rummage around my makeup bag, trying to figure out how to look even remotely festive. Everything feels frivolous. Finally, I fish out a pot of thick, silver glitter and dab some on my eyelids.

Stella flips over onto her back and plants her feet on the bed so her knees point toward the ceiling. She reaches for her phone and starts texting furiously. Whoever's on the other end is making her smile just slightly.

"Stella Steckler, are you *flirting* with someone right now?" I say, reaching for her phone.

Stella turns bright red and shoves her phone under her butt. "Maybe don't go," she says, changing the subject. "We can watch a movie or something."

I take a step back. "Okay, whatever *this* is," I say, motioning to her, "is weird. When's the last time you asked me to stay home and watch a movie with you?"

But just like that, the soft expression on her face is gone. "Whatever."

"I'm going to show face, pay my ten bucks, and get out of there," I say, already regretting the fact that I'm going. "If I don't, that'll just inspire more talk about the Steckler sisters." I wipe a few loose specks of glitter from my cheeks.

"Your funeral," she says, then winces. "Bad line."

"The worst."

She looks up at me in the mirror. "Who are you supposed to be anyway?"

"A disco ball, I guess."

She rolls her eyes.

"It's last-minute, okay?"

"Call me if you need me to come get you," she says, walking right out my door.

There's a cavernous pit in my stomach when I arrive at the party alone. It takes every muscle in my body to push open Noah's front door, and when I do, it seems like the entire school is here. A handful of zombie brides shimmy their chests while a werewolf passes a tray of tequila shots around the room. I spot a whole crew of Mario Kart characters in the kitchen playing Quarters, and I see a few cats, a bottle of sriracha, and someone I don't recognize wearing what can only be described as a "sexy avocado" outfit.

The music is so loud, the walls vibrate. It's as if everyone at Edgewater High is about to explode. Here they are, expending all of their pent-up energy, acting out their most depraved desires in fear of what's happened, of the unknown. There's a feverish energy that fizzles and cracks as the music swells and the stench of sticky beer spreads throughout the main floor. Suddenly, I'm suffocating and I get a creeping feeling that I just should have stayed home.

I push my way to the back of the house and open a sliding door that leads to the deck. The cold air stings my bare skin, and I pull my denim jacket tighter around my middle, hiding my silver sequined top. The backyard is lit up from the fairy lights hanging in the trees, and kids sprawl around on lawn chairs and in little circles on the grass just beyond the deck.

I've been here a few times, over the summer, when Noah's parents were out of town. I know that if I spin around and look up to the right, I'll see Noah's bedroom window. His pale-blue wallpaper would show through, as would his cross country trophies that line one wall. You wouldn't be able to see his plaid comforter or the plastic *Simpsons* figurines he keeps on his nightstand. Or his seven-foot stack of books from the seventies, the overflow from his bookcase in the corner.

I got to see all of that this summer, the real him, the guy who always kept a paperback in his bag, who wrote silly notes on the dedication pages, and knew a freaky amount of presidential trivia. But now it's like that part of him doesn't even exist. All I know, all I can see, is the bro I decided to intertwine myself with in the worst of ways. He's just a dude who turned my life inside out without a second thought.

"Oh, hey." I turn at the sound of Raven's voice behind me. She steps out of the sliding door and shuts it behind her. Her eyes are painted with bright green eyeshadow and she's wearing a neon-lime bodysuit. Poison Ivy. "We didn't think you'd show up." Then she looks me up and down. "What are you supposed to be?"

"A disco ball," I say, a little defeated.

"Sure," Raven says. "You okay? You've seemed distracted in practice and stuff. I mean, I even beat you yesterday," she says, a smile curling on her face.

I look at her with a blank stare and scramble for something to say other than *Fuck off.* "Yeah, I mean, Mila and everything . . ." I let the sentence trail and Raven's face falls.

"Of course," she says. "So devastating." She takes a big swig of a drink and from the face she makes as it goes down, I'm guessing it's more than half booze. I cross my arms, wondering what the hell she'll say next. "But we still have to worry about our times, you know? The season is still, like . . . happening." She takes another gulp. Her glassy eyes meet mine. "Whoever killed her must've known the toll it would take on Edgewater's best runners."

I feel my stomach lurch. "What do you—" But Raven cuts me off and points to an old swing set over in the corner of the backyard.

"Come on, everyone else is over there." She grabs a beer from the cooler behind us and hands it to me. I follow her, but my feet are heavy as bricks.

"Well, look who it is," Bader says, a beer can clenched in his meaty hand. "The lesser of two evils."

My cheeks burn but I will myself to be strong. "Shut up, Bader. You're just mad that Stella and I can both beat your PR."

He grimaces and takes a long swig from his can.

"I'm here to donate to the PI fund, obviously," I say, the words sounding forced and hollow in my mouth. I swallow hard to keep my dinner down.

"Guess your *sister* couldn't do the same," Julia says under her breath.

I know I should fight back and stand up for Stella, but in this crowd I'm outnumbered. Nothing I could say would change that right now. So I let the conversation flow toward regionals, then State, then back to regionals. It's all so boring, so ordinary. I can sense Noah trying to catch my eye the entire time, but I avoid him, pretending the can I'm holding is super interesting.

But then I hear a bang coming from the house. I turn to see Tamara slamming the door behind her, looking frazzled and clutching her phone. She's dressed as Diana Ross, wearing a full Supremes get-up and holding an inflatable microphone. Her sparkly dress shimmers in the moonlight as she rushes toward us. "Did you see?" she asks, shoving the phone into the middle of the group.

"What?" Julia asks.

"Mila." Tamara breathes heavily and her eyes roam the circle until they land on me. "Parker held a press conference tonight. Look."

Tamara presses play on a video. Parker takes over the screen and his voice plays through the small speaker. We huddle close to hear him over the music and the cheering from inside the party.

"We are here tonight to release new information about Mila Keene's disappearance and death. Here is what we know: Mila left her home around dawn on the morning of October 15 to go for her usual run around the Ellacoya Lake Preserve. Until recently, we thought she might have been alone, but we now know that Mila was *not* alone. She was joined by a female friend, most likely a teammate on the Edgewater varsity cross country team."

Someone gasps next to me. My hands go numb and my head spins. I look up from the screen to find Noah staring directly at me, terror in his eyes.

"We do not know *who* she was with, but we have leads that we will be following."

Tamara's hands shake as she tries to hold the phone for us. The tension in the circle is palpable, a beating heart about to burst. Back on the screen, Parker clears his throat and continues speaking.

"We are now ready to release more information about Mila's death. We hope doing so will encourage those of you who may have tips to share them with the police department." He takes a deep breath. "Mila was found on the Oak Tower trail, inside a deep pit, which had been covered in a blanket of leaves and brush. That's why it took so long to find her. She was wearing black spandex leggings, a blue long-sleeve Edgewater cross country shirt, and one lilac Nike sneaker. Her other shoe was found fifty yards away with its shoelace missing."

Someone in the circle gasps at that last detail, a freaky similarity to the cold cases.

"Our medical examiner found two broken ribs, a head wound, and a twisted ankle, all sustained pre-mortem," Parker continues. "The cause of death has been determined as blunt force trauma. Right now we are treating this as a homicide."

I cover my hand with my mouth, trying not to barf or cry or scream. Julia ekes out a small sob.

"While Miss Keene's death somewhat resembles the Edgewater cold cases, we are not convinced that this crime was committed by the same perpetrator or perpetrators," Parker says. "As many of you know, it rained in the days following Mila's disappearance, thus compromising the crime scene and much of the evidence. We are imploring you, our community, to come forward now if you know anything about Mila's untimely death. She was a bright girl with an even brighter future and her tragic death was avoidable. Please help us find justice for Mila and peace for the entire Keene family."

The screen goes dark and no one says a word. They just keep staring at Tamara's phone where Parker used to be, until finally Tamara shoves it back into a hidden pocket in her sparkly dress and pushes her hair off her face. I wrap my arms around my stomach to try to steady myself, to understand what this all means, what the evidence says.

"It's a copycat case," Julia says, shaking her head. "Some monster is trying to make everyone think the serial killer is back." She looks at the ground and mutters, "Probably Stella."

"What did you say?" I bark, but Julia holds her ground, narrowing her eyes at me.

"I said, probably Stel—"

"Jesus, Julia, that's not helping anything," Tamara says.

Raven clears her throat. "It seems like the killer is back. I mean, the missing shoelace. The Oak Tower trail. Blunt force trauma." She shrugs. "But honestly, everyone here knows about those cases. I wouldn't be surprised if someone *else*"— she glances over at me quickly—"did a little extra reading and—"

"Stella didn't do this," I say, my voice trembling.

"Sure, she's your sister, Ellie, but the text messages," Julia says. "She sent those. She's the only one who had a motive."

"Just stop it!" I scream, surprising even myself. "Stella had nothing to do with this. She was working out at home in our basement like she does every morning. I was with her doing circuits," I say, echoing what Stella told Parker. The lie burns like poison on my tongue.

Everyone in the circle turns to me and all of a sudden I want to melt into the ground.

"Oh, yeah?" Julia says, sneering.

Bader cuts in. "Didn't Parker say that someone was running with her? And that they have evidence to back that up?"

Tamara nods. "Who was it?" she asks, looking around the circle. "Who went running with Mila that morning?"

My toes begin to tingle and a chill runs through me. No one says anything and I can feel Noah's eyes on me, daring me to speak.

"Clearly no one's going to come forward now," Julia says. "Cowards. But the truth will come out."

Tamara nods, her eyes welling with tears. "And you don't want to be on the wrong side of it."

34

STELLA

I WAKE WITH a jolt, sweat dampening my brow, and before I open my eyes, I remember the press conference from last night. Parker's unwavering voice. His steady gaze. Mila had two broken ribs. A head wound. A twisted ankle. Parker said she was found in a pit, the one by Oak Tower, the forbidden trail. But you don't get those kinds of injuries from just falling into a pit and trying to climb out. Something must have happened. Someone else was there. Someone on our team.

I reach for my phone and when I see there's a text from Naomi, my heart beats fast.

I can't even begin to wrap my head around this. How are you holding up?

Wow. Even through all this, she thought to text *me*. I want to respond. I want to call her and hear her voice. But my screen says she sent that at two a.m. and it's now close to five. I resist the urge to wake her.

I roll over and pull the curtain back from my window. It's pitch-black outside, but I just need to run. I change my clothes in silence and shove my feet into practice sneakers. I tiptoe down the stairs and carefully slide open the side door. The air is cold, whipping at my cheeks. But as soon as I put one foot in front of the other, my mind begins to clear.

I watch a dark, quiet Edgewater go by in a blur of trees and houses just as the first signs of sun begin to peek out over the graying horizon. Soon I'm in town. I pass the public library, where the windows are frosted, and the small bowling alley Bader's parents own. I look up past the quaint brick buildings to the mountains in the distance, and for a second I feel like I can't breathe, like I'm trapped here in Edgewater, caged in by the peaks that surround us on all sides. People come here to feel free, to have space, to run away. But I've been running my whole life, and I'm still stuck here.

The sun is rising now, a mix of pinks and yellows and dull whites. I pick up my pace, trying to outrun the light. But all I can picture is Mila inside the pit.

"Stella Steckler."

The voice is loud and gruff, almost a little surprised. But I know it immediately. It forces me to stop.

Detective Parker is standing right in front of me, outside Mo's Diner, dressed in wrinkled khakis and a thin down jacket zipped up to his chin. He's wearing a wool beanie and clutching a paper cup of coffee in one hand and a manila folder in the other. We're the only two people on the street.

"Parker," I say. I rest my hands on my hips and try to catch my breath.

"What are you doing out here so early? Don't you know there's a 'no running alone' mandate right now?" He looks concerned. Not about my safety, though, but about the information he revealed last night.

I don't say anything.

Parker takes a step toward me. "Look, I won't tell if you don't, but we have some unfinished business, Miss Steckler."

"I saw the press conference," I say, my voice small and shaky.

Parker nods and cocks his head. "Then you must know that Mila was with someone the morning she disappeared. It appears she went on a run with someone on the cross country team. A girl. A friend."

I know where this is going, but I remind myself I have nothing to hide.

"Can you just tell me again where you were that morning, Stella? Where were you the morning of Mila Keene's disappearance?" Parker takes a sip of coffee and purses his lips.

He knows my answer and it won't change. It's the same thing I told him when he questioned me after practice weeks ago. "I was at home," I say. "I went down to the basement, like I always do, and lifted. I did a few arm circuits, mostly working on my biceps and triceps."

Parker nods. "Right, right. You mentioned that," he says, looking toward the diner. The light's on inside, but no one's there except Mo, filling salt shakers at the counter. I want to run, but I plant my feet firmly in the ground. "Walk me through the timing of it again, will you?"

"Don't you have all this written down somewhere?" I ask, exasperated.

Parker narrows his eyes. "You want me to bring you in for real again? With lawyers? Your parents? You want me to alert the school, Stella?"

I can't tell if he's bluffing but I squeeze my eyes shut and try to remember every single detail I shared last time. "I started around 5:15 a.m.," I say slowly. "That whole first part takes about twenty minutes, and then I did an ab workout." This is the part where I have to lie. "That's when Ellie came down, too. It's basically impossible to get her up before 5:45. So she joined a little after that."

"Mm-hm," Parker says, staring at me with dark eyes. He's quiet and the discomfort shifts inside me. "That doesn't prove much, though," Parker says. "The photo we have was time stamped at 6:07 a.m. Plenty of time for you to get to Mila after that."

I suppress a gasp. "What photo?" I ask.

Parker raises his eyebrows and rocks on his heels. He looks the same as he did when he called me in for questioning in the Allison Tarley debacle. Like he knew he would win.

"We found a photo on Mila's phone. That's how we know someone was with her that morning."

Mila's phone. That first search feels so long ago now.

"Can I see it?" I ask.

Parker smiles thinly. "No."

"But if you have a photo, wouldn't you know who was with her?" My mind is moving too fast for me to keep up and I don't understand what he has, what he knows.

Parker's mouth turns into a firm line and he sets his coffee down on the ground. He opens the folder he's carrying and sifts through a bunch of papers. Then he stops. "You may have gotten away with what you did to Allison Tarley, but this is not a game, Stella. This is not another Shira Tannenbaum situation. A girl is dead. You were too young to understand what it was like when the other murders happened here in Edgewater, but I remember," he says, his voice rising in the quiet, cold street. "I will not let this crime go unsolved. I will not let this town be known as Deadwater ever again. Someone has to pay for what happened to Mila. Do you understand me?"

I open my mouth to respond *Yes* but my throat is sand. I know what he's saying. He's willing to pin Mila's death on just about anyone if it means saving Edgewater's reputation—*his* reputation. And I'm the only lead he has. But I'm not willing to take the fall. Not now. Not again. I step back and swallow my words.

Parker mutters something under his breath. He looks at the piece of paper in front of him and cocks his head. His mouth turns into a small knowing smile. Then he flips it around and thrusts the photo toward me so it's only a few inches from my face.

Mila's smile fills most of the page. It's a selfie taken at the beginning of the trailhead. I can tell by the mountain range behind her and Ellacoya's main lodge in the distance. The sky is all purples and blues and pinks signaling dawn. She's making a peace sign at the camera, her eyes shiny with hope.

But there, in the top left-hand corner, is something else—*someone* else. The back of a head. Another set of limbs. Another girl, facing away from Mila so only her ponytail can be seen. Her dark, wavy ponytail. Hair that is shiny but just a little frizzy, probably from the mist. Her shoulders are square and tense. She's almost out of frame and sort of blurry. From any other angle, she would have blended right into the background, the dark woods behind her. But in this light, it's clear—at least to me.

The girl is Ellie.

"You're telling me this isn't you?" Parker asks.

I shake my head and will myself to speak. "No," I say. "That's not me."

"Well, then, who is it?"

I shrug and avert my gaze.

"Nothing?" Parker says.

My face reddens and an icy breeze whips between us. Store-fronts are starting to open and I know I have to flee before anyone sees us together, before more threads of gossip begin to float through town.

I shake my head again and spit out the words. "That's not me."

Parker looks at me, suspicious, and before he can say any-thing else, I turn and run—away from Parker and that photo of Mila and Ellie, now burned into my brain. I run until I get to our street, still silent and sleepy in the gray morning. Porch lights are only just starting to turn on. I run until I get to our driveway, the grass damp with morning dew. I slow and clasp my hands behind my neck, gazing up at Ellie's window. *What have you done, Ellie? What do you know?*

I shake my head, trying to find the answers. But there are none. All I know is that I have to find a way to protect myself. Everyone is going to continue to point fingers at *me* until they have another suspect, someone else that fits the bill. But if that someone is Ellie, I have to find a way to protect her, too.

35

ELLIE

THE FRONT DOOR slams hard and I know Stella is home. She takes the old creaky steps two at a time and I hear her bound from the landing straight to her room. It's nearly seven a.m. and the article has been up for an hour. I was dying to talk to Stella when I first saw it, but her room was empty, and she wasn't answering her phone. My stomach flips as I approach Stella's bedroom.

"Stell?" I ask cautiously. "Can I come in?"

Stella grunts and I push open her door. She's pulling on a hoodie, her hair damp with sweat.

"Where were you?" I ask.

"Out," she says, not looking at me. "Close the door. We have to talk."

I do as she says and take a step farther into her room.

Stella turns to me with expectant, furious eyes. She's about to say something, but I cut her off. "Wait, there's something you have to see," I say, and toss her my phone.

Stella catches it and her eyebrows shoot up as she looks at the screen. "What . . ."

"Read it," I say.

I've already seen the article, but I take a seat next her and read it again over her shoulder. Stella's mouth drops open just a little and her eyes move over the words. At first I didn't recognize the blog, but as soon as I saw who wrote the post, my heart dropped.

I Broke My Own Collarbone So I Could Stop Running

By Allison Tarley

I was always the fastest girl in Langston, New York. I won races, trophies, and a scholarship to a Big 10 School. I was told I could go pro. I was told I had Olympic potential. All I had to do was work harder, run faster, train longer, and fight harder. Seems great, right?

Wrong.

When I started junior year, I was healthy and strong. By December, I was not. I lost over twenty pounds in a semester. At the time, I thought this meant I was doing everything right. I was eating what my coach wanted me to eat, even if I only subsisted on dry grilled chicken and steamed spinach. I was training harder than I ever had before, even if that meant my bones were brittle and I had stopped getting my period.

But what I didn't realize was that none of this was normal. No girl, no athlete is supposed to push her body to the point of breaking, over and over. But I did. Because that's what my coach told me would put me over the edge. He said no college would want a flabby runner who had to be trained and disciplined. They wanted machines. Girls who don't think. Girls who perform. So I became just that.

I tried not to care when he berated me in front of my teammates, saying that I needed to train more because I was better than them, that they would never be as good as me. I tried not to care when he caught me sneaking a protein bar after a meet and snatched it out of my hands in front of the whole bus, calling me a pig.

But I finally broke when I lost the New York State championship. Another student, Stella Steckler from a neighboring town called Edgewater, came in first, and I didn't even place in the top three. Which makes sense now that I know my body was rebelling against what I had put it through. Sure, I might have had potential at some point. But not after running more than I ever had before, subsisting on no nutrition, and dealing with anxiety and depression that totally consumed me. My coach, who I trusted to help me succeed, to help me be the best, destroyed my mental health and made me more prone to injuries.

That's when I decided I wanted to quit. But I knew I couldn't. Well, that's not fair. I was scared to quit. I was scared of what my parents would say, I was scared of losing my identity as a runner, and of course, I was scared of what my coach would do.

So at the final race of the year, one that was supposed to be just for fun, I did something awful. (This might be the moment where my name starts to ring a bell. Maybe you ask yourself, *Oh, yeah, isn't this that girl who was attacked by that violent runner in the Catskills?* The answer is yes. But you don't know the whole truth just yet.)

In the final moments of the race, I found myself fighting with Stella Steckler for gold. But I didn't want to win. I just wanted a way out. So I asked Stella to hurt me. I wanted a reason to never run again.

Stella said no. Stella kept running. Stella stayed focused.

So, I flung myself at her and forced my body into her path until we collided. I tripped and tumbled off the trail. I broke my own collarbone. It was my fault. Stella was blamed for the whole thing, and I let her take the blame. I even pressed charges against her because that's what my coach told me to do. We dropped the suit eventually, but the damage was done. Stella lost her spot at her dream college and I descended even deeper into a depression.

Now, after nearly a year of therapy and recovery work, I realize how wrong I was, how much damage I actually caused.

I'm coming forward because I want to be a voice for all the other athletes out there who find it so difficult to stand up to their coaches, who trust them implicitly only to have their dreams stolen.

But I'm also coming forward for another reason. Recently, a talented runner, Mila Keene, was found dead in Edgewater. The police think it's a homicide. They also think that because of what happened last year between Stella and me that she had something to do with it.

I don't know Stella well, but I know that she is not violent. When I asked her to push me, to hurt me, she didn't. Yes, she's fierce. Yes, she's a fighter. But she's not a

killer. I know this because I had her branded as one. And
that was so, so wrong. I hope everyone else in Edgewater
can see that too.

When Stella finally looks over at me, she has one hand over
her mouth. "She told the truth," she says.

"You never told me what really happened," I say, the words
chalky in my throat.

Stella shakes her head. "I didn't think anyone would believe me."

"I would have," I say, choking up. "I would have, Stella."

"It doesn't matter now," she says. "Mila's dead and we don't
know who killed her. Do we?" She looks up at me with a scowl
and disappointed eyes.

I wish I could tell her about everything, let the words tumble
out and ask for her help. But all I can do is shake my head and
say nothing at all.

36

STELLA

I THOUGHT ELLIE would tell me the truth about where she was that morning. I really thought she would.

37

ELLIE

I CAN'T GET out of bed on Monday. My stomach hurts and my head pounds, and I know it's not the flu. It's fear.

"Ellie, you're going to be late!" Mom calls. She swings open my door and looks at me with worried eyes.

"I can't, Mom," I say. "Sick day."

She walks into the room and presses a cool hand to my forehead. "You do feel a little warm. I'll call Principal Pérez."

I roll over and listen for my family's routine. Dad's jangling keys. Mom heading downstairs to make eggs. Stella blending a smoothie. She doesn't even say goodbye when she heads off to school. I keep replaying our conversation from yesterday over and over.

We don't know who killed Mila. Do we?

Soon the house goes quiet. Doors slam and engines start. Then, when I'm all alone, time starts to disappear. I lie on my side and look out the window, watching the sun pass through clouds. The branches on the big oak shake, a few dead leaves fluttering to the ground below. But even that is too light to bear, too full of life. I don't deserve to see that kind of beauty. Not when Mila is dead.

I pull the covers up tighter around my chin and close my eyes. I am raw and numb, a slab of salted meat waiting to be seared.

My phone buzzes on the side table. But I don't have the energy to look at who's texting, trying to wake me from this nightmare. Instead I roll away to face my blank wall and wonder what will happen next. How I'll survive this.

But then something taps hard up against the window. At first it sounds like a branch, thwacking against the house. But when I look over my shoulder, I see a hand, curled into a fist, knocking against the glass. It's a big hand, almost the size of my face. Noah.

His profile appears as he swings his legs up off the trellis and crouches on the angled roof. Before I can leap up to shut the latch, he lifts the window and climbs into my room. "There you are."

I try to push myself up in bed, but my arms are weak and my joints are creaky. I slump against the headboard. "You look like shit," he says.

My mouth is dry but I search for something to say, something that for once is true. "Maybe that's because I can't live with myself now that everyone is blaming Stella for what *we* did to Mila."

Noah's face turns gray, but he doesn't say anything.

"You were there too, you know. What do you think everyone's going to say when they find out? You think Mr. Johnson will help you get into Princeton *now*?"

Noah comes closer, towering over my bed. "Ellie, come on," he says. "I came here so we can talk about all this. So we can come up with a plan."

"We have to go to the police," I say, shaking my head, tears falling down my face. "I can't do this anymore." I push the covers back and stand on the other side of the bed so it's in between us.

"Calling the police is out of the question," he says, running a hand through his hair. Hair I used to love touching. It was always so soft against my fingers. "It would ruin everything."

"We already *have* ruined everything."

Noah is quiet for a second but I can feel him thinking, the gears in his brain turning as he tries to figure out how to handle me, how to shut me up. But I won't let him. Not anymore.

"*You* ruined everything," I say, nearly choking on the words. "If you hadn't made me feel like getting an abortion was the most shameful thing in the world, none of this would have happened." The tears are flowing now and I don't want them to stop. I want him to feel the fury swirling inside me, to understand that it didn't have to be this way. I start pacing across the room, the wood floorboards cold and hard against my feet.

"Babe—" he starts.

"Don't *babe* me," I say, turning to face him. "You don't get to call me that ever again. You can save that for Tamara, who you've spent months lying to. You know what? I should have told her instead of Mila. Then everyone would know who you really are."

Noah's fists are clenched and I'm immediately transported back to the lifeguarding shack, when he punched a hole through the wall after I told him I was pregnant.

"Jesus, Ellie," Noah says. The words are acidic. "You don't know when to stop, do you? I never should have gotten involved with this fucked-up family."

"And I never should have gotten involved with a selfish asshole who only cares about getting laid."

Something snaps in Noah's eyes and I see the same deep anger there I saw once before. He reaches for the lamp on my side table. The movement happens so fast that I don't see him throw it across the room at me. I only feel the ceramic base collide with my chest and all the air leave my lungs. The lamp crashes against the floor, shattering. I gasp for air and slide down the wall, trying to right myself, to stand, to breathe.

"Shit," he says, his voice barely a whisper. Noah rushes toward me and I can't tell if he's going to save me or kill me. He crouches down, ceramic shards crunching underfoot, and I feel cornered, trapped. "Ellie, I didn't mean it. Ellie, I'm sorry."

Then I hear a voice from downstairs. "Ellie?" Stella yells. Noah whips his head toward my bedroom door, then back at me. He puts a finger to his lips, telling me to be silent. Always to be silent. "What the fuck was that noise?" Stella calls. "Are you okay? I left my physics book here. Have you seen it?"

I try to scream, to call out for her, but I'm paralyzed and my vision is spotty. I wonder if this is how it feels to lose control. Am I letting Noah's violence absolve me of my own guilt, my own crimes? I am an accomplice, after all. I deserve this. I deserve to be punished, to pay for Mila's death.

But then I hear footsteps, pounding up the stairs and just outside my door. Stella knocks once, then pushes the door open.

"Ellie, what the . . . ?"

38

STELLA

THE WORDS DISSOLVE when I see Noah standing over Ellie, his arms outstretched and his eyes wide with shock. Ellie's folded into a ball clutching her stomach, her bedside lamp in pieces beside her.

"Stella," Noah says. He steps toward me and I instinctively push him out of the way and throw myself over my sister, shielding her.

"Get the fuck away from us," I shout. I turn to Ellie. "Are you okay?" I push the hair back off her forehead. She's more shaken than I've ever seen her. Pure terror fills her eyes. But Ellie nods and I grab her hand, pulling her to stand. "Whatever just happened, you need to get out of here, Noah," I say, succumbing to the anger I always knew was inside of me.

Noah holds up his hands in surrender. "I'm sorry," he says. "I'm so sorry." All of a sudden, he bursts into tears, covering his face with his hands and dropping to his knees. "I didn't mean . . ."

Ellie pants hard behind me and grips my wrist.

"Stella," she says. "You need to know the truth."

Noah sobs on the floor and I know what Ellie's going to say. I want to shut her up, to make it stop, to hold the world still and travel back in time to when none of this had ever happened, when Mila was still alive.

"No," I whisper.

Then Ellie says what I knew all along.

"We killed Mila."

39

ELLIE

IT WASN'T SUPPOSED to be like this. We were just going to talk to Mila, to explain what could happen if she told anyone about the abortion, to show her how high the stakes were. To convince her to stay quiet.

Noah suggested Mila and I go running together, that we could casually bump into him in the woods as if it were no big deal, like it was a coincidence. It seemed to make sense. It seemed so easy.

Getting her to invite me was no big deal. In fact, she practically begged me. And I was happy to do it. Stella never wanted to run with me, and I was sick of running with the other girls who couldn't keep up. Only Raven could, but she was no fun because her panting was so loud it was distracting.

Under any other circumstances, it would have been like breaking ground on a new friendship. But on that day, everything went wrong.

I left before dawn, when the sky was still dark and dewy, and met Mila outside her house, on the wraparound porch. I suggested we take the Oak Tower trail, just like Noah said, so we wouldn't come across anyone else. Mila didn't hesitate. Her eyes sparkled and she nodded enthusiastically. "Creepy," she said. "I'm into it. Tamara says that all the bartenders sneak up there to smoke weed after their shifts at the restaurant."

We took it slow over to Ellacoya. I wasn't paying attention when she snapped a selfie at the trailhead, but I figured I wasn't in it since I was stretching beside her. That was my first mistake.

"Ready?" I asked, flashing my best smile, trying to cover my nerves.

Mila nodded and rubbed her hands together. "Let's go."

We took off together, our legs stiff from the early-morning cold, and made our way up the dirt trail over the hill. If we looped around for a mile, it would lead toward Foxfire Point, one of the most beautiful vistas in Edgewater. But if we veered to the left, we'd head up to Oak Tower, where Noah and I agreed to meet. Our sneakers hit the ground together in a series of *thwap-thwaps*, running over crunchy leaves and tangled roots.

We ran in silence, but my brain was on fire, curious how this would go, if Noah would freak her out. He promised to make it seem like no big deal. Soon we trotted up the hill, sidestepping the rocky pit covered in brush. I remember thinking how strange it was no one had filled it in, but then I remembered that no one maintained this trail, not after they shut it down.

That's when I heard Noah's footsteps coming from the other side of the hill. I worked hard to keep my gait steady, to not give anything away. But Mila turned to me, her face a question mark. "Is that—" she started to ask.

"Oh, hey," Noah said nonchalantly, and only a little out of breath.

"Noah," Mila said, surprise creeping into her voice. "What are you doing here?"

"We just wanted to—" I said, but I already knew I chose the wrong words.

"We?" Mila asked, confusion on her face. "Are you guys talking again?" She knew how badly Noah hurt me. I should have known she would be on my side. Or what she *thought* was my side.

"Well . . ." I started.

"Seriously, Ellie? You're still hanging out with this douche?" she said, scoffing at Noah. "Let's go." She turned and motioned for me to follow her, but I stood grounded into the earth and looked to Noah. His eyes were pleading.

"Hold up," I said, my voice wobbly.

Mila turned back to us and crossed her arms over her chest, annoyed at the whole situation.

"We just wanted to talk to you," Noah said. "What Ellie told you . . . we just wanted to make sure you wouldn't tell anyone, okay?"

Mila raised her eyebrows, as if she couldn't believe he had to ask that. She tilted her chin up toward him, defiant. "Tamara is my friend," she said. "But Ellie is too. When someone asks me to keep a secret, I do. I value trust and loyalty, unlike you two, obviously." She threw me a disappointed look. "But you should seriously come clean to her," Mila said. "This is only going to end in disaster for you."

"You don't understand anything about this town," Noah said, fear and frustration filling his voice. "We need you to keep quiet."

"That kind of sounds like a threat, Noah," Mila said through gritted teeth.

"Mila, please," I said, trying to fight the tears, the raw scratching in my throat. "I don't want anyone to find out. It could ruin

Noah's chance of getting into Princeton." I was feeding her lines that Noah fed me, but there was nothing else to do.

Mila rolled her eyes. "That's what this is all about? You want Mr. Johnson to help get you into Princeton? There are other schools. And maybe you should try to get in on more than your girlfriend's dad's word." Mila threw her hands up. "You know what? Maybe everyone *should* know what liars you both are." Her voice was sad and unsteady. She looked at me with pained eyes. "I can't believe you set me up like this, Ellie." Then she turned toward the ridge in the woods and took off.

Before she could get beyond the clearing, Noah took after her, his stride so much longer than hers. "Noah!" I called out. "Stop!"

But it was too late. Noah barreled toward Mila and shoved her hard, over the edge of the pit we had passed only a little while before. All I could hear was a strangled scream stretching into the woods and the rustling of dried leaves as she tumbled down through brush and roots and stones.

"Mila!" I called.

She yelped from below and called back to us. "What the hell, Noah?"

I peered down into the pit and saw her there, clutching her ankle, dirt smudged on her face.

"Ellie, help me!" she called. "I think it's sprained."

I turned to Noah and saw fire in his eyes, fear curling at the edges of his mouth. "What did you do?" I yelled.

"Ellie!" Mila called again. "It really hurts. Can you get help?"

I opened my mouth to respond, to say *Yes, of course.* But Noah clamped a palm over my face, blocking air to my nose and mouth. "No," he hissed. "We have to leave her there."

I wanted to protest, but I couldn't breathe. I formed my

hands into fists and started pounding on his chest. But he grabbed them both in his other hand and I was trapped.

"I know you want to play nice, babe, but you can't," he whispered. "Not now. We need to scare her. Make her think we're going to leave her here for dead if she tells your secret."

Fire filled my lungs. *Your* secret. As if this whole mess was mine and mine alone. As if he played no part in my trauma, my pain. As if he was just here to clean up the mess. As if me having an abortion was even a mess to begin with. But I nodded in that moment. I just wanted him to let me go.

"We'll come back after school," he said. "We'll help her then."

I wanted to tell him it was the dumbest plan ever. That there was still time to right this. But Noah gripped my face and my hands tighter, pushing me back toward the ledge of the pit. I nodded again and Noah finally dropped his grip. I took a sharp breath in and rubbed my sore wrists.

"Mila," Noah shouted down to her. "We're going to leave now."

"*What?*" she screamed. "You fucking asshole! Are you serious?"

"Mila," Noah said again, calmly, like he was talking to a child. "We need you to agree that you won't tell anyone about Ellie. If you agree to that, we'll come back after school and get you. We'll help you."

I could hear Mila breathing, panting in pain. "Bullshit," she said. "I'm calling Coach." I could hear her fumbling for her phone and then her voice rang out, small and defeated. "Shit."

"There's no cell service up here," Noah said. "But if you agree to keep quiet, we'll come back later and pretend like none of this ever happened, okay?"

Mila was quiet for a beat until finally she said one word. "Fine."

My stomach dropped and I knew this was bad. But I couldn't speak.

Noah turned back to me. "Let's go," he said, his voice barely a whisper. "Meet me back at the entrance after practice. We'll figure it out then."

The rest of the day was a blur of classes and notes and pens scratching paper. But by the time Coach dismissed us from practice, it was pouring rain and fear quickened in my heart. We had to get to Mila soon. Her mom would be worried. She would miss a shift at Ellacoya. One day of hooky was fine. Not coming home at night was something else. Especially in this town.

I arrived at the clearing that led to the trail, soaking wet and clutching my windbreaker around me. Noah was nervous when he got there, too. His eyes were wide and he couldn't stop touching his face, cracking his knuckles. "Come on," he said. He had brought a rope and some bandages, and I could tell he was weighing what he had done, what *we* had done.

We walked in silence, our footsteps squelching in the mud. It was getting darker then, colder. And I started to worry about what state Mila would be in now, what we would find when we reached the pit. A half mile into the trail, we could barely see our hands in front of our faces, and I whipped out my phone to use as a flashlight. I shone it around at the trees, the sky, the brush as rain pelted down, obscuring my vision.

"It's just up ahead," Noah said.

"Mila," I called. "Mila, we're back. I'm so sorry. Let's get you out of there. Let's get you home." But no one answered.

I snuck a peek at Noah and he looked scared for the first time. His jaw was clenched and his eyes were wide.

"Where is she?" Terror filled my voice. My heart was in my throat.

"Mila!" Noah screamed.

We both picked up our pace, nearing the entrance to the pit. I held my breath and angled the flashlight on my phone so it cast a spotlight down below.

But I didn't see Mila. The pit was just a sea of wet, dark mud, filled with brush and fallen leaves. I couldn't get a good look inside. I couldn't see anything. There was nothing.

No sign that a human had ever been there at all.

Except . . . except for the blood. A thin trail dripping down the side of the hole. It was dark and shiny, almost blending in with the mud.

"Mila!" I shrieked. But no one answered. I spun around, trying to catch my breath, trying not to look at Noah, to imagine the possibilities.

"Come on," Noah said, clipped and scared. "Let's go."

"No. She has to be here somewhere," I said, desperate. "We have to go down there. There was blood. You saw it too. I *know* you did. What if she's trapped?" But Noah grabbed my hand and yanked, pulling me after him, toward the road.

I don't remember saying yes or no or doing anything but moving. All I knew was that within minutes I had followed Noah off the trail and down behind the Ellacoya Resort's boat launch, stumbling over rocks and trying to keep my lunch from coming up out my mouth. Tears and rain blurred my vision as I tried to keep up. At one point, I tripped over a root and let out a sob. Noah turned around and clamped a hand over my mouth for the second time that day. His hair was matted to his forehead and his eyes were wide and bloodshot. When he released his grip, my jaw ached and I continued following him until we got to the other side of the resort, which spits out onto a side road.

"Noah," I started. My voice trembled.

"What, Ellie? What?"

"We have to call someone—the police, Coach, her mom," I said, quietly, pleading. "We have to do something. Anything. She could be down there still. Or somewhere on the trail, hurt."

Noah ran his hands through his hair, like he was clawing for the answer. "No," he said. "She probably got herself out of there and is already home. Don't you think?"

"We would have heard about that at school."

"Call her, then," he said, throwing up his hands. "Call her."

I pulled my phone out of my pocket with shaky hands. "Shit," I said. "There's still no service. We have to get back to the main road." I bolted and continued to dial, waiting for the phone to connect. Finally, after another half a mile, the call went through. I held my breath, waiting for someone to pick up, to hear Mila's raspy voice, to get yelled at for what had happened. But it went straight to voicemail. I tried again. Same thing.

I brought the phone down from my ear. "What if—"

"Don't say it," Noah said. His hands were shaking and he sped up, taking off down the road. "Don't you dare say it."

"We left her there to *die*," I said, trailing behind him.

Noah turned around fast with his pointer finger outstretched. "Shut up, Ellie," he said, the words cutting through the air like a knife.

I stumbled backward, like I had been punched in the gut, like all the air had been knocked out of me. I sank to my knees, trying to understand what just happened.

A few months before, this exact scene would have been my best-case scenario. A nighttime run alone with Noah. Feeling his sweaty, heavy body syncing up with mine, our breath finding each other's, our gait in time. It would have been magical, a moment I could capture and replay on repeat to help me fall asleep.

But all I could do was stay crouched on the ground, gravel digging into my knees, rain pelting down on my back.

"We didn't . . ." Noah shook his head. "I'm sorry," he said, stepping back. "I'm sorry. We just . . ." He crouched down beside me. "We have to go," he said. "I have to go."

Then he stood and sucked in his breath. He looked back to the trail where we had left Mila and then the other way, back toward town. I squeezed my eyes, willing this to be a dream, but when I opened them, Noah was gone.

I stumbled to my feet and walked to the gas station down the road, the one with vintage signage, cheap beer, and the only pay phone in town. I knew Noah was wrong, that we had to do something, that we had to *tell* someone. I fumbled in my pocket for a quarter and picked up the receiver. I dialed, knowing it wouldn't be traced back to me.

"911, what's your emergency?" a perky woman asked.

"There's a girl up on the Ellacoya trail," I said with a chalky voice, barely able to get the words out. "A runner. I think she's hurt."

"Can you be more specific, dear?" the woman said.

"Up by the clearing near Oak Tower on the forbidden trail, there's a pit. She was there before. Now she's gone. She's missing." I sobbed into the mouthpiece. "Help her."

When I stop talking and finally look at Stella, her face is white and her mouth is small. She wraps her arms around her middle and whispers, "No." Then her eyes pop wide open and she looks directly at me. "How could you?"

There's nothing to say. I have no way to defend or explain myself. I take a quick look at Noah and he's just standing there, his hands clasped behind his neck, like he can't believe he's gotten himself so entrenched, so tangled up with the Steckler sisters. Like this isn't his fault too.

Stella starts pacing around the room and I can see her brain trying to piece everything together, fit all of the lies into a neat little story. "So you knew someone would find Mila's phone at Ellacoya?"

My head snaps up. "No," I say. "No. I have no idea how her phone ended up there."

"And what about Mila's school ID? Remember it fell out of my locker? You got rid of it before Parker could find it, but how did it get there in the first place?"

I'm silent, stunned. I forgot about the ID. I never even questioned why Stella had it. I just knew I had to protect us both. "I don't know," I whisper, shaking my head. "I don't know how it got there, I promise you."

"Naomi had no idea either," Stella mutters.

"Naomi?" I ask. "Like, Mila's best friend? You know her?"

Stella nods and the gulf between us grows even wider. How many secrets have we kept from each other? How much do we still not know?

"I met her at the funeral," she says. "We went to visit Mila's dad together, to see if he had anything to do with this. But he was in rehab in Malibu." Stella's face contorts, like she's confused. "But the phone," she says. "The ID. I just . . . Something isn't right." She grabs my hands and turns to face me. "Ellie," she says, her gray eyes piercing mine. "This isn't you."

My lip trembles and I know Stella's wrong. This *is* me. This is who I have become, and no one even noticed.

"We're missing something," she says. "I know it."

But there's nothing to miss. I was there. I left Mila to die. I did nothing to stop it.

Noah clears his throat and speaks. "You're saying you think something happened to Mila after we left?"

Stella ignores him and keeps looking at me. "She didn't die down there from starvation. She didn't die of frostbite. She died of a head wound. And she was found *in* the pit, remember? That's what Parker said during the press conference. How could that all have happened? She only had a sprained ankle when you left her. Right?" Stella's voice cracks when she speaks and I know she's trying her best to hold it together, to keep me from harm, even though I'm the one who ruined everything.

I squeeze my eyes closed and force myself to remember the morning I tried so hard to forget. The frigid air. The way her scream sliced through the trees.

"I don't know," I say, breathless.

"Well, someone must have been there after you," Stella says. "How else did her phone wind up by the boat launch at Ellacoya? That's miles from where the pit is. And what about the shoelace?" Stella asks, exasperated. "Parker said one of her shoelaces was missing, just like the cold cases."

For a moment no one says anything and we're all standing there, silent, unable to comprehend what has happened, what we've done and what we haven't.

"I mean, maybe the Deadwater killer is back," Noah says. "Maybe Kendall Fitzwater returned to Edgewater and has been hiding out in the woods. Maybe he found Mila in the pit after we left her there and decided she was his next victim."

Fire burns in Stella's eyes. "You expect me to believe that on the same day you lured Mila out into the woods, the old Edgewater killer just decided to show up in town, stake out his old terrain, and kill Mila when he found her there?"

The words hang between us, unfathomable.

"I mean, maybe," Noah mumbles.

"You're pathetic," Stella says.

Right then, Noah's phone buzzes in his pocket. He pulls it out and looks at the screen. "It's Tamara. She's with Julia and Raven over at Ellacoya. Wants to know if I'll swing by to hang out."

Stella narrows her eyes. "Tell her we're on our way," she says. "Someone's gotta know something, and we need answers."

I shiver in my thin, oversized T-shirt and look around the room. The lamp is still broken by the door and my sheets are tangled on the floor. Dirty laundry is strewn about and everything smells stale. My gaze lands on Noah, who only a few moments ago tried to hurt me, tried to shut me up, *again*. But all I can do is feel pain and pity and sorrow for the boy I thought I loved, the one I thought held the answers to everything. I think of the secrets he made me keep, the trauma from which he never helped me heal. Finally I realize I'm not afraid of him anymore. I'm not afraid of anyone.

"Okay. Let's go."

40

STELLA

WE DO WHAT we always do. We run. This time to Ellacoya at a frantic pace, one that sets my lungs on fire. Ellie is slow, stumbling over herself, rubbing at what I'm sure is the massive bruise on her chest. Noah keeps a steady jog, eyes straight ahead, focused and far away. I hate him. What he did to Mila. What he did to Ellie. But now we're tied together in an unlikely trio out for the truth. It doesn't make sense, but nothing does these days.

When we hit the entrance, Noah slows and pulls out his phone, blinking with messages from Tamara. "They're down by the boat launch," he says.

I nod and follow him, walking briskly down the path, past the A-frames and the tennis courts. Ellie tenses beside me and I grab her hand and squeeze it hard. She squeezes back.

Soon we hear voices coming from the picnic table next to the canoes, still roped off with yellow caution tape, even though we know that's not where Mila took her last breaths.

Noah pushes through the branches first and Julia calls out to him. "Finally!" she says. "Did you bring any beer? Tamara won't let us steal any from the bar."

Ellie and I step through the opening and Julia's face falls.

Raven frowns only slightly and Tamara raises her eyebrows in surprise.

"What are they doing here?" Julia asks.

Noah's silent. What can he say? That he's the reason Mila died but . . . maybe not? That we want to know what they know?

Ellie steps forward and wastes no time with pleasantries. "I was the runner who was with Mila that morning," she says, her voice strong and firm.

Their mouths drop open.

Ellie nods. "Noah was there too."

"What?" Tamara asks.

"I'm so sorry, Tamara," Ellie says, turning to her, tears forming in her eyes. "We have to tell you the truth." She looks at Noah, but he doesn't say anything. "Noah and I were together over the summer."

Tamara's face stays still, unreadable.

"And something happened," Ellie continues, trying to keep her voice calm. "I got pregnant and I had an abortion."

Tamara presses her lips together and her whole body tenses.

"I told Mila after homecoming," Ellie says. "And we were scared it would get out, that she might tell you. That's what we were doing that morning, trying to convince her to stay quiet."

My stomach is in my throat and I stare at my sister, shocked at her verve, what she just said, and the way this is all going down.

No one speaks for a second but then after an awkward moment, Tamara lets out a long breath. Then her eyes flash open and she widens her stance. She looks right at Noah. "I'm not surprised."

"What?" Ellie asks.

"I mean, Noah isn't exactly a mastermind when it comes to

sneaking around," she said. "I suspected something was up. I just didn't want to believe it." Tamara's lip trembles. "But you, Ellie? Seriously? I know we're not *friends* or anything, but, shit . . ." She wipes an arm across her nose, sniffling into her sleeve.

Ellie swallows hard, blinking back tears. I want to wrap my arms around her, hold her close and shield her from all this. But she needs to face this completely. She needs to hear how badly she hurt Tamara. She needs to know her actions have consequences. We all do.

Noah covers his face with his hands, seemingly trying to hide from that fact that suddenly he's an open book, all his secrets on display. "Why didn't you say anything, Tam?"

"Are you joking? I knew you would have just said I was crazy, that I was making things up," Tamara says. "Plus, I always assumed we would break up when you went off to college, even though you're obviously using me for my dad's connections."

Noah looks like he wants to crawl inside himself. His shoulders are hunched over and he gazes straight at the ground.

"Yeah, asshole," Tamara says. "It was pretty obvious. Figured it was less stressful to stay together for a few more months than dump your ass or cause any drama. I'm used to pretending in this town and I thought I'd rather have a pleasant, phony year than have you and Bader make the rest of my time in Edgewater a living hell," she says, nodding at Noah. "But now? Fuck that. I don't need to deal with this shit anymore."

"I never would have made your life . . ." Noah starts.

"Yes, you would have," Julia says. "Your pride couldn't have taken it." She scoffs. "Honestly, fuck you both." She shoves her pointer finger toward Ellie and Noah. "But this explains nothing about what happened to Mila."

We wait a beat. None of us is sure how to explain what happened. Then Julia's eyes go wide. "Wait, are you saying . . . ?" Her voice quivers. "Did you kill her?"

"No," I say. It comes out louder than I meant it to. "They didn't. The evidence doesn't add up."

Ellie picks at her lip and looks around the circle, terrified that we got this all wrong.

"Bullshit," Julia says, standing. Her face hardens. "You totally did, you liar," she says and takes a step toward Ellie. "I'm calling Detective Parker." Julia reaches for her phone in her pocket, but I take a step toward her and knock it out of her hand.

"No," I say.

"What the actual fuck?" Julia calls out. "Tam, call security."

Tamara straightens her back and pulls at a few of her braids, loose around her shoulder. Her gaze lands on me and some kind of acknowledgment passes between us. "I want to hear them out."

Ellie inhales deeply like she's summoning all her strength. "Noah pushed Mila into the pit," she says, making direct eye contact with Tamara. "He wanted to make sure you never found out about us or what happened. She had a sprained ankle and we decided we would come get her after school. But when we got there, she was gone. Nothing was left. Only a trail of blood. I called 911 when we left the woods. That's where the tip came from," Ellie says. "But Raven found her phone at the boat launch."

Ellie's bottom lip trembles and I place a hand on her shoulder, urging her to keep going. "I don't know how that got all the way down here or how Mila ended up with head trauma or broken ribs. She only had a twisted ankle when we left her. And then there's that missing shoelace." Ellie's voice breaks and a tear slides down her cheek.

"It just doesn't make sense," I say. "Someone else was there in the woods. Someone else must have found Mila after Noah and Ellie left."

Everyone is quiet for a sec, but Tamara is the first to speak. "So what now?"

Beside her, Raven coughs and pushes herself to stand. "I gotta go," she says. "I should have been home a while ago." She doesn't make eye contact with anyone and fumbles to zip up her jacket.

"Wait," Tamara says, tugging on her sleeve. "You're the one who found the phone. You spoke to Parker about it. What do you think happened?"

Raven pulls her arm away, almost violently. "Let me go, Tam." Her voice is urgent and small. Something about it reminds me of the way she looked at me when she saw Mila's ID fall out of my locker. It was almost like she was expecting it to happen.

"What's wrong?" Tamara asks, grabbing for Raven again.

"Nothing," Raven snaps. She doesn't look at anyone, but her strawberry-colored ponytail swings around her shoulder as she stumbles. "I just have to go."

When Raven lifts her head, her face is pale and worried. Julia stands and reaches for Raven too. "What's going on?" Julia asks. "You're freaking me out."

But Raven takes a step back, out of Julia's reach. Then she turns and starts running, her feet flying in front of her.

That's when I see it. A flash of lilac, long and thin, trailing from her pocket.

"Raven!" I call, but she keeps going without turning around, without slowing down. Ellie gasps beside me. She sees it too, and in an instant we're both off, racing after her, up the hill toward the main Ellacoya lodge.

Ellie collides with her first and they tumble to the earth in a ball of tangled limbs and fleecy coats. Raven shrieks as I grab at Mila's shoelace and wrap my hand around its end.

I hear Tamara, Julia, and Noah scramble up behind us. "Hold her!" I say to Ellie. But she's weak, hurt from Noah's outburst, and Raven starts to wriggle away. Her eyes are wide and terrified, and her cheeks are wet with tears. She's trying to breathe, to gasp for air, but it sounds like she's choking and screaming all at the same time.

Finally, I yank the shoelace from her grasp and leap up, jumping back and falling into Tamara. She steadies me and I can finally breathe.

"What the hell is going on?" Julia screams, coming up behind us.

I hold up the shoelace, not wanting to believe it's real, that it was Mila's.

"Holy shit," Tamara says. We both know it is. There, at the end of the fabric, swinging in the wind, are Mila's initials embroidered on the edge. *MK.* "How did you get this, Raven? How?"

Raven screams, a bloodcurdling wail that makes my ears ring. I spin around just in time to see her shove Ellie to the ground and bring her knee right up into Noah's groin. He bowls over with a hard *oof*, and Raven stands, looking right at us. Her face is a ball of rage and she's breathing hard, her shoulders heaving up and down.

Julia takes a few steps back, horrified. Tamara covers her mouth, as if holding back vomit.

"Raven," I say. "What have you done?"

41

RAVEN

THEY'RE ALL LOOKING at me like *I'm* the crazy one. Like *I'm* the one who ruined everything. And that might be true now, but it didn't have to be this way. I never meant to kill Mila. At first, it was the Stecklers who had to go. A broken femur for Stella and a dislocated shoulder for Ellie, perhaps. I thought about it all summer while I was working in the kitchen at Ellacoya, stuck with the deep fryer so I smelled like grease every day.

I knew Stella would come back from that camp faster than she had been and that Ellie's natural ability would only get better with her lifeguard training. I didn't have a shot at beating either of them. I knew that the first day of preseason.

But when Mila showed up, I had to rethink everything. There would now be three girls on the team who were better than me. Three people to beat. Three obstacles between me and an exit from Edgewater, where everyone knew me as Shira Tannenbaum's sister. The *good* sister. The one who wasn't nearly as fast or as special but would never run away and force the police to try and find a girl who didn't want to be found. I had to live up to that since Mom put all her hopes and dreams on me. I was our family's last chance of making it out, making it *somewhere.* Winning was my only option and I couldn't even get that right.

It took a few weeks, but the plan started to come together just after homecoming. First I noticed that Mila and Stella actually got along. Mila cracked Stella open in a way no one else in Edgewater ever did. Stella was happy. She was laughing. But she was also distractible. Off her game at that first meet. Mila only got stronger, though, beating Stella over and over.

And then I overheard Ellie's admission on the party bus. That she was *with* Noah and got pregnant. She thought no one was around. But I had come back to pick up my purse at the perfect moment.

I knew I could tell Tamara what I heard on my own, but I thought it would be more compelling coming from Mila, the person who Ellie actually confided in. I figured it would be the ammo I needed to turn Mila against the Stecklers. All I had to do was get her alone and convince her that we were *both* better off if they were out of the picture. I figured we could use that knowledge to force Ellie into quitting the team and that Mila might be down to mess with Stella's head a bit, throw her off her game even more. I thought she might be as desperate as I was.

And so that October morning, just as dawn began to break, I walked over to Mila's house. I knew her schedule by then, that she got up at 5:45 and hit the trail a little while later. I showed up at 5:30 to be safe and watched as she came trotting out, wearing her fancy lilac shoes. I hated those sneakers. I missed out on them by thirteen seconds.

I was just about to call out to her, but that's when I saw Ellie jog toward her from the sidewalk.

"Ready?" she said, flashing that annoying Steckler grin.

Mila nodded and rubbed her hands together. "Let's go."

I watched them take off together, up the trail toward Ellacoya. I couldn't help it. I followed them, watching as they chitchatted while they ran, and as Mila snapped a selfie at the trailhead. But then Ellie made the surprising move to lead Mila up the Oak Tower path. I tried to keep a steady pace, but they were fast and I fell behind, tracking them by sound.

Little notes of laughter floated up through the sky and a bubbling fury boiled in my stomach. Why was it so easy for them? To joke around. To be happy. To go fast.

None of that has ever been easy for me. Nothing has. Not after Dad followed Shira's lead, ditching us for a new family in Putnam County, and Mom had to take the job at the school that pays like crap. Not after we had to move from our big farmhouse to a run-down cottage by the pizza place. Not after I had to stop shopping at Julia's dad's shop and wear hand-me-down running clothes from the thrift store.

I had to claw my way into Tamara's good graces back in middle school, stake my claim in her crew, and do *everything* right to stay there. I let Julia walk all over me, copy my tests, and treat me like garbage. I worked my ass off, running sprints and lifting weights long after everyone else went home, to land my spot on the varsity squad. Keeping these things was a battle I had to fight every single day.

I was breathing heavy then, tracking them as they reached the top of the hill, just after the pit. But that's when I heard another voice. Low with a fake casual lilt to it. "Oh, hey," Noah said.

"Noah," Mila said, surprise creeping into her voice. "What are you doing here?"

"We just wanted to—" Ellie said, and I knew at once it was

a setup. I crouched lower so I couldn't see their faces, but I got close enough to glimpse the backs of their heads, Ellie's shoulders tensing.

I listened to them quibble, to Noah spew his brutish bullshit. "We just wanted to make sure you wouldn't tell anyone, okay?"

Mila argued with them both and I was impressed by her confidence. She was mad. Mad at being ambushed, mad at being made to feel like she was a pawn in these dumb Edgewater games. I could tell because that's how I felt too.

But when Noah said, "We need you to keep quiet," I knew she didn't have a chance.

"You know what? Maybe everyone should know what liars you both are," Mila spit. "I can't believe you set me up like this, Ellie." Mila spun around, ready to leave, but then Noah set off after her. In one enormous push he sent her over the edge of the pit, down, down below.

Ellie and Noah huddled together, and I tried to inch closer to hear what was going on. Finally Noah raised his voice. "Mila," Noah shouted down to her. "We're going to leave now."

Noah grasped Ellie by both shoulders and shook her hard. Then Ellie, seemingly still in shock, nodded and allowed herself to be steered away from the path, out of sight and back toward the road.

I don't know how long I stayed crouched in my position, but the sun was halfway up the horizon when I heard a muffled grunt and then her voice, mumbling to herself in anger. Mila was trying to climb out.

I scrambled up to the top of the ridge, and when I stood where Ellie and Noah had been, I could see straight down into the pit. Mila was there, with dirt stains on her shirt and her cheeks, clutching her ankle. Dark red blood crusted above her eyebrow.

"Raven?" she called. "Is that you?"

I froze mid-step, and in that moment, I knew I had a choice. I could turn around and leave her there, letting Noah and Ellie come back and have all the power. Or I could take control of my own life, for once. I could convince her that it was the right thing to do to tell Tamara about everything—that *she* needed to be the one to do it. It would throw both the Stecklers off their game, paving the way for me to beat them all. The decision was easy.

"I need your help," Mila called. "Did you see what they did?" Her voice was trembling now. "Help me, Raven. My ankle's twisted and I can't get out. I need help."

"Hold on," I said, sidestepping toward her. "I got you."

"Oh, thank god," Mila said, desperation in her voice. "I'm going to throw my shoe up there, okay? My foot's swelling and I can't wear it."

One lilac sneaker sailed over the edge and landed right beside me. It was flashy and absurd for a casual morning jog. A reminder of what she had achieved—and what I hadn't. I wanted them. I wanted them so badly.

"You wore your State sneakers on a morning run?" I asked.

Mila laughed. "Kinda silly, right? They remind me of why I run. How hard I've worked." Her voice broke at the end. "Damn it, I really hope I'm not out for the season."

I stared at the shoe, replaying all of the meets I lost, all of the ribbons I let slip away. A few years ago, life seemed like it would open itself up to me and that I could be anything I wanted. I could be a winner. But after Shira disappeared, and I saw the way hard work did not always pay off, I knew that was just the dream of a child.

"I'm so glad you're here. Everyone always said you were so reliable," Mila said with relief. Her words snapped me out of my thoughts.

Reliable. I hate that word. People only say that because Shira proved to be the opposite. I didn't have the luxury of being flighty or unpredictable or spontaneous. Shira stole all of that. And now the Stecklers and Mila stole my only way out of this town. But maybe there was still a chance for me.

It happened quickly then. My plan took shape.

"Raven?" Mila called. "You still there?"

"Yes," I said, my voice a hoarse whisper. I tried to drown out my thoughts and focus on the task at hand. I spun around and saw a branch, heavy and long. I grabbed at the wood and heaved it over my shoulder, dragging it to the pit. "Here," I said. "Can you climb out with this?" I dropped one end down below so Mila could use it as a way to get out.

I gripped the branch, holding it steady while Mila pushed herself up.

"You got it?" I asked.

Mila grunted, exhausted. "I think so," she said.

She climbed farther up. She was almost at the top when I did it.

I could feel my grip slipping. I tried to summon my strength—at least I told myself I did. But then I let it go, the wood sliding out of my gloved hands.

"Raven!" Mila called, scared and confused as she fell backward into the pit.

I heard her skull collide with a large flat rock at the bottom in a screeching, cracking sound that sliced through the air and turned my insides into ice. The air went still and I tiptoed toward the pit. I peered over the edge to see her sprawled out on the ground where Noah and Ellie had left her like an animal. The branch was next to her, leaning against the side like it had fallen right there, just another act of nature.

"Mila," I whispered. But no one responded. The birds rustled their feathers overhead and I knew whatever had happened could not be undone.

I scanned the scene, trying to see what could tie me to this place. I saw a flash of red. Mila's phone, facedown in the dirt. I picked it up carefully with my gloved hands, more out of curiosity than anything else.

And when I saw the shoe, just sitting there, another memory came back to me. The Edgewater killer. He always took his victims' shoelaces as a sick trophy. It was almost too easy. When the police eventually found Mila, they'd assume that either Kendall Fitzwater was back or that a deranged copycat killer had come along. Neither would lead back to me, and with a few key pieces of planted evidence, I could blame the whole thing on Ellie *or* Stella. With both sisters tied up as suspects, the season would be mine for the taking.

My brain spun with possibilities. I gently nudged the shoelace out of its holes and stuffed it inside the pocket of my leggings along with the phone. Then I ran.

Within an hour I was sitting in the passenger seat of Julia's SUV, on our way to school, singing along to an old Britney Spears song like we always did.

Mila was gone. And only I knew the truth. For the first time in a long time, I felt powerful.

At first it seemed easy enough to set my traps. Once I

charged Mila's cell phone, I found the incriminating texts about Georgetown from Stella and the selfie that featured Ellie's head bobbing in the background. I knew dropping her phone during the search party would lead Detective Parker to the Stecklers.

But when Parker became even more fixed on Stella instead of Ellie, I tried to help their investigation along. I slipped Mila's mud-stained ID, which had been in her phone case, into Stella's locker and watched as it fell while she was talking to Tamara. It was easy to tell Principal Pérez like a concerned witness.

I thought they would assume that Stella killed Mila to knock her out of the competition. I mean, she basically tried to do that with Allison Tarley last year.

But as time passed and no body was found, I started to get worried. Maybe Mila survived somehow and had made her way home. But that was impossible, wasn't it? Was there any way I could be found out? I stayed calm by reminding myself that there was nothing tying me to Mila or the pit. No evidence, no clues, no obvious motive. I had, I told myself, committed the perfect crime.

They did find Mila, though. Buried under brush and mud, the earth taking hold after the wild storm that tore through town that day. That only caused Parker and his cronies to focus even more intently on Stella.

I never once worried that Ellie would turn herself in. I assumed she would let Stella take the fall. She had too much to lose, and they never seemed that close anyway. Plus, her mental game would be too rocked to focus on winning.

But I didn't think about the invisible tether that kept those sisters so chained to one another. Shira and I were never like that. We always kept our distance from one another, orbiting each other carefully with no intention of making contact. I thought I could break Stella and Ellie individually. I thought they would turn on each other. But I was wrong.

It's only now that I realize who could have saved me from this year. Who I could have turned to. And I killed her. I let her die. Mila and I were cut from the same cloth. Two betrayed girls desperately trying to exchange the cards we'd been dealt. We had dreams. We had grit. And I took that all away.

But what can I say to the people in front of me? To Tamara and Julia, who thought they knew me. To Noah, the scumbag who threw everything off the rails. And to Stella and Ellie, who started all this, who ruined my chances at getting out of this hellhole over and over and over again.

There's nothing to say. All I can do is run.

42

ELLIE

IT WAS RAVEN. Sweet, vanilla, almost-as-fast Raven. She's the one who framed Stella. Who killed Mila. Whose want was so big, she burned everything to the ground. I thought only Stella and I were like that. That the hungry need, the desire to win, the explosion of fury we experienced when we lost—I thought that was only ours. That we were the weird ones, the exceptions.

But now I know that's not true. We all have that in us somewhere. What differentiates us is what we do with it, how far we take it.

"Ellie Steckler?" Detective Parker calls. He's holding a clipboard and leaning up against the doorframe of the waiting room at the police station. The room is dingy, like every wall could use a fresh coat of paint or a good scrub.

"Ellie?" Parker calls again. I stand this time and walk over to him, wrapping my fleece tighter around my middle.

Stella stands behind me and reaches for my hand. "She's a minor," she says. "You can't question her without our parents." Stella straightens her back, nudging her chin upward. My heart crumbles, grateful and weary. I'm so undeserving of this protection after what I've done, what I've put her through.

Parker runs a hand through his hair. He turns to me. "You wanna wait or what?" But I know what I have to do. I shake my head and squeeze Stella's fingers.

"No," I say. "Stella can come in. I'm ready."

"Ellie, no," she says, her voice sharp. But my mind is made up and I float by Parker. The room is sparse, with two chairs on either side of an aluminum table. There's no two-way mirror, no cameras. Just . . . us.

I sit down in one of the wobbly chairs, and tell Detective Parker everything.

43

STELLA

ELLIE SPEAKS WITH a strange calm I didn't know she possessed. I don't let her hand go. Not to flinch when she tells Parker how she led Mila into the woods or when she explains what happened over the summer and that Noah convinced her that their lives would be ruined if anyone found out. That she now knows that was bullshit.

When Ellie finishes, she leans back in her chair, deflated, and looks to the stucco ceiling. "I deserve to be punished," she says.

Parker rests his elbows on the table, ready to say something. But then the door swings open and Mom and Dad burst into the room.

"Girls, we're leaving," Mom says, furious. "Now."

I start to stand but Ellie's butt stays planted in the seat. "I'm part of this," she says. "I set the plan in motion. I deserve this."

"Not another word, Ellie," Dad says. Mom's eyes are pleading and I wonder if she wants a drink, if this may be what finally breaks our family for good.

Parker clears his throat. "Ellie, you can go now," he says in a soft, kind voice. Then he turns to Mom and Dad. "We'll be in touch," he says.

Mom mutters something under her breath and turns to the door. "Come on," Dad says, resting his hands on our shoulders. "Let's go home."

I follow Ellie out the door. The station is quiet. Through the windows I see the sun setting outside, turning the walls pink and orange. When I take another step, the light streams through the window, blinding me for just a moment. I avert my gaze and swing my head toward another interrogation room, where the door is wide open. Inside, I see Raven, sitting at a table just like the one we were behind. Her red hair has fallen out of its ponytail and her skin is pale, her freckles muted. She sobs silently, her shoulders heaving up and down, and all I can think is *Good*.

Principal Pérez asks us to stay home from school for the rest of the week while they "figure everything out," she tells Mom. But there's nothing to *figure out*, really. We all know the truth now.

In the morning, my phone buzzes. It's Naomi, and when I see her name flash on the screen, I bite my lip to keep from smiling. After I told her everything that happened, we've been texting nonstop.

> *What's on tap for hooky today?*

> *Idk yet. Run forever?*

> *I wish you could run all the way to me. It'd be so much easier to get through this together.*

Another text pops up. *Okay, that was weird and forward. Don't hate me! Disappearing forever.*

I lean back against my pillow as heat spreads through my body. I didn't know this kind of hope was possible.

I'd like that. Not today, though. Soon.

Naomi sends back a smirking face and I shove my phone in my pocket. I throw back the covers and pad downstairs, a smile tugging at the corners of my lips. I wish Mila were here to analyze every word in these texts with me, but maybe that's the thing about Naomi. There aren't any misleading moments to obsess over. Everything's just there, out in the open. Honest.

"Jeez, Stell, you scared me." Mom says, clasping a hand over her heart. She's never up this early and she looks like she maybe hasn't slept at all.

"Sorry," I say, and mean it. We've put them through hell this year, and last year, and forever, honestly, and it all hits me at once how much they've tried to do for us, how *normal* they've tried to make everything.

And look what they're stuck with. Us.

But Mom isn't mad. She wraps me up in a bear hug and squeezes hard. "I love you, Stella," she says into my hair. "I love your sister too. More than you know."

She releases me then and I see tears in her eyes, though her gaze drifts above me, where Ellie comes into the room. Her eyes are sunken into her head and her hair is frizzy around her shoulders. Before she can say anything, Mom envelops her too and cries softly into Ellie's neck.

"I'm so sorry," she says. "That you felt like you couldn't come to me. That you both were so alone in all of this. I'm not perfect, but I'm your mother. I'll always be there for you. I'll always love you."

Ellie swallows hard and blinks back tears.

Mom holds us tighter and that's when I lose it and let the tears come. Ellie does too and the three of us stand there together, shoulders shaking, sobs heaving, until my throat becomes raw and scratchy.

Dad walks into the room just then and lets out a big breath. His lip trembles like he's going to cry too. "My girls," he says, wrapping his arms around Mom from behind her. "We're all such disasters."

"But we're *our* disasters," I say, and that's all it takes to get everyone laughing. Soon I have to hold my stomach to keep myself standing up. Finally Mom wipes her face with a dish towel and we compose ourselves, if only for a moment.

"Good to know we'll get through this," Dad says. "We are Stecklers, after all."

44

ELLIE

MOM KEEPS TELLING me to spend the day resting, to lie down and take it easy. To do nothing. To feel nothing. To relax. But I can't. Everything feels uncertain, like I'm standing on ground that's too soft to stay solid. The air in my room is too heavy, and the lamp is still broken in the corner, all its shards swept into a pile I'm too scared to clean up. The scene is reminder of what I've done, how I let someone else have so much control, so much power. It's a reminder that I'll never let anything like that happen again. Looking at the damage from the other day, I need to get out of here.

I pull a sweatshirt over my head. I reach for my sneakers and tie the laces with shaking fingers. I need to run. To feel the air rush between my fingers. To pant and sweat. To move. To breathe. To be me.

I take the stairs two at a time and when I push the front door open, I hear Stella's voice from the living room.

"Where are you going?" she asks, her head popping up from behind the couch.

I don't know what to say or where I'm headed, just that I

need to feel normal, to feel anything at all. But she eyes my sneakers.

"How many miles you thinking?" she asks.

"Who knows?"

Stella smiles just a bit. "Can I come?"

"Really?" It's the first time she's ever asked.

She stands and stretches her arms above her head. "Gimme two."

In a few minutes we're out the door in matching hoodies and practice kicks, taking it slow through the quiet Edgewater streets. This isn't a real run, one we'll log on our spreadsheets. This is a run for us. A run for survival.

We don't say much for the first mile through town. We pass the diner and the wine shop, the cheese purveyor and the nursery. Only a handful of people are out today, and they crane their necks to see the Steckler sisters they've heard about. They don't hide their stares. But I'm not worried, not anymore. They'll never catch us.

Even if they did read the papers this morning. VARSITY RUNNER CONFESSES TO MILA KEENE'S MURDER. If I close my eyes, I can still picture Raven in the station, her stringy red hair hanging limp around her face. Her shoulders hunched up around her ears. She didn't look like one of those murderers you see in documentaries, like the disheveled Fitzwater brothers, photographed in black and white in the newspaper. She looked like the same girl we've known our whole lives.

The article didn't mention me by name. But it doesn't have to. Everyone knows what I did and didn't do. Everyone heard about Noah and me, about our little trip to Newburgh. It's just what happens in a small town. But now that it's out in the open, I don't feel any shame about making that decision. I just feel free.

"Come on," Stella says, a slight huff in her breath.

I let her lead us up toward Ellacoya. The hairs on the back of my neck prickle when we get to the service entrance. Gone are cops and the crime scene investigators, but everything else is as it was the other day when the truth came out. I can even see the patch of ground where Stella pinned Raven down. Footprints from her sneakers. A slick scraped edge of dirt.

We don't stop. Stella's gaze stays straight ahead and I suck air in between my teeth, trying to be brave and face reality. For a second, I think she's going to lead me back to Oak Tower, but then she veers left toward Foxfire Point and motions for me to follow her. I slow, unsure if I can take these first few steps.

"Come on, Ell," she says softly. "If you can't do this run, how can you expect to keep going?"

I hesitate. How can I tell Stella that I can't bear to face anything right now? How can I tell her how sorry I am for ruining everything and leading Mila to her death?

Stella keeps her eyes on me and extends an arm to rub my shoulder. "We're in this together."

Her softness takes me aback. So different than the sister I've grown accustomed to. The one I spent years trying to avoid. But as soon as she touches me, I turn to putty, blubbering and heaving, snot and tears running down my face.

"Hey," she says softly, pulling me to her in an hug. "Hey, it's okay."

That only makes me sob harder and I wonder how many gallons of tears I've cried in the past month, the past day.

"I got you," Stella says softly. I choose to believe her.

We take the first mile of the trail slow, slower than usual, and I steady my breathing as we climb the hill. Farther and farther up we go until we reach a break in the path and make the left toward Foxfire Point. It's the best view in Edgewater, three hundred and sixty degrees of scenery stretching almost to the Berkshires. Swaying trees extend for miles and I suck in air, overwhelmed by it all. I'd forgotten how beautiful Edgewater can be.

A branch snaps behind me and I spin, my heart pounding. "Hey," Tamara says. She's sitting on a rock off to one side of the trail, knees curled up under her chin.

"Hey," Stella says.

Tamara's braids are tied at the base of her neck and her cheeks are wet. She rubs them with the underside of her sweatshirt. Her gaze moves to me and her eyes soften. "Guess we're all in the same boat."

Stella walks to her and sits next to Tamara, so close their shoulders are touching and they both face out, taking in the scenery. I stay put, my feet too heavy to move. But Tamara motions to me. "Come on," she says.

I stumble to them and sit next to Stella, feeling her warmth seep into me. I close my eyes and listen to the sound of the leaves rustling and the water lapping at the shore of the lake below. I let my heart rate slow.

"She fooled everyone, you know," Tamara says, shoving her hands inside her pockets. "Raven, I mean."

Stella nods but we don't say anything.

"She just wanted everything so much, so badly. We all do, I guess." Tamara kicks at the ground in front of her. "Reporters are all over the school. They'll be here for a while." She tilts her head toward the sun. "It's the perfect story, really. No tabloid could ignore it. Especially since it happened here in Edgewater. Another tragedy." She pauses. "A copycat killer."

Stella starts to open her mouth, then snaps it shut.

"What?" Tamara asks.

"Well," Stella starts. "I'm sure there will be another story waiting in the wings, something else that will make headlines soon. Who knows how long they'll pay Mila any attention." She chews over the words as if she's trying to decide how to phrase this next thought, whatever it is that's about to come out of her brain. "Why don't we give them something to pay attention to? Something for Mila."

A slow smile spreads on Tamara's face and my heart starts racing, thumping at a rhythm I can barely keep time.

Tamara turns to us and her eyes sparkle. "What do you have in mind?"

45

STELLA

IT WAS EASY to get the rest of the girls' team on board now that the "team" consists of only Ellie, Tamara, Julia, me, and three sophomores who had been plucked from the junior varsity squad to compete at State.

They were sick of being pitted against one another too. Sick of Coach Gary's rules, of his menacing bark. Sick of the way this town treated us like prizes to be won. Sick of being known as the girls from Deadwater. They were still hungry and lean and knew they had a few more years to break records. Once Tamara gave them the speech, the one we had written together in the Ellacoya den, they were eager to help, to make a scene.

No one says anything on the bus ride to State. We sit together for two hours of mellow silence, undisturbed meditation. A sacred ritual. If Coach thinks anything is off, he doesn't show it. Every few minutes I feel Ellie tense, clench her hands into fists. But when I press my thigh more firmly into hers, she presses back, and I know she's going to be okay. I know she's going to do this like we planned.

When we finally reach our destination, the team files off the bus in a single line. The air is frigid and coarse, colder than it's been in Edgewater. Bitter and sharp, like it could slit your throat if it blew too hard.

I shiver and zip my fleece up around my chin.

"Let's go," Coach yells, and we follow him like we always have, to the area of the field sectioned off for us. I look to the stands and see Mom and Dad, their hair hidden under blue Edgewater beanies. They wave at us with supportive smiles even though they know what's to come, what we're about to do. My heart lifts a little, knowing they have our backs. They're on our side.

I spot the scouts a few rows in front of them. Coach does too and hurries over to them, offering hearty handshakes and pointing back at us over his shoulder. His trophies. His bounce-back girls. Look what they've been through. Look who they've become. Look how much they can survive. But he doesn't know what we've planned or what we're capable of.

The guy from Georgetown won't even look at us, disgusted by Edgewater blue. But someone else, a white woman from a small college in the Midwest, makes eye contact with me and smiles. She jots down a note on her clipboard and takes a sip from a thermos branded with the school's logo.

"They're restarting their program," Ellie says next to me. "Division Two. No full rides. Partials, though. Not nothing."

"Huh," I say. "Maybe there's hope for us yet."

Ellie gnaws on her nail. She looks like she doesn't believe me, and that she's trapped in her own body, miserable. Beyond repair.

"You know that, right?" I ask. "We're going to get through this. You and me forever."

Even though she seems skeptical, Ellie places her hand on top of mine. "You and me forever."

"All right, girls," Coach calls as he jogs back to us. "Do your stretches, hit your marks. You've got about twenty minutes until go-time." Then he hops in place and makes his way to the boys' huddle, where Noah is noticeably absent while everyone figures out his punishment.

If this were a normal race, I'd have my noise-canceling headphones on, my stomach in knots. My head would just be beginning to clear. But today I sit on the ground and stretch my legs out in front of me, mulling over what's about to happen.

"Are you sure you're ready to do this?" Tamara says. She drops down next to me. "You have more riding on this than I do. I'm not even trying to run in college anyway."

"Yes," I say. "We have to. For Mila."

She nods once in approval. "Mila would have loved this," she says.

My chest tightens. Tamara's right. She would have.

"Is Naomi here?" she asks.

I swivel my head to the stands and scan the rows. "There," I say, pointing to the far-left corner, all the way in the back. "In the gold jacket." Naomi's staring right at me, her hand cupping her mouth as she calls my name loudly, hooting and hollering. She waves and my heart flutters, wide open for once. At last.

Tamara looks at Naomi and then at me. "Oh, shit," she says with a grin. "I see what's happening here. Get it, Stella Steckler."

I can't help but laugh and give a little shrug. "She's cool."

"Uh-huh, sure sure," Tamara says, elbowing me in the ribs. "Looks like she's with Mila's mom. And some random white dude."

I nod, refocusing my gaze on Thomas Keene. "That's Mila's

dad." There in the stands, he waves to us, his other arm wrapped tightly around Shawna's shoulders.

"Varsity girls!" one of the refs calls over the loudspeaker. The crowd erupts and together we stand, unzipping our layers, kicking our heels up into our butts. We look the part. Athletes. Heroes.

I breathe in deeply and remember what this meet means. We line up at the start and I feel Ellie on my left, Tamara on my right. Julia peers around from Tamara's other side with expectant, big eyes. I press my lips together and remember to breathe, to trust the girls I used to be so wary of.

"On your marks!" the ref shouts. We all crouch in unison, playing our roles. "Get set," he calls. I swing my arms back, ready to fly. "Go!"

I close my eyes and stay still. We all do.

The girls from other teams sprint out of the gate as us Edgewater runners stand up straight and firm, unmoving. Then Tamara extends her hand to me and I reach for Ellie's. Together we form a chain, our chins tilted toward the sky, away from the stands.

A collective gasp rises, and from the corner of my eye I can see people scramble to their feet.

"What the fuck?!" Coach yells from the side. "Run! Run!"

I hear his feet pounding the ground, rushing toward us.

"Hold steady," I whisper, and the others nod in agreement.

"What are you doing?" Coach screams, in front of us now. Spittle flies from the sides of his mouth and the vein in his neck bulges, thick and blue.

But we stay silent, knowing at least the next time we run, it will be for us.

ACKNOWLEDGMENTS

Thank you to my agent, Alyssa Reuben. You are my greatest champion and the most trusted voice in my head. I'll always be awed that you pulled me out of the slush pile.

Thank you to Jess Harriton, who edited this book with such generosity and was a true partner in its creation. This story would not exist without you and your brilliant brain.

Thank you to Casey McIntyre, who shepherded me through the publication process with much-needed humor and enthusiasm, and who has shown me the kind of support authors can only dream of.

Thank you to Elyse Marshall, whose publicity prowess I would be lost without and whose steady guiding hand I am so appreciative of.

Thank you to Ruta Rimas, whose excitement over what's in store is truly contagious.

Thank you to Kim Ryan and the Penguin Teen foreign rights team for bringing my work to so many readers around the world. Thank you to my international publishers, who I hope to meet after this whole pandemic thing is over.

Thank you to Kristin Boyle and Lilia Cretcher for creating *such* a stunning cover and letting me come along for the Zoom photoshoot ride. Thank you to Katie Bircher and Marinda Valenti for polishing this manuscript with your copyediting expertise.

Thank you to everyone at Razorbill and Penguin Teen who works tirelessly to make sure our stories find the readers who need them most. You are the *best* support system and I'm so lucky to be part of this wildly smart team: Kara Brammer, Christina Colangelo, Gretchen Durning, Felicia Frazier, Alex Garber, Carmela Iaria, Jen Klonsky, Bri Lockhart, Jen Loja, Shanta Newlin, Debra Polansky, Emily Romero, Jocelyn Schmidt, and Jayne Ziemba. Extra special thank-you to Felicity Vallence and the social media team for basically being fairy godpeople.

Thank you to Sydnee Monday and Rachel Porter for spending time with this story and offering excellent, thoughtful notes. Additional gratitude to Katelyn Dougherty and Alaina Belisle for your honest feedback and guidance.

Thank you to everyone at Paradigm Agency, including Alaina Belisle, Aaron Buotte, and Katelyn Dougherty. You make everything so much easier. Thank you to Matt Snow for thinking bigger than I ever could.

Thank you to the team behind *The Players' Table* for believing in the magic of *They Wish They Were Us*.

Thank you to Marley Goldman, my first reader, who never coddles me and always has ideas for how to make these stories better.

Thank you to my fellow writers-in-arms, who became lifelines during a year of isolation: Emma Gray, Stephan Lee, Hayley Krischer, Kelsey McKinney, Caroline Moss, Zach Sergi, and Jordyn Taylor.

Thank you to the Nieman Foundation and the 2021 class of fellows and affiliates for making this strange year feel warm and inviting.

Thank you to Steve Almond, Maria Bell, and Marla Kanelos for expanding my view of what writing can be. I'm so grateful for your instruction.

Thank you to Andi Bartz, Jessica Knoll, Megan Miranda, and Kara Thomas, whose early support for *They Wish They Were Us* buoyed me in so many ways.

Thank you to my friends—all of you—for the socially distanced picnics, hikes, roller blading sessions, and sweatsuit selfies.

Thank you to the booksellers, teachers, bookstagrammers, librarians, bloggers, and readers who devoured and shared *They Wish They Were Us*. This is the best job in the world and I could not do it without you.

Thank you to the Lund Strachan family for letting me lock myself in a room to write and not asking too many questions when I came out bleary-eyed—and for all the laughs around the dinner table.

Thank you to Mom, Dad, Halley, Ben, and baby Luke. Your strength, support, devotion, and unyielding love helps me stay motivated to keep at it and to make you proud. I love you endlessly.

Thank you to Maxwell Strachan, who, after more than a year of quarantine, I only love more. Thank you for reminding me that home is where we are together.

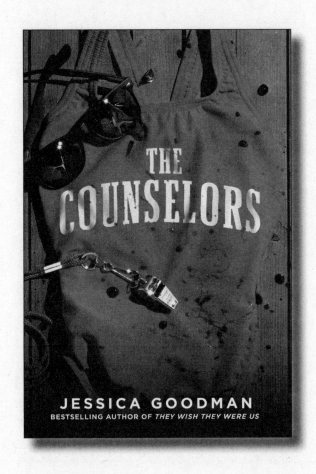

PROLOGUE

Evil doesn't exist at Camp Alpine Lake. Not inside the wrought-iron gate that separates camp from the rest of Roxwood, and not at the waterfront, where far-out buoys keep us isolated from the rest of New England. Everything here is safe. The tennis courts. The arts and crafts shed. The cabins. The Lodge. Camp is a bubble, made for bonfires and sing-alongs and friendships formed under the beam of a flashlight.

Even when I was eight and the group leaders would huddle us together on the man-made beach in neat little rows so we could watch the lifeguards line up in the water to practice safety drills, we knew they were all for show. We were never in danger. Not here.

We'd watch the lifeguards dive in unison, touching the ground beneath the surface, even if it was eleven or twelve feet below. They'd come up with nothing, handfuls of dirt. No harmed child, no limp arm. They'd do this over and over until they reached the end of the boundaries, never screaming in horror. Never fearful that a precious camper was gone.

Even when I became a counselor and was tasked with keeping the children alive, healthy, and well fed, I knew there was never any real danger here. Not in the edges of the forest up by the cliffs where loose rocks threatened to fall silently into the abyss. Not along the ropes course where harnesses always stayed buckled. And certainly not in the lake, where I wore my red lifeguarding suit like a superhero's costume.

But that was before I knew what kind of dark secrets were hidden in the corners of Camp Alpine Lake, out of sight of campers, of counselors, of lifers like me who would give everything we had to keep this place whole.

That was before we learned the truth. About Ava, Imogen, and me—and how far we'd go to protect each other even after we had been exposed.

Before this summer, Camp Alpine Lake was a haven. An escape from what I could not face back home in Roxwood, only a few miles outside the gate.

But now, Camp Alpine Lake is another place where I'll never feel safe.

CHAPTER 1

Now

The summer will begin like it always does, with me wandering the grounds of Camp Alpine Lake alone. It's the first day of maintenance week, when all the counselors arrive to get the place ready for campers. But I'm the only one who can come early.

No one else gets to experience how the cabins smell like cedar and lemon when they're empty, not yet filled with twelve-year-old boys who don't know about deodorant. How the sun bounces off the lake when there aren't any swimmers bobbing in the lap lanes. Or how you can stand at the edge of Creepy Cliff and scream, loud and long, listening to your voice echo all across New England.

"This place is your home, too, Goldie," Mellie has always said. I've heard the words enough times to believe them, even though my *actual* home is only a few miles away in Roxwood, right down the road from Truly's, the dive bar we go to on nights off.

But this summer is different. And Stu and Mellie are the only people at Alpine Lake who know why.

Mom and Dad insist I shouldn't break tradition. "You can't let what happened ruin every single thing you love," Dad says, gripping the steering wheel of our old Subaru as we pull up to the gate. "You deserve to have fun. We'll see you later at orientation."

Mom turns around from the passenger seat and squeezes my bare knee. "You're going to be okay."

I nod, unable to find words, but I know she's right. This place has always calmed me. Always washed away whatever sorrow I held on to at the beginning of the summer. If anything could heal me, it was a summer at Camp Alpine Lake with Ava and Imogen, who have been my best friends for a decade. I may not have told them about my school year, but eight weeks with them will erase the damage and the pain. Even if we've barely spoken in the past few months. They always make everything better.

I get out of the car with shaky legs and heave my duffel over my shoulder. I walk through the gate and inhale deeply, smelling freshly cut grass and woodchips. I'm home.

I make my way to the gazebo and sit down, pushing my sunglasses up on my head. The clock on the dining hall says it's only nine in the morning. I've still got an hour before Ava and Imogen arrive on the buses. They'll bring with them all the other former campers who are now counselors. The lifers. People I've known since I was eight years old. Later today, we'll meet the foreigners. The ones who fly from Argentina, South Africa, and Australia to experience eight weeks in America. There are always a handful of Brits, mostly teaching tennis or soccer. Men with silly accents who will offer you tallboys and cigarettes at bonfires. Women who order gin and tonics on nights off and sunburn easy. Some come back year after year and some we never see again.

"Goldie!" someone calls.

I swivel around to find Stu jogging toward me in a polo shirt and long khaki shorts, belted at the waist. An Alpine Lake baseball hat covers his bald head and he's holding a clipboard like it's an extension of his arm. For a second, my stomach cramps. *Does he regret how they helped me?*

"Hi, Stu," I say, my voice smaller than usual.

"There's our golden girl." I half expect him to ruffle my dark curly hair like he used to do when I was little. But he smiles at me like nothing happened this year. Like he and Mellie didn't save my life. "Do you want to know your cabin assignment early? Drop your stuff off before the buses pull in?"

I nod eagerly, pulling one knee up under my chin. There's no way Imogen, Ava, and I would be staffed in the same cabin since we're all going to be lifeguards, but hopefully we'll be in the same group so we have the same schedules. Last year was our first time on the staff side of things and we were all assigned cabins so far away from each other. It sucked. Nothing like the years we spent as campers. I wonder if that's when the gulf between us began to widen.

"Let's see," Stu says, tapping his clipboard with a pen. "Here you are, my dear. You're with the Ramblers. Nine-year-olds. And you'll be in Bloodroot. Best view on camp, but you know that already. Your bed was in the back left corner, right?"

That's the thing about Stu. He always remembers what cabins you were in, what your favorite activities were, and if you preferred chicken patties over wing dings. He knows my dad likes to stock the infirmary with neon-colored Band-Aids so the little ones can wear them like badges of honor, and that Mom blasts Queen in the woodworking shop to soundtrack the buzzsaws. Last year, he got her a vintage shirt from their Live Aid show for her birthday, and I swear it's her most prized possession.

I smile up at Stu, blocking the sun with my hand. "Any chance you can give me a hint about—"

"Ava and Imogen? I thought you'd never ask," he says with a wink. "Don't worry, they're with the Ramblers, too. Ava's in Ludlow and Imogen's in Ascutney. You're smack dab in the middle."

My shoulders relax and all I want to do is text them the good news, but I know there's no use. There's no service at Camp Alpine Lake. Barely any in the town of Roxwood at all.

"Why don't you get settled and we'll see you when everyone else gets here, okay?"

"Thanks, Stu. Holler if you need anything."

"You got it, golden girl."

He tips his hat in a playful way and heads toward the office. But as he walks off, his face falls, a furrow forming at his brow. For a second, I wonder if his worry is related to me. If he regrets letting me come back.

But I don't know what I would do if, after everything, I lost this place, too. The promise of spending the summer at Alpine Lake was the only thing that helped me get through the year. The stares. The whispers that echoed through the halls of Roxwood High. Whenever someone left a nasty note in my locker or shoved me hard in the shoulder, I would close my eyes and think of this place. Of the first day of camp. Of being reunited with Ava and Imogen.

They never treated me different even though I'm not like them. I'm a local—a *townie*. Someone who bypassed camp's exclusive admissions exam and five-digit price tag because my parents work here. But Ava and Imogen don't care about that. We're all the same—the kids who live ten months for two. That's all that matters.

I hope that's still true.

The walk from the gazebo to Bloodroot only takes a few minutes but you can see just about everything. I pass the volleyball court, the softball field, the upper picnic tables, and the first set of tennis courts. My cabin is fourth in a row on a big hill and it's right in the center of all the action. Everyone has to pass it on their way down to the waterfront, so it always feels like you're at the center of everything. Plus, like Stu said, killer views. You can see all the way to the lake from the counselor room.

But I love Bloodroot for different reasons. Ava, Imogen, and I lived here the first summer we had been assigned the same cabin. The previous year, when we were eight, we begged the counselors to let us switch but they never did. And then finally, a few weeks before we were due to be Ramblers, Ava's mom called and worked some fancy-person magic so we were not only assigned to the same cabin, but also beds right next to each other in the far corner of the room, right by the big window that faces the waterfront. Like Stu remembered.

I push open the door and as the metal springs squeak, tears prick my eyes. *This* is my home. I dump my duffel on a top bunk in the counselor room and walk slowly through the main cabin, running my fingertips along the wooden bed frames, the rafters overhead, and the cubbies that will soon be crowded with little girls' linens.

I stop at the entrance and look up at the plaques. There's one commemorating each year that camp's been open, with the names of those who lived here painted in dramatic fashion. I recognize so many names. Girls who fell in love with each other and the friendships you can only make at a place like this. I search the plaques until I find ours.

There we are, along the bottom. Three lines of the same phrase, repeated over and over with our names signed below. *Sisters by choice.* Our handwriting still looks the same. Mine neat and tiny, like I'm trying to fit as many letters as possible. Imogen's loopy and bubbly, and Ava's a quick scrawl.

I close my eyes and hold my breath, keeping this feeling in my lungs. It's the first time since before the accident that I feel free. That I feel like *me*. But I can't think about that too much because I'll break into tears, and if I do, Ava and Imogen will know as soon as they see me. They always know. And then I'd have to tell them the truth.

They don't need to know yet. Maybe ever. It won't do me any good. I'll still be Goldie Easton, the most hated girl in Roxwood. I'll still have to repeat a semester of high school. And Dylan Adler will still never walk again.

I was lucky I didn't go to jail. That's what people said around town.

It's because she's associated with that camp.

Those directors saved her ass.

Stu and Mellie pulled some strings for her.

She should rot in hell.

What if Ava and Imogen thought I was a monster, like everyone else? We've shared everything with each other. Complaints about the bumps on our bikini lines, the jelly donuts Ava special orders around Hanukkah, the secret things that make our bodies hum alone in the dark. But not this. I don't want them to know about this.

It was easy to dodge their calls and the three-way FaceTimes right after the accident, and as the semester stretched on, they both became busier and busier, and their texts became less frequent. Now, six months later, I don't know how I would begin to explain that my whole life had changed without them even knowing.

Plus, Ava's got enough to worry about with her shitty invest-ment banker dad who's happy to write her checks for her Upper East Side prep school but refuses to visit from Palm Beach. And Imogen's busy with auditions after landing a cell phone commer-cial that plays before basically every YouTube video.

Whenever they asked about life up here, it was easier to say it was boring. The same. To flip the question and ask for stories about New York, to say I couldn't wait to get out of this hellhole. No one expects anything else when you live some place like Roxwood.

For now, I want to enjoy the summer. Eight magical weeks at Camp Alpine Lake. Nothing exists outside this place. Not even the past.

CHAPTER 2

Then

It was hard not to notice Heller McConnell at the haunted house orientation. There were nine of us, all seniors from Roxwood High, who had been cast to work the season at the old abandoned psych ward off Route 16, and Heller was the only athlete.

I was picking through a box of fangs when Heller walked over to inspect a roll of mummy wrapping. His curly dark hair swooped over one eye and a soft smile tugged at the corner of his red mouth.

"Didn't peg you as a vampire lover," Heller said, holding up a plastic knife.

His voice was low and smooth, the same way he sounded over the loudspeaker at school while making the morning announcements.

"I could get into it," I said. "A gender-swapped Dracula situation."

Heller laughed like he was impressed. "Goldie, right?"

My brow shot up in surprise, and Heller snapped his mouth shut.

"Sorry, that's weird. It's . . ."

"We've been in the same class since kindergarten," I said. "It'd be weird if you *didn't* know my name."

A smile blossomed on his face, and I licked my lips, trying to ignore the warmth spreading through my chest.

In that moment, I wasn't Goldie Easton, the quiet girl who was always head down in her phone or an old mystery novel, never present. I was something new and sparkly, full of possibilities. I cleared my throat and hunted for something to say.

"Why are you here?" It was the wrong question. I knew it as soon as I saw Heller's face fall.

"College fund," he said. "Pays more than leading hayrides at the nursery."

"Dartmouth?" I'd heard their hockey coaches had been court-ing him since sophomore year. It was pretty much a miracle, a Roxwood kid going Ivy. I expected Heller to puff out his chest and be all aggro about it. But instead, he averted his eyes like he was embarrassed. It made me like him more.

"It's not a sure thing," he said, shrugging. "I still have to get in." Then he leaned forward into the bin of costumes and dug out a black pointy witch's hat, setting it on my head at an odd angle.

"Everyone said there was a reason no one took jobs here." Heller smiled right at me and took a step closer so the space between us almost disappeared, so I could smell him, all mint and flannel and firewood. "But I think I'm going to like it."